ALSO BY SAV R. MILLER

MONSTERS & MUSES

Promises and Pomegranates
(includes the novella "Sweet Sin")
Vipers and Virtuosos
Oaths and Omissions
Arrows and Apologies
Souls and Sorrows
Liars and Liaisons

Endless Anger

Endless Anger

SAV R. MILLER

sourcebooks
casablanca

Published by Sourcebooks Casablanca, an imprint of Sourcebooks
P.O. Box 4410, Naperville, Illinois 60567-4410
(630) 961-3900
sourcebooks.com

Cataloging-in-Publication Data is on file with the Library of Congress.

Printed and bound in the United States of America.
WOZ 10 9 8 7 6 5 4 3 2 1

For the ones who hide their
anger behind a mask.

Now hear, you blissful powers underground—
answer the call, send help.

Bless the children, give them triumph now.

—AESCHYLUS

Content Note

Endless Anger is a dark academia romance containing material that may not be suitable for all audiences, including: explicit sexual scenes, graphic violence, on-page sexual assault/violence/rape, gore, murder, and other mature situations.

For a full list of content warnings, please visit savrmiller.com

Endless Anger is the first book in the Monsters Within series, which is a second generation spin-off of the Monsters & Muses series. Though it is a standalone, if you'd like to meet the first generation, you should start with *Promises & Pomegranates*.

In addition to US academic institutions, Avernia College (and Fury Hill) was heavily inspired by ancient Greece and Rome, as well as their mythologies. Some words, phrases, and spellings may have been altered to fit within the context of the story.

AVERNIA COLLEGE

The White Mountains
Tenarus Cave
Quarry
Lake Lerna
Abandoned Building
Graveyard
The Primordial Forest
Curator House
Kore's Garden
Staff Housing
Amphitheater
Visio Aternae Clubhouse
The Obeliskos
Law Center
Elysian Dorms
Recreational Fields
Daughters of Persephone Clubhouse
Erebus Hall
Blessed Hall
Chapel
Cadmus Hall
Rhadamanthus Hall
Observatory
Dean's House
The Lyceum
Science Wing
Greenhouse
Theater
Refectory
Campus Store
Morning Fields
Archives
The Apollodorus
Jean-Claude Dupont Gymnasium
Courtyard
Administration Building
Student Health Center
Main Gate

Secret Societies

Secret societies move in the
shadows and write their histories
in blood. Can you follow their
trail through Avernia College?

The
Curators

Death's
Teeth

Daughters of
Persephone

Visio
Aternae

Playlist

"In a Week"–Hozier feat. Karen Cowley

"Thistle & Weeds"–Mumford & Sons

"Savior Complex"–Phoebe Bridgers

"To You Alone"–Tom Rosenthal

"Lover, Please Stay"–Nothing But Thieves

"The End of Love"–Florence + The Machine

"I Will Follow You Into The Dark" (cover)–Miya Folick

"Euclid"–Sleep Token

"rosier/punk2"–brakence

"that way"–Tate McRae with Jeremy Zucker

"Your Call"–Secondhand Serenade

Chapter 1

Asher

THIRTEEN YEARS OLD

ACCORDING TO MY FATHER, NEXT TO DEATH, ANGER IS THE ONLY constant in life.

When Mom and Grandma aren't around, *his* father, my grandpa, says anger is a part of our heritage—unforgiving and endless.

So I have to be too.

"*Daddy!* Asher and Foxe are fighting again!"

My older sister's scream echoes down the beach, bouncing off the water as Foxe's elbow catches my right eye.

I wince as pain shoots across my forehead. He's not supposed to *fight back*. That's not part of the deal.

If Mom were here, she'd have come running to break things up already. She always gets to us before we can do too much damage.

Dad is another story entirely.

I sense the moment he steps out from the rosebushes partially hiding our backyard, impossibly tall and foreboding, like one of the ash trees lining our property.

He stuffs his hands into his dress pants pockets, walking over casually. There's no urgency with him, no rush to correct bad behavior. Everything is calm, like the moment before a storm rolls in.

I grab my cousin in a headlock and drive my fist into his face. Blood spurts from his nose, painting my knuckles, and I wait for a beat of excitement to pulse inside my chest the way it normally does when I let rage win.

Nothing happens.

Glancing over Foxe's head at the sandy shore, I search for the cause of the fight.

Well, not that she *did* anything. I just like sticking up for her. Sometimes she's too nice to do it herself.

Right now, though, Lucy's not even looking in my direction. I wonder if that's why I feel so *stupid*.

She's with some of the others, plucking wilted flowers from my aunt Violet's garden. They drop the petals on top of a wooden lockbox and repeat some Latin prayer that none of them even understand.

The box isn't that big—just enough for the ashes of the mutt her family's had since before she was born—but there's a fresh carving of a wolf with an arrow between its teeth on the lid, which is why she insisted on using it for the memorial.

She lives for symbolism like that.

Black hair falls out of the double braids her mom did this morning and sticks to her face, hiding her expression from me.

But I don't need to see her to know she's crying.

Don't need to hear the sniffling or watch her nose get all red to want to beat the crap out of Foxe anyway.

He grunts when I lift my knee and wedge it into his stomach. A heavy hand comes down on my head and then on Foxe's.

I see the flash of a black wedding ring.

It doesn't match Mom's, but it fits him.

"Aren't you two tired of this yet?" Dad asks in that level, almost bored tone of his. "There are much better ways to spend your time, don't you think?"

"I didn't even *do* anything!" Foxe snaps, growling when Dad wrenches us apart. "Ash-tree is just a freaking psycho."

Swallowing, I slide my fist over my bottom lip, tasting blood. My knuckles are already throbbing and turning purple; I tuck that hand beneath my armpit, glaring at my sister Noelle, who's at the back gate watching everything, because she's a nosy bitch.

She's always the first to tattle. Quincy, the oldest of us three, would have walked inside without a word. Unfortunately, she's off at some stupid fancy college, and I'm left to fend off the brat here all by myself.

"Name-calling seems unnecessary." Dad bends slightly, gripping Foxe's jaw and tilting his head to inspect his bloody face. "Your mother's in the kitchen. Please go see her so she can clean you up."

I cringe internally. Aunt Violet'll be pissed that we got into another fight, and I know she'll tell the rest of the parents. The adults in our family gossip more than anyone I've ever met, and since I started eighth grade at Aplana Academy this year, that's saying a *lot*.

Foxe tries to frown but winces as Dad releases him. He touches his nose. "Is it broken?"

"Don't think so. The swelling will be a pain though. Put some ice on it."

Tossing a dirty look my way, Foxe huffs and storms off, leaving us alone. I feel other pairs of eyes on us, but when Dad lets out a long sigh, I know better than to give anyone else my attention.

I glare at my feet, keeping my gaze down even when he starts man-handling my face like he did with Foxe. His skin is always a little chilled at the fingertips, but I'm used to it by now. It's almost calming on my flushed, enraged flesh.

"What was it this time?" he murmurs, pressing my lip with his thumb.

"Nothing."

His black eyebrows arch. "Sure about that?"

"Yes." My frown grows, and I cross my arms. "Where's Mom?"

"Still in town with her sisters. Why do you ask?"

"I don't know." I scuff my toe across some sand. "She gets me. I don't have to explain myself to her."

"Yes, your mother once enjoyed throwing punches without thinking too. Although I don't believe I asked you to explain anything besides what happened."

"Yeah, and I said nothing. You don't believe me." Now, I glance up into his dark, almost black eyes. He towers above me, even though I hit a huge growth spurt this month, and I'm starting to wonder if I'll ever catch up.

The kids at school call him the Grim Reaper. I don't understand why—aside from his height, he looks just like me, and *I* don't look like the collector of death.

Mom says so.

Still, I guess if you don't know better, he does seem pretty scary. To anyone else, the look in his eyes might spell trouble, but I can see the laughter hidden behind his brown irises. The grin he's trying to keep from me.

He *knows* what happened.

And he thinks my misery is funny.

Pulling my chin from his grasp, I shoot the little trio down the beach a glare and then move past my father. "I'm going to my room."

"Leaving partway through a funeral is a bad look, my son."

I press my teeth together. "It's a funeral for a *dog* who was, like, a hundred years old. Who fucking cares?"

He shrugs. "Is that really how you feel?"

No. I'm just repeating the same bullshit Foxe said that ticked me off and made Lucy burst into tears after I spent the entire morning trying to cheer her up. When her mom, who the dog belonged to first, dropped her off for the unofficial ceremony, that was her single request to me: make Lucy feel better about all this.

Death, the circle of life. I don't know why that's *my* responsibility, but here we are.

And I fucked it up, letting Foxe join. He's such an idiot. No one ever asks him to comfort their kids, even though he'd be good at it if he put some effort into the gesture. He's goofy and lighthearted where

I can't help being angry and violent, but he can't seem to take anything seriously either.

Maybe that's why he keeps coming back after our fights. I guess I should count my blessings. A plastic punching bag wouldn't be as satisfying.

"Asher!" Aurora calls from down the beach, waving her hands over her blond head. "Where'd Foxe go?"

"Why don't you go look for him?" I snap.

"He's inside with his mother," Dad says.

I glare at him. "Don't tell her that. She just wants to give him googly eyes all day long."

Dad chuckles. "What's so wrong with that?"

"It's *gross*."

"Ah. Sounds like you're projecting."

Aurora calls out again to me, not having moved from her spot beside Lucy and Lachlan. "Asher, come back! We're gonna spread the ashes in the water!"

I glance over at them, at *her*, but don't respond. She's looking at her brother now, laughing at something he says, all sunshine and happiness. Her fingers cling to that box though, the only sign that she's still giving the dead dog her silent attention.

How do you compete with that?

If I go over there now, I'll be playing second fiddle to something that isn't even alive.

Dad seems to read my mind. "Doesn't have to be a competition, you know. There's enough of that girl to go around."

My nostrils flare. *Yeah, that's the problem.* She's already spread thin, and I don't want to be another *thing* she has to balance her focus on.

Especially since she's really bad at it, anyway.

Shooting my father a look, I step away from him. "You are way more annoying than Mom."

"Oh, I'm devastated. Wait until I tell her about the *googly* eyes you have for her best friend's daughter."

Cutting my gaze to his, I watch for a moment as Dad's facial expression softens slightly as if in understanding.

Or because he was baiting me, the jerk.

Dad clamps his hand down on my head again. "Come on." He nudges me forward, nodding toward the house with his chin. "Let's get you cleaned up before your mother comes back and assumes I've let all hell break loose."

Keats, my short-haired calico kitten, curls up at the foot of my bed later that night. He kneads at the blankets, pulling them away from me, and I shift my focus from the thirty-second volume of *Berserk* in my lap to him.

A sliver of darkness peeks in through the partially open bedroom door; I'm usually the last awake at night, unable to ever fully feel at ease in this big, creepy mansion. Despite Mom's best efforts to make the fancy, overly furnished former hotel into something family-friendly, there's always been something *off* about the place.

Or maybe it's the inhabitants who are off.

I grip the book and Keats's nape when the door begins to slowly creak, and the darkness is swallowed by the lamplight. I'm expecting Mom, who likes to check in before she goes to sleep, or Noelle, who insists on sneaking out to visit her endless parade of boyfriends, even though our parents let her see them any other time.

She says she enjoys the rush, but maybe I don't get it because I've never been attracted to anyone before, so there's no thrill to be had there. Or maybe it's because my room is always the one being snuck into, rather than me trying to leave.

Lucy Wolfe's thin frame slips from the shadows. Her hair is still in those two braids, pieces of her bangs sweeping into the corners of her eyes. The bright blue of her irises is undercut by the red rimming her lids, and I ignore the way my heart seems to pound extra hard inside my chest.

Get a grip, loser. She's your best friend.

I've known her our entire lives, and I think that's part of the problem. Maybe you can know a person too well, and your relationship starts to break apart in the midst of familiarity.

That's how I reason away my reaction to her, at least.

She's wearing plaid pajama pants and a black zip-up hoodie over a red tank top. Wolf slippers cover her feet, and I wonder if she came all the way from her house across the island in them.

I bet she did. They're her favorite. Really anything to do with canines or their ancestral relatives interests her.

Walking over, she reaches a hand out, stroking the top of Keats's head. He immediately starts purring, and the hint of a smile pulls at her mouth.

That smile feels like the eighth wonder of the world.

The stupid, selfish part of me wishes she'd direct it my way, but she's always favored animals over humans.

Everything over me.

"Foxe got you pretty good, huh?"

I touch my fingers to the outside of my eye, which is still tender and hot. "Whatever. You should see him."

"Is that supposed to impress me, pretty boy?"

My heart skips a silent beat, but I pretend not to notice.

Rolling my eyes, I close the manga and toss it down the bed where Keats is. He barely flinches.

"Why would I be trying to impress you, *pup*?" I ask.

She hates that nickname, and I've never cared. It keeps distance between us. Not enough to freak her out but enough that I can somewhat breathe when she's around.

When she sniffles, wiping her nose with her sleeve, I slide over in the bed, pulling back the comforter.

Without a word, she kicks off her slippers and joins me, stretching out on the edge of the mattress.

My gaze darts around the room. There's a cobweb in one ceiling corner that I'll tell our housekeeper, Marcelline, about tomorrow. Everything else is in its regular boring place—all my sketchbooks and the trays with my charcoal, ink pens, and pencils sit neatly on my desk, while the floating shelves above it house my manga collection and a few of the classics I stole from the library downstairs.

The only person who ever disturbs any of my drawings or books is in my bed, sulking. I don't mind that she makes the room chaotic just by existing.

"You left," she says finally.

I roll over on my side, facing the wall away from her, and tuck my arm under my head. "Surprised you even noticed."

"It was kind of a shitty thing to do, Ash. You loved Laurel too."

Big, soft brown eyes and black fur appear in my vision, but I ignore the way my heart twists. This is the circle of life. Everyone and everything dies, no matter how hard you try to put it off.

No matter how good and pure something is, death is the one thing that will eventually touch it.

The sooner Lucy learns that, the better.

"Well, it's not like he knows I wasn't at the stupid ceremony," I grumble.

"But *I* know."

"You didn't need me."

"That's not true. It's never true."

My fingers buzz with some unknown sensation. "You shouldn't say never."

She huffs, and the bed jostles as she rolls toward me. "I *mean* it, you big dummy. You make everything easier to deal with."

"Oh, so you want me around because I'm useful?"

"Why do you do that?" she snaps. "You're putting words in my mouth."

I roll back over, now facing her, but I'm not expecting her to be so close.

Her lips are mere inches away, and my stomach tenses, my chest growing tight. Sticky with something warm, something I don't fully understand.

She's glaring at me, her blue eyes hard as sapphires, but all I can focus on is the shape of her mouth.

I want to cover it with my own. Make her look at me differently.

What is wrong with me?

"I'm sad," she admits after a few seconds, sniffling again.

Throat burning, I clench my teeth. She's sad a lot these days, what with each failed project at school, being kicked out of the Aplana Youth Club for being too polarizing, and now her first animal death.

Somehow, even though her mom has been fostering and running the island's animal shelter since before we were born, they've been lucky enough to avoid any demise.

But Laurel was old, and we all knew it was coming. Turns out, that doesn't make it any easier.

Still, you'd never know about the weight on her shoulders. Lucy buries everything inside, and then when she comes here late at night—this is where she lets herself bleed.

"How do you do it?"

My jaw relaxes slightly. "Do what?"

"Well, you don't really ever seem sad, right?" She blinks at me, rubbing her nose. "How do you do it? Is there, like, a switch you can flip?"

Embarrassment floods my face. "I don't know, Luce. It's not really something I put any thought into."

She frowns, seeming to contemplate this, and I shove my trembling hands beneath the comforter.

It's a flaw I wish she couldn't see.

I don't know how to fix it. Almost like there's so much anger within me, there's no *room* for anything else.

Just anger and her.

After a few seconds, she scoots a little closer. Swallowing becomes difficult as the scent of her coconut shampoo surrounds me.

That's something I never used to notice.

Funny how everything changes in the blink of an eye.

"I miss him," she says, her breath brushing the skin on my neck above my T-shirt. "Do you think I'll ever stop?"

"*You?*" I scoff. "Doubtful."

"Yeah, I didn't think so either." Looking down at Keats, a soft little smile tugs at her lips, replacing the frown from before. "I kind of like that though. It'll be like he's always with me. One day, when I open up a big conservation center and rescue all kinds of endangered species, I'll dedicate it to him so he can help me watch over the animals."

"Corny."

She kicks me. "Sorry not everyone wants to be a cynical jerk like you all the time."

"That's how you keep the sadness away though."

Those blue eyes swivel up. "Are you sad, Asher?"

Only when you are.

"Nope. Just angry. Mostly at Foxe for being an asshole earlier."

"Eh, he can't help it. Serious stuff makes him uncomfortable. He's not like you and me."

"You're too forgiving."

She sighs. "Thank you for the box. It's pretty."

Warmth spreads across my cheeks. I spent the morning carving that design into it, unable to think of any other way to help.

Her fingers brush against mine under the covers. I stop breathing for a moment.

We don't mention how her forgiveness benefits me or our friendship. When her hand slides closer, her fingers interlocking with mine, I feel I might explode into a million little pieces.

I think this must be what death is like, and I wonder how she'd react if I told her.

Dying doesn't seem all that bad. Not if it's like this.

Not if it's with you.

"You won't leave me again, right?" she asks, moving her head to my shoulder.

My heart pounds a wild rhythm against my ribs.

Glancing down, I note the deepening of her breathing and how she gets heavier on me within seconds.

She's asleep, her long black lashes resting on top of her pale, freckled cheeks, and there's no point in me answering.

Still, I can't help it.

My "no" is whispered into the dark room, drowned out by Keats's snoring and the hum of the mini fridge on the far wall. The crickets outside and Mom's rustling down the hall as she gets ready for bed—all of that is louder than the single syllable I utter, yet the weight of the one word is unbearable.

Because it makes me a liar.

Chapter 2

Asher

I DON'T WANT TO BE VISITING QUINCY ON THIS STUPID CAMPUS. IT'S dull and dark, the clouds hanging so low in the sky that it looks like they're clinging to the buildings.

I'll never understand why my sister chose this tiny college over the bigger and less expensive schools she was accepted into, except that she was going through a box of things from Dad's childhood—*one* singular box—a few years back and discovered an old brochure from Avernia College in Fury Hill, New Hampshire, where our grandmother had apparently graduated top of her class.

Dad's dead, biological mom, not Aunt Violet's mom. I doubt Grandma would step foot anywhere as creepy as this. She likes sunshine too much.

From there, Quincy did a deep dive into the school's history and discovered we had an ancestor who helped found the place, and her obsession only strengthened.

Lucy *begged* to tag along on the trip because she worships Quincy. And Noelle. And my parents. Everyone except me, it seems, even though I'd do pretty much anything for her.

Noelle says I want it too much. I don't know what *it* is.

But I told Lucy there wasn't room in the car. There's no way I'm spending a weekend listening to her drool over my boring sisters or fantasize about how cool this school is and how she can't wait to go here one day.

Ever since Quincy ditched Aplana Island for higher education, the idea that Avernia is Lucy's ticket to getting out is all she can fucking talk about. That and the litter of puppies her mom is fostering.

Frankly, I'd rather let Foxe take a whack between my legs than listen to her talk about either one.

My hands are in my pockets as I trail behind my family, not paying a lick of attention to the campus tour guide as they explain the school's "rich, vibrant history" and the influences of ancient Greek and Roman cultures on it.

The thick trees lining the property and the stained glass windows in many of the pointed stone structures don't make any of this less soul sucking.

I don't even really understand why we're here—Quincy's been a student for two years now and never invited us to a family weekend before. The tour feels unnecessary, but Dad wouldn't let me skip and hide out in the car, waiting for Lucy to call me.

Mom hangs back like she's worried I might slip away at the first opportunity.

"And this is the Obeliskos—the largest and oldest library on campus." Our tour guide is a tall person with spiky white hair and thick, purple glasses resting on the bridge of their wide, pale nose. "Legend has it that certain floors are haunted by the spirits of students who've passed on before graduation."

They point up at the building, which looms behind a clock tower that doesn't appear to tell the correct time.

I glance at Mom, who's already reaching for me. The diamond ring on her left hand catches in the sunlight as it pokes through a cloud.

"Kallum," she says to Dad. "Asher and I will meet up with you three in a bit."

He nods once. "At the dorms."

Noelle frowns. "You're going in there? Didn't you just hear them say it's haunted?"

Quincy rolls her eyes. "They say everything is haunted on this campus. Fury Hill residents are extremely superstitious and paranoid."

"Dates back to the founding families," the tour guide tells us. "Lot of conspiracy theories surrounding the creation of the school and how the joint venture turned into an undead bloodbath."

"Undead?" Dad cocks an eyebrow. "As in zombies?" He glances at Quincy, his expression skeptical. "Are we sure you should be attending a school that promotes the existence of the supernatural? What happened to art and science?"

"Mr. Anderson, you don't think humans are alone in the world, do you?" the tour guide questions. "You think all the stories about ghouls and goblins are fake?"

Dad's jaw clenches. "If there's a creature out there worse than a human, I've yet to be convinced."

He continues walking, leaving the five of us standing at the library's entrance. Quincy exhales, her shoulders slumping, and starts after him. The tour guide follows suit, marking something off on their clipboard.

Noelle purses her lips, glancing at us and then the Obeliskos. Something unreadable flashes through her gaze...like the passing of a shadow behind an empty window, rustling the curtain. "He has a point, but I still don't want to go in there. I bet you'll fall through the stairs. This place doesn't look like it gets inspected often."

Sprinting after the other three, Noelle's dark brown hair swishes against her back, which is rigid despite her excited gait.

I look up at Mom, who simply watches her daughter with eyes that seem sad.

I'm not sure why, and I don't bother asking.

Snapping out of it, Mom drags me through the Obeliskos's revolving glass door and into a lobby with a giant circulation desk and rows of tables with desktop computers behind it. Two staircases and an elevator punctuate the center of the room, splitting the halls beyond that seem to go on for miles.

Sturdy bookshelves lines the walls, cut so they fit beneath more stained glass windows, and the dark wood floors creak as we walk on them.

Mom sighs wistfully. "Nothing beats a campus library."

We migrate slowly through the many rows of books, circling around study areas and tiptoeing past the offices toward the back. Eventually, we come to another elevator, where a sign with the building's levels is plastered above the buttons.

"Fury Hill archives and world encyclopedias," I read, tracing the words with a finger. "Thirteenth floor."

"Looking to prove your father wrong?" Mom asks, reaching for my hand. She squeezes as the elevator doors slide open, tugging me inside.

"He's never wrong," I mutter.

"Never say never, my darling boy."

The thirteenth floor is as creepy as it sounds like it would be. The first level had decent lighting and enough human paraphernalia that, despite its emptiness, still gave it a sense of agency.

Up here, it's like time is stuck in a bottle and hasn't moved for centuries. City archives are locked in glass display cases alongside rare leatherbound classics and an endless collection of encyclopedias.

Posters on the wall instruct visitors not to touch the books without proper handling equipment and not to remove them from the premises.

I grab one from a shelf and flip to the middle, searching until I find something mildly interesting. The entries are mostly about the founding of Fury Hill, but there's a name that continually comes up, making me pause when it gets to the actual person.

Cronus Anderson (born c. 1550—died unknown). One of the six founding family members, Cronus is attributed with the conception of Avernia as a learning institution, the construction of town around campus, and promoting drilling near the base of the White Mountains for raw minerals that would boost Fury Hill's economic growth.

Eventually, like the other founders, Cronus would go on to establish his bloodline and grow his wealth. Though he survived the consumption crisis, Cronus was excommunicated before his death.

There are no records of the death of Cronus Anderson. It is likely they were destroyed in a fire that eventually burned down his farm or perhaps intentionally erased at the behest of his daughter.

Similarly, documentation of his time during the height of the crisis in Fury Hill have all but disappeared. Witnesses recall his intervention with unconventional methods of medicine and how he was one of the few who seemed unaffected by the illness. He is often blamed by residents for having taken advantage of the situation to gain ownership of the school and town.

While still revered as a medical marvel and important piece of Fury Hill history, it is important to note that the Anderson bloodline is—

See index for more information.

The last part of that paragraph cuts off, having been scribbled out with a permanent marker. I glance up, a strange feeling clutching at my chest. Mom's a few rows down, flipping through a tattered copy of some town periodical.

Beneath the entry for Cronus is a host of others, each with the same surname, indicating direct relations. My stomach twists as I drag my finger along each bullet point, pausing only when I get to the bottom few.

Deidre Anderson.

Kallum Anderson.

With quick fingers, I turn to the index and find my apparent ancestor's name.

A note is written in the margins—in fact, the entire back end of the book is handwritten anecdotes, some pages falling out as if they were stapled in after the fact.

The bloodline is tainted. Cronus placed this fate upon their heads. If a descendant steps onto this campus, it is the duty of Avernia to ensure they do not remain if we are to avoid the curse that plagues them.

Remember the law of three. Unity will result in our failure—they will be the destruction of us all.

Snorting, I snap the book closed. What kind of an encyclopedia includes a call to action?

And *curses*? Tainted bloodlines?

It almost feels like a prank, and I'm tempted to ask Quincy about it when we meet back up later, just to see if she's aware of the apparent connections we have here too. Maybe that's why she stays—she's always wanted a deeper family history.

What could possibly be *deeper* than fable?

"Find anything interesting?" Mom asks when we finally exit the thirteenth floor, heading in search of the rest of our party. "Not a good selection for fiction, and unfortunately, I'm not that interested in the town's story. But at least there were no ghosts."

"Oh, there's fiction up there all right. Some of those entries were just plain weird." I pause, looking at her from the corner of my eye. "Did Q ever tell you why she *had* to come here?"

"Well, historically, Avernia was a place for students to step into the world of liberating thought and social practices. They emphasized and highlighted the arts and humanities as tools to bridge histories and psyches, and they've created many loyal alumni from those practices. I assume she wanted to come here based on that, and because it was one of the top colleges in the country for classics studies."

Glancing up, I meet her soft gaze. "Do you think this is a normal school? I mean, they have books about town curses and conspiracies. That's weird, right?"

"Everyone has their lore." She lifts a shoulder. "It seems normal enough. They're incredibly difficult to get into, they have rigorous programs, their endowment is impressive, and Quincy says student life is pretty typical, even in the classics department. Parties, tailgates, fundraisers. Why? Does it not appeal to you?"

I swing my face forward, staring at the ground. "College never has, but Lucy wants to go here so bad. She thinks it'll be some miracle worker for her. I don't see the point."

"Ah." She quiets for a moment. "You know who you sound like?"

"Who?"

"Noelle."

My face twists into a mask of horror. "*Gross.* You think I sound like that spoiled brat?"

Laughing, Mom tugs me closer. "Don't for a second think you're any less spoiled there, my sweet son. Your father and I are just as indulgent to your whims as we are Q's and Noelle's. It's just that usually yours have to do with Lucy."

Grumbling under my breath, I lean into her and stop talking.

We meet up with the others as they're walking past the four dormitories, which sit in their own square a ways off from the main academic building and close to an entrance into the Primordial Forest, the woods that surround the school and block it off from the mountains.

Dad kisses Mom's forehead but allows us to stay toward the back, continuing our conversation even as our group moves on with its tour.

"Mortui vivos docent." I pause under the iron gateway, staring up at the words.

"The dead teach the living," Mom translates, squeezing my fingers.

"Does that mean I could learn more if you told me about your parents?"

She bristles, tugging me forward. "Any lessons you'd take from my parents would just be a laundry list of how to not be a shitty human. Don't you think your father and I have already drilled that into you at this point?"

I consider this as we weave between trees, coming out eventually at a rocky clearing that overlooks a dark, pitch-black lake many feet below. Shitty humans probably don't make their friends cry by lying to them about their car being full, but I don't tell Mom that.

If she wants to believe I'm good, I'll let her. Maybe if she thinks it long enough, it'll become true. A reality that takes over others.

Ahead of us, I catch Dad's eye. His expression doesn't change, but I know he heard what she said. They don't go into depth when it comes to their pasts, but from what I understand, Mom's parents are a particularly sore subject. Not even Aunt Ariana or Stella will talk about them, which makes it as though they never even existed.

Which is just as well, I guess.

My gaze flickers along my father's rigid back as he walks ahead of us. I wonder if *he* thinks I'm good. Compared to what the people back home say about him, the bar is pretty low.

But as they also say, the apple doesn't fall far from the tree.

"As you can see here, this is the quarry. It's home to some beautiful natural minerals and gemstones," the tour guide says, sweeping their hand out. "We haven't had anyone drill in a long time, but it's always a possibility that the city will bring excavators back, so campus administrators tend to try and keep this place under wraps. Though, Quincy, I'm sure you've found that students venture into the woods anyway."

My sister grunts, and I know she's annoyed that she isn't the one giving us the tour. Noelle's face is buried in her phone, and she keeps stepping on Quincy's heels.

"Now, if you'll follow me over here, we can take a look at some of the cave systems under the mountains surrounding campus, although again, these are off-limits to the public. Unlike the Primordial Forest in totality, the caves are completely blocked off…"

I stop listening when Mom lets go of my hand, jogging to catch up with Dad. He wraps an arm around her waist, tugging her close without even a moment's hesitation, and I kind of wish I'd let Lucy come with us.

Not that she'd ever let me touch her like that, but at least I wouldn't be the lone straggler.

Crouching down to tie my shoe, I exhale, doing my best not to think about how much Lucy would love it here. The gloomy atmosphere, the promise of progress, and the wide-open outdoors mostly untouched by humanity? She'd thrive, and maybe that's part of the reason I didn't want her coming.

Back home, she depends on me. I'm her only friend besides Aurora and Foxe, and I like it that way.

If she leaves and comes here, that all changes.

Unless I go with her, and frankly, college doesn't seem like it's for me. All I want to do is draw, and I can do that anywhere. Why would I do it at a place designed to make me miserable, even if there is a familial connection to it?

Especially a school that believes in bullshit curses.

When I stand back up, I realize I'm alone. My parents and sisters, even the tour guide—they've all disappeared, leaving me in the middle of fucking nowhere.

"Fantastic," I mutter, gritting my teeth as I start in the direction they were all heading. Noelle talks so loud that I'm positive I'll be able to find them if I move quickly enough.

Eventually, I come to a small fork in the path, and I stare at it for several seconds. Pulling my phone from my pocket, I try not to roll my eyes at the odds of having no service.

Hooking right, I cross my fingers and hope for the best. I can already hear Dad's lecture on keeping aware of my surroundings, one I've gotten from him dozens of times before, although usually because Lucy wasn't paying attention to *hers* and I stepped in to help.

And she thinks I'm trouble.

I don't find my family though, instead stumbling upon a smaller clearing with a white gazebo, bright among the greenery surrounding it. Just beyond is a decrepit house with a half-collapsed roof, while the entire side of the building is rubble, as if someone took a sledgehammer to it.

Seems strange that this wasn't included in the tour, but maybe it's something from before the school came to be, and no one's bothered to remove it yet.

As I circle the gazebo, I tilt my head all the way back, admiring the intricate carvings along the curved top—vines and flowers mostly, along with little symbols I can't fully make out. At the center, hanging lower than the rest, is a three-headed beast.

It looks like the one my mythology books say guards the gates of the Underworld, and given Avernia's obvious inspiration, I'm not at all surprised to see it.

Branches snap in the distance, and I whirl around, trying to figure out where the noise is coming from. I suddenly feel like I'm encroaching on someone's territory, and I shouldn't be here at all.

The air around me seems to thicken, pressing down until breathing becomes difficult.

Panic, maybe, or something sinister clinging to the atmosphere.

Turning, I start back the way I came, though I walk too fast for my feet to catch up fully, tripping over a tree root rising out of the ground. My face smacks the dirt, and my palms scrape against gravel, the little rocks tearing into my skin.

Hissing against the burn, I push to my knees, dusting my hands off. An eerie sensation crawls down my spine, but I lift my chin despite it, meeting the hardened gaze of a complete stranger.

Their short hair is in disarray, but their dark eyes feel unmistakable. For as long as I live, I'll remember their deep sheen and the feral glint hidden within.

Living doesn't seem to be much of an option, though, when they hold up an arm to reveal a butcher's knife, their fingers gripping the handle so tight that their knuckles are almost translucent.

My eyes widen, and I fall back on my ass.

"You're not supposed to be here," the person says.

"S-sorry," I choke out, fear clouding my throat. "I got lost and took a wrong turn—"

"No," they interrupt, moving closer. "Here at all. You'll bring destruction to this campus, all of you. This family is not welcome."

It is the duty of Avernia to ensure they do not remain.

I have no qualms about leaving, so I scramble to my feet, prepared to dart into the forest. As soon as my foot moves in that direction though, the person launches themselves at me, knocking me back to the ground.

My vision temporarily goes black as my head hits a rock, but when I come to again, the person is looming over me, straddling my waist, and holding the sharp edge of the knife to my throat.

Clenching my jaw, I don't make any sudden moves as the blade gently presses against my skin. I feel the moment it slices through, and guilt washes over me that this will be how my parents find their only son: lost and decapitated.

How fucking embarrassing.

There's no doubt in my mind that disappointment would be a forefront emotion when my dad discovers my corpse; he spent half our childhoods teaching us not only to be aware of our surroundings but to utilize them to our advantage.

As the person swaps the knife for their hand, strangling me instead of trying to cut through flesh and bone, my fingers stretch out, slowly groping the ground for something to use.

Anything.

I don't know what the hell is happening, but I do know I don't want to die.

My thumb grazes something long and oddly shaped, and I wrap my fingers around it quickly, pressing the tip into the dirt until I can feel it splinter off. Sliding my hand beneath, I curl the object in my palm as my head begins to swim and use every ounce of strength I can muster to drive the broken branch into the side of their skull.

The force of the blow knocks them back, and they clutch their head instantly.

Without pause, I throw myself over the knife and draw it upward, slamming the thing into the center of their forehead before they have a chance to blink.

Their eyes are wide open as I withdraw, repeating the motion again. And again.

And again.

My entire body trembles, adrenaline and fear pumping through me. Nausea curdles in my stomach, but I swallow over it as the assailant drops, blood spurting from the wound in their head.

I don't remove the knife when they go limp.

Sitting back, I fall on my ass again, reaching up to where they cut my throat. The wound doesn't feel too deep, so I tear a piece of my T-shirt off and try to stop the bleeding.

More branches crunch in the distance, and I jump to my feet, diving behind the gazebo this time. Breathing hard, I lean my head against the wood. If I'm attacked again, it's unlikely I'll make it out of here alive.

"Asher?"

Tears spring to my eyes. I fly out from behind the gazebo, almost tackling Dad as he jogs in my direction. His arms wrap around me, holding me close while a terrified noise comes from my chest.

"What the hell happened? I turned around for a minute, and you were gone, and then..." He trails off, and I imagine him glancing around, then at the dead body a few feet away. Pulling back, he puts his hands on my shoulders and looks into my eyes. "What happened?"

I don't say anything. I'm still not sure myself.

His fourteen-year-old son just murdered someone. That much seems obvious.

"What if we went to that little diner down the street for lunch—oh my *God*!" Mom's voice enters the clearing, and I peek past Dad to see her standing at the edge, eyes wide and mouth agape. "What the fuck did you do, Kallum?"

Dad exhales, turning with me still in his grip, and makes me face her. She gasps louder this time, horror etching into her delicate features. I wince, hating that I'm the cause.

"What the fuck did you let him do?"

"Elena."

She rushes over, yanking me into an embrace. Her hands pat me down, feeling for fractures and abrasions, and I close my eyes for a moment. When she pulls away, she smooths her thumbs over my cheeks, giving me a little shake.

"Are you okay, baby?"

"He's fine."

"I wasn't asking you," she snaps, glaring at Dad. He's now standing over the corpse, rubbing his chin. "Who the hell is that?"

"No clue. I was just with you, looking for our son, you know."

She drops her head to my shoulder, sighing. "I know, I know. I just…" Clutching me tighter, she makes a weird sound and then releases me to walk over to him. "What do you think?"

He says something too low for me to hear. Not that I'm really paying much attention as my vision swims in and out of focus.

This wasn't like my usual fights. I don't feel any excitement—only thick, unending dread.

"…actually fucking dangerous. I'm not sure what they want with us, but maybe we should talk to Q about this place."

"We can, but you know she won't want to leave without a good reason. She thinks this is her destiny, and she's convinced Lucy of it too."

"So let's *give* her a reason. Destiny or not, our son was just randomly attacked."

"Was it random though?"

They get quiet, and I wonder if they know what *I* know. If they've seen the encyclopedia too somehow.

Mom exhales long and slow. "I don't want this following Asher in the meantime."

"Well, I'm afraid there's not much we can do to lessen the emotional impact—"

"No, I mean." Mom waves her hands between the four of us. "On paper. Can't you…fix it?"

For a long time, he doesn't say anything, but his gaze eventually slides to mine. His chest puffs up with a deep inhale, deflates slowly, and then he nods at Mom. "Be sure what you're asking me to do is really what you want, little one. There's no coming back from this."

She bites her lip, then holds an arm out, beckoning me. "I know what I'm asking, Kallum. For you to protect our child. You promised you would no matter what."

"You don't normally let me go to such extremes."

"Not if it means compromising our child's trust, no." She points at his chest. "That is not the case here."

I don't know what the hell is going on anymore. They seem to be more aware of things that I'm not in any shape to comprehend, but when Mom tells me to come over, my feet carry me to her.

"I'm going to go find your sisters and take them back to main campus," she says, kissing my forehead before removing the scrap of fabric from my neck. Her jaw clenches when she notices the gash there, and she tucks the piece into my fist, curling my fingers inward. "You two come find us when you're finished."

It's more than a little unsettling how calm she seems about all this, but I don't get the chance to comment, because she's gone within minutes. Dad looks at the trees she slipped through, and I wonder if he's about to lecture me again or ask for more details I'm not ready to give.

Instead of doing either, he reaches into his pants pocket and fishes out a matchbook. Holding it up with two fingers, he raises a dark brow at me, something easy and foreboding passing between us.

"That cut on your neck," he deadpans, moving my hand for a moment to inspect it. He clicks his tongue, then places the fabric back into place. "Keep that there until we get to the car. I've got a med kit—I'll patch you up once we're out of here."

I nod.

"Now." Turning, he faces the corpse. "One of the most important things I will ever teach you," he says in a low, steady voice, like he's been waiting for this exact moment, which I find fucking weird, "is how to properly clean up your messes."

Chapter 3

Lucy

SIXTEEN YEARS OLD

WHEN WE WERE BABIES, OUR PARENTS PUT ASHER AND ME IN THE same crib because there weren't any other safe places for a colicky infant to nap. Our moms, best friends at that point, stayed in the room, making sure eight-month-old Asher didn't stir and cause problems.

As the story goes, the intrusion did wake Asher, but only long enough for him to reach out and grab hold of the sleeve of my outfit, which they said had an immediate calming effect on me.

I was out like a light in seconds, and we've been inseparable since.

That small gap in our ages never really seemed like much—it's a mere six months—maybe *because* we've always been together. But lately, as the spring rolls around and Asher's being fitted for his graduation gown and doing grad prep, the divide feels impassable.

I'm sitting on his bed with my legs crossed, Keats purring in my lap, watching from the corner of my eye as he tosses another college brochure in the wastebasket by his desk. Floating shelves above the wooden structure are lined with various books—from classics like *Moby Dick* and *Beowulf* to manga and blank sketchbooks.

His black hair is a little longer than usual, falling limp when he leans back in his chair, shaking the strands loose from the collar of his plaid button-down. The sharp angles of his face are mesmerizing, but then he opens his mouth and ruins the illusion.

"You know, I'm starting to think my parents signed me up for some mailing lists," he grumbles.

"Have you decided where you want to go?" I ask, trying to make it sound casual. Like I don't mind that he'll be leaving me behind.

If my parents had bothered having me earlier in the year, we'd be in the same grade, and I wouldn't feel like I'm suffocating now.

Asher swings his gaze lazily in my direction. His eye is a purplish-yellow color from a scuffle at school last Friday, and there's a hint of blood on the collar of his shirt.

Violence doesn't faze him in the slightest, and as a pacifist I should probably care more that his solution to every problem involves his fists, but…they're usually *my* problems that he's trying to solve.

There's a small, slightly deranged, part of me that likes how he always has my back.

"According to these fucking recruitment letters, I pretty much have my pick of the lot," he tells me.

Acid burns in my stomach. *Must be nice.* All three of the Anderson kids have had that experience.

"Yeah, but where do you *want* to go? It probably won't do you any good to just pick a random school."

"All I want to do is draw," he says, shrugging. "I can do that any-where. Don't even need school for it."

"Sure, but—"

"My mom didn't finish her degree, your mom has one she doesn't use, and they both seem to be doing pretty well," he continues, propping his arms behind his head.

I catalog the bulk of them, which has increased in the past year or so, and I quickly look away as heat fans my face.

"So are you saying you don't want to go to school at all?"

"Who knows. Maybe I'll take a gap year and wait to see if something else piques my interest." His warm brown eyes meet mine. "Where are you wanting to go?"

"Avernia."

"Ugh. Still? I thought Quincy'd convinced you to stay away from that stupid place."

I frown, confusion screwing up my face, and dig my fingers into Keats's fur. "What are you talking about? Your sister *loves* Avernia. She's constantly singing its praises. Plus, it's one of the only schools in the country to keep expanding its art and humanities courses where the others keep shrinking theirs."

"Do you even know what you want to major in yet?"

"Well, no. But I have some time to decide. I'm stuck between some kind of environmental preservation program and political science—"

Asher snorts.

"—but a planned trip to see the campus next fall will help me pick, I think. Avernia graduates go off to do really cool things, and I...I want to do them too."

It sounds pathetic when I say it, but it's the truth. Where else can I whisper my basest desires if not in the comfort of Asher's bedroom?

My *dream* has always been to open up a sanctuary for endangered wildlife and to fight for the conservation of the planet and its natural resources. While Avernia is best known for its classics, theater, and literature departments, it's a top-tier location for the kind of work I'm interested in, and has superior science programs with lots of important faculty to network.

Not to mention Quincy going there makes me feel like I *could* do it. I trust her judgment.

Asher gives me a droll look. "There are better schools out there, pup. Closer to home even. I bet your parents would love that."

"I'm sure they would," I say, thinking of the disappointment that lines my dad's face with each day that brings us closer to my graduation. "But my long-term decisions shouldn't be about them. That's what they've always told me anyway."

"They're lying."

The way he says it, with such assurance and finality, makes my skin crawl. It feels like he's holding something back, which he never does.

We tell each other everything.

"Why would they lie?"

"Parents do that sometimes. Maybe they're trying to spare your feelings."

"If they wanted to control my decisions, couldn't they just threaten not to pay my way?" That's what happens in the movies and books, anyway.

My parents aren't like that, but maybe Asher knows something I don't.

Ever since he came back from that weekend trip a couple years ago, his attitude about school and the future in general has been worse. While he has never been a terribly positive person, this still seems excessive.

"What aren't you telling me?" I ask.

He pushes from his desk, kicking off his Converse before face-planting beside me. The mattress jostles with his added weight, and Keats launches off my lap, retreating to the hallway.

"No more school talk," he says into the bed, his voice muffled by the sheets. "It's depressing."

"How so? Your grades are great, and you don't even have to try. Mine, on the other hand…"

"If you're worried about getting in, don't be. I'm sure Quincy would write a great recommendation, and having an alumna on your side would go a long way."

"That won't make me a better test-taker. Not even the extra time helps."

"There's more to the application than test scores, Luce. Plus, your parents can convince anyone to do anything. I doubt the school would want to piss off a former governor."

"Yeah," I agree, but his words weigh heavily on my chest.

I don't want my parents to have to charm my way into school.

Given my academic record and history of "civil disturbances" in the name of the greater good, I doubt I'll get in anywhere based on extra-curriculars alone.

My community merit outshines everyone on this godforsaken island. I'm the twice-elected leader of our school's wildlife conservation club, I've helped my mother run countless fundraisers to find stray animals homes and offer affordable spay and neuter clinics, and I spent last summer volunteering at the Society of American Foresters helping plant trees along the East Coast.

But Avernia is still a business at its core, so the likelihood of them caring about community action when considering retention possibilities is low. Even Quincy says there's a certain expectation of the students to be exemplary learners and social butterflies.

Unfortunately, my academics leave a lot to be desired, although not for lack of trying. It's just that concentrating on stuff I don't find interesting is hard, and when I lose focus, it just kind of snowballs into an uncontrollable mess.

Still, if I end up having to use my parents to get me into Avernia, I suppose that wouldn't be the worst thing. Maybe the change of scenery will help reset my brain or at least give me a chance to get away from the people who have always disliked that I'm not outgoing or exciting enough.

Anything that takes me away from this island.

"Asher! Lucy! Dinner's on the table if you're hungry!" Asher's mom shouts from somewhere in the house, her lilting voice carrying across the dark wood floors and disappearing into the tall ceilings.

"She made vegan mac just for you," Asher notes, lifting his head. "Don't tell her Italian ancestors."

I mime zipping my lips and tossing the key. "Mum's the word."

When I get up from the bed, reaching for my jacket, I turn around and wait for him to join me. He rolls over, propping his head on his hand, and stares at the wall.

"Are you okay?" I ask, crossing my arms over my chest. "You're being weird."

"I'm fine, pup. Don't worry about me." When he sits up, there's a distant glint in his gaze that makes me shiver. After a beat, he refocuses.

"Sometimes I think you forget I know you better than anyone." Reaching forward, I smooth the indent between his brows. "I can always tell when you're keeping secrets."

He swats my hand away, but catches it at the last second, holding me still. "Oh yeah? What sort of secrets might those be?"

"If I knew, I wouldn't have to ask."

"Then maybe you don't know me as well as you think."

It feels like he's just slapped me. I recoil, snatching my wrist out of his grasp.

Sighing, he drops his head into his palms. "I'll go with you."

"Thanks, but I don't need an escort to get food—"

"No, not downstairs." He plants his feet on the floor, lifting his eyes to mine. "To Avernia. If that's really where you want to go."

I can't stop a smile from splitting my face in half. "Are you serious?"

"Yeah. I don't mind waiting around a year for you." He clears his throat, straightening his spine. "That's what best friends are for, right? So you don't have to do anything alone?"

"But three seconds ago you were just trying to convince me to enroll somewhere else."

Asher shrugs. "An exercise in futility. You hate being told what to do, and you've never listened to me before."

Squealing, I throw myself at him, not thinking about the position it'll put us in when he falls under my weight. I just wrap my arms around his neck and squeeze tight, trying to memorize the clean cotton scent of his shirt and the hint of some woodsy cologne he and Foxe bought a few months back.

For once in our friendship, he doesn't smell like fresh blood or sweat, even though I can see the evidence of today's fight blooming on his knuckles. Beneath one eye. A scar on his lip from a few weeks back with Foxe.

"No take-backs," I say, jabbing my finger into his chest.

He chuckles but doesn't reply as I bury my face in his shoulder, too delighted to speak.

At this moment in time, he's not the angry, unhinged kid I've come to think of as a savior.

Right now, he's just my best friend.

The only boy I've ever loved.

And the one I know will never break my heart.

Chapter 4

Asher

"DO YOU THINK OUR PARENTS HAVE EVER FUCKED?" LUCY ASKS.

Foxe makes a gagging noise from one corner of Lucy's bedroom, where he and Aurora are taking shots of tequila and attempting to use a Ouija board. I'm seated on the counter in Lucy's bathroom, swinging my legs while she steps between them with an alcohol-soaked cotton ball, swiping it over my nostril with a shaky hand.

"Why the fuck are you thinking about your parents' dirty business?" Foxe calls, running a hand through his disheveled brown locks. His shirt is off, displaying the recent muscular definition afforded him by being promoted to quarterback of Aplana Academy's football team, and Aurora can barely disguise her drooling.

I pretend not to notice though, because I don't want them calling me out for my own inability to rein in my emotions. With Lucy between my thighs in a low-cut tank top, it's nearly impossible to keep my stare above her head.

"Hold still," she orders me, scrubbing at a particularly raw cut on my cheekbone. The fight I was in this afternoon was with some asshole who didn't like Lucy's science project on the alternatives to fossil fuels, so she doesn't admonish me for the fact that I showed up tonight bloodied and bruised.

They called her stupid. I broke their jaw.

She quietly cleans me and then marks my nose with a purple felt-tip marker, moving on to the task we had planned.

My hands flex against the granite counter, gripping tight as I ignore the effect her bossiness has on me.

"But also answer the question," she says, lowering her voice.

"Do I think our parents have ever fucked? Like, each other?"

She nods, and I lift my shoulders.

"I can't say I've spent much time thinking about it. Most days, I consider myself lucky that my mom and dad seem to keep their sexual weirdness to their bedroom after dark. I don't really want to wonder if they're bringing in others to watch."

Lucy's blue eyes widen. "Oh my God. That's what they do, isn't it? They just have orgies together. I *knew* our moms were too close."

"What does that have to do with anything?" Foxe chimes in, leaning away from the board as he reaches for a vodka bottle on the floor. He unscrews the cap, taking a huge gulp without wincing. "You and Ash-tree are close, but you're not fucking. Right?"

My throat constricts, and Lucy's mouth drops open. She whirls toward him, hurling the bottle of rubbing alcohol in his direction.

It smacks Aurora in the back of her blond head, and she groans, glaring at her cousin. "Hey! I didn't do anything."

"Jeez, Lulu, work on your aim," Foxe snickers. "And learn how to take a joke."

Aurora kicks his shin. "Don't be a dick."

"That's my drum-pedaling leg," he tells her, passing the drink. "You break it, you'll have to explain to my dad why I didn't get to follow in his musical footsteps."

"He's a professor," she replies.

"A *music* professor."

"So? It's not like you're on track to follow in *those* footsteps. You're closer to becoming a washed up rock star like your uncle."

"Aiden is not washed up. He retired to produce."

Aurora waves her hand dismissively. "Basically the same thing."

"Okay, well, let's not forget how *your* dad spends all his time at his bar—"

Bringing my gaze back to Lucy while those two bicker, I note the fuchsia color staining her cheeks. "What's wrong with you?"

"*Nothing*," she snaps.

"You look like you're about to pass out. Are you hot?"

"I don't know, Asher. *Am* I?"

"What?"

Scoffing, she reaches for the piercing clamp on the counter and shakes her head, clutching my chin again as she positions the metal prongs over my nostril. "Forget it. Just hold still so I can do this."

"But I want to know—"

She slides the needle in so quickly, I barely even register the bite of pain before she pulls it back out, quickly filling the hole with a small sapphire stud.

My skin vibrates a little at the foreign sensation tickling the inside of my nose.

"There," she says in a monotone voice. "The deed is done. You now have a hole in your face, just like my mom."

Foxe whistles. "Your mom is *smokin'*, so by default, this is too."

"Gross," Aurora complains. "He's your cousin, weirdo."

"I can't appreciate an attractive person if they're related to me?" He huffs, leaning back against the poster-covered wall. "I mean, we're all practically related. Our parents are closer than most cults."

"Not sure that's a great comparison," I note.

He rolls his hazel eyes. "Back me up here, Lulu. You think Asher's attractive, right?"

My pulse mobilizes, ratcheting to extreme levels in my chest.

I don't want her to answer.

No. Not true. I just don't *know* why I want her to answer.

Or at least I don't want to *admit* that I do.

Still, every atom of my being strains to hear the slightest shift in

Lucy's breathing or to see the blush staining her face darken. She turns away from me, cleaning up the tools she purchased specifically to pierce my nose.

No eye contact is made. It's almost as if I'm no longer here to her.

And she doesn't answer at all.

"*Boring*," Foxe says, staggering to his feet. He glances around the room at her desk and bookshelves cluttered with pet paraphernalia—dog tags, collars, leashes she and her younger sister, Logan, have crafted into key chains—and a raw mineral collection, finally finding his T-shirt on top of a pile of discarded clothing.

Bugs in resin line Lucy's white dresser, next to a bottle of perfume and a picture from the day she buried her first dog.

It's the three of them on the beach behind my house, plus her brother Lachlan. I'm nowhere to be seen, though Foxe's nose is swollen and packed with cotton, so my legacy is unmistakable.

Still, I can't help noticing it's the only picture in Lucy's room, aside from a few of her immediate family and the many animals the Wolfes have fostered over the years.

Almost like I don't exist at all.

I'd expected there to be a disconnect once I graduated, because Lucy is the kind of person to withdraw when she feels too much, but I hadn't planned on the erasure happening before then.

"We should head home," Foxe tells me, tugging his shirt on over his head. He smirks at the piercing as he gets closer, nodding once. "Yup, just as I suspected. Hot like Aunt Cora."

"If you want to bang Lucy's mom, you should just say that," Aurora grumbles from the bed. She's fuming, even as she pulls up a random compilation video on her phone.

"Everyone in Aplana wants to bang Lucy's mom." Foxe shrugs, slinging his arm over my shoulder and dragging me from the bathroom. "Except Asher, who doesn't want to bang anyone, ever. Right?"

I stare at him, resisting the urge to look at the raven-haired girl to his right.

"My dad would hunt you down if you even looked at her for too long," Lucy says finally, washing her hands in the sink. "So I wouldn't suggest trying anything."

There's a hint of wistfulness in her tone, a reverence she keeps in place for the few people she admires.

Is that the kind of thing she's into? Extreme jealousy and overprotection?

Have I not been doing enough?

Internally, I shake my head. It's not like it fucking matters. None of this means a damn thing, because I'll never act on it anyway.

Not in this lifetime at least.

Some people are simply destined to watch greatness from the sidelines. I'm a man cursed by his own want, a slave to captive desire.

She'd never go for it. For me.

I wouldn't even know how to ask.

"Yeah, yeah." Foxe rolls his eyes, pulling me toward the door. "The fantasy's always better anyway."

That, at least, I can agree with.

The fantasy is all I've fucking got.

"What made you decide not to continue school?" I ask Mom a few days later, aware that she doesn't like to be disturbed when she's in the middle of a project deadline but willing to risk her wrath anyway.

The thing with Mom's anger is that it burns out quickly, whereas Dad's is a quiet flame that builds and consumes slowly.

Mine is…eternal. That's all I know about it.

It's this disease that pulses inside my stomach on a constant rotation, ready to push me into action no matter the circumstance. I can't seem to ever let it go, ignore it, or move on.

It's just there.

It *is*.

Mom glances up at me from her laptop, a thoughtful expression on her angular face. Her golden-hazel eyes are soft at the corners, and she purses her pink-painted lips as if genuinely contemplating her answer.

"Well, I married your father, for one." She leans back from her desk, folding her hands in her lap. "And I was *really* into him. At that point, I couldn't imagine ever leaving him."

My face screws up, and I close the tattered copy of *For Whom the Bell Tolls* resting on my knee. "Didn't he force you into the marriage?"

"Force is a strong word. Your father is a man of action, and I like to think he just didn't know how to ask back then."

"You'd have married him if he asked?"

"Probably. I had a fiancé, and he was terrible. I'd been infatuated with Kallum for practically my whole life. The decision would've been an easy one."

"But he didn't let you make it."

"I suppose that's where the force comes in. Not that I minded." She grins, seemingly at the memory, pushing some dark brown hair from her shoulder.

"Ew," I mutter, resting my head on the back of the armchair I'm in.

The library at the Asphodel, our family home, is *huge*. Dad had it renovated before I was born to accommodate his and Mom's love for literature, and the built-in mahogany shelves stretch all the way to the ceiling, with attached ladders giving access to the books out of reach.

"A library is a place of worship," he told me at one point, and I often wondered if that was why we didn't go to church. If my parents found religion within the pages of these bound masterpieces.

When I was little, I'd spend my time here curled up on the floor in front of the black stone fireplace, listening to Mom read from whatever classic she chose that evening. Lucy could rarely stand to sit still long enough to join, but I used to love nothing more than the sound of my mother's soothing voice before bed, lulling me to a place where anger felt a little less prevalent.

It seems such an infrequent sensation for me these days.

I'd hoped as I got older, that might change.

"Why are you asking about school?" Mom continues, tilting her head at me. "Have you been thinking about what your plans are for after graduation?"

"I certainly hope that's been on his mind, considering how close it is." Dad's voice echoes through the room as he strides in, bringing Mom a steaming mug of tea. He places it on the desk by her elbow, bending to press a kiss to her forehead.

She leans into the gesture, smiling up at him.

A private smile.

One she keeps just for him.

"Maybe you should worry more about your globe-trotting daughters," I point out. "Has anyone heard from Noelle recently?"

"She had an audition last night and got brunch with her agent today. And Q's ferry should be here in an hour or so," Mom replies easily, winking at me. "I can worry about all three of my kids at the same time."

"Kind of feels like I'm getting all the focus these days."

"Well, Ash, you're the only one left." Dad comes over, dropping into the chair across from me, and picks up a copy of the *Aplana Times* from the coffee table between us. "Maybe if you seemed more interested in your future, we'd be able to think about something else."

I scrub my hands over my face. "Do you think I should go to Avernia?"

Dad's dark eyes meet mine over the newspaper. "No."

Nodding, I slump back and glare at the ceiling. "Great. Then what the hell am I supposed to do?"

"We were under the impression you weren't interested in going anyway, what with everything that happened when we visited." Dad cocks his head, studying me. "Did something change?"

"What if all that was just a fluke? I mean, Q's doing grad school there, and the place is up and running. Surely—"

"I've yet to fully understand your sister's insistence on remaining at the school for her master's," Dad says. "But I sincerely doubt she's there because it's a *good* place to be. Especially for our family. You read what was in those books that day, and the more we've looked into it the more clear it is that you kids are targets to the people in that town."

Mom comes over, perching on the arm of Dad's chair. She adjusts the neckline of her wine red robe, and he wraps an arm around her waist.

I look at a piece of warped hardwood floor.

"Avernia's belief system is wrapped up in its city's history," Mom says. "And that means they don't want Anderson blood around at all. It makes the campus a dangerous place to be, and since we don't *really* know what else they have planned or how far they're willing to go...I'm just not sure it's a good idea, Asher."

"Quincy's there."

"In violation of my wishes," Dad replies. "If I'd had my way, we'd have yanked her out immediately after I disposed of two corpses the day we visited."

Two corpses? I frown, opening my mouth to question where the other came from, but a memory flashes in my mind before I can speak.

Noelle, tucked tightly into the back seat of our car, huddled under a blanket in the corner. The smell of alcohol and sweat as I climbed in beside her, casting a glance at her unmoving form.

It was past midnight, and she'd gone to some party with Quincy, so I'd just assumed she was drunk or tired.

But unlike the times I'd actually seen her inebriated, she never spoke a word on the whole ride home. Even when we got back to the Asphodel, she just went straight up to her room, and I heard the shower run for hours before I finally fell asleep.

Is it possible that something else happened that day?

That Avernia is even worse than I'd initially thought?

"Quincy insisted on staying, and since Avernia credits are nontransferable, pulling her would've done more damage than good," Dad finishes. "Though I maintain that the Kellys could have easily fixed *that* issue for us, but *no*—"

"You'll be an adult," Mom interrupts, placing her palm on Dad's thigh. "We can't tell you where to go or what to do, nor can we force your sisters to listen. That is why Q remains on campus. We trust you all to make the right decisions for yourselves and your safety, so ultimately, if you choose to attend, we won't stop you. Just... Keep all this in mind, okay?"

"They never reported those deaths," Dad notes. "Not the person who attacked you or the...other. No one questioned anything, and it's just like those two people didn't exist. I barely had to clean up beyond the technical scrubbing. That school has way more secrets than just the desired downfall of a founding family."

When I'm alone in my room later, I spend hours researching Avernia College on the web, trying desperately to find out what sinister things lurk within the grounds there. Mostly, it seems to just be a conglomerate of centuries-old buildings with a student body that supposedly embraces modern progress while honoring tradition.

Yet the evidence of some strange, deadly plot is damning.

Mortui vivos docent.

The school's motto, plastered at the top of their site's homepage and on the garish iron gates leading onto and off campus.

The dead teach the living.

Is that their goal? Did the school have a hand in the attempt on my life, and that's why it was never reported?

Do they intend to kill people because of something that supposedly happened centuries ago and use them as a lesson for future generations?

To stave off some ridiculous idea of a curse?

If that's the case, then I should steer clear of it entirely. I've no desire to go somewhere I'm not wanted, much less where I'm threatened.

Still...

Lucy's *convinced* this place will be her reckoning, her shot at greatness, because of how Quincy's hyped it up over the years.

But no one's told Lucy about how the Andersons tie in.

She doesn't *know* it's dangerous for us, and I'm not sure I should tell her.

I stare at the ceiling after everyone's gone to bed, with Keats curled up in my lap over the comforter, and wish the Asphodel would collapse on top of me so I didn't have to make the decision.

If I don't go, Lucy will hate me.

But if I do go, it sounds like I won't come out the same person. If I come out of it at all.

Chapter 5

Lucy

EIGHTEEN YEARS OLD

"THIS SCHOOL FITS LULU'S PERSONALITY PERFECTLY," MY YOUNGER sister, Logan, mutters under her breath, leaning over the dining room table to study the brochure. "Look how creepy and dark it is! Why are we still debating where she'll end up?"

Our mom gently guides a brown Chiweenie foster dog off her lap, then scoots her chair in. Her blue hair is pulled back into a low bun, and the tattoos covering her arms are fully displayed in the Aplana Animal Society T-shirt she has on.

At her side, our father, with his slightly unbuttoned dress shirt, suspenders, and the slicked-back black hair with gray peeking over his ears, feels like a massive contrast.

He's smooth edges and she's a messy canvas, yet somehow they work.

Mom takes a sip of her water, giving my sister a look. "No one is debating anything, Logan. Where Lucy goes is entirely up to her."

I glance at Dad, whose jaw tightens as he dutifully stares at his phone. She looks at him too, then shoves her elbow into his side.

"*Right*, Alistair?"

"Of course, *m' eudail*," Dad says in his English accent, putting his phone down next to his dinner plate. His icy blue eyes find hers, and he leans in to flick her nose. "You needn't worry about me. I said I would respect Lucy's decision, and I meant it."

My gaze narrows. "Is that why my Avernia pamphlets keep magically finding their way to the garage trash? Or in the pool? Or why they're usually shredded and unusable by the time I find them?"

He blinks at me, the picture of innocence. "How can you possibly accuse your doting father of such things when we have a house full of rabid beasts?"

"It's not like your room is clean and a dog wouldn't be able to grab something," Lachlan adds, always coming to Dad's defense. His shaggy black hair obscures his brownish-gold irises as he digs into the steak in front of him, but I can practically see him salivating for the older man's approval.

"Don't blame the dogs," Mom replies, glaring over her water. "I've worked very hard with the current lot to scale back their destructive tendencies."

"If it's on the floor already though, I'm not really blaming them," Lachlan says. "That's just the natural course of evolution happening. Maybe Lucy should clean her bedroom."

"Maybe you should mind your business," I snap, jabbing my fork in his direction. *Little shit.*

Dad laughs, raising his eyebrows pointedly at me. "You're going to miss this if you move too far."

"Alistair," Mom scolds. "Stop manipulating her."

"What? I'm only stating the facts. Do you or do you not love our meals together?"

I shrug, pushing a piece of garlic tofu onto the portobello mushroom patty at the center of my bowl. I'm the only one not eating steak. "Maybe it'll make each future one more special?"

"She's gonna go wherever Asher Anderson goes anyway," Logan interjects. "It's not like there's any convincing her otherwise."

"Why would *Asher* factor in at all?" Dad asks with a frown.

"Uh…" Logan makes a face, her golden gaze—a mirror of Mom and Lachlan's—volleying between the four of us. "Because she's in love with him?"

White-hot shame slashes across my face, flames of embarrassment snaking their way down my neck and over my chest. "I am *not*."

"Liar, liar, pants on—"

"All right," Mom says, setting her utensils down. "Is this really appropriate table conversation?"

Dad bristles, sitting up straighter. "I'm certainly interested."

"Because you're a busybody," she tells him.

"I am, yes, in more than one sense of the word." He lets his gaze drop down over her, and something in the air shifts between them.

Something wildly uncomfortable.

"*Okay then.*" I shove back from the table. "I've got to get to Foxe's, and I don't want to catch the live-action Cora and Alistair show. I've been scarred by that enough at this point."

"Oh please." Mom scoffs, though her cheeks are flushed. "We've never done anything with you all awake in the house."

Logan pretends to gag. "That doesn't make it better."

"You three should be glad your parents have such a healthy appetite for each other," Dad adds, slinging his arm over the back of Mom's chair and tugging her close. "We're fantastic role models."

"Pillars of affection, really." She grins at him, tilting her head back for a kiss.

Logan and I retreat from the dining room, but Lachlan remains at the table, scarfing down the rest of his meal without making eye contact. He'll probably wait until they disentangle themselves and then follow Dad outside to talk about archery, Lachlan's only real hobby outside of being an annoying shit.

"Sorry if you didn't want them to know," Logan says as she pauses at my bedroom. "I…kinda thought it was obvious."

"What?"

She blinks. "You know, the whole Asher thing."

"Oh." I shake my head, inching into my room. "Nonissue. I'm not in love with him."

One of her eyebrows arches. "If you say so."

Throat tight, I watch her skip down the hall to her room, and a few minutes later I can hear her whisper-yelling at the computer as she hops on some sort of game for a live stream.

I spend several seconds staring at the closed door, wondering if I'm really *that* transparent.

And if I am, how come *he* hasn't noticed?

A while later, Dad knocks on the wall, strolling inside with his hands in his trouser pockets. He glances around my room, smiling softly to himself as he runs a finger over the dog tags on my dresser.

"You know I don't care where you go to school," he says, turning to me as I slide my boots on. "I just like riling up your mum."

I roll my eyes but give him a small smile. "Yeah, I know. She makes it super easy."

"That she does. I think she secretly likes it though." He runs a finger over my desk, collecting dust. "Only reason we've gotten through two decades of marriage."

"Because she'd kill you if she didn't like it?"

"Precisely."

Brushing off his hands, he continues until he reaches my side, plopping down on the bed next to me. The mattress shifts, and I inhale deeply as he crosses his ankles, finding comfort in the familiarity of his cologne and warmth.

Everything else feels like it's changing so quickly, it's nice to know that this is a constant. That when I'm gone, I'll be able to come back and see things the way they are now.

The way they'll always be.

"I'll miss you no matter where you go," he says, bumping my knee with his. "It won't be the same in this house without you yelling at us to conserve water when we brush our teeth or trying to convince us that tofu is good."

"It's not like I'm dying. I'll be back." I pause, placing my foot on the floor. "And tofu *is* good, you just cook it wrong."

"Whatever you say, Lucy." Dad nods. "But when you come home to visit, it won't be the same. It never is. I guess I'm just having a bit more difficulty adjusting to this major change than I'd anticipated. I apologize for throwing out your brochures and burning the student tour invitation you got last week."

My eyebrows arch. "I didn't know about that one."

He smirks. "I'm very good at erasing evidence, my girl." Pausing, he leans back on my bed, stretching his long legs. "Can I ask a question?"

"It's a free-ish country."

The former governor smirks. "Why Avernia College? There are plenty of private liberal arts schools scattered across the states and bigger universities we'd be able to afford. Similar programs, some farther away. Better reputations. So why *that* school?"

"Do you believe in fate?" I counter.

"Absolutely."

"Well, I was in the attic with Quincy Anderson when she first found out about Avernia and how her grandmother attended a long time ago. I watched her sift through this box of their dad's old stuff. Pictures, letters, scraps of clothing, and hospital bills. Random stuff Uncle Kal kept that she hadn't seen before."

"That stuffy old doctor is terrible at sharing."

I nudge Dad with my knee. "Yet he's one of your closest friends."

"Well, it isn't like I had much say in the matter. Your mum and Elena clicked far too well for me to sit back and let her have all the fun."

My mind flickers back to the question I asked Asher long ago about our parents' relationships behind closed doors, but I quickly push it away. No fucking *way* am I asking my father for more information.

"Anyway," I continue, "Quincy was just so elated at the prospect of this historical tie to the university, and I swear I'd never seen that look on *anyone's* face before. It felt like fate had brought that box out of hiding. And the way she talked about the school after enrolling, it just feels like the close-knit, forward-thinking community I really want. A place where I can be myself and not feel like I need to wear a mask around everyone. You know?"

Dad glances down at me. "I get it. Plus, watching people you know go through it makes the journey seem less terrifying. Right?"

I smile, nodding. "Exactly."

"Oh, for fuck's sake." Arms crossed over her chest, Mom enters the room, already glaring at Dad. She's in a fuzzy orange robe we got her several birthdays ago, apparently having changed after we left downstairs. "Would you stop harassing our daughter?"

"Does it look like she's being harassed, *m'eudail*?"

She grabs his arm and hauls him to his feet; the significant difference in their height, him being over a foot taller than her, is almost comical. "Lucy, baby, get ready for your party. I have something for you to give your aunt Violet if you don't mind taking it for me."

I nod. There's no arguing with her.

"And for the record," she tells me, pausing in the doorway with Dad glued to her side, "wherever you go, you're gonna do great. So don't let anyone else's opinion sway you, and pick whatever's in your heart."

They leave, and I spend a few extra minutes sitting there, swinging my legs back and forth.

Would it be the end of the world if I didn't wind up at Avernia College? I doubt it'd matter at all in the grand scheme of things, and I know I could get in elsewhere. Probably.

I just…don't want to.

For years, I've had my eyes set on this one place. Any time I looked anywhere else, I'd be drawn right back to those hallowed halls, and since I've spent a lot of my life resigned to the fact that I can't have everything I want, this is something attainable.

Something I can do that might actually have an impact on the world around me. Maybe if I can get away, burying myself somewhere no one knows my name or my history, I'll feel like I've accomplished something.

It's stupid to hang on to such a surface-level dream, but at the moment, it's all I really have. With everything else changing so quickly, this feels like the one thing I have any semblance of control over, and I want it.

I *need* it.

Exhaling, I eventually get up from the bed and make my way downstairs again, taking the tray of seed starters Mom shoves into my arms.

Avernia will be different, I tell myself.

The way Aplana never was.

All I have to do is make myself believe it.

Chapter 6

Asher

EIGHTEEN YEARS OLD

I SHOULD PROBABLY TAKE THE BOTTLE OF VODKA AWAY FROM FOXE right now. I'm not sure how many drinks he's had, but as we make our way through the massive sunflower field behind his house, he keeps tripping over himself.

Once we get to the big clearing in the middle of the field, a few of the kids Foxe and Aurora invited from school start setting up plastic chairs and picnic blankets, and two guys whose pale biceps are almost fluorescent in the moonlight get to work on a bonfire.

We've been using this place for small get-togethers since middle school, though back then, there were fewer of us. That was how I liked it.

Now, I'm forced to babysit my overindulging cousin while he pauses to puke off to the side somewhere and watch as some pricks I don't recognize make Lucy blush.

I hate that I can tell the moment her cheeks pinken.

She's buzzed, presumably; normally at these things, she hides in the corner until she's had enough to drink or smoke to become somewhat sociable. Even then, her niceties are short-lived and generally devolve into rants about social injustices by the end of the night.

"How much do you want to bet she winds up making out with one of them tonight?" Foxe asks, nudging my shoulder with his.

"I don't think *you* should be gambling."

His mouth falls open. "I'll have you know the five big ones I lost last weekend at the track were only because I had too much to drink, and I filled out the wrong slot. Otherwise, my odds were great."

My gaze drops to the glass bottle in his hand.

He rolls his eyes and ditches me for the blond coordinating the lantern setup on the outer edge of the gathering.

Speculating on who Lucy might gift with her attention—or more—isn't a game I want to play, anyway.

Maybe these guys are interested in hearing her talking points. I know I'd listen to her for eternity. But somehow, their interest feels more nefarious.

Perhaps it's the way their stares occasionally drag down the length of her slender form, clad in a short red plaid skirt and a T-shirt layered over a long-sleeved shirt. Her legs are on display, wrapped partway in tall black boots. She'd tempt a saint with those pale thighs, and there are none of those on the island.

Least of all me as I fantasize about murdering the two students before her.

I could do it. I am my father's son after all.

Passing by Foxe as he argues with Aurora, I shove my hands in my pockets and head in Lucy's direction. I'm unable to take my gaze off her, especially when the spiky-haired blond leans in, brushing something from Lucy's cheek.

She freezes, and so does he, their eyes locked.

Jealousy roars to life inside my chest, making it burn.

"I'd love to know your thoughts about the governmental versus individual impact on the current state of the climate crisis," the blond tells her in a slow, smooth voice. His hand remains on her face, his fingers opening to cup her jaw and tilt her head.

The other guy, with long dark hair hidden beneath his jacket, slides a little closer, almost edging her out of my view.

My heart thumps deep and heavy, anger pumping slowly from the organ to the rest of my body.

"Individuals have a responsibility," Lucy says, slurring just slightly. "But the main blame should be on the govern—" She hiccups, interrupting her own sentence, and sways on her feet.

Spiky slips an arm around her waist. "Careful there, sweetheart."

"Yeah," the dark-haired one agrees with a smile. "Don't get yourself worked up just yet. Save your energy."

Lucy frowns, pulling away from the blond. "What is that supposed to mean?"

"Nothing, just—"

As I skid to a stop behind them, I snatch a box of matches from the girl bent over the bonfire, trying to get it started. With a flick of my wrist, the match in my hand flares up, and I mimic tripping over myself, sending the little stick flying.

It lands on the blond guy, and in a split second, a spark erupts on his tweed jacket, catching on the fabric.

Flames spread instantly, engulfing the immediate area. He releases Lucy, jumping back and frantically patting and swatting the arm, trying to get the fire to go out.

He shrugs the coat off, dropping it to the ground, where his friend stomps on it.

"Jesus fuck, man!" he shouts, drawing the attention of the rest of the crowd. The flames go out after a moment, but his eyes are still wild, his breathing labored.

I blink at him. "Oops."

"*Oops?* What the hell is your problem?"

"I tripped."

His eyes blaze, and he steps closer, trying to shove his nose in my face. I have a few inches on him though, so it's not an easy feat.

A grin stretches slowly across my mouth. "Do *you* have a problem?"

"Apparently, I do, Anderson. I should fuck up your face for trying to set me on fire."

"Go ahead," I tell him. "I don't have to go to school Monday and explain to the principal why I ended up with a broken nose and missing front teeth though, so I'd think it through before you hit me. I might enjoy it."

Excitement tingles beneath the surface of my skin, heating me in ways Lucy's presence never has—the *only* way she never has, because the anger isn't something she touches.

She's a balm to it most of the time. Yet right now, I suppose, she's the source.

Fear flashes in the blond's eyes, just for a moment. He clears his throat, shrinking back an inch. "That was a brand-new coat. Cost sixteen hundred dollars."

"Maybe you shouldn't wear flammable clothing to a *bonfire*."

"All fucking clothing is flammable, douchebag." Bending to collect the jacket, he huffs, glancing at Lucy. Nodding to his friend, he makes a noise of disgust, turning away from us. "Whatever, man. She's not fucking drunk enough to be worth it."

My knuckles ache to drive into his face, but they traipse off before I can do anything more, likely to find other unsuspecting inebriated girls to prey on.

So goddamn predictable. If they were going to be creeps, they could at least be creative about it.

Lucy crosses her arms, her face falling with their departure. She lifts her chin, glaring daggers at me. "Why did you have to do that?"

"Oh, sorry, were you enjoying their sleazy attention? I can ask them to come back if you're into that."

"I'm obviously not," she snaps, reaching out to jab me in the chest. She reeks of Malibu and pot, and her sapphire eyes are a little glassy, but somehow she manages to focus on me. "But I had it under control, *pretty boy*. I don't always need you coming to my rescue. I'm not a damsel in distress."

"Didn't say you were," I reply, taking her elbow and heading off in the opposite direction those two guys went in. Farther away from the fire, the soft pop music playing from a portable speaker somewhere, and the crowd.

I drag her into the sunflower stems, forging a path through the overgrown flora. We've practically had this place memorized since we were kids, but I doubt she'll be able to find her way out in her current state.

At first glance, she doesn't seem or sound that off, but I can see it: the subtle flush of her cheeks, the wide stare, and how she keeps looking down at her feet so she doesn't fall over them.

Small things you only notice when you've spent a lifetime watching.

Still, I didn't step in to *save* her. There's no doubt in my mind that if she needed to, she could easily take care of herself, even if she often chooses the path of no resistance. If it were her life or theirs, I want to believe she'd pick hers.

Stepping in was for *me*. Because I'm a jealous piece of shit who doesn't want to see her smile at anyone else.

But I can't admit that. I don't even know if she feels the same, and if she doesn't?

There's no way she'd ever forgive me for ruining our friendship and making things awkward.

Eventually, we come to another much smaller clearing, and I stop walking, dropping to my ass as she seems to contemplate going back the way we came.

"Aplana emergency officials don't know the full scope of this field," I tell her, leaning back with my palms on the loose dirt. "It'd take them a while to find you."

My uncle Grayson's been cultivating the massive sunflower field for as long as I can remember; it was a project he began specifically to make my aunt Violet's green thumb happy and then evolved into some sort of game with the Aplana Island city officials, who consider the plants an invasive species.

If anything, that only incentivized him more to make it bigger. Thicker. The entire back of the Jameses' house is obscured by the giant yellow and green plants through the autumn, providing us a place to escape when we really need it.

Lucy doesn't turn around, crossing her arms over her chest as she continues staring into the stems. "You can't keep doing this."

I pull my phone from my pocket, opening some random game. "Doing what?"

"*This*. Cutting in when I'm just trying to live my life." She spins around, stumbling a bit, and throws her arms out to the sides to catch her balance. "You're making it hard for me to exist."

"And here I thought I made your life easier."

"No." She stares at me, her blue eyes shadowed by the moonlight. "Not for a long time now."

Despite the dark sky, I can see every soft line of her face, and I hate it.

The divide between us that cracked open when I graduated in the spring seems to grow infinite in this enclosed space. I'm watching it split, standing on the edge, ready to jump, but there's no time before it becomes insurmountable.

I suppress the curdling in my stomach, ignoring how her words feel like a serrated knife to my gut as she walks over, dropping to the ground beside me.

"How am I supposed to get through this school year without you if I'm reliant on you always being around?"

"But I am around," I say. "Just because I'm not there—"

"You being somewhere on the island isn't the same as you *being there with me*." She sighs, extending her legs and folding her hands between her thighs. Her feet swing from side to side, as she's unable to ever fully sit still. "We're barely a month in, and I can feel the difference. I didn't mind that people were no longer speaking to me or certain clubs were shunning me, because it'll all be over next year, right? We'll go to Avernia, as long as we both get in, and the people here will forget I ever existed."

Impossible, I think, gritting my teeth. *No one could ever forget you.*

Still, the other part of her sentence fills me with dread, bleak and hollow.

"In the meantime though, I think it'd be smart if I learned to live without you a little bit. You're not around to take notes for me or stop by and make sure I get somewhere on time. It just feels like I should take some responsibility, don't you think?"

"I didn't realize my friendship was such a burden." I'm not sure why I say it—hate the way her eyes seem to dim with the accusation.

"Not a burden," she replies, shaking her head. "A crutch. I don't have to worry about anything, because I know you're there."

Throat burning, I look away, down at my lap. I don't know what to say.

Use me. I don't fucking mind.

"Hey," she says, interrupting my thoughts as she leans in.

I shift, turning as she does, noting the way her eyelashes sweep over her cheeks.

"Can I ask you something?"

"Never been able to stop you before."

"Whatever our souls are made of, his and mine are the same."

I cock an eyebrow. "Is that a question, Ms. Brontë?"

Lucy snorts, losing her balance. Her hand comes down on my thigh, gripping tight as she catches herself. "I'm a little drunk, I think."

The breath *whooshes* from my lungs, disappearing into the air around us. "It's definitely possible."

"Oh," she says, tilting her chin down to stare at her hand. She flexes her fingers, and I suppress a full-body shiver. "You have really muscular thighs."

I don't—*can't* reply. I can barely hear anything she's saying, my brain and nerve endings too focused on the contact. Even through my jeans, her touch feels like an open flame, threatening to swallow me whole.

"Do you... Could I try something?" Lucy asks softly.

Somehow, my tongue finds enough moisture to unstick from the roof of my mouth. "Is that your question?"

She nods.

Clearing my throat, I shift, straightening my spine as I try to subtly move out from under her grip. She doesn't seem to get the hint, scooting closer even as I inch away.

"S-stay still," she bites out.

I want to make a quip about how that's a rich command coming from her, considering the way she can't seem to stop squeezing me, but then she's moving in, and I forget how to speak at all.

Her mouth hovers dangerously close to mine. My heart lurches into my throat, expanding so I can barely breathe. I can't think, certainly not enough to push her away or put a stop to this.

I should put a stop to it.

This is *bad*. A terrible idea, all things considered.

But I obey her single command and remain as still as a statue. She pushes up, using my leg as leverage, and pinches her eyes shut.

Mine are wide open the entire time.

Sweat lines my palms, but I keep them on the dirt, sure that I'll fall if I move. I wouldn't know what the hell to do with them anyway.

If I touch her now, I won't be able to restrain myself.

"What are you—"

When her mouth meets mine in the gentlest of kisses, I black out.

For several seconds, not one thought crosses my mind—it's blank, my vision completely obscured, my brain paused as it tries to process my elation.

Euphoria pulses in my chest, like a sky full of fireworks or supernovas.

Seconds later, I'm back in the clearing, my fingernails digging into the soft earth to keep from tangling in her raven-colored hair or grabbing her hips and pulling her on top of me.

Fuck. My cock stiffens just at the thought, and I shift, attempting to shield the evidence of what she does to me. Not that she's paying any attention; her eyes are still closed, and her breaths come in short, shallow waves as she parts her lips the tiniest bit.

She tastes like cherry lip balm and booze. I hope I remember the flavor combination for the rest of my life.

Suddenly, I'm curious to know what the rest of her tastes like. If she'd be sweet or tangy—if she'd want me to find out.

My fingers ache to reach for her. To draw her into my arms and release every ounce of tension I've been holding onto since realizing that I *liked* her.

Only her.

These aren't feelings I've harbored for anyone else, and I used to think it was because there was something else going on, like maybe I only liked men or wasn't interested in sex at all.

Turns out I'm interested, but only where Lucy Aberdeen Wolfe is concerned.

I only want *anything* with her.

Which is why I know I should stop this kiss and put an end to things before they get any worse.

I don't.

Stop, that is.

Fuck me, I don't.

Instead, my hand comes off the ground, slides along her jaw, and dives into her silky hair. I use her roots to angle her head, letting my tongue sweep past her lips to deepen the kiss.

It's the opposite of stopping.

And when she exhales into me, her palm flattening against my chest, I realize it's the brightest green light. An invitation if ever there was one.

Her tongue tentatively touches mine, a silent plea. My knuckles feel like they might break from the restraint I'm exercising, resisting the urge to haul her into my arms and never let her leave.

Fuck, fuck, fuck. This is bad.

"Asher," she breathes, pulling back for a second before diving in again, redoubling her efforts.

I shiver when her hand falls to my lap, her fingers softly pressing down on the zipper of my jeans.

A small gasp escapes as our mouths switch positions, but I can't tell if it comes from me or her.

I think I'm in love with you.

My brain screams those seven words, desperate to push them from my lips and into hers.

"What?" she says against me, her teeth bumping mine.

When she squeezes my dick, sending a rush of blood south, panic settles into my bone marrow.

I think I'm in love with you, my brain repeats.

My mouth moves with each syllable, and it takes several seconds for me to realize the words have been spoken out loud.

Heat sears my face, rising to my ears. I withdraw abruptly, keeping my fingers tangled in her hair.

Her eyes shine as she blinks at me, a question flickering in the oceanic depths. "What did you say?" she asks quietly.

Clenching my jaw, I release her and move backward. *She didn't hear me.* "I said you need practice."

Lucy's wonder fades immediately, like a bucket of cold water splashing on us. "Well, that's fucking rude."

"You're drunk," I offer, searching for some explanation that'll fix this. Put things back the way they were. I know she didn't mean for this to happen. She wouldn't have kissed *me* if she hadn't been drinking. "It's fine. I'm sure the next guy you kiss will be under different circumstances."

"I'm not *that* drunk, Asher. And that was a good kiss."

Fuck. I don't know what to do. Or say. Instinct has me locking up, pushing her out. My lips move before I'm ready. "You're lying."

Her mouth falls open. "What the fuck is your *problem*—"

"*You* are my problem, Lucy. Always have been."

It's mean. Too mean.

It's not even what I want to say.

But at the end of the day, I'm a coward. My anger bleeds too heavily into every other emotion, and I'm afraid it'll stain her too.

Fear and anger are driving forces that seek the same thing: complete destruction.

I just let them fuck everything up.

We stare at each other for several beats. Maybe even minutes.

My heart pounds in my throat, closing the airway as silence stretches thin between us. It feels like a million miles separate the distance, though we could probably close it in just a few steps.

Deep down, I yearn to erase the space. Indefinitely.

But I don't.

Instead, I get up. Brush the dirt from my pants while she continues sitting there, watching me with a stunned expression haunting her face.

And I leave.

"You're home early," Mom says when I burst through the front door a half hour later.

She's sitting in the living room, drinking lavender tea with her younger sister, Ariana, and Ariana's husband, Cash. Dad's off to the side, talking quietly on his phone, and I wonder if it's Foxe's dad calling to let him know I left the party already.

They lounge on our dark furniture while the television mounted above the gray stone fireplace plays some silent trivia show. The glow of the screen dances on the far dark green wall, and I focus on that while I try to regulate my breathing.

Cash adjusts his glasses, crossing a leg as he takes me in. One of his dark blond brows arches, but he doesn't say anything.

I'm sure I look like a wild animal, so I appreciate that his judgment is unspoken.

His wife's, however, is not.

"Jeez, what the hell happened to you?" Aunt Ariana asks, leaning over the arm of the sofa to peer closer at me. "You look like you got dragged three miles through the mud and then took a dip in the ocean to rinse off."

Glancing down, I note that my clothes and hair are drenched in sweat. I hadn't even realized it until this moment.

I don't know when it happened. Maybe when I sprinted across town to get here? Or when I ditched Lucy in the clearing?

Concern wrinkles Mom's forehead as she gets a better look at me. "Good God, Asher, are you all right?"

"I'm fine," I bite out. "I just walked here from Foxe's."

"It's unlike you to come home without Foxe or Lucy in tow," Mom notes, gripping her mug with both hands. She gives me one last lingering glance before taking a sip. "Was the party okay?"

"Ah," Ariana says, slumping back on the cushions. "I'll bet they had a fight."

I narrow my eyes at her, and she seems to hold back a grin.

"Oh, not again." Mom's face contorts into a mask of worry.

"There was no fight," I say, kicking the front door shut. I walk into the living area, holding my hands up. "No blood or bruises, see? I'm fine."

"We wouldn't be able to see a cracked rib," Dad chimes in, joining the conversation.

"Better lift up your shirt and show us," Ariana says, gesturing at me. "Come on, kiddo. Chop-chop. We don't have all day."

I look at her husband again, though I already know it's pointless. Even if he could stop her from being a lunatic, I doubt he would.

"Ariana," Mom scolds, hiding a smirk behind her wrist.

"Just trying to lighten the mood," she replies with a shrug, leaning her head on Cash's shoulder. Her chestnut-colored hair falls over his suntanned arm. "Your kids are always so serious. As the fun, childless aunt and uncle, it's our job to provide levity."

"For the record," Cash adds, like the lawyer he is, "I never said anything."

Dad chuckles, squeezing Mom's neck gently. "Trust me, it's all in the eyes anyway."

"Going to my room," I mutter, though they're no longer even paying attention to me as I head out into the hallway. I take the stairs two at a time, just in case any of the four try to come and get more answers.

I don't want to talk about this shit ever again, but especially right now. *Stupid, Asher. You are so stupid.*

My hands tremble when I get to my room, slamming the door shut with more force than I mean to. I slide my phone out of my pocket, reading the sixteen missed calls and texts from Lucy and Foxe. There are even a couple from Aurora, who normally doesn't care whether I live or die, so Lucy must've pressed her to reach out.

> **Lucy:** Are you ok? Did you get sick or something?
> **Foxe:** Where tf did you go?
> **Aurora:** If you went for more booze, could you try to get some of those seltzers we had last time? I'll pay you back probably.

I delete the notifications, and another comes in.

> **Lucy:** I'm sorry if that was over the line.

Goddammit. I can practically feel her disappointment and confusion.

For *years* I've been starving to kiss her, and when I finally get to, I run away.

Keats scurries out from under my bed when I lie back on it, dropping my phone and covering my face with my arms. My fingers itch, the desire to work out my feelings through sketches welling up inside me, but tonight I punish myself by refusing to create anything.

I'd always hoped to give Lucy Wolfe my first kiss. Nothing else would've ever sufficed.

In a perfect world, that would have been all it took for me to get over my insecurities and decide I'm worthy of her.

Tonight should've been amazing. My dream come true.

It was, a small voice in the back of my mind insists.

Except now I've woven action in with a lie she doesn't even know about yet, and I have no clue how I'll ever disentangle myself from this without ruining both our lives.

Chapter 7

Asher

EIGHTEEN YEARS OLD

QUINCY'S SITTING IN FRONT OF MY BED, HER LEGS PULLED TO HER chest and her arms wrapped around her knees. Her dark brown eyes—just like mine and Dad's—have purple bags beneath them, and her black hair is pulled back, her bangs almost hiding her expression.

Complete and total terror.

I shrug out of my hoodie and toss my headphones onto my desk. "Didn't know you were home."

She doesn't respond, so I kick out of my sneakers and move to my dresser, finding clothes for after my shower. Running with Foxe this morning was the only thing that could keep me from heading to the Wolfe residence and making an even bigger fool of myself.

I'm covered in sweat, seriously unpracticed from miles-long runs, but somehow Foxe was *glowing*. Despite finishing his night pissing Jägermeister and fucking who knows what, he'd been prepped and ready to go before I even showed up.

That's been his routine for the past few months, really. Could be a problem, but as long as he's functioning, who the hell am I to intervene?

I'm not his mother, and I've got my own problems.

Growing irritated with Quincy's prolonged silence, I slam my dresser drawer shut and spin around, pinning my sister with a look. "What are you doing in my room? Don't you usually poke around in Noelle's when you visit?"

"She's not home," Quincy whispers.

It takes me a moment to realize she's shivering—no, *trembling*. My throat constricts, and my hands ball into fists at my sides, wrinkling the clothes.

I think about the one time I saw Noelle in a similar state years ago, when she'd spent several hours in the shower and came out bloodred all over.

Back then, I was just a kid, so I didn't mention anything. She never said what happened, and I think to this day it's a secret, but I'll never forget that look in her eyes.

Shallow and broken, so similar to Quincy's now.

"What's wrong?" I demand.

Finally, Quincy moves, shaking her head just slightly. When she lifts her gaze, I try not to react over how bloodshot it is. The whites aren't visible. At all.

There's dirt dried on her jaw and a scrape across her cheek. Yellow bruising on her neck.

My heart beats faster.

Faster still.

So fast, I think I might pass out.

Inhaling slowly, I inch a step toward the door. "I'm getting Dad."

"*No*," Quincy rushes out, her eyes widening.

It'd be comical—*me*, the Anderson family vault, threatening to tattle on one of my sisters—if she didn't seem so panicked.

Thing is Dad's got forty or so years of life on me. Vengeance is much easier for him to navigate with a calm mind, whereas the idea swallows me whole.

Already, I want to taste the blood of whoever made Quincy look like this. I want to feel it pump beneath my fingers before the life leaves them for good.

"I told him and Mom. They're aware. That's why I came home."

"All right." I scratch at the back of my neck. "Then what's going on? Why are you here?"

She frowns, bringing her hands into her lap. I watch, silent, as she twists them together, the delicate gold rings on her knuckles shifting with each movement.

"You're not going to Avernia." She glances up at me. "Right? Mom said you weren't sure—"

"Are you asking or warning me against it?"

It takes her another minute to respond. She's always been like that though. Methodical and precise, so concerned with how she presents to the rest of the world.

"I'd advise you against it," she says finally. "It's...not a good place. There are people there who'd love to see you suffer."

"Why am I always getting singled out?"

"Not just you," Quincy says. "All of us."

Frustration zips through me, and I fold my arms over my chest. "Stop being cryptic, and just tell me what's going on. You can't say stupid shit and expect me to accept the vagueness. If it's okay for *you* to still go there, why can't I?"

"There are things I *can't* escape," she tells me, her voice somewhat pleading. She's always so quiet and put together, it's unnerving to see her unravel before me. "I've got it under control. Mostly. Things have been going on, and tonight... Something rattled me."

"*What?*"

"The details aren't important. But you should know there are forces at work there who are hell-bent on keeping us Andersons away."

My irritation mounts. "God, Q, have you been brainwashed? Stop talking in fucking riddles. What is going on?"

Quincy hesitates. "I'm not sure exactly. I just know we're not wanted."

Reaching into her jacket pocket, she pulls out a scrap of paper. I unfold it quickly, instantly recognizing the handwritten entry from that encyclopedia in the campus library four years back.

"It was a mistake going there," she says softly.

"So it's real? The students, the faculty… They really believe this curse bullshit?"

She nods.

"What does elimination even mean, exactly? Are you in danger?"

"As long as you and Noelle don't step foot there again, no."

Sighing, I collapse into my desk chair. None of this makes any goddamn sense, nor does it explain why she's still attending or why she looks the way she does. "Lucy still wants to go."

"Tell her not to."

"I can't fucking do that, Q. You spent the last several years talking about how much you loved the place. She thinks it's a utopia."

"Well, I was wrong. Can't you explain that? She'll do whatever you tell her to."

That unsettles me. I spin around, facing the wall, and stare at the book spines hovering above my laptop. Even if I had that kind of power over Lucy, I wouldn't want to use it.

What's the point if she doesn't have freedom? To choose and to be her own person?

Isn't that what she was just begging me for?

Dropping my head into my hands, I ignore the persistence in my bones. The nagging desire to listen to Quincy and convince Lucy to stay here, where I know she'll be safe.

"Give me something to offer her," I tell my sister. "If there's a concrete threat, then she should know—"

"No." She shakes her head. "You can't tell her about any of this."

"Why not?"

"Because she'll tell Aurora, who will tell Foxe, who will tell his parents. Then we'll have thirty days before the school is shut down. If that."

My eyebrows hike up. "It sounds like it *should* be shut down."

"Shutting the place down would erase all I've been—it would leave a ton of students displaced, and ruin a decent institution being corrupted by a secret few. Totally dismantling it does no good."

I stare at her for several seconds, a frown firm on my lips. *What the hell has she gotten herself into?*

"Lucy would be okay if I weren't there," I note quietly. "Right? She's not an Anderson. They'd have no reason to target her if I didn't go too."

Quincy's eyes shimmer. "Well, I guess so, yeah. If she's *really* dead set on attending, she'd probably be fine without you by her side. But is that something you'd be okay with?"

I don't have much of a choice. Lucy's mind is made up, and if I try to convince her not to go now, she's going to assume I'm just being an asshole and making all this up to keep her from gaining any independence.

She doesn't know how much her choices and freedom matter to me. It's *all* I fucking care about, and this is the most important thing to her right now. Independence and getting away from the shadow of her reputation, her family, the inside of her own head.

Avernia would be okay for her without me.

That's how I justify this betrayal, at least.

Chapter 8

Lucy

THE WIDE WHITE ENVELOPE IS HEAVY IN MY HAND AS I SPRINT UP the paved drive of the Asphodel. On the southern side of Aplana Island, the Andersons' stone mansion looms over its secluded beach like a haunted gray landmark, the corners hidden by shadows this time of night.

Crunching noises fill the air as I step off the pavement, darting around the house like I've done a million other times before. Until my senior year, this was the routine.

I feel a little dizzy as I stop beneath a darkened window on the second floor in the back. Adrenaline still courses through me, buzzing, from my rush to get over here and reveal the good news.

At least I think it's good news. Dad says colleges don't send big envelopes if they're rejecting you.

Since this is my dream, I'm choosing to believe he isn't lying.

Wrenching my cell from my pocket, I send a quick text, even though I know the recipient despises that form of communication. He always wants face-to-face interactions or nothing else, which is why I spent so much of my childhood totally wrapped up in his orbit.

There was never any other way to maintain his friendship.

Me: I'm outside. Come down or open up. Have something
to show you!

I pretend there aren't a dozen unanswered messages already from
the last week.

It's a little chilly tonight, so when I don't get an immediate reply,
I stuff my phone back into my coat and bury my fingers beneath my
armpits.

Despite the cold, I'm positively giddy. If I concentrated hard enough,
I could probably use my excitement to scale the side of the mansion and
just propel myself into his room, but the rope ladder Asher keeps tucked
under his bed is safer.

I wait, hopping from one leg to the other. We saw each other earlier,
but the mail hadn't run yet. I'd been perched at my bedroom window
all afternoon waiting and ran out the second our postman showed up,
snatching the envelope before anyone else could see that it'd come.

Asher must've gotten his too. Since he graduated last year, he's been
doing random odd jobs with his parents, helping his mom with book
tours or his dad with… Well, I don't really know what they do, since his
dad's a retired physician, but I imagine it's busywork. Whatever keeps
Asher out of trouble.

But we decided to tackle Avernia next fall. Together.

There's no one else I'd rather have by my side for this next chapter.

Even though we've been seeing much less of each other since Foxe's
party, my sentiment remains. Supper earlier this evening was a bit awkward, but considering the thousands of arguments we've had and moved
past, I know this is just a little blip on the radar.

Still, something quietly aches in the center of my chest. Heartbreak
in physical form as I involuntarily recall the party.

Asher's face, bright red and stunned, as he pulls his lips from mine.

*The back of his head as he scrambled away, like he couldn't run from
my kiss fast enough.*

My brain flips through the memories like snapshots.

Nothing has ever stung more.

Above me, his window remains dark, and I start to grow irritated. Stepping back, I scan the ground and find a pebble among the rows of rosebushes, then cock my arm with it in hand, aiming for the glass pane.

"You break it, my mom will probably make you buy it."

Startled by the sudden voice coasting in over my shoulder, I jump, dropping the pebble as I whirl around. Asher's six-foot-four frame is cloaked in darkness, his pale face partially lit up by the overhead moon. Jet-black tendrils of hair fall in damp strands over his forehead, and the blue stud in his left nostril seems to sparkle as he looks down at me.

His brown eyes are indiscernible, completely masked by the shadows.

Yet I feel his stare in my stomach.

Clearing my throat, I give him a dirty look. "Let's be honest here, pretty boy. Your mom would make *you* pay, because you took too long to come out."

I can't tell if his expression changes at all. "I was busy."

"You always say that, but you never really are."

"Except when I'm doing something for you."

For some reason, that makes my cheeks heat. I shiver, shaking it off. "Well, I don't think I asked you to do anything for me tonight, so consider yourself pardoned."

A few unbearably awkward beats of silence follow. He just looks at me, and I feel my heart beating in my chest—can feel it in my throat as every muscle in my body begins to itch beneath his scrutiny.

Or maybe it's the standing still. I've never been very good at that. Something within me, like a spiritual need, is always rearing to go. It's like my body is made up of a million little worker bees who will die if they stop moving.

Finally, Asher exhales, his breath collecting in a plume between us. It smells vaguely of mint toothpaste and nutty alcohol.

That gives me pause. Asher doesn't drink or even smoke. Never has.

I don't ask him about it though. It's probably my imagination anyway.

"What did you want?" he probes eventually.

I try not to let the muted irritation dull my excitement and shove the envelope forward, bouncing on my heels. "I got this in the mail today."

"What is it?"

My eyebrows arch. "Is the big gold A on the front not enough of an indication?"

When he doesn't respond, I groan, tossing the thing at him. He catches it against his broad chest, holding it in place.

His fingers are stained with smudged ink, and I imagine him sitting upstairs all evening, working on his sketches. Endless stacks of drawing pads fill his bedroom, and I let myself dream a little bit of how his dorm will look with them.

I wonder if he'll tape any pieces to the walls or gift them to me like he used to.

Silly aspirations but, standing here right now, they feel attainable.

"It's my Avernia College acceptance letter. Well, maybe. I haven't opened it yet. I wanted to, uh, do it with you."

That makes my face burn even more, and I reach up, pushing my hair behind my ears just to have something to do. I don't know if he's tracking my movements, but it feels like he is, and it makes me fidget more.

I tuck another piece of hair back, then scrub my palm over my jaw.

"You got in?" he replies.

"I...I don't know. We'll have to open it and see."

More silence. Fuck, I'm starting to get nauseous. Why is he being so weird?

"Why are you being so weird?" I cringe when I realize the question has been verbalized.

"What am I doing?"

"You're just..." I trail off, waving my hand in his direction. "I don't know. Something is up, so tell me what it is so we can move on."

"There's nothing—"

My hands fly to my face, abruptly cutting him off. "Did you not get in?"

"What?"

"To Avernia. Did you get a rejection letter?" Panic bubbles in my throat, but I force an exhale, ignoring it. "Okay, well, that's not the end of the world. I'm sure your parents can pull some strings, especially since your sister is an alumna, and—"

"Lucy."

"—maybe she can even write a letter of recommendation, like she did for me? Or Uncle Grayson probably has some weight to throw around up there, since he teaches at—"

"*Lucy.*"

It takes a moment to register that he's calling me by my actual name and not any derivative he's concocted over the years. Not pup or Luce or Lulu. Not even L or Lucille, my least favorite.

Just Lucy.

My heart seizes a bit in my chest.

More so when he speaks again.

"I didn't apply."

Several seconds pass before my brain comprehends his words. I blink, glancing down at the envelope he's still holding, then back up. Annoyance pulses in my veins over not being able to see his face that well.

"What do you mean, you didn't apply?" I ask. "We did it together at my house. I watched you hit Submit and pay the application fee."

He sighs. I feel it in my chest.

"I didn't apply," he says again, like I didn't hear him the first time. "I clicked out of the page before it could finish processing. I just...I couldn't. No part of me wants to go there."

My mouth falls open. "Since when? This has been our plan for the last two years."

"Your plan," he corrects, and I hate that it feels like a slap to the face. "I don't want to go."

Blood rushes between my ears, making my skin hot to the touch despite the cold. My throat swells painfully as tears brim my eyes, and I take a step back, crossing my arms over my chest.

"But you said…" Inhaling shakily, I wait for the tears to subside and glare at his shoes. "If this is about what happened last week—"

"It isn't."

I swallow, nodding. "Sure, sure. But you know, I've barely seen you other than today with everyone else, and when I do see you, it's like we don't even know how to talk to each other anymore. And now you're saying you don't want to go to school with me, so I'm just a little concerned, you know?"

Fire burns my esophagus, the burden of honesty scorching my vocal cords. I've never in my life been afraid of telling him how I feel though, so I don't know any other way to be.

"Luce." Now when he uses my nickname, it feels like a precursor to disappointment.

I take another step back, my hands trembling. "What are you doing instead?"

He hesitates. "Does it matter?"

"Yes," I say softly. "It matters to me."

How can you even ask that?

Asher doesn't respond.

Every atom of my being deflates with the prolonged silence.

Shaking off the sadness crushing my rib cage, I turn away, back toward the gated entrance of the Asphodel. There's a humming sound between my ears, blocking out my ability to process any thoughts except *he's not coming.*

You're on your own, Lucy.

Despair scratches at my bones, and I want to stop and demand he go with me anyway. I want to tell him I need him there—I've always needed him, the way a plant needs water or the moon needs gravity to keep from flying off into space.

But it sounds stupid, even spoken silently in my head.

Asher doesn't need anyone, so why would I expect him to understand?

What am I supposed to do without you around?

There's never been a moment when that was something I had to wonder. He's been here since before I was born, always hovering somewhere in my peripheral if not directly at my side.

"Luce."

My heart squeezes. I twist my body, facing him again. "You're supposed to be my best friend."

He holds out the envelope.

I shake my head. "Keep it."

"Don't want it."

"Well, neither do I."

"Stop being ridiculous. You were so excited a few seconds ago. Don't let my choice ruin this for you."

Anger boils inside my stomach, spewing out and upward.

"You won't even tell me why you don't want to go," I snap. "For years, it's just been these vague little 'oh, Avernia is a terrible school,' with nothing to back up your claims, so what the hell am I supposed to think? Either you're letting me go off to a place that's no fucking good, or you're not going just because you don't want to go there with *me*."

His nostrils flare. "I can't explain—"

"Then you're right, Asher." I'm seething now, seeing red instead of the darker hues where he stands. "I shouldn't let you ruin things. I'm happy I got in, and I don't give a shit whether you go or not. In fact, maybe we should skip the formalities completely and just stop caring about what the other person does for good. Does that sound like a plan to you? Since you've decided to abandon the other one we had mapped out, I figured maybe I should ask."

More silence. My head grows dizzy, defiance running through me like a live wire. If I was a different person, maybe I'd hit him. Hurt him somehow, the way he has me. I doubt it'd do much—he's probably got some huge tolerance built up from a lifetime of picking fights with his peers—but it would make me feel better to see him bleed from the nose once because *I* was angry and not because he wanted to.

I consider it for a moment. My fist aches to drive into him.

Or maybe that's my heart. I don't know.

If I cared less, maybe I could.

"Is that really what you want?" he asks after what feels like a lifetime. "You want this to be it for us?"

"You make it sound like we're breaking up."

But that would require him to have feelings for me, and this has made it obvious he doesn't.

He moves forward, his shoes crushing the leaves on the ground. The sound is loud, drowning out the ocean past his house. He drowns out everything.

I can still feel the intensity of his mouth on mine, covering the world as I knew it a week ago.

He's as terrifying as he is intriguing, and I hate that.

I hate that I'm going to miss him.

"Answer the question, Luce. You're that mad at me, you're fine if I walk away and don't contact you again? Ever?"

"Yes." A single syllable, spoken with courage I don't particularly feel. "I don't think I can be friends with someone who lies to me."

"Because the only liar in this relationship can be you. Right?" Disgust drips from his words, and he comes close, shoving the envelope into my stomach.

I don't grab it, so it falls between us, landing in a shallow puddle.

"When have I ever lied to you?"

"Actions can be lies too."

Lifting my chin, I pretend his insistence that my feelings are untrue doesn't bother me. "So this *is* about last week."

Asher scoffs, shaking his head. He keeps his face turned toward me for several seconds, but I can't tell if he's looking at or past me. It's unnerving either way, but I curl my toes inside my boots and keep my spine straight.

"It is now," he answers finally, sidestepping me before taking off.

I'm frozen in place, unable to move as he abandons me. Forced to listen to his retreat grow more and more distant, until his footsteps are inaudible and the ocean beyond the trees takes their place.

I half expect him to turn around and come back. To glue himself to my side until our anger has diluted and we can speak again.

He never does.

My shoulders slump when I realize I'm really alone out here, no longer able to celebrate with the one person I wanted to.

Some fucking birthday.

Chapter 9

Asher

NINETEEN YEARS OLD

"YOUR CALL COULD NOT BE COMPLETED AS DIALED. PLEASE HANG up and try the number agai—"

Grinding my teeth together, I slam my thumb into the red End button and toss my phone at the sofa across the room.

Foxe comes in with a white towel wrapped around his waist, drying his hair with another, as steam billows in the doorway behind him. "Still no answer?"

I don't respond, irritation licking a debauched path down my sternum. It's worse than her simply not answering my texts or calls for the last year—now I'm blocked entirely.

Drives me fucking mad knowing she's out there and I can't get ahold of her.

Serves me right, I guess, but still.

I *hate* it.

Dropping his hair towel to the floor, Foxe strides to the minibar in the hotel suite's kitchen, frowning when he realizes there are no alcoholic beverages inside. Jaw clenched, he retrieves a tiny water bottle, turning toward me as he unscrews the cap and takes a long sip.

His suntanned skin is covered in tattoos now; since graduating and setting off to NYC to join his cousin's label as a debut artist, ink seems to be his favorite form of expression outside music.

Better than the alternative of getting blackout drunk every night, I suppose.

Personally, I can't commit to tattoos. The idea of anything being permanently etched into my skin is about as appealing to me as a lobotomy.

My gaze slides back to my phone. I might as well not even bother charging it at this point, although if my parents can't get ahold of me, they'll track me down and drag me home.

Not that it'd matter much. I'm Foxe's glorified babysitter. Guess all the worry about my future plans takes a back seat when someone else turns out to be a bigger threat to themselves.

"Tatiana booked a private club for after tonight's gig," Foxe says, putting the bottle on the counter. "I heard the stars of some local reality TV show might be around. You in?"

"Do I have a choice?"

He rolls his eyes. "Obviously. I don't want to drag you out if you're going to be a fucking bummer the whole night. If I can't drink, I'm going to need you to. As my proxy."

"Not interested."

"Oh, come *on*. You can break your principles *once*. For me?"

"No."

"Are you really gonna make me fly River out here? You don't mind corrupting my baby brother like that?"

I roll my eyes as a knock sounds at the door. Aiden James, Foxe's cousin, pokes his head in before entering, followed closely by his short, pink-haired wife.

"Getting River to do something other than junior champion orchestra would be the real challenge here," Aiden says, crossing his tan arms over his chest. They're covered in sleeves of tattoos from when he still toured back in the day. "And you're not going out tonight, anyway. We have to be packed and on the bus by four."

"Ugh, Riley, can you please explain the importance of R&R to your husband? I think retirement is warping his brain."

Her blue eyes glitter, her pale cheeks flushing. "Sorry, Foxe, but I'm in agreement. We told your parents no parties."

"So the adults who gave me my first joint as a teen have taken the side of my oppressor." Foxe shakes his head, throwing his hands up. "It's a sad day."

He groans when no one refutes the assertion, then stomps into one of the two adjoining bedrooms, slamming the door shut with his heel.

"Speaking of parents," Aiden says, taking a seat at the table in the corner. He runs a hand through his brown hair, his gray eyes finding mine. "You check in with your old man today?"

Though not related to me, Aiden and Riley have known my parents for decades, and they're as much a part of the family as my other aunts and uncles. Mom likes to say Dad adopted pretty much every stray human he met after they got married, as if he was making up for the fact that he'd been alone most of his life.

In contrast, he's made sure his kids have never known a moment of peace in theirs.

"I'm an adult, you know," I tell Aiden, though I get up to grab my phone anyway.

"But a baby adult," Riley says, walking over to perch on Aiden's knee. She gives me a small grin. "The world is your oyster, but you've barely even begun to see it."

"Which means you can still use the guidance of those older than you," Aiden adds. "And, also, I don't want your dad calling *me* if he doesn't hear from you. So get on it."

Grunting, I get up and head for my bedroom, leaving them in the living area. Keats meows loudly as he traipses out from the darkness, rubbing against my shins. I sit on the bed and scratch behind his ears, sending Dad a quick text. While I wait for his reply, I open an old—long-dead—thread and stupidly pray to a god I don't believe in for its revival.

Hope swims in my stomach when a notification flashes on the screen, but it's dashed immediately when I note the caller.

Exhaling slowly, I lean back and close my eyes, bracing myself as I answer. "Noelle."

My sister squeals at the sound of my voice, and I take the phone away with a wince, waiting for her to stop. It takes a full ten seconds, and then she's babbling like we didn't just speak last weekend.

"Asher! What are you doing right this second?"

"Sitting in my hotel room."

"Oh good, so you're not occupied."

"I didn't say that—"

"Your boredom is implied!" she singsongs. "Luckily for you, I'm right outside the Carlyle, and I've got somewhere you'll definitely want to go."

"I seriously doubt that."

"Would you just come on? Jeez. Act like you miss your big sister, you little rat."

Biting back a smirk, I get up and shrug into my jacket. Foxe hasn't come back out, so I tell Aiden and Riley where I'm going, and head down to the lobby.

My sister stands at reception, twirling a piece of her long, dark brown hair around one finger.

"...you can't beat LA views, but New York does come pretty close," she tells a short, stocky bellhop behind the counter. "NYC wasn't quite far enough from home though, you know what I mean? Sometimes, you just have to fly across the country and start fresh."

He's not paying attention to a word she says, too busy staring down the plunging neckline of the dark green romper she's wearing.

If she notices, she doesn't seem to mind. Attention is currency to her.

I mind though. It's fucking weird.

Snatching her hand, I tug her away from the desk before she can say any parting words, and she lets out a small yelp, jerking out of my hold.

"Hey!" She tenses and whirls on me, her hazel eyes wide and hand outstretched as if to slap me. When she realizes who I am, she lets that arm fall, breaking into a smile instead. "Oh yay! You're here!"

Throwing her arms around my neck, she launches against me, giving the tightest hug I've ever received. Even from her, the most touchy-feely person I've ever met.

I pull back, holding her away with both hands on her shoulders. She seems thinner than before, and there's something off about her smile, but I don't say that.

"What are you doing here?"

Her lips form a perfect pout. "Aren't you happy to see me?"

"I just saw you at Q's birthday party."

"Months ago! Don't you miss me at all when I'm gone?"

I'm not really sure what to say to that, so I don't reply to it. "You seem weird."

"How so?"

Squinting at her, I note the mascara smudged beneath her eyelids. The shallow curves of her cheeks, the way she can't seem to fully maintain eye contact, instead volleying between mine like she's vibrating.

Quincy's the calm and collected one, and Noelle is the glamorous one, but there's nothing glitzy about the way she looks right now. Like Los Angeles has somehow sucked the soul right out of her body.

"I don't know," I say finally. It doesn't feel right to pry.

I'm sure if something were wrong, she'd have told our parents anyway.

"All right, whatever." She grabs my hand, yanking me toward the front entrance of the hotel. "Let's go."

"This is kidnapping," I mention as she drags me outside into a waiting SUV.

"Kidnapping is our family legacy," she says simply, shoving me into the passenger seat. "Shut up and enjoy the ride."

Several blocks past the Carlyle, she stops at a gas station, turning the engine off and hopping out. She extends her palm across the console, waiting.

I arch an eyebrow.

"Gas money please."

My other eyebrow hitches as well. "You're asking me to fund my own kidnapping?"

"Well, just the trip." She reaches behind her head, rubbing the back of her neck. "I'm a little strapped for cash right now."

"Pretty sure Mom and Dad give you the same allowance they give me and Q."

"Do you want a copy of my receipts or what?" she snaps. "LA is expensive, and so are headshots and agent retention fees and networking dinners. Do you have money or not?"

Annoyed, I shove my fist into my pocket and draw out a wad of cash. I start to sift through the bills, but she leans over the seat and snatches them all.

"This is perfect!"

"That's several hundred bucks."

"Should've held a tighter grip!" she sings, hopping out and slamming the driver door shut.

I check my phone again. Still no messages. This is going to be a long fucking night.

Six goddamn hours later, and we pass a stone WELCOME TO FURY HILL sign before entering the city limits of a town I haven't visited in years.

Not since I was fourteen.

I didn't go at all when Lucy toured. That should've been her first red flag.

Though I suppose blaming her isn't fair when I was stringing her along with false promises the entire time.

"What the hell are we doing here?"

Noelle's wrists are draped lazily over the steering wheel as she navigates the town's main two-lane highway. "Well, it's the end of the first month of the semester. I thought we could pop in and say hi."

My stomach churns. "To whom exactly?"

"We only know two current students…"

I clench my fists. "No. Absolutely not, Noelle."

"Oh please!" she whines, drooping her shoulders. "You guys need to talk. You're making holidays awkward."

"I've not been attending holidays."

"Precisely! Mom's miserable."

Thick trees blur past the car windows as she turns onto College Road, the central activity hub in the small town. Most of the residents live much farther out, packed within the mountains or the forest, as if they don't want to be bothered by campus life.

I can't blame them. Not when it's *this* school.

Noelle pulls into a lot in front of a small brick building. Strobe lights flicker inside, visible through the frosted windows, and a blinking green neon sign hangs off the front awning, clutching the fabric for dear life.

Lethe's.

"Just one conversation," Noelle says, shutting off the vehicle's engine with a nod.

My jaw works from side to side, and I rub at it, my head pounding in anticipation. "Fine. But if anyone touches me, we're out of there."

"Please," she snorts. "Like you're that hot of a commodity."

I turn my hands over in my lap; the bloodstains are long gone by now, but I can still see their shadow. No matter how many times I've washed them since, the memory of what happened five years ago never fades away.

Glancing over at her, I think back to what Dad said about there being two corpses he had to clean up that day, and then to Quincy's words of caution.

Does Noelle know more than she lets on? Is that why she wants me in contact with Lucy—because she's afraid for her too?

Shoving open the passenger door, I stretch my legs and climb out.

I pause, waiting for my sister. She doesn't follow, instead scrolling through her phone while she remains buckled.

Clearing my throat, I tilt my head at her. "Are you coming?"

"Nope." She grins, but it seems forced. "I've got a big audition tomorrow morning. Don't want to jeopardize my slot."

"So why do *I* have to go in?"

"Because your best friend is in there, and she deserves more than what she's been getting from you."

"Why do you even give a shit, Noelle? It's none of your business."

"As your older, wiser sister, it is actually my business. Plus, I love Lucy, and I'm tired of her being sad because you're too stupid to fix things." Her face grows solemn for a moment. "Don't be an idiot and let the resentment foster. It won't do you any good."

"Are you speaking from experience?"

"How else does one gain wisdom?" Her grin wobbles. "I've realized some stuff while living out west, that's all. Time is fleeting, and so are people. You have to latch on to them while you can."

What the hell is going on with her?

She leans over, pulling the passenger door shut. A second later, the locks click into place, and she cracks the window. "Go get 'em, tiger!"

Growling under my breath, I make a mental note to get her back for this. Whether it's by somehow sabotaging her big audition tomorrow—honestly, she's been out in California since she graduated from high school, and *every* audition seems to be her potential break until it isn't—or forcing her to ride in the trunk while I drive home later, I can't decide.

Both sound appealing as I make my way to Lethe's entrance, the scent of sweat and cheap booze growing immensely the closer I get.

Not a great sign, considering the door isn't even open yet, but oh well. I've made it this far, I may as well see it through.

I push inside and am met with low lighting and a wall of dancing bodies, writhing around as they either wait at the bar for service or stand just outside the illuminated dance floor in the middle of the big room.

Circular tables sparsely decorate the worn wooden floors on the edges of the crowd, and several bass speakers thump so loud at the front that the bottles behind the bar rattle on the shelves.

I swallow over the knot in my throat, unwilling to retreat, even though parties are the furthest thing from being my scene. Even Foxe's in high school, I'd only tag along to be the designated driver and make sure no one tried anything with Lucy.

My heart thumps an uneven rhythm in my chest, echoing against my rib cage as I glance around for evidence of her. I don't even know if she's actually here—Noelle's notorious for bad intel, and this feels like one of those sloppy-as-fuck plans that she threw together at the last second for no reason.

Seriously. I don't buy that my rift with Lucy was upsetting Mom. Maybe Noelle isn't giving the woman enough credit.

Making my way to the bar, I weave through the throng of folks waiting in line, propping my elbows on the counter. Dozens of eyes swing in my direction, but I ignore every one of them.

I doubt they'd know who I am just by a single glance, but I don't need to draw extra attention.

A girl with a dark brown complexion and wide eyes skips over, her curly hair pushed back with a sparkling pink headband.

"Can I get you something?" she asks.

"A name?"

She smiles, displaying a full set of perfect white teeth. "Muna. Head of student relations and campus activity through the week and part-time bartender at Lethe's on the weekends." Extending her hand, she gives me a nod. "Nice to meet you."

I blink at her offer and let my arms fall from the counter. "I didn't mean your name."

"Oh." Her face deflates, and someone at my side snickers into their drink. "Are you looking for someone then?"

"A friend," I say, stuffing my hands in my pockets.

Muna tilts her head, studying me. "You don't go here, I presume?"

"Is it that obvious?"

"Well, most Avernia students trip over themselves when they talk to me," she replies, reaching for a glass that someone sends her way. "Half the campus won't dare look in the eyes of the Curators' electoral body."

"The Curators?"

"Student organization," she tells me. "Kind of like Avernia's version of Greek life. There are four orgs: the Curators, the Daughters of Persephone, Death's Teeth, and Visio Aternae—but their name is incorrect. The founders came up with it, though, so for the sake of tradition it remains."

"I see."

"The Curators are by far the most prestigious. They're invite-only, have the most alumni donors on their side, and the best networking groups. Kind of stuffy compared to the others, but great for your résumé. Visio Aternae is comparative, but *way* easier to get into. They focus more on philanthropy and school programs."

"And the others?" I ask.

"The Daughters of Persephone was created just a few years back by two students who felt some voices on campus were being suppressed. The administration does *not* like them." She hesitates. "Death's Teeth… Well, no one really knows what they do or who they are. Some say they're anonymous vigilantes, other say it's some kind of sex cult. Mostly they just seem to vandalize university property, which is why they're not officially recognized by the dean or higher-ups."

Interesting.

"But really, the only one that matters much is the Curators. They're top dogs on campus for sure."

"Hence the lack of eye contact."

She points a long finger at me. "Exactly. Now, who was it you were looking for?"

"Lucy Wolfe."

Muna's dark eyes go round for a fraction of a second. I reach up, twisting the stud in my left nostril, and wait for her to recompose herself.

"I'll take it you're familiar with her?"

Snorting, Muna nods. "Oh yeah. No organization will take her because she's always clashing with the administration or because her grades are subpar. They don't really mesh well with difficult students around here. Avernia likes order."

My heart skitters to a halt.

Fuck.

So much for a clean slate.

"Oh, I've only met her once though," Muna continues, leaning over the bar. "So take my account with a grain of salt. She's nice but not really…"

"Approachable?"

"Right." Her gaze narrows, surveying me once more. "Kinda hard to believe you're a friend of hers."

"Why's that?"

"Well, she hates everyone except that blond fashion design major. If you even try to recruit her for something she hasn't organized herself, she'll bite your head off."

That sounds like Lucy, but I'm not really interested in spending my time in Fury Hill talking *about* her. I want to see her. "Any chance you know where she might be tonight?"

"I don't think she usually comes to this kind of place," Muna answers. "I can't tell you how many Curator parties she's turned down just since I've been VP. As the first freshman to win that slot, I try to invite even the outcasts—makes the org look better to the sponsors, y'know?"

My stare must turn hollow, because Muna shrugs and pulls away.

Instead of sitting around and wasting more time, I shoulder back the way I came, then set off for the bathrooms. The rear hallway splits in multiple directions, no more illuminated than the front area itself, and I pick the one on my right just so I don't have to keep waiting.

Music pulses in my skeleton as I shove past couples making out and people standing in line to piss.

There's a skinny door at the very end of the hall marked EXIT, and I make a beeline for it, my annoyance causing me to twist the knob harder than necessary. It swings open, the handle getting caught in the plaster with the sudden force, and instead of an exit, I'm practically shoved into another room.

Inside is a single leather sofa, a standing lamp in the corner, and a coffee table with several half-smoked joints on top. Two people sit on the couch—one the blue-eyed siren who's haunted my dreams since she left town.

The other is a dead man.

Chapter 10

Lucy

NINETEEN YEARS OLD

I BLINK AT THE SILHOUETTE SHROUDING THE DOORWAY, THEN RUB my eyes, certain that I'm imagining things.

Surely Asher Blake Anderson isn't standing in the same room as me, glaring at the boy beside me with his hand on my bare knee.

That's two birthdays in a row the asshole's ruined now.

Maybe ignoring him wasn't a good idea, but since Aurora decided to take Asher's place with me at Avernia, she spends most of her time suggesting I avoid communication with him. Not that I've wanted to reply to anything he's sent, but still.

The easiest way for me to stop sulking was to just shut him out completely.

He's been blocked on my phone for months. I wouldn't have even known he still called or texted if Foxe didn't harass me nearly every day, begging me to answer him.

Like I give a shit if Asher's despondency ruins Foxe James's precious little tour.

The only reason he's out there having so much success anyway is that he signed to his cousin's label. His *famous* cousin, who has nothing but time and money to pour into Foxe's career.

I sound bitter—and maybe I am. But so far, college is *not* all it was cracked up to be, and Asher being here is only amplifying that sentiment.

If he really is here. The figure in the doorway hasn't moved a muscle, and I'm starting to think maybe I'm hallucinating.

What the hell was in that joint?

The guy with his hand on my knee—whose name I can't recall at the moment—makes an irritated noise in the back of his throat. His fingers are cold now, and I reach down to pry them off one by one.

Asher's brown eyes aren't totally visible with the bar lighting spilling in from behind him, but I can sense them tracking my movement.

For some reason, my stomach feels hollow. I craved Asher's attention a year ago, and now I'm no longer interested.

"You're lying."

Anger boils inside my body, threatening to explode.

"This room's occupied," Sofa Guy says, pushing my hand aside and squeezing my leg.

"Leave." Asher's voice is barely audible over the bass bleeding in from the front of Lethe's, but I hear its deep timbre anyway.

"No," I reply immediately, like a reflexive defiance. "*You* leave."

Even though I'm not sure I want to be stuck in here with this Avernia student anymore, the battered pieces of my heart still prefer him to my former best friend.

"Yeah." Sofa Guy scoffs, sliding his hand higher. "Fuck off and find your own place. We're busy."

Without saying another word, Asher stalks over to the couch, his arm lashing out before either of us has a chance to process what he's doing. I assume he's grabbing for me, but the contact never comes. Instead, seconds later, Sofa Guy is flying off the seat and face-planting on the floor.

He groans, placing his palms on the ground as he tries to push to his feet. Asher fists the guy's hoodie and drags him toward the door without letting him up.

My skin feels warm, watching the whole thing unfold, and I chide myself silently for it.

Asher isn't stepping in for my sake. He's just being a dick.

Sofa Guy's face squeaks across the floor, and he moans the whole way but seems unable to pick himself up. Asher hauls him onto his hands and knees, then gives him a shove over the threshold, sending the guy's limbs flailing.

He launches into the wall across the hall, grunting at the impact.

Asher turns slowly back toward me, kicking the door shut with his heel. He reaches behind him, and I hear the lock slide into place, trapping me in the small break room with him.

It's the first time we've been this close since my graduation, and then we barely spoke. I try not to focus on the sweat sprouting beneath my arms or the way my knee is bouncing again as the effects of the weed start to wear off.

"What a change in scenery, pup," he says finally, sliding his large hand up the wall. Is it possible his fingers have gotten longer since I saw him last? "You can't hang out, smoke pot, and get groped anywhere back in Aplana. I see why you had to come here so badly."

Clenching my fists, I get to my feet, ignoring his glare in the low light. Lifting my chin, I smooth my hands down my short plaid skirt and head for the door.

He doesn't move at first, and I think maybe he'll let me through.

My fingers close around the doorknob, pinching to unlock it. Freedom is within my grasp, but as soon as colorful neon lights pour in through the crack, Asher's palm slams into the wood surface right next to my head, closing us in once more.

His clean scent surrounds me, and I hate how comforting I find it. I'm so accustomed to his presence, even after so many months of his absence.

"Let me go," I grind out, growing more irritated by the second.

"I can't do that," he says, his voice lowering as it caresses my ear. "What if he's waiting to accost you right outside? What sort of friend would I be if I just let that happen?"

"Maybe I *wanted* to be accosted."

"Oh yeah?" With his free hand, he grabs my shoulder, spinning me around. My back collides with the door, and the air struggles to reach my lungs as he presses in closer, leaning his forearm next to my face.

His forehead grazes mine, and I swallow whatever emotion's trembling in my stomach.

"Tell me what you wanted from him then," Asher whispers. "I'll do it for you instead."

A laugh bubbles out of my throat. "I don't fucking think so, *pretty boy*. That ship has sailed."

"Aw. Off at college for a month, and she already thinks she knows everything." He touches my chin, tilting my head up.

"I know a fuck of a lot more than you do. Always have."

"True. Your problem has always been in the application of that knowledge."

I'm not sure why, but that assessment stings more than anything else.

"Whatever. That's not even the point. What are you doing? How did you know I was here?"

"Apparently Noelle is still a big enough fan of yours that she felt the need to intervene after months of us not speaking." His jaw twitches, a slight crack in his formidable armor. "I didn't know where she was taking me until we were past state lines."

Pain slices through me, increasing the effects of the earlier stinging sensation. Some sick, desperate part of me—stuffed way down where I can never really hear her—had been hoping he'd come of his own volition.

After all this time and the start of the school year, I'd still been stupid enough to think maybe he'd change his mind.

Turning my head, I break eye and skin contact. He pulls back, though his gaze doesn't leave my face, the heat of it searing into my cheekbones where I'm sure I'll be able to feel it for the next week.

"Well, great," I mutter. "Thank her for ruining my night, would you?"

I twist myself away from his hold, but he comes too, bracketing me in against the door once more.

"Wait a second." Two of his fingers find my chin again, forcing me to look at him again. "Is that it? You don't have anything else to say?"

Blinking slowly, I let myself linger on the harsh angles of his face, the warm brown hues of his irises. The sapphire stud in his nostril and the mostly impassive expression he wears.

A strand of inky hair pops out from the mess on top of his head, swinging into his eyebrow. My fingers twitch, eager to push it back, to grab the normalcy his presence provides.

Standing here with him is the first time I've felt like myself in months. The first time I've felt like I could breathe on my own and think clearly.

Avernia College isn't what I expected.

It isn't even really like anyone else said it'd be either. There's a sinister film that clings to the campus air, sure, but in general, the state of the university itself is just sort of strange. Macabre in a way that's still somehow trying to pretend it isn't.

My student advisor swears it's just the massive change in scenery and that I'll adapt to the atmosphere eventually. But so far, I'm not convinced.

Even my coming out tonight was only because I've spent the first four weeks of classes holed up in one of the libraries, alternating between studying feminist poetry of the eighteenth century and wondering if the floor I like to study on most is haunted. There's not much else to do unless you're in one of the many campus cliques, and those are nearly impossible to break into.

My eyes find Asher's, and I swallow.

Unless you're a founding family member. Then it's practically your birthright, because the organizations want donors, and there's a very strong superstition among the residents that disfavor from the founding bloodlines will result in the crumbling of their community.

I still can't believe Asher didn't tell me about that connection. Instead, I had to find out how deep his family ties go during orientation, when they went over the school's dark history and all the deaths that have happened on the property over the centuries.

A strange introduction but powerful nonetheless.

The Andersons are the only name on the founders' statue in the quad that's been scratched out.

They're somehow revered and feared at the same time.

"What do you want me to say?" I finally ask, because there's no way I can broach the subject of his secrets.

Or admit that I get it now—why he didn't want to come here.

Maybe if he'd been honest about it, I'd have been less offended. Maybe I would have *understood* and gone wherever he picked.

But he didn't give me that choice. He just did whatever he wanted, same as always.

"Don't you—" He cuts himself off, chewing on his lip for a split second.

My eyes trace the indentations his teeth make in the soft flesh. My stomach tenses, and I pretend not to notice.

He releases his lip with a soft breath. "Don't you miss me at all?"

His thumb smooths over my chin.

Gravity pulses between us, an electromagnetic field of opportunity. Heat expands in my blood, rising as he sways forward, temptation welling in his heavy gaze.

I've never seen him look at me like this.

It'd take so little effort to push up on my toes and close the distance. To do what I've dreamed of for the past year, after convincing myself the first time in that sunflower field was a hallucination brought on by alcohol.

We never talked about it after. Really, we barely spoke past that night, but I could never tell if things were awkward because of the kiss or because our lives were splitting in different directions.

He taps on my skin, bringing me back to focus.

I shake my head, dispelling the want. Ignoring the strange, almost wistful look on his face. What good will it do me now anyway?

"No. I don't miss you, Asher. Not even a little bit."

For a few more seconds, he continues touching me. Staring at me.

Finally, his expression drops slightly, something blank replacing the emotion there. His arms fall from the door, releasing me from the prison he concocted, and without another word, I reach for the knob, wrenching it open.

Laughter and loud music spill into the small room. Perfumed air filters in with the warmth from a bar packed with college kids, and I spin on my heels, then slip through the opening.

Because if he can lie, so can I.

Chapter 11

Asher

SHE LEAVES ME BEHIND WITH MY TAIL TUCKED BETWEEN MY FUCK-ing legs, wishing I could wring my sister's neck for dragging me here in the first place.

How did everything get so fucked up?

I would have crawled on hands and knees to my death for Lucy Wolfe. Now she doesn't even want to see me.

Was my own self-preservation worth it? Was keeping her out of the loop worth *anything* if I don't get to see her, speak to her, or exist near her?

Leaving the room with my heart in pieces, I head toward a side exit through the narrow hall, pausing as I work the door open. A glance over my shoulder proves that no one's paying me any attention—though I see the asshole from before find Lucy in the crowd.

My teeth grind together, and a shot of adrenaline pumps through my limbs. I want to stalk over there and drag him out with me.

But that'll just irritate Lucy even more, and knowing her, she'd fall further into his arms just to spite me.

Instead, I walk outside, snatching a cigarette from someone hunched in a corner, and flick it into the brush at the building's base. It catches instantly, an explosion of bright orange flames consuming the grass and crawling quickly up the wall.

A few people inside notice immediately and scatter. It only takes minutes for the door to become mostly unusable, blocked by the fire. Covering my face with my jacket sleeve, I step over it, ignoring the heat scalding my shins.

I reach back inside, my hand connecting with the wall and pulling a lever there.

An alarm begins blaring throughout the bar, lights flickering against the smoke slowly creeping in, and the sprinklers activate, soaking everyone in the vicinity.

That ought to get her out of there.

Jogging back to where Noelle's parked, I slip into the passenger side silently. She hangs up with whoever she's on the phone with, turning to greet me with a big smile.

"Well? Did you—" She cuts off, her gaze darting past my head as the crowd begins evacuating Lethe's. Her expression flattens, and she slumps in her seat. "Should've fucking known."

Yeah, I muse to myself as she starts the vehicle, *you should have.*

Still, my hand whips out when she shifts gears, keeping the car in place.

She gives me a questioning look, trying to move, but I squeeze her fingers tight. "*Ow*, you fucker! Jeez, sorry for trying to help."

"I didn't ask for assistance." I keep my eyes fixed on the bar. Waiting.

Obviously I'm fucking waiting.

I'll walk back in and carry her out if I need to.

My heart pounds like a kick drum in my chest, loud and perturbed.

Maybe I shouldn't have done that.

A reddish-orange glow grows behind the building, smoke billowing into the night air. My lungs feel heavy, weighed down by my impulsivity.

Finally, I see that familiar head of raven-colored hair. She comes out with her arms wrapped around herself.

Alone.

My pulse slows a little. I let go of Noelle.

When Lucy's attention shifts, instantly finding the car, I lift a hand in some sort of wave or parting gesture—I don't know. My limb moves of its own accord.

She doesn't respond. When she turns away, I can't help the glee that surges within me when she finds a familiar blond in the crowd, heading off to stand with her instead of the guy from before.

As we drive away, I fold my hands in my lap, noting the fresh red welts on the backs of my palms. I imagine they match the lightly charred skin on my calves, though none of that felt worse than seeing Lucy again after all this time and knowing it hasn't changed a fucking thing.

All I wanted to do today was wish her a happy birthday.

Chapter 12

Asher

TWENTY YEARS OLD

LUCY DOESN'T UNBLOCK ME. I'M NOT SURPRISED.

Another year passes in which I don't speak to her on her birthday. She doesn't reach out, and no one says she's missing me.

Noelle doesn't try to mend things for me anymore, preoccupied with her own bullshit, and our parents seem to have accepted the rift. They lament in private, if at all.

Quincy finishes grad school and gets a job at the Aplana Island city archives with Alistair's assistance. She seems restless and bothered, just like Noelle, but nobody questions it.

I go on with my life. Sort of.

Foxe says I'm becoming unhinged—barely sleeping, spending all my time drawing the same things over and over, holing up in whatever hotel room we're staying in at the moment. Rich coming from him, but I never say that.

I can't help feeling like I fucked up majorly with Lucy, and now I'm not sure how to fix it. I can't extract her from the school, can't convince her to transfer without any reason, and she probably wouldn't believe me now anyway.

Dad says I should tell her what happened, but I can't fucking make myself do it. Every time I contemplate driving up there and spilling my guts, I break out in hives like a goddamn pussy.

I don't want her to look at me differently. In fact, I just want her to look at me the way she used to.

Or look at me at all.

Chapter 13

Asher

TWENTY-ONE YEARS OLD

SILENCE AGAIN THIS YEAR.

Sometimes I dream of her, but mostly I dream of blood.

Rivers of it, drowning me.

I think I'm losing my fucking mind.

Speaking to her would probably cure me.

Chapter 14

Asher

TWENTY-TWO YEARS OLD

I CAN'T DO IT ANYMORE.

She'll speak to me this year.

I'll make certain of it.

Chapter 15

Lucy

THE SCENT OF INCENSE AND MUSTY, STALE BOOKS IS OVERPOWER-
ing as I exit the Obeliskos.

I time my propulsion through the revolving glass door efficiently,
holding my breath in case I miscalculate and a foot gets caught. But I
don't pause—just *move through*.

If you hesitate at this hour, you'll get stuck. Something about the
way the night air changes. The old building's heating system is unable to
keep up with the demand from the outside, causing the doors to swell.

Some say it's ghosts. That the biggest library on Avernia College's
campus is rife with supernatural activity, and we shouldn't go there at all.

I say that's a load of fucking horseshit and continue to give the
building my patronage anyway. The thirteenth floor—with bookshelves
stretching out as far as you can see and all the way up to the domed ceiling
with gorgeous, vibrant murals painted on it—is the only place I can get
any sort of peace and quiet.

No one cares much about the city archives and encyclopedias except
the library staff, who don't allow checkouts of thirteenth-floor items.
Some of the books even have to be handled with gloves and face guards.

Since my Landscape Ecology class insisted on sourcing firsthand accounts of Fury Hill's predeveloped environment, I've spent my entire Friday hiding out there.

Well, I was hiding out to do the assignment at first, but that quickly morphed into me completely losing track of time by switching between archives with town lore and trashy reality television. My project was all but abandoned a few hours in.

It doesn't help, I guess, that I was trying to escape thoughts about my earlier meeting with the dean and that trashy reality shows are the easiest way to push things from my mind. Otherwise, I just fixate on them until my brain feels like it's going to explode—and wind up losing track of time, anyway.

But it's why I'm now rushing, hurriedly shoving papers into my backpack as I jog past the big clock tower in front of the building.

In seconds, the deafening chimes will signal midnight. No one wants to be next to it when that happens.

My skin prickles, goose bumps sprouting along my arms. A gust of freezing air washes over me as I approach the Lyceum and its courtyard at the center of campus.

Awareness sits high on my back, digging its claws into my neck. I hate walking alone this late, but since I'm running behind, I have no choice.

Once I'm beyond the Lyceum—the main academic building—the clock rings out, echoing in the cool night air. I startle at the sudden noise even though I'm expecting it, quickly scanning the immediate vicinity. Multistory, French Gothic–inspired buildings loom like the backdrop to a bad film noir. Their ornate peaks seem to scratch the clouds hanging low in the sky, and the clock tower fully blocks the moon from sight.

A few lampposts decorate the paved walkways, occasionally punctuated by those call boxes meant for people in distress.

My fingers itch, and I curl one hand around the strap of my backpack, eyeing the blue lights.

No movement occurs in my peripheral vision, and it doesn't appear that anyone else is around. Not in this spot at least.

Altercations aren't unheard of, even somewhere as small and prestigious as Avernia. I suppose not even a billion-dollar endowment can eradicate evil.

Might even lure it in.

It's a short walk from center campus to the Elysian Dorms, where four gray-stone buildings house the majority of the student body. Normies like me who aren't in any of the official organizations and the lowerclassmen who haven't been given the opportunity to join their ranks and reside there.

Past that, it's an extra thirty minutes to the Primordial Forest that encircles the school grounds, cutting it off from the White Mountains and the rest of Fury Hill.

Technically, the forest is off-limits to students, but no one really seems to give a fuck.

Legend says—and by legend, I mean Pythia, the anonymous editor of *The Delphic Pages*, our school's online newsletter—the best parties are thrown out there, where the admin staff rarely wander.

Not that I care about anything that bitch Pythia says. All she does is spew gossip most of the time anyway.

I don't stop at my room to drop off my backpack, although once I hear the bass thumping from the quarry, regret starts to seep into my bones. I'm sure no one else has their fucking school stuff with them, since it's a Friday night, and they're all able to shut it off for the weekend.

Jimmying open the broken wrought-iron gate leading into the woods, I'm engulfed by massive trees within seconds, most older than the school itself and protected by the town's historical and conservation societies.

Probably the only reason Fury Hill hasn't torn them down and sold the land to greedy developers.

A worn dirt path twists through the trees, carved into the earth by the thousands of students defying authority before me. It disappears in the distance, but I've come this way enough times that I can practically trace the steps with my eyes closed.

The air starts to shift the closer I get to the quarry, growing cooler yet thicker somehow. Wind picks up, blowing through each strand of my hair, and I doubly wish I'd stopped at my room now. My oversize cardigan and tights do very little to protect me from the mountain breeze.

Styx becomes visible the deeper into the foliage I trudge; that's what they call this corner, consisting of the quarry above the bottomless lake, blocked-off cave systems below, and an old abandoned house with a half-burnt gazebo, both of which supposedly belonged to the first-ever Avernia dean.

There are a couple of Range Rovers and Jaguars backed up to the eroded rock wall overlooking the water. On the other side are the mountains, under which the lake eventually disappears into. Students mill about, some with their Burberry overcoats buttoned all the way up, attempting to stave off the chill. Others are half-undressed, participating in keg stands, or doing dramatic reenactments of their favorite lesser-known Marlowe or Shaw play.

A few are tangled up in each other, their hands disappearing beneath muted layers, their passion evaporating into the air around them.

Someone shoves a red Solo cup in my hand, slurring incoherently. The liquid inside sloshes against me, and I wrinkle my nose, glancing around to see if there's some sort of waste management the students remembered to set up.

But since this is a Curator party and not one by a more socially conscious organization, I see nothing. A couple of kids roll empty beer bottles down piles of crushed rock, leaning over to see whose shatters first.

They don't rush to pick up the glass, and why would they? Most Avernia students grew up with someone else to clean their shit for them.

I lift one of my hands, scratching behind my ear repeatedly until it feels like my skin is starting to chafe—

"*Lucy!*" a loud, melodic voice bursts from over my shoulder like an alarm, drawing the crowd's attention to me.

Cringing, I turn toward it; across the flat pavement, Aurora waves a vodka bottle over her head. In her other hand is her cell phone, which she shakes at me as I approach, her spray-tanned skin flushed, blond ponytail loose, and her pink lip gloss smudged.

She's clearly been here for a minute.

"Uh-oh, the reigning bitch queen has arrived," a male voice snickers from the sidelines. "Get ready to be ratted on for not recycling your cigarette butts."

"Yeah," someone else joins in. This person I recognize, but I act like I don't hear him. "Better not look at her too long, or she might try to set another bar or refectory on fire."

My shoulders tense up, but I refrain from taking the bait. They want the reaction, and I refuse to give it.

Besides, I didn't start either of those fires..

I just got blamed for them.

Aurora's blue eyes narrow, and she slings her arm around my shoulder as she approaches. "Ignore them," she says, giving me a squeeze.

Glancing down at the beer in my hand, I slowly bring it to my lips, ignoring the warning bells in my head. I shouldn't drink at all since I remembered to take my meds this morning, but fuck it.

The clock tower strikes again, reverberating through the trees and echoing in my chest. The noise seems to ricochet off the rocks, then get carried across the water, where it falls silent.

"I always do."

Chapter 16

Lucy

AURORA LEANS ON THE PORTABLE PING-PONG TABLE THAT A COUPLE of guys have set up. "*Dean Bauer* told you to drop out?"

"Not in so many words," I say after recounting the events of this morning. My knee trembles, bouncing lightly. It started earlier in the dean's office and hasn't really stopped since. "But he suggested I might feel more *at ease* at a different school. Said there were ones better designed to accommodate my needs than anything in Fury Hill."

"Your *needs*?" My roommate, Celeste, scoffs as she picks a twig from her platinum-blond bob. "Do you suddenly require rare resources or something? Expensive testing accommodations?"

"I'm pretty sure that'd be discrimination on his part if she did," Yuri, a student who moved here from Okinawa a few years back, adds, opening a convenience store cupcake with her teeth. She glances at me, her dark brown eyes widening. "You've got ADHD, right? Maybe we should bring a case against the administration."

"Like I need another reason to pit them against me." My brain hurts at the thought alone, knowing they don't fight with logic or justice but money and alienation. "Besides, if I try to do anything, my parents will join in for sure."

Celeste reaches into her purse, pulling out a small bottle of lotion, which she proceeds to slather over her pale pink skin. "So? Your dad is a former governor, girl, and your mom is hot as hell. Not to mention totally terrifying. You should really be using them to your advantage more."

I have no doubt that if my mom knew even half the things that go on at Avernia, she'd have flown in months ago and packed up my room without question. But only after spending an afternoon in the dean's office with my father, arranging to have the school's multibillion-dollar endowment revoked and the administrative faculty made eunuchs.

My father, who has always been totally powerless against Cora Wolfe's chaos, would offer his full support. The accused would probably be missing before sundown if he had any say in the matter.

While on paper, that's the kind of parenting some people would kill for, it's always felt like more of a detriment to me. Learning to be human and interact with my peers has been enough of a struggle my whole life without adding my over-the-top parents into the mix.

I've never wanted people to feel like they *had* to be my friend *or else*.

Avernia was supposed to be different from Aplana, yet I'm no less of an outcast. Their involvement would make that worse.

"Poor Lucy," Yuri mocks around bites of pastry, which are sticking to her flushed beige cheeks. "'I have loving and supportive parents, boo-hoo. My life is so hard.'"

Without looking up, I give her the finger, and she howls with laughter. *Jeez, is everyone here drunk?* I take another sip of my beer, trying to catch up.

Aurora chucks a Ping-Pong ball away from herself. "Why are they even spending so much time harassing you when it's obvious to anyone with a brain that you had nothing to do with the refectory fire?"

I track the ball's movement as it bounces once and then sails right past the back row of red plastic cups. "Who knows? I made it onto the dean's hit list, and that's what matters, I guess."

It's easiest to punish the pariah, because no one gives a rat's ass whether they live or die. Even at Avernia, a university *supposedly* revered for championing the underdog, there's a social hierarchy that must be adhered to. It wouldn't make a difference if I had an iron-clad alibi placing me in another state when the refectory fire broke out last week— since it was during a small demonstration I organized to protest drilling in the quarry.

The faculty want me to be guilty, so I am. They just can't pin anything directly on me, so they're trying to make me uncomfortable in the hope I'll withdraw voluntarily.

But I don't say that to Aurora. She wouldn't appreciate the sentiment—or understand it. Most people around here love her because she's outgoing and fun, so this isn't an area she's experienced in.

I can handle the heat. It's not like I came here hoping to make nice with the administration.

The small crowd we've amassed—and by *we*, I mean the three of them—erupts in a fit of cheers as someone makes a point. A field hockey player named Donovan or Kerrington or *something* equally douchey shoves the offending beer in Aurora's direction.

My knee still won't stop bouncing.

"Drink up, PW," the guy tells her, grinning wide like a literal wolf lying in wait to attack its prey.

She bats her long, thick eyelashes and lifts the cup to her lips. Several *whoops* of excitement echo around us, and she guzzles it down in seconds before tossing it to the opposite end of the table.

"Boys' turn," she announces, swiveling her attention back to me. I roll my eyes, and she giggles. "Oh, lighten up, Luce. It's a party. We're supposed to be having *fun*."

"I hate fun." I don't—not really. I don't even particularly hate parties or half the students that attend them.

Interacting with them is just not something I know how to do. It always feels like I'm trying too hard or not hard enough, and I've never been able to strike a balance. I've spent my entire life watching, absorbing, and mimicking, only to feel like a total fraud anyway.

Even now, as I drink my beer and stare at those dancing around us or reciting their top ten composers and forcing one another to strip for each incorrectly placed answer, I'm only doing so in the hopes of seeming like the rest of them.

Instead of blending, I end up on either extreme end of the spectrum and have nothing to show for it except people who are my friends because we're related or we were forced into proximity.

If not for my room assignment with Celeste or the dates I went on last semester with Yuri, I doubt either of them would be hanging out right now.

Angry brown eyes flash in my vision for a millisecond, making my heart ache inside my chest, like a gaping wound that no one ever bothered stitching up. My mood plummets, and I shrink into myself more.

Bounce, bounce, bounce.

"Yeah, I know, but can't you pretend?" Aurora pouts, handing me a second Ping-Pong ball. "Wanna play?"

"Not even a little bit." I let the white sphere fall while my foot continues its assault on the ground.

"I bet you'd feel better."

"The only reason I'm here at all is because you said you'd let me bitch about my morning."

"And that was only if you came to lunch with me, but instead you spent the day in the library. Your punishment is unfolding, dude."

"*Ugh.*" Celeste groans, pushing to her feet and downing the rest of her drink. She doesn't toss the cup aside though, at least. "You guys are harshing my buzz."

"Drink more," Yuri suggests, then points to the bong. "Or try something new?"

Celeste shakes her head. "I didn't spend all summer at the Ren faire with my family to come back to school and not have at least one full-moon rendezvous. I'm going to get another beer and try to find someone's mouth to ride."

Yuri makes a face. "Don't you mean dick?"

"In this economy? Yeah, right." Celeste fluffs her hair with one hand. "Avernia students should be so lucky."

She traipses off, walking sideways, before being swallowed by the crowd. I watch until the very last piece of her blond bob is no longer visible.

Perching on the rock beside me, Aurora nods. "Go ahead then. Tell Auntie Aurora what all the mean dean said to you."

"Cousin." I don't mean to correct her, but I can't help it. Even though she's joking.

I hate myself for it.

A chorus of boos drowns out whatever she says next as the boys' ball flies off the table. Field Hockey Guy glares at me, running a hand over his brown crew cut.

"Maybe Lucy should go," he tells Aurora, reaching out to stroke the side of her face. "We were winning before she came."

Her smile deepens, but it's not a kind one now. Not if you know her. "What's that supposed to mean?"

Yuri takes a hit from the bong, averting her gaze as she coughs up clouds of smoke.

He shrugs. "Maybe her negative energy is affecting the play."

My knee ceases moving. "Or maybe you're not as talented as you think."

"You boys and your silly superstitions. Your team hasn't won a game all year, and *that's* certainly not Lucy's fault, since she never goes to them." Aurora slides a slender hand up, hooking her index finger over his thumb, and yanks downward. The crack of bone is audible, even with the crowd.

Field Hockey Guy lets out a yelp, immediately withdrawing. He cradles his hand to his chest, glaring as Aurora plops down beside me once more, taking her phone from her pocket and tapping away. Her lack of attention seems to leave him irritated as he walks back to the other guys, who snicker quietly at his expense.

"*Bitch*," he mutters, although I know it's not aimed at her. It never is.

Exhaling, I hand my empty cup to my cousin and push off the rock, combing my fingers through my hair. "I'm going to get another drink."

"Get me one too!" Yuri says, leaning back with her palms behind her, closing her eyes.

"The keg's on the side where all those vehicles are, but there are coolers with good stuff in them too." Aurora points in the opposite direction, down the flat part of the quarry to where more jagged stone walls block off another section of the forest. "Don't get distracted picking up empty bottles you find on the ground though. I *will* come find you."

Waving her off, I make my way over the crushed rocks where the majority of the party convenes, passing a heated argument on Albert Cohen's effects on the modern scholar. My head throbs, unable to keep interest in the debate for even a second.

Who knew college would mean so much *discussion*?

A few students turn to stare as I continue, head down, my arms wrapped tight around my middle. I'm used to the attention because of how small Avernia is, but that doesn't mean I *want* it. Unless I'm trying to convince people that they should give a shit about their environment, I'd rather people didn't look at all.

Not because I'm afraid or ashamed but because I never learned how to react properly when they do.

All I know how to do is bite.

The crowd thins the farther out I go, but I find the coolers, lifting one to pull out a few mini bottles of tequila.

Unscrewing a cap and downing the first immediately, I keep moving away from the party, in search of a reprieve from the ghosts and everything else haunting this school. The town even. All of it's tainted.

Two bottles down, and I realize just how far I've walked. Now I'm past the quarry itself, weaving through the trees on the very outer edge of the cliffs. When I turn around, all I'm met with is wide trunk after trunk, obscuring my view of the gathering.

I can't hear them, and I find the silence soothing, so I continue forward. Mom used to say that if you get lost and circle around long enough, you'll eventually find yourself back where you're supposed to be.

Dad says not to listen to her wildlife survival advice, but it's not like I can really go very far anyway. The mountain will block me off.

An eerie feeling sweeps over my shoulders, blanketing my arms like black slime.

Glancing behind me, I try to see if maybe someone followed me into the forest, but it appears I'm alone.

But I don't *feel* alone.

Distantly, a branch snaps. I spin toward the noise, scouring the shadows, but come up empty again. The muscles in my arms cinch tight, tension threading through them. My vision is a little fuzzy, but I swear I see a figure dash between two trees.

I turn around again, not fully certain which way I came.

Any footprints on the ground have been swallowed back up by the soft earth.

Laughter reaches my ears next, and I swivel in its direction, hopeful over how feminine it sounds. I follow it, my heart pounding, sticking close to the trees as I move.

"If that's you, Aurora, I'm literally going to gouge your eyes out."

A shiver coasts over my spine, getting caught in the ridges. I don't get a response, but the laughter suddenly stops.

Moaning ensues instead.

I freeze as sounds of pleasure fill the air. Grunts and groans float to the treetops, getting caught and plummeting back down like heavy rainfall.

Fascination skitters along my arms, buzzing all the way to my fingertips. Again, I move toward the noises, clinging to the shadows as they get louder. Closer.

With trembling hands, I peer between two trees, coming face-to-face with the complete opposite, empty end of the quarry. This side morphs into the mountain, connecting us to the barrier while bracketing Lake Lerna below the cliff.

Several feet away from the edge, a group of people are twisted up in one another. My chest tightens as I watch the shadows move together, their bodies writhing on the ground.

One shadow stands over the others in front, and I watch silently as the person seems to reach for their waist, undoing their pants. They're just barely visible in the moonlight, and I lean forward, trying to make out the identities despite the white masks and black hoodies some of them are wearing.

Death's Teeth members? They're notorious among students for public excursions like this one, especially during full moons, but I can't imagine they'd be so bold during a Curator party.

An anonymous student organization, they tend to hide in the dark and commence their activities where they have time to clean up the messes afterward. Typical vandalism and occasional drug-induced sex fests are their legacy at Avernia, though there are rumors about more violent traditions as well.

Some say they're vigilantes, seeking justice for those who've been wronged by the other organizations. Others say they're self-serving, seeking control of the entire town, and that the increase in student suicides over the last few years can be traced back to them.

I say nothing at all. I don't want their attention.

Their iconography—some sort of three-headed beast emblem—is carved in the biggest trees in the forest, spray-painted on quarry rocks, and etched into bathroom stall in the dorms. A calling card of sorts that they tend to leave after they've been somewhere.

For some reason, everyone thinks I'm a member.

I couldn't even get Visio Aternae to accept me. There's no way a shadow group would risk its reputation for me. But since they're notorious, people just assume I'm involved.

"Oh, *shit*," one of the orgy partakers cries out—a woman's voice I'm awfully familiar with. That must be who's in the middle of the human sandwich, and I roll my eyes. So much for *no dicks in this economy*.

Gurgling cuts off whatever she's about to say, and I see the person before her ram their hips forward, shutting her up with what looks like a cock. Celeste gags, and it takes a moment before she's given any reprieve; then she's yanked off, gasping for air.

Heat singes my entire body.

"Christ, Beckett, she's gonna pass out if you keep doing that."

The heat evaporates with that one sentence, and when I squint, I can make out his black hair and the outline of his dimpled chin. He's the only one not wearing a disguise.

Beckett?

Of course, Celeste is out here with the president of the Curators. I don't know why I'm surprised, really, given that she's a member of the organization. Maybe I thought our association would have her excommunicated, but clearly—

"Who fucking cares if she passes out," Beckett replies, shoving his way back into Celeste's mouth. "It's not going to matter in a few minutes anyway."

When he pulls off again, Celeste sputters. "What the hell is that supposed to mean?"

"Shut the fuck up, you dumb bitch." Beckett grabs her head with both hands, forcing his cock between her lips. The other two people continue their own ministrations, thrusting from below and behind, and something unsettling spasms in my gut. "You literally asked to be a part of this."

I move back a step, my fingers spreading on the trunk beside me.

She manages to break away after some more gagging, and I hear her spit. "You're *hurting* me—"

My heart lurches to my throat when a dull thud abruptly ends her sentence.

Ice solidifies in my veins.

He *hit* her.

I can't tell if it was Beckett's hand or another person's, but someone hit her.

Celeste screeches, flailing as she apparently tries to push the people off her, dragging her mouth away long enough to let out a shrill scream.

This time, I watch someone's fist drive right into her face, and shock washes over me, giving my feet roots. I can't move, can't run or rush in to help.

My stomach churns violently, twisting so hard that I wince from the onslaught of pain.

She goes slack without protest. Unconscious by the way her body slumps, held up only by the cocks still moving inside her.

"Fuck, man, I'm close—"

"Knocking her out does it for you?"

"Don't *judge* me. She's really hot. Are you sure we have to do this?"

"It's not up to us. Periculum in mora. Just don't fucking come in her."

"Aw, man. That's so fucking boring."

I glance down at my feet, trying to will them to move. This is—they're going to hurt her. They already are, and I'm just standing here watching...

Oh my God. I was aroused earlier.

Putrid shame pulses into my heart, filtering into my bloodstream. For once in my life, I'm completely fucking immobile, but my body is trembling. I want to move, but I can't—*I'm stuck*—

Simultaneous grunts spill out around the group, each person halting their gyrations with a final thrust.

Vomit surges up the back of my throat, and I buckle, falling to my knees as it pushes past my lips. I hurl into a bush, digging my nails into the dirt, and let out a small sob.

"What the fuck was that?" one of them asks, and my heart seems to stop beating inside my chest.

Lifting my head, I shuffle against a tree. I don't move a muscle, fear keeping me totally still.

The trunk across from me has the three-headed beast carved into it and outlined in some dark liquid. Paint, I *hope*.

"Is someone out there?" one of the guys calls.

I cover my mouth with my palm, trying to regulate my breathing. No part of me knows what to do. My brain is short-circuiting, attempting to run through dozens of scenarios at once and coming up totally empty, unable to focus on any one thing.

How the fuck can I ever face my roommate again, or look in her bright blue eyes, after this?

The group remains quiet for several minutes before they finally pull away from Celeste. Listening for me.

Eventually, they seem to move on.

"Who fucking knows," one says, walking toward a backpack lying on the ground a few feet from their tryst. "Let's just get this over with."

"It's the worst part," someone else says.

But not Beckett.

He doesn't say anything. Just stares out into the forest, right in my direction.

I retch silently, afraid I may puke again, and keep my hand in place.

Finally, he turns away, but I don't feel an ounce of relief. Only raw terror exists in my body right now, resurfacing when he tells the other two to hoist Celeste up.

A flash of shiny metal glints in the dark. Beckett raises his hand, lifting Celeste's chin, and he murmurs something quietly to her. The other two murmur back, and I know it's that Latin phrase from before. It *has* to be—the Curators love their dead languages.

He drives the metal object directly into her throat.

My mouth drops, a silent scream trying to escape. I slide my foot back, my limbs moving before my brain has fully caught up to what I'm seeing.

Horror courses through me, shaky and unending. Operating on autopilot, I push from my place beside the tree slowly, keeping my gaze on the group. Beckett pulls the knife from Celeste and then assaults her with it again. And again. And *again*.

She doesn't make a single noise through it all.

When they start to bind her hands and feet together with some sort of rope, I *run*. Back the way I came, my body vibrating with a vengeance.

I don't get very far before someone grabs me from behind.

A large, warm hand slaps over my mouth, cutting off my shocked cry before shoving me against a tree trunk.

Milliseconds pass with me standing as motionless as possible, confusion and trepidation rendering me totally useless. Pinching my eyes shut, I mentally prepare myself for death and inhale slowly, catching an oddly familiar scent—metallic, like I'd expect, but also something soft and comforting, like cedar and grapefruit. The hint of cologne. Soft, clean cotton.

I open my eyes, letting them adjust to the moonlight again, and a new sense of dread fills my gut.

There's no way...

My assailant reaches up with one arm, running a hand over his face. Several strands of his obsidian hair drape across his forehead, long enough to look effortlessly tousled. His sharp, clean-shaven jaw tightens, his pale skin smooth and glistening with perspiration. A silver hoop piercing his left nostril temporarily draws my attention—the sapphire stud is gone.

There's a scar that cuts into his upper lip, making the full flesh bow, and I hate that I know exactly which fight with his cousin caused it.

The longer I stare, I realize that somehow, witnessing my roommate's murder isn't the worst thing that I'll experience tonight.

Because before me are the fiery, endlessly angry brown eyes of a man I haven't seen or spoken to since he ditched me three years ago.

And *he's* covered in blood.

Chapter 17

Asher

"LONG TIME, NO SEE, PUP."

Even though it's never been her MO, I half expect Lucy to try and hit me when I pin her against the tree. If she had any sense of self-preservation whatsoever, she'd knee me in the balls before I could effectively cut off her escape.

She doesn't move a muscle. Shock lines the dark edges of her ocean-blue irises, mixing with the white-hot glint of betrayal. I can't fault her for that, considering I swore to myself that I'd never step foot on this godforsaken campus again.

Things change. *People* change. All we can do is roll with the punches.

I soak her in, noting the years of distance have been kind to her. Two bright red streaks of hair frame her heart-shaped face, the rest as black as the night sky and just as silky smooth. It's shorter than I remember, sitting just below her collarbone, and there's a cut on her pale cheek, caked with dried blood and dirt.

My heart taps slowly against my rib cage, as if it can sense her presence.

I fucking hate that.

The scent of sweat and alcohol clings to the air. Her hand comes up, fingers curling over mine, and she tugs her mouth free.

"What the *hell*—"

A branch breaks somewhere close by, as if someone is hovering a few feet away. Lucy immediately goes quiet. Footsteps thud on the forest floor, drawing nearer with each second that passes.

I recover her mouth and press farther into the tree trunk, moving slowly to make as little noise as possible.

My arm slides up, looping behind her neck, and I tuck her into me. She clutches my hip, clawing at my sweater.

It's a tight fit. Our pelvises line up, every inch of our bodies plastered together while we wait in uncomfortable silence.

Her pulse beats a panicked rhythm against my chest.

I wonder if she can feel mine too.

She mumbles into my palm, her eyebrows knitting. I lean harder, sliding my gaze past the tree in a wordless explanation.

Her breaths start to come in thicker, uneasy bursts; they brush over my knuckles, and I focus on them as the noise dissipates.

Still, we don't move.

A small whimper escapes her, crawling from the back of her throat. My eyes find hers; they're tense and laced with confusion.

"Do you know who that was?" I whisper, straining to hear in case the hooded strangers return.

She nods.

Shit. "They killed her?"

I'm not sure why I phrase it as a question—I watched them pitch the girl's lifeless body over the edge of the quarry and heard the distant splash as it plummeted into the water below.

If I witnessed all that and could put two and two together, there's no way Lucy wouldn't catch on. She's the smart one.

Lucy blinks. Nods again. Tears well up in her eyes, and I grit my teeth, instantly desperate to keep them from spilling over.

I guess some things *don't* change.

"Were you—"

The sudden, frenzied sound of hastened footsteps interrupts my question. A startled noise rips from behind my hand, and her tears break through, sluicing over my fingers. My head swings toward the quarry, noting the group has dispersed, and I realize I may not have pulled us back far enough.

Every muscle in Lucy's body is taut, on high alert, and I'm wishing I hadn't fucking come to Fury Hill at all.

Relaxing my hold on her, I twist my torso, peeking out past the trunk.

She grips my biceps, her nails penetrating even through my sweater. When I look back at her, those blue eyes are wide and vast and completely terrified.

"It's *fine*," I murmur.

I can't blame her for the fear. Three years of not speaking and me showing up on the night a classmate is murdered—I'd be hesitant too, at the very least. Though it's a little irksome that she thinks I'd ever endanger her.

Bar fires notwithstanding.

Scanning the area, I don't see anything alarming, but I resume my position anyway. She's easy to hide from plain sight; I cover her body completely, tucking her in. Just in case.

My nose grazes her soft hair, and I involuntarily inhale the sweet coconut scent.

She trembles, shaking violently as we wait for the footsteps to cease.

When they do, they're accompanied by, "Whoa, hey, sorry for interrupting. I'm looking for my cousin, not Casanova."

Even though I roll my eyes, relief sags in my shoulders at the smooth tenor voice. I turn us toward Foxe, whose six-foot, six-inch frame feels small compared to the forest. Moonlight spills in from behind him, illuminating his form like a god stepping down to earth.

His brows disappear beneath his messy umber locks as he gets a better look at us. A knowing grin twitches against his mouth, and he pockets his hands in his black distressed jeans, rocking back on his heels.

"Ditching me for Lulu again, I see." Dark amusement dances in his eyes, hidden in the shadows. "Just like old times."

After a single beat of silence, Lucy starts thrashing. She shoves at me, so I let go of her, stepping back. Lifting her chin, she tucks those red pieces of hair behind her ears, revealing a row of piercings decorating the cartilage on the left, and adjusts her plaid skirt where it's ridden up her tight-clad thighs.

Foxe gives her a once-over. "Still loving those short little skirts, huh, Lulu?"

I let my gaze linger on her legs a little longer than necessary.

"Do *not* call me that," she snarls. Storms rage in her eyes as they volley between us, and she crosses her arms over her chest. "And what the *hell* is going on? What are you two doing at Avernia?"

"Is this Avernia?" Foxe asks, glancing around. "I'd have expected a better reception. Most college campuses love having a rock star in their midst."

She stares at him. "Avernia is a private school for the country's best and brightest. The students here aren't like your groupies."

"You think I don't have pretentious groupies?"

Her focus swings to me, ignoring him. "Well? What are you doing here?"

"Attending a party, if that's allowed?" I pause, lifting a shoulder. "That's what I *was* doing anyway. Now, I guess we're all accomplices to murder."

"Uh, what?" Foxe's brows shoot up as he places a hand over his heart. "I know Ash-tree is a violent prick, but you too, Lulu? I thought you were a pacifist."

Lucy doesn't respond, pushing past us and heading back to the empty quarry.

Foxe looks at me, his expression lazy. "Didn't take you any time at all to find her, did it?"

I roll my eyes, checking his shoulder with mine as I stalk after her. "It's why I'm here, isn't it?"

Dozens of bloody footprints mark the dirt path to the rock clearing, and I try not to cringe at what just happened or the fact that Lucy saw it all go down.

"Actually, you never told me why you wanted to come here." Foxe falls into step beside me. "Just that you had to leave the tour to come slum it with a bunch of nerds."

I feel his eyes rake over me, silently absorbing my disheveled state, but I don't respond.

"I'd be lying if I said it didn't feel like I missed a very important bullet point in your journey though. Were you covered in blood when Aiden's security team dropped us off?"

"Do you really want to know?"

He seems to consider this. "Good point."

We stop a few feet away from where Lucy's standing at the quarry's edge, contemplating the lake below.

She doesn't move at first, and Foxe slings an arm around her shoulders. "Thinkin' about going for a swim, Lulu?"

Her hands ball into fists, and her spine tenses beneath the oversize cardigan she's wearing. "They just…threw her down there."

The lake is black, impossible to see through even during the day— according to my sister. Fury Hill residents say things that go in don't come back out.

Because of the poor visibility, the girl they tossed has a low chance of being found, even if the local police department was to get involved. Fury Hill cops are notorious for their corruption and generally terrible solved-case stats. Avernia campus police are even worse.

Everything just gets covered up and ignored so this town can continue on with its pretend idyllic image.

It's *bullshit*.

"Who threw who?" Foxe asks, letting her shrug out of his hold. "What's going on exactly?"

Lucy swallows. "I…I don't…" She trails off, a tremor caught in her words. Her fingers flex at her sides, and she just keeps staring at the water, her blue eyes wide as the full moon above.

Shock. She's in shock.

Of fucking course, she would be. Watching a classmate be brutally murdered isn't a daily occurrence, and despite her rough exterior, Lucy's heart bleeds hard. She's the kind of person who absorbs everyone else's pain, and I've always envied her for it.

The only thing I've ever been capable of absorbing is other peoples' anger. I store fury in my heart like I'm afraid I'll forget how painful it is if I don't.

Like father, like son.

Taking a step forward, I reach for Lucy's wrist; my hand dominates it. Always has. She looks down just in time for me to tug her away from the edge, her legs struggling to keep pace with my easy stride.

"What are... We need to call someone, don't we? This needs to be reported..."

"Later," I tell her, keeping my voice firm so I don't cave to whatever she desires.

"*Wait!*" She digs her heels into the dirt, halting me with every ounce of strength in her body.

I clench my jaw, slowly turning around.

She's breathing heavily, an unmoored glint rippling her irises. Her chest rises and falls in short, rapid bursts, and her eyebrows draw inward, frustration coloring her features.

"You're covered in blood," she whispers, dropping her gaze to my shoes.

"Not exactly headlining news."

"And you showed up here out of *nowhere*," she continues.

I can almost see the cogs rotating in her mind as she tries to piece together a puzzle she doesn't understand. Her eyes lift, seeking mine, and she shuffles backward one step. Then two.

"How did you know I was here?"

"I followed you."

Another step away from me. My chest aches with the distance, even though it has no right to.

"That is…beyond creepy." She glances at Foxe without turning her head, but he's leaning against a tree, not even facing us. "Still, how did you know I was *here*, at this party? Why are *you* here? You don't go to Avernia, and you don't live in Fury Hill. Last I knew, you wanted nothing to do with this school or town or m—"

"Can I explain some other time? I really don't think we should be hanging out when there are murderers running around in the fucking forest."

"Good Lord," Foxe mutters. "As if this place wasn't creepy enough."

I surge forward, reaching for Lucy's wrist once more, and she jumps back out of my reach. My teeth grind together, irritation sewing into the enamel.

"No, no." She shakes her head vigorously, her hair flying in front of her face. "I'm not going with you."

"Lucy."

"*No.* I—I don't know what you were doing out here. You could've been—you could have done something like the others. I'm…I need to go find Aurora, and then we can go to the police."

She moves to sidestep me, her entire body shaking, and I take the opportunity to catch her from behind. Wrapping one arm around her neck, I palm the back of her head and gently tilt it forward.

Her hands come up, scratching at my skin as I increase the pressure to the sides of her throat. She bucks wildly, but I'm bigger, and she's never fought anyone off in her entire life.

Why would she need to when she always had someone else around who was willing to step in—even when she didn't ask him to?

"Stop!" she manages to choke out, but I don't release her, and within seconds, she goes totally limp in my arms.

Foxe comes over, whistling low. "Goddamn. You Andersons really know how to make an entrance."

I roll my eyes and shift Lucy toward him; he grabs her arms, holding her so I can haul her over my shoulder. The forest is starting to feel like it's bearing down on us, the darkness beneath the full moon cloaking the air like a vile film. Almost as if everything about this town is as putrid and evil as I always said it was. Not that I ever told Lucy that, nor do I think she would've listened.

Stubborn girl.

My arm envelops her legs, and I tug on the hem of her skirt, pulling it so her ass is fully covered. Foxe purses his lips, watching me silently.

He doesn't ask again about what I was doing before I found Lucy, and I'm glad. I don't need him to know that I'm making them accomplices to my own crime.

"This really does take me back, you know?" he jokes, nudging me as we start toward campus.

"Shut the fuck up, and let's just get her back to the dorms in one piece."

"Aye aye, captain."

Chapter 18

Asher

THE DORMS ARE OUTDATED AND STUFFY. DESPITE THEIR LAVISH, historically preserved exteriors, each hall feels like a time capsule, catapulting us back to when Avernia was first built. Of the four main housing buildings, Erebus Hall is the worst offender and, of course, the place Lucy's called home since she enrolled.

At one end of her floor is a private suite, and I slide a key from the back pocket of my pants, unlatching the lock and pushing the door open. My hand gropes the wall, searching for the switch as Foxe slips in behind us, kicking the door closed.

The light flicks on, casting a warm glow on the neat, unpacked room. Boxes are stacked on the desk and in front of the twin bed, while a welcome kit sits on top of the sole dresser next to the window.

Lucy wakes as soon as we've closed ourselves inside. As she stirs, I bend, slowly placing her feet on the ground and giving her a moment to gather herself.

She blinks, then quickly twists out of my grip. "I cannot believe you did that."

"You were panicking."

"*Rightfully so*, you fucking asshole! Someone was murdered out there tonight. I think that's a pretty valid thing to freak out over."

"Sure, but you having a panic attack when the killers are at large would have drawn unnecessary attention. Did you want to join your classmate?"

Scoffing, she crosses her arms over her perky little tits, turning her head from me. "This is"—her brows furrow as she pauses, eyes darting around the small space—"not my dorm room. Uh, this is the RA's assignment. We can't be in here."

Snorting, Foxe grabs the first volume in a volleyball manga series from the top of one of the boxes, flopping down on the mattress as he flips open to a random page.

She gives him a dirty look, then narrows her eyes at the cover of the book. Slowly, her gaze slides to my face before slinking around the room again and then back to me.

"Okay, seriously. What the fuck is going on?"

I shove my phone into her hands. "Don't you think you should email the dean or campus security? We need to report a crime after all."

"That's what I said." She pauses. Swallows. "Answer my question, Asher."

"Aw, *Asher*." Foxe pouts from the bed. "What ever happened to *pretty boy*? Do you not think he's handsome anymore, Lulu?"

"Oh my God." Whirling around, she chucks the phone at his head.

He drops the book, catching the device effortlessly.

Lucy seethes, gritting her teeth. "If you don't tell me what you're doing here, I'm going to report *you* for murder."

Smothering a grin, I reach for the hem of my sweater, tugging it over my head. "Jeez, Luce. Can't your new RA unpack before you start accusing him of horrible crimes?"

"My…" Her eyes widen, two endless pools of clear ocean. She studies my face, shaking her head. "No, that's…impossible. You don't go here."

"As of this morning, I do."

I'm not sure what I'm expecting to happen. Maybe for her to get angry or sad. It's unlikely that she'll hit me but not totally out of the realm of possibility, I suppose. In the three years since I saw her last, maybe her aversion to violence has changed.

She *did* almost assault Foxe after all.

I think she wanted to hit me in Lethe's that night too.

What I don't expect is for her eyelids to flutter or her forehead to break out in a sheen of sweat. But when Keats shimmies his way out from behind a stack of boxes, reality seems to slam in on her at once. She collapses before she can say anything more, and I dive forward, catching her so she doesn't hit her head.

Her skin is warm and clammy to the touch. It must be the shock finally catching up. Or maybe the oxygen deprivation from my choke hold earlier.

I should probably call my dad to double-check.

One shoulder of her cardigan is falling off, so I push it over her arm to try and cool her down.

Cradling her unconscious form to my chest, I steel my jaw and guide us to the floor. Eyeing Foxe, I lift a brow. "You didn't call the cops, right?"

"Do I look like an idiot?"

Turning my attention back to Lucy, I don't reply. Instead, I slump against the wall, gently stretching her so she can comfortably put her head in my lap. She'll bitch about the contact when she wakes, but whatever.

It's the least she can do after ignoring all my calls and texts for years. As if I was the only one who broke our friendship into tiny pieces.

Fuck. No, that's not true. The end of our relationship was a joint effort, but only one of us lit the match, and it wasn't Lucy.

She wouldn't have done that.

I should've never let her come here alone.

Sighing, I lean my head back, listening to the sound of her breathing. "Well, thanks for coming with. I know going out in public isn't always the easiest thing for you to do."

Foxe shrugs, lifting the book again to hide his face. Keats hops onto the bed, curling against his side and purring loudly. "Couldn't let you hog Lulu like you did when we were kids."

I grunt. "Sure it has nothing to do with a certain blond who goes to school here?"

"Nope. Although you'll probably want to call her and let her know you stole her cousin. She'll come looking for her soon enough."

He snaps the book shut, throwing it at his feet, and scrambles up from the bed. Traipsing to the door, he wrenches it open, checking the hall before stepping out into it.

His hand grips the frame, and he leans back in with a ridiculous grin that shows both rows of straight, white teeth. "By the way, I didn't call the cops, but I definitely contacted someone on your behalf."

Freezing as I push hair out of Lucy's face, I look up, my heart hammering. "Who?"

"I called your dad."

Lucy still hasn't woken when students start returning from the party, completely unaware of the danger in their midst. When I get back from my shower, I watch through the square window on the far wall as they filter into the dorms across the yard, giggling and stumbling without a care in the world.

Idiots. Every single one of them.

Phantom sensations reverberate beneath my fingertips; I turn my hands over, seeing blood caked where I've scrubbed everything clean.

If Lucy knew what I'd been up to before I found her, she'd run for sure.

Now that I've got her back, I don't want to risk that.

Eventually, I move her to my bed, telling Keats to keep her company as I kick my feet up in front of my desk, lean back in my chair, and call my father.

He answers on the first ring. "Asher."

"Dad."

"What was the one caveat we agreed on when you decided to leave Foxe's tour and head up to New Hampshire?"

My chest deflates. "That I wouldn't cause trouble."

His silence is fucking deafening. I clear my throat, and he finally speaks again. "And how is that going?"

"*I* didn't do anything. I've been a perfect angel all day." I fold my hands in my lap, balancing the chair on its back two legs.

As far as he knows.

"So you didn't harass Lucy Wolfe until she fainted from annoyance?"

"What the—how the hell do you know about that?"

He chuckles, the sound rich and dark. "I know everything. And Foxe is a tattletale."

Duh. It's a wonder Foxe is so popular, both as a private citizen and renowned musician, considering how much of a narc he's always been. But I guess the Goody Two-Shoes act really works on some impressionable teenagers. And my parents.

If his mother weren't my dad's younger sister, I'm not sure we'd be close at all.

"When did he even have time to tell you?" I mutter.

"This is a dangerous game you're playing, you know," Dad adds, glossing over my question. "Ignoring the one thing Lucy asked of you may not end as favorably as you think. I imagine she's had a lot of time to reflect, and she's not exactly known for letting go of grudges."

My gaze swings to her on the bed, sleeping semi-peacefully. *Should I have gotten her checked out at the campus clinic?* That choke hold wasn't particularly powerful, but now I'm wondering if she should still be unconscious.

Turning back around, I set my chair on the floor. "Are *you* really trying to lecture me on boundaries right now?"

"As your father, I feel uniquely qualified to do so. I do know a little bit about angry women, you know."

"Yeah, Mom tells the story about how you two got together at every holiday party. It's super fun and not at all concerning."

And, I imagine, stories of betrayal and kidnapping are probably why we spend holidays at home, where everyone's trauma can be contained to those who were directly impacted by it.

Theirs is the kind of trauma passed on to future generations, even when you spend almost three decades trying to reverse the effects. Not everything can be fixed, and sometimes the consequences are residual.

Sometimes the anger lingers.

"I'm just saying, she may not forgive you still. That's something you'll need to earn."

An ache the size of the Grand Canyon cracks open in my chest. "I know."

"Look." Dad's sigh filters over the line—that chest-deep exhale of relief and concern he's perfected over the years. The man's the master of *I'm not mad, I'm disappointed.* "You're okay?"

I blink hard at the wall. "Yeah, I'm fine. All of us are." *For now.*

"Then that's all that matters." He pauses. "You didn't have anything to do with…"

My skin grows tight. "No, and I'm a little offended you'd ask that."

"Well, you are my son after all. I know you."

That makes something uncomfortable lengthen in my throat. I hate lying to him. "Right. Tell Mom I love her. I'll call her tomorrow."

"Will do. Be good." I snort, and he amends his demand. "Or good adjacent. Don't cause more problems for your sister."

"Yeah, yeah. Two Andersons on campus for the first time in years, and shit's *bound* to hit the fan. Imagine what'll happen when Noelle shows up too."

"I did not raise the three of you to cause chaos at every turn."

"No, you didn't," I agree, smirking to myself. "Mom did."

We hang up, and I place my phone on the desk, a prickling sensation traveling slowly down my spine. It's cool awareness, the feeling of being watched.

Without looking, I smother a grin. "Eavesdropping is rude, pup."

From my peripheral vision, I see Lucy push the comforter away and sit up in my bed. She presses her palms into the mattress on either side of her thighs, breathing deep.

"What's *rude* is your existence."

"Glad to see the mountain air hasn't warped that silver tongue of yours."

I spin all the way around, and her eyes are burning—blue flames that I know I shouldn't stoke but can't help wanting to anyway.

"So, what? You go here now? You're an RA in my dorm? After the bullshit you said three years ago about how you had no interest in attending school with me."

"Can't a guy change his mind?"

"You rarely do."

Hurt flashes in her gaze, dimming those flames in a way that makes my chest feel like it's being crushed. But she quickly drops her eyes to the floor, glaring at her bare feet for a second before getting up to find her black Doc Martens in the corner.

"Where are you going?"

She bends down, slipping the shoes on. "Privileged information."

"Oh?" I get up at the same time as she straightens, stalking toward her. Unlike earlier, she's not caught off guard, so she doesn't cower or fold when I stop an inch away, so close I can almost taste her shampoo. "We don't speak for a few years, and suddenly I'm not important enough to warrant knowing your whereabouts?"

"You gonna tell me what you were doing out in the woods? Or why you were covered in blood?"

My mouth snaps shut.

Her frown is insidious. It almost makes me smile. "Then that's *exactly* what I'm saying. Thanks for helping me out, but I'm going to go report my roommate's murder because it's the right thing to do. Maybe I'll file a restraining order while I'm there."

"A piece of paper wouldn't keep me from you," I tell her, leaning in to finger the red hair brushing her face. "Besides, we've waited too long to report the incident. Anything you say now will look suspicious. You don't want to get us in trouble, do you?"

She glares at me, then jerks back, ripping her hair from my hand. "See, you haven't changed a bit." Pushing past me, she heads for the door, pausing just once as she grips the knob. "Don't contact me again. Avernia's big enough that we don't need to see each other, and I'm...not interested in rekindling our friendship. I'm not interested in anything when it comes to you, so leave me the fuck alone, *pretty boy.*"

My mouth twists up when she leaves, slamming the door behind her.

Such a ridiculous notion, that I haven't changed in three years. As if all that time I've been sitting in some sort of growth stalemate and not lamenting the fact that I didn't go with her when we graduated.

I would have followed Lucy Wolfe to the ends of the goddamn earth.

I was just too chickenshit to admit it.

And now that I know better, I'm definitely not going anywhere.

Chapter 19

Lucy

I DON'T TELL ANYONE WHAT I SAW.

That would make this real, and a part of me is still trying to convince myself that what happened was some sort of nightmare.

Incidentally, I don't sleep either. Instead, I vacillate all night between staring at the dorm room ceiling and pacing until the soles of my shoes feel worn.

I do, however, check to make sure none of my belongings have been disturbed. That feels like a normal thing to do when your roommate's been murdered—just in case it was premeditated and you're next.

The first thing I look for is the Vyvanse; I'm shit at remembering to take it, but I know some students around here would steal it if they knew I had it, and admitting to my parents that I don't regularly keep it on me isn't something I want to do.

Truly, the medicine is great when I think about it and a low enough dose that my irregular ingestion only really seems to affect my sleep schedule, which is awful anyway. But Mom would be on my ass if she knew.

I'm not abusing the stuff, but I suppose I'm not correctly using it either.

I just fucking wish I didn't need it at all. Wish my brain could regulate on its own and my body didn't feel like it needs to be in constant motion, or else.

Or else what, I don't know. Nobody does. Death, it sometimes feels like. Spontaneous combustion, maybe.

Anger. Lots of anger. Racing jumbled thoughts turn to overstimulation and then systemic shutdowns.

When I was little, I had no idea why I felt so isolated and disconnected. I had energy and tried to be friendly, but there were needs I was pushing down to try and fit in that kept me from the others.

My interests came at higher, more concentrated speeds. What didn't interest me made me uneasy.

I tried *desperately* to blend in with my peers, and when I realized I couldn't, I left. Thought a change of scenery would alleviate the hyperactivity and attention deficit.

A lot of fucking good that did me.

At some point, a loud knock raps on my door, and I press myself as close to the corner of my bed as possible, huddled beneath my blankets and wishing I could disappear into the wall. Fear paralyzes me, keeping me in place as I replay the scene from the quarry over and over on a loop.

Celeste's muffled noises—first pleasure and then pain.

Terror.

Pure and unfiltered.

The knife as it slicked right through her throat.

And I just sat there, watching, listening, witnessing the darkest and final moments of her life.

A metal trash can next to my bed becomes a vomit bucket. I empty acidic fluid into it until my skin is clammy and my hair sticks to my forehead. My throat burns with the effort.

The knocking ceases eventually, but the images don't stop. Dark crimson stains my vision, blurring everything in sight. I try to read, attempting to catch up on Archaeological Theories and Methods coursework, but my focus is completely shot.

My attention span on a normal day is part of the real reason Dean Bauer called me to his office; it's unprecedented for an Avernia student to be doing as badly as me so early in the semester, but here I am. Breaking records.

I doubt these are ones my parents would be proud to display on the fridge though. Lachlan and Logan likely have much loftier achievements.

The sun comes up at some point, spilling in through the sheer curtains bracketing the sole window in the room. Celeste's side is completely intact from when she was here last, her gold satin sheets made up, waiting for her return. A bag of makeup sits on her desk next to her open laptop, and when I wake the screen, it still displays a research paper she'd been working on.

One of the outfits she'd been debating on wearing to the party hangs up on her closed wardrobe, abandoned as she ran out of time before a seminar.

My hands tremble the longer I stare at her half, nausea churning in my gut.

I stuff my feet into a pair of sneakers and sprint to the door. Panic swells in my chest like wind catching in a sail, and I scramble to unlock the knob, breathing erratically when I throw the damn thing open.

Aurora's on the other side, her fist raised as if poised to knock. Her blond hair is a tangled mess, her blue eyes smudged with last night's makeup, and she's holding two to-go cups from Gaea Beans, the only vegan coffee shop in Fury Hill.

"Dude, what the *hell* happened to you? I watch you walk off to find something to drink, and the next thing I know, you've completely disappeared." She pushes into the room, irritation rolling off her in waves. "Do you know how worried I was? I couldn't even get into Erebus to find you, and then you weren't answering your phone—"

"I'm fine," I cut in, swallowing thickly. "Clearly."

"Fine?"

She sets the cups down, hauling me by my bicep, and stops in front of Celeste's wall mirror. I bite the inside of my cheek as my palms grow sweaty, trying to convince myself it's just the heat from the coffee.

I wait for her to mention the mess and disorganization on my side, but she doesn't even seem to notice.

"Does this scream fine to you?" Her fingers squeeze my arm, so tight I can already feel it bruising. I don't even flinch. "Good God, Lucy, you're covered in dirt and...*blood*? What did you *do* last night?"

I'm not looking at my reflection.

I...*can't*.

My eyes won't focus. They're too afraid to see what she sees, to face the nightmare looking back.

Why isn't she asking about Celeste?

Did I make up everything that happened?

I feel like I'm losing my fucking mind. Was Asher even here last night, or did I just dream that too?

Wouldn't be the first time I'd dreamed about him.

"Have you seen or heard from Celeste?"

Aurora drops my arm, and I track her movements in the mirror as she places her hands on her hips. "Uh, no, but someone said they saw her go into Rad Hall around midnight, so I figured since she didn't come back, she was just hooking up. Isn't that normally how she spends her weekends?"

Whirling around, I snatch Aurora's wrist, yanking her toward me. Confusion bounces in my chest, making me dizzy. "Who saw her? What was she wearing, do you know? Who was she with?"

Her eyebrows knit together, and she gives me a horrified look, tugging on her wrist. "Let go, dude. You're freaking me out—"

A figure stops in the open doorway of my room, hands in the pockets of their cigar pants. Slightly tanned arms are revealed as the person comes forward over the threshold, then short black hair and a familiar grin bearing white teeth.

His eyes show last, dark blue and smug.

I wonder if that was the final thing Celeste saw before she plummeted to her death.

Beckett, the current acting president of the Curators and Fury Hill founding family member, smiles at me.

My skin crawls.

"Room check." He cocks his head to the side, eyeing me with a predatory glint in his gaze. *Or maybe I'm imagining it?* "Just making sure you girls got back safe after last night's little shindig. You know us Curators like to keep track of those things."

Aurora glances between us, then slides her foot in my direction. "Uh, yeah, we're good. Thanks for coming twelve hours later, I guess?"

"Oh, it was the least I could do, *Rory*," he says to her. "You never know what's lurking around at night, especially out in the Primordial Forest. Lots of people go missing there, ya know. You've probably heard the rumors about human sacrifices, secret fertility ceremonies, and death god sightings, right?" Looking back at me, his grin widens. "I don't know about that last bit, but you look like the kind of girl to warrant meetings with unsightly deities, Lucy."

Bile churns in the base of my throat, burning me from the inside out. "And *you* look like a guy who'd be at the top of someone's hit list. Maybe you should shut the fuck up and worry about yourself."

Smirking, he glances past me, and something sinister slithers along my sternum as the memories from last night continue repeating in a ceaseless, spherical motion.

"Where's your roomie, *Wolfe?*"

My stomach somersaults, and I feel my arm tense beneath Aurora's hold.

His eyes are taunting when they return to my person. I'm not imagining that.

I shift on my feet, swallowing, my gaze darting around his face to look like I'm not avoiding the question.

"I'm not her keeper," I manage finally.

"So you don't know then?"

"Do *you?*"

Tension stretches in the space between us. He knows. I *heard* him out there.

But he doesn't know I know he knows. I need to keep it that way.

Aurora clears her throat. "Lucy and I were just on our way to get breakfast. We'd better get going, or we'll miss the two-dollar mimosas."

"Ah." Beckett grunts, nodding. "Of course, of course. I'd hate to stand in the way of Lucy Wolfe and the shit she likes to devour. Who knows what she might burn down this time if she doesn't get her way?" He moves back from the room, rapping his knuckles on the wooden doorframe once more before shooting us a toothy smile. "Glad you're okay, ladies. See you next weekend."

"What was *that* about?" Aurora asks once he's gone.

Shaking my head, I shrug. "Just a Curator being a Curator. You know they can't help but insert themselves into things."

She makes a clicking sound with her tongue. "I'll never understand what you saw in him."

As I change and wash off in the little sink in my room, I consider her comment. The truth is I didn't see anything in him; he was just one of the few people to give me the time of day when we were freshmen.

The attention was nice, and I missed Asher. Back then, I didn't know Beckett was the human equivalent of a dirty toilet.

Without answering my cousin, I drag her from the room, leaving Erebus Hall in a hurry just in case he plans on returning.

Or in case the new RA makes himself known today.

Once we're in the student parking lot outside the front gate, I clutch my biceps tight, trying to warm myself. It isn't that cold out, but I can't seem to get the goose bumps on my arms to go away.

"So…" Aurora begins. "What *did* happen last night?"

"Nothing," I tell her, though the lie feels like cinder blocks filling my body. "I got lost looking for more drinks, and then—"

I'm cut off as I collide with a massive wall of flesh and muscle, clad in a soft cashmere sweater. My grunt is swallowed by his chest, and two big hands come up to steady me.

"*Asher?*" Aurora gasps, immediately trying to tug me away from him.

He doesn't release me though. I lift my chin, meeting those tumultuous brown eyes, and regret it instantly.

In the daylight, I notice things I didn't see hours ago: the hint of gold circling his pupils, which seem to dilate in the sun, and the jewelry adorning his left ear.

They mirror the piercings on mine, though his are just plain silver hoops in his lobe and cartilage. He didn't have those three years ago.

"What are..." Aurora trails off, as if at a loss for words for the first time ever. She reaches up, rubbing her eyes with her fists, and then shakes her head. "What the hell are you doing here?"

"Just returning Lucy's cardigan," he deadpans. He lets go of my arms, holding up a scrap of black fabric I don't remember taking off last night.

Aurora's eyebrows shoot into her hairline. "Is that the one from—"

Not bothering to stick around and answer, Asher shoves the piece of clothing into my hands and then continues on his way through the front gates. I wonder if he's serious about *being* here now.

One more person I'll have to try and avoid, I guess.

Aurora's mouth gapes when I turn to look at her.

"Please don't ask," I say, tying the cardigan around my waist. He must have washed it in the Erebus basement, because it's not dirty at all. "It really isn't what you think."

"Yeah, *right*." She laughs, looping her arm through mine as we begin walking toward her bubblegum pink BMW. "The boy you've been crying about since graduation suddenly shows up with your clothes, and I'm supposed to believe nothing happened?"

"Does that mean when I found you and Foxe naked in my pool four years ago, you guys were definitely screwing around?"

"Screwing around?" Again, she laughs, and I hate the little stab of envy I feel in my gut. She clearly has no clue what went down last night, and I refuse to be the one to ruin that for her. "No, babe, we fucked for sure. He was my first, you know?"

My eyes shoot to hers. "What the hell? Why are you just now telling me this?"

"Well, it wasn't a particularly good time. He'd had *way* too much to drink, and neither of us knew what we were doing..." The lights on her vehicle flash as she unlocks it, and she slides away from me. "Besides, what's it matter when he's probably out fucking the whole world on tour these days? We've both moved on, and that's where I'd like to keep things."

I stare at her across the hood, running a finger over the car's shiny coat of paint. It would probably be in our best interest if I gave her a heads-up that Foxe is, in fact, on campus with Asher, but there's a difference in her eyes when she talks about him versus the one I know I get when I think about Asher.

If there's unfinished business with them, she doesn't care. It can stay in the past as far as she's concerned.

Maybe she already had her closure.

Should I have sex with Asher?

Horror—and something else, something sort of magical—pulses through me with that thought, and I shake my head, trying to clear my foggy brain of all its chaos.

Why in the world would I have sex with someone who made it clear years ago that he wasn't interested in me?

The shame from how he acted after I kissed him still burns bright in the back of my mind—as bright as that fucking fire he set at Lethe's because he was mad at me. He doesn't give a shit about anyone but himself, and I don't want to get tangled up in that sort of mess anymore.

I flop into the passenger seat, squeezing the cardigan in my lap. Aurora slides in beside me, checking her lip gloss in the rearview mirror.

"*So*," she says, drawing out the *o*. "Are you going to tell me what else happened, or do I have to wait for the next holiday back home to get the deets from my parents? We both know our dads are going to be talking about this forever."

"He just showed up, all right? I don't know why or how or…anything, really. One second, I was lost, and the next, Asher Anderson was manhandling me back to my dorm."

"Classic Ash-tree. Did he even try to cop a feel at least?"

I shoot her a look. "Why is everything about sex with you?"

"Not *everything* is about sex. Just the important things, if Shakespeare and Victorian lit have taught me anything." Grinning, she jabs me with her elbow. "Besides, you two are just a long time coming—"

"Please stop."

"All right, but I demand to know the second it happens so I can tell you I told you so."

Gritting my teeth, I clench the cardigan in my fists, ignoring how his scent clings to the fabric. Almost like he sprayed his fucking cologne on it.

Sex is off the table. I don't even *know* him anymore.

Last night, he was covered in blood and showed up out of nowhere, somehow just *happening* upon the exact place where Celeste was being gangbanged and dumped into the lake.

If I believed in coincidence, maybe that wouldn't bug me so much. But at Avernia, I've learned that everything is calculated or purposeful, and coincidences only seem that way when someone wants them to.

Nothing is left up to chance or accident. Our fates are written in the stars, the mountains, and the bathroom stalls.

Often in blood.

I spent my whole childhood thinking Asher Anderson would always be at my side. Something in me died a bit when I realized he hadn't been planning the same. There's no way I'll believe now that he just decided to change his mind.

Aurora shifts gears, backing up. "We'll stop at Lethe's and then head to the diner. Please don't make me try their vegan bacon again though. I almost threw up last time."

I roll my eyes. "Why Lethe's?"

She smirks. "After the night you probably had? Getting drunk is the only solution. We need hard liquor."

She has no idea. "It's morning. Isn't day drinking kind of...pathetic?"

Aurora considers this. "It's only been a few hours since we left the party. We'll just pretend we never stopped drinking in the first place."

Chapter 20

Asher

AVERNIA DOESN'T CHANGE AT ALL THE NEXT DAY, DESPITE ONE OF their very own—a presidential scholar—being MIA.

No one even seems to notice, in fact, that anything is amiss. Multiple killers waltz around campus freely, living their lives the same as everyone else, and not a soul bats an eye.

Granted, I suppose it's possible they're unaware of the crime that has taken place, but still.

Students seem to care more about *my* presence than they do the absence of a peer, which I find unnerving. Not because I'm unfamiliar with the level of scrutiny but because it shouldn't be so commonplace that someone goes missing.

Yet the archives and encyclopedias in the Obeliskos tell another story—one filled with disappearances, unexplained suicides, and that goddamn curse.

If you want to believe that bullshit.

I think higher education is just corrupt in general, and there are certain places where malice breeds well. Schools like Avernia, who pride themselves on prestige and elitism and then use the exclusivity as a weapon to keep students quiet.

Even outside their strange desire to eliminate a supposedly cursed bloodline, it's clear this university has *many* pockets of darkness, all waiting for the chance to consume the people.

Not that it matters. I'm not sticking around here long enough to give a shit about how Avernia treats its student body.

Just one student's body in particular.

It takes all my effort not to stalk into Lucy's dorm room and keep an eye on her when she gets back from breakfast with Aurora, but I have other things to do. I already spent the night listening to her pace a hole in the floor from the hall; maybe now that she's had some normalcy in her routine, she'll be able to calm down.

That logic is how I force myself to leave her, anyway.

When I get to the quarry, I'm only half surprised to find it sparkling and spotless. After a party like the one from last night, I'd have expected a certain level of cleanup, but this feels like overkill.

The Primordial Forest itself is no less intimidating during the day; dense eastern hemlock and American beech trees surround the campus on all sides, so thick it's impossible to know how deep they run before you hit alpine terrain.

Deep enough that you start to feel lost the minute you step foot within.

Goose bumps prick along my arms as I remember the first time I entered them. What changed within me when I left.

I find what I'm looking for behind the half-burnt gazebo a ways off from the quarry. A wooden lockbox with some matches, small tools, and an envelope stuffed full of dirty, wrinkled papers.

When Foxe and I showed up yesterday, I ducked out after he was accosted by a couple of naive freshmen, stashing the wooden storage piece where I could access it later.

An hour before the Curators started their party, putting some sinister plan into action, I was already out here.

Cleaning up my own mess.

"You're late."

Carefully placing the envelope back in the box, I close and lock it. Slowly, I turn around and come face-to-face with Muna—the bartender from Lethe's. Her dark brown skin shines with a glittery bronzer in the sunlight, the long, pleated skirt she wears swishing as she approaches.

She clutches a tan satchel to her chest, and at her side is a broad-shouldered redhead with a ponytail and heavily freckled face.

I glance between them, settling on her familiarity, though I'm certain she doesn't remember ever meeting me. "We said three."

"It's three-oh-five," Muna states, her gaze falling to the box behind me. "If you're trying to bury a time capsule here, you'll need to submit a formal request to the Student Initiative Board as well as the Fury Hill Historical Society. There is a lot of paperwork involved with—"

"Muna," the redhead interjects, reaching up to rub the back of his neck. "Why don't you let the guy explain what he's doing before you start lecturing him?"

She rolls her eyes. "Are you seriously suggesting I ask questions after he's violated school and city policy? God, Tiernan, at least pretend you know me. We've only been on the Curators governing body for the last three years together."

"Right, I forget you want to be queen of Mars one day. I guess a policy violation would get in the way of that."

"Mars isn't—" Muna cuts herself off, holding her hands up in mock surrender. She looks at me again, rolling her shoulders. "*Anyway*. Are you ready for the grand tour?"

My head already aches. "What's so grand about it?"

She cocks her head. "Well… You're only standing on the property of one of the greatest schools in the country. Maybe even the world. I think the better question would be what *isn't* grand about it?"

"Feels like I could name a few things."

"Like?"

"Poor security, unstable blockades at the cave entrances, and all the rumors about ghosts, for starters."

"This place definitely *is* haunted," Tiernan tells me. "When students die—"

Muna elbows him in the gut. "I'll give you the first two things, but the rumors are unfounded. Don't believe everything you read on *The Delphic Pages*, and you'll thrive here."

"The what?"

"Our school's community forum. That's where you heard about the rumors, right?" she replies, though she doesn't wait for my answer. "And since you're new, I'll let your attitude slide. By the time I'm done with you, you'll be seeing Avernia in a whole new light."

I have no doubt that's true, though probably not in the way she's hoping. The only reason I accepted the tour invitation was in the hopes she'd let her guard down and show me the ugly underbelly without meaning to.

Between Muna and Tiernan though, I'm not sure they're the best option for that. I need a higher-ranking student. The president of the Curators, maybe, or one of the Daughters of Persephone.

I'd ask Quincy, since the latter is her project, but I'm not supposed to bother her unless it's an emergency. Since it's her first semester as part of the faculty, she doesn't want me causing issues.

Like I'm a beacon for trouble, or something.

"Okay, so if we hit up the Morning Fields first and then the Lyceum, we can do the Meadows after lunch." Muna takes a notepad from her satchel, scribbling something down with a small pink pen. "Which do you want to see first?"

Glancing into the deeper forest, I wonder if my bloody footprints from last night are still visible in the soft dirt, and try to guess how long it'd take for someone to trace them back to me.

I was fucking sloppy, too focused on finding Lucy. Dad would be pissed.

"...most people use the gyms in the Morning Fields recreationally, but the observatory and greenhouse are really nice. I know the Daughters of Persephone are working on a *huge* campus garden renovation right now, so they probably don't want us over there. The outdoor theater is nice this time of day, and Professor Dupont usually hangs out there with his org, if you'd like to meet him."

It takes a second to realize she's talking to me. "Professor Dupont?"

Tiernan raises a thin brow. "Did you enroll at Avernia on purpose or just throw a penny onto a map and head wherever it landed?"

"*Sutton* Dupont is the premier professor on campus," Muna says with an incredulous look aimed my way. "He's an alumnus and part of the Dupont family, which is the most revered founding bloodline in town. They run *everything*. Plus, he's an acting phenomenon and fantastic teacher."

"As far as legends go," Tiernan adds. "he's about as close to one as we'll get around here."

Muna eyes me, tilting her head. "You're an Anderson, right? Shouldn't you, like, know this sort of thing? I know your family isn't exactly on great terms with Fury Hill, but—"

"My interest in what the other families do or don't do is nonexistent." Shoving my hands in my pockets, I stand up and start in their direction. Probably shouldn't have told her my name or association, but she hadn't wanted to give me a tour until I did. "Now, what exactly are the Morning Fields?"

"Campus is split up into sections," Tiernan answers. "The Elysian Dorms are, obviously, student housing. Org residences, the dean's house, and some admin buildings are also found scattered along this quadrant. The Lyceum is the main academic building and the center hub, with the big courtyard out in front, and the biggest library behind it. Which then leads us to the Morning Fields—essentially, areas you might need access to earlier in the day, or places that might make you cry, like the smaller libraries, the gyms, or the student health center. It's a play on words… morning, *mourning*. Studying, exercise…get it?"

He grins wide at me, and I just blink back. "Clever."

"It was the founders' idea to tie in Greek myths so heavily with the structure of the school. Their fascination with the ancient beliefs ran deep and are inescapable now." Waving that off, he continues. "The Meadows are basically everything not included in main campus or the forest beyond. Mostly just whatever's outside but still within city limits."

"Great." Taking off, I start past them but sense hesitance.

"Um…" Muna's gaze shifts back to the wooden box. "You're not just leaving that there, are you?"

I don't reply, because I don't really know what to say. It didn't cross my mind that she'd be so interested in the damn thing.

One of Tiernan's feet slides forward as if he's tempted to investigate. "I'd take it if I were you. That Wolfe girl will be out here doing her week-end forest cleanup, and if she sees that, you'll never hear the end of it."

"Wolfe girl?"

Nodding, Muna shudders. "Lucy Wolfe. The cleanup is part of her community service sentence."

My eyebrows arch. "Her *sentence?*"

"For starting a fire at Lethe's a few years ago." Muna smooths a hand over her dark curls, adjusting the silky red headband above her forehead. "The place nearly burned down. It's a wonder there were no deaths, hon-estly. A couple of injuries and serious internal damage to the bar though. Since the dean is good friends with the chief of police, they let him decide her fate, and she chose community enrichment over jail time."

"Still went on her record though," Tiernan says, crossing his arms. They seem to move on from the box's presence, turning and heading toward the school. "Plus, everyone pretty much stays away from her now. Well, except Beckett and Eli. I think they just want in her pants though."

Something bleak and angry simmers in my gut. I follow after them. "How do they know she did it?"

"Hell if I know," Tiernan replies. "Dean Bauer finds out everything."

"She'll give you a formal citation for littering," Muna notes, looking over her shoulder one last time. "Lucy seems to get off on the power dynamic. Probably because she has none otherwise here."

Tiernan scoffs. "You and she would be best friends, I bet."

"Please." Muna shakes her head, shoving her notepad back into her satchel. "She's a little too gruff for my tastes. I like people who smile."

My teeth grind together. "Maybe she'd smile more if she wasn't on the hook for something from three years ago."

"Nah. She started a fire a week ago too." Tiernan slings an arm around Muna's shoulders. "We tried to befriend her during orientation. She's like this…rabid dog someone just recently let out of a cage into civilized society. Practically bit our heads off for suggesting she join a student group." He pauses, seeming to consider something. "Hey, maybe that's where she gets her name! Because she's a bit—"

I kick my foot forward, hooking around the front of his ankle, cutting him off. He grunts, tripping over the blockage; Muna jumps out of the way, disentangling herself from him before he can pull her down too.

He face-plants in a puddle of mud and comes up furious.

"What the *fuck*, man? Watch where you're fucking stepping, with your ridiculous Slenderman legs."

I stare down at him as he slings mud from his eyes with two fingers. "Oops."

Without waiting for them to catch up, I keep on the path back to Avernia.

Fuck that guy.

I should've just killed him.

Chapter 21

Lucy

"THIS IS *SO BORING*," WILLA CRAWFORD MOANS, STABBING A PIECE of Styrofoam with her pickup stick. Her short, light brown hair points outward at different angles, likely disturbed by the wet air around us. "Why can't you ever take me anywhere fun for our dates?"

I glare at her from over my clipboard. "This is *not* a date, Willa."

"Yeah, you're telling me. I like to wait for the fifth or sixth before I invite an audience."

Clenching my teeth, I pivot away from where she's crouched down, one of a dozen other Avernia students cleaning up the lake this afternoon.

Not that they're helping out of the goodness of their hearts. Like me, these students are doing community service to avoid jail time or expulsion.

Though if my sentencing is any indication, I'd be willing to bet at least half of them haven't actually done what they've been accused of.

Which is *irritating*, all things considered. My goals are in jeopardy because Dean Bauer's a bitch.

"Back me up here, Eli," Willa calls out to the student a few feet away from her, who continues carefully crushing pop cans before stuffing them into his compostable bag. "You thought Lucy was inviting me on a date too, right?"

He looks over at her, his green eyes not really revealing any emotion. Eli's a Blackwater, and they're notorious around Fury Hill for their quiet demeanors and pale skin that tans without burning in the summertime.

Unlike the other founding families, the Blackwaters don't seem to wade far into the sociopolitical sphere of the school, so I don't mind them as much. They're spineless, which means they go along with whatever decisions the rest of the assholes in charge decide, but I tend to think even their silence is a calculated move.

A lack of response is manipulation too.

Plus, they have a history of being Visio Aternae members, which makes running community service projects like this one easier if I have them involved. Not even Dean Bauer wanted to stand in my way when he learned Eli would be participating.

"You don't even like girls," I tell Willa when Eli ignores her, needing to fill the air. I might not be attracted to her, but the fact that she's willing to speak to me at all matters.

I hate that it does, but I can't change it at this point. Allies are too few and far between to reject.

Especially now that Celeste is gone.

"That's true," Willa agrees, making a face as she overturns a large rock.

"So why are you crying about a date with me?"

"Just curious if I could tame the Wolfe queen."

That makes Eli snort, but he doesn't say anything else, moving several feet down the lakeside.

"Terrible nickname. And you can't," I tell her, marking through her signature on the check-in sheet. "I'm not interested."

"But if you *were*, who'd be your ty—"

"Ms. Crawford," an authoritative voice says, joining the conversation, and I grit my teeth against the sound. "You're talking an awful lot for someone with so much work left to do on your side of this embankment."

Willa shoots me an apologetic look, spinning around so she's no longer facing the dean. I tuck the clipboard under my arm, biting the inside of my cheek to keep from immediately demanding to know why he's out here.

Part of the agreement is that he makes random appearances to ensure the students are doing what they're getting credit for. As if I'd let anyone sign up and leave without doing their fucking job.

I could clean the lake up on my own, if that were all it took. I'd be out here doing it for longer, but at least I wouldn't have to deal with anyone else either.

Dean Bauer clasps his hands in front of him, surveying the scenery behind me. He doesn't say anything more while he scans the area, presumably trying to make me sweat as I wait.

It works. I shift on my heels, my gaze darting up and down the front of his tweed jacket. There's a hole in one of the elbow pads, and the lapels are almost threadbare, but my eyes can't stop circling the little brown button holding the two sides together in the middle.

Swallowing, I rub the back of my wrist, trying to let that ground me in the moment. I can feel my focus slipping, struggling to remain in the present as images from Friday filter in, disturbed by his presence.

Him berating me in his office, though not outright. He slices with thinly veiled jabs and questions about my intelligence, suggesting I'm not suited for a place as precious as Avernia.

But my mind doesn't stay in his office either, jumping right ahead to Friday night and what happened in the quarry above us. Until this point, the cleanup effort was doing a decent job at distracting me from those thoughts, but now the scent of blood returns along with the fear in my chest, and it takes several beats of dissociation for me to even notice that Dean Bauer's talking to me.

I blink, scattering my thoughts like a blanket of fog over my brain.

"...not sure this is the most productive use of school resources," he says, though the first part of his tirade is lost to me.

"What?"

Dean Bauer's face reddens. "Ms. Wolfe, it would behoove you to not be insubordinate in public. You send an atrocious message to your fellow students."

My fingers curl into my palm. "I didn't *hear* you." *Moron.*

"Goodness, do you ever pay attention? No wonder your grades are suffering." He scoffs, shaking his head. "I'd like to see you in my office Monday morning."

"Couldn't we just discuss whatever it is now—"

"Eight a.m., sharp. I hope I don't need to send the campus police after you, but please note that I am not above such measures." Turning on his heel, he levels me once more with spite lacing his bright gaze. "I've invited your parents to this one."

An hour later, Yuri meets me at the abandoned building a mile from the lake, helping me pack away the cleanup equipment as students begin tapering off.

"What do you think he wants to see you for this time?" she asks, blowing a bubble that smacks against her lips.

I shake my head, pacing back and forth. "No clue."

"Involving your parents feels…bad." She looks at me, gnawing on her bottom lip. "Like, really bad. Did you do something?"

Again, I shake my head, though I know better.

Here, it doesn't matter whether you've actually done something, just whether someone important *thinks* you did.

Yuri takes out her phone, grunting in frustration. "What is *up* with Celeste, by the way? She's ignoring my calls, and leaving me on read. I have half a mind to bust into your dorm room and pour some leftover Jägermeister on her mattress for being so fucking rude."

My chest grows tight, and I stare at her hand as she types furiously. "The texts are being read?"

"Yeah." She frowns, turning the screen so I can see the dozen or so messages that have gone unanswered since last night. "Weird, right?

Did I do something to piss her off, you think? My dick comment was a joke…"

"I doubt that has anything to do with it," I mutter, wrapping my arms around myself.

"You're hurting me!"

"Let's get this over with."

"Periculum in mora."

"Well, if you see her before I do, tell her to get over herself or I'm not writing her Anthro essay." Yuri slaps the top of a plastic bin, pushing the lid down on the neon orange vests the volunteers wear.

My stomach aches. I turn away from her, trying to regulate the sudden erratic nature of my pulse. Bile burns my throat, bubbling up as reminders keep resurfacing.

I feel like my head's been shoved in the lake, and I'm being held down, unable to take a breath without inhaling water into my lungs.

"Hey, boss lady! Look what we found!" Willa singsongs, skipping over to me with Eli on her heels.

He's holding a varnished oak box, clutching it like he thinks it houses something sinister within.

I stare at it with painfully wide eyes, studying the design etched in the top.

Two laurel branches curling around a wolf with an arrow between its teeth. Messily carved into the lid and not sanded, as though done by some amateur vandal instead of a practiced artist.

"Where did you find this?"

"By the lake over there," Willa says, hiking her thumb over her shoulder. "It's locked and sort of heavy, but I figure we can easily break that open."

I take the box, sliding the worn lock between two fingers.

"So what do you say?" she continues. "Should we toss it in the lost and found? Eli says he wants it for his little rock collection."

"Skull and bone collection," he corrects, threading a hand through his dark blond curls. "I collect rare finds and plant them to keep Fury Hill from drilling out here for more."

Willa holds up her hands. "Hey, man, you don't have to explain your strange hobbies to me."

"Uh…Luce?" Yuri's soft voice drifts to me, and I snap out of my reverie, noticing that she's now standing at my side, gazing down at the box too.

Clearing my throat, I exhale. "Sorry. School policy is that we surrender any nonperishable items found out here. You know how Avernia is."

Deflating, Willa pouts and walks away, muttering something about how unfair the system is. Eli lingers a little longer, and I pretend I don't notice his eyes narrowing on my fingers.

My knuckles blanch from how tightly I'm holding the container.

After a few more seconds, he lifts his gaze to mine. Silence ripples between us, and I wonder if he can tell I'll be keeping the find and if he plans on reporting me to the dean.

But he doesn't mention it. Just turns and follows in the direction Willa just ran off in, hooking his thumbs in the pockets of his khakis.

A splash of red on the hem of his pant leg catches my attention, only for a second though, before I'm back to the box resting between my fingers, wondering what the fuck Asher Anderson's angle is.

Chapter 22

Lucy

DEAN BAUER SITS WITH HIS HANDS FOLDED BEHIND A MASSIVE OAK desk, staring like he wants to squish me with the heel of his Italian calf-skin shoes.

I slide my hand over my knee, trying to absorb its bouncing. It doesn't work. "Can we get this over with already? I've got class in forty minutes."

"You've got quite the mouth on you for a delinquent, you know that?"

"Well, if you'd *actually* invited my parents like you said you did, you'd be able to see where I get it from."

"Don't worry, Ms. Wolfe," he says, leaning back in his chair and unbuttoning his jacket. "Avernia is well aware of who your parents are and how they operate. Frankly, wanting to avoid the wrath of a former governor is the main reason you're still enrolled here. It wouldn't look good to the board, you know."

"Perception *is* more important than merit and safety."

"See?" He clasps his hands in his lap, giving me a humorless grin. "Perhaps you aren't so stupid after all."

That word is a slap to the face, but I ignore it, stuffing down my feelings before they get me into more trouble. If I were a different person—Asher, maybe, or even Aurora—I'd launch myself across the desk and gouge his beady little eyes out.

Maybe I'd even feel good getting his blood on my hands.

But I'm *me*, which means the thought of harming another person makes my stomach revolt. God forbid I fucking defend myself beyond a few scathing remarks.

"Now, if we could get to more pressing matters," he says, cocking an eyebrow at me, like I'm the reason we've been sitting here for ten minutes already. "Where were you Friday night around one or two in the morning?"

My knee freezes, my foot halting in midair. "Well, I left the Obeliskos around midnight—"

"I didn't ask where you weren't. I asked where you *were*."

"Why?"

His thin lips fold together for a moment, and he sits forward, bringing his interlocked fingers to rest on top of his desk. His dark hair is combed back neatly from his face, revealing a forehead glistening with perspiration.

For some reason, the fact that he's sweating makes me more nervous.

"Have you been getting along with your roommate this semester, Ms. Wolfe?" he asks. "I know she was the third or fourth reassignment you've had since enrolling here. Normally, we don't change rooms unless there are serious issues, but you're a bit of a special case."

My throat swells.

All my room reassignments were people deciding *they* no longer wanted to share a living space. Like they were afraid being a pariah is contagious.

Celeste was the first one who didn't seem to care about any of that.

"Is it safe to say things between you and Ms. Hawthorne were going well?"

I shift in my seat. "Yes, things have been fine."

Dean Bauer stares at me long and hard. "When was the last time you saw your roommate?"

Silence ensues.

My heart kicks against my chest, and my foot flattens on the floor.

Behind the dean, through a large frosted-glass window, the outline of campus is visible. The courtyard with its massive marble fountain and the circle of matching statues, mostly just Greek gods carved into stone, as if holding court over the mere mortals attending here.

I keep my gaze on the glass, wishing I were out there instead. Even if it meant being stared at like some sort of lab rat by my peers.

It would be preferable to the vitriolic shame raging in my gut now.

Celeste's bloody corpse flashes across my vision, staining everything in sight. Nausea churns in my stomach, and I shove the image away.

"Um…" I rub my fingernails together in my lap. "I saw her at a party in the quarry. After I left the library. There were lots of other students there, so they can vouch for that."

"And did Ms. Hawthorne leave your group?"

"My group?"

"Whoever you were there with. Did she leave? Did she tell you where she was going or suggest anyone go with her?"

"She…" I trail off, pinching the bottom of my palm. It doesn't feel right to talk about her plans with the dean. "I don't know."

He blinks. "You don't know?"

"That's what I said."

Sighing deeply, Dean Bauer's shoulders slump. "When was the last time you saw Ms. Hawthorne then? Friday night, shortly after your arrival at the party?"

Suspicion claws at my sternum.

I narrow my eyes. "Are you accusing me of something?"

"Well, *if* that was the last time you had any sort of contact with your roommate, then it should come as no surprise to you that Ms. Hawthorne was reported missing this morning by her parents. They haven't seen or heard from her since Friday either."

My hands grow clammy, and sweat beads under my arms, sticking to the cotton fabric of my sweater.

I'm not sure how to react. My body stiffens, my spine goes ramrod straight, and I stretch my fingers over my thighs, drawing quick circles on my tights.

I can't stop *fidgeting*, my discomfort mounting the longer I'm forced to sit here and try to stave off the memories.

A knock sounds at the door, and seconds later, the thick wood divider is being pushed open, and my parents are shoving their way into the office. The dean's mousy secretary gives him an apologetic bow as she stands in the hallway, unable to corral the intruders.

Bile pushes into my esophagus, threatening to spew.

Dean Bauer moves to greet them. "Mr. and Mrs. Wolfe, what a pleasant surprise—"

Mom holds a hand up, her expression malicious. "Save it, Bauer. I want to know why the school didn't notify my husband and I *immediately* when they thought there was an issue involving our daughter."

The dean's eyes widen. "Well, we did call over the weekend with our concerns, but out of respect for your presumably busy schedules, we thought it best to simply deal with the incident internally."

She crosses her arms, her sleeve tattoos only partially obscured by a sheer white blouse. Her pierced nostril flares, anger radiating off her in waves. "And what is the incident exactly? Why is our daughter here at all?"

He swallows, reaching up to adjust the knot in his black tie—the only tell that my mother makes him nervous.

She has that effect on most people, whether it's because they think she's beautiful or because she doesn't take no for an answer. Powerful, compelling women are as alluring to some men as they are intimidating, and they either embrace the attraction or aim to squash it altogether.

With her, she's too far gone for anything they say to make her wilt. Especially with my father in the room, who would rip funding from the school himself if they even hinted at disrespect.

Me, on the other hand—I'm a different project completely. One Avernia isn't yet afraid of.

Primarily because I don't like to involve my parents in these situations, because they tend to exacerbate my problems when they're gone. Not on purpose—just the residual effects of power.

"To be quite honest, Mrs.—may I call you Cora?"

"No."

I catch my father's smirk in the corner of my eye.

"R-right." Dean Bauer clears his throat, leaning back in his leather office chair. "Lucy's roommate is, unfortunately, missing. Allegedly. Now, we've had similar instances in the past—a party gets out of hand, and a girl finds herself in over her head and can't take the heat from the experience. Or maybe she's wandered off and gotten herself lost or headed home to recuperate for a few days. I'm sure it's nothing *serious*, but there are certain protocols we have to follow when official reports are made."

"Is it protocol to harass your students until you find an answer?" Dad chimes in.

The dean's face pales.

Dad leans forward. "Surely, you didn't think these old walls were soundproof."

"Mr. Wolfe, I assure you, our students' safety and happiness are of the utmost importance to us at Avernia College. Alongside ensuring they get the richest, most fulfilling education during their time here. My intent wasn't to harass your daughter but simply to—"

"Get to the point." Dad's voice booms in the office, bouncing off the bookshelves, and I swear someone walking past in the hall outside comes to a halt. "You think Lucy had something to do with the Hawthorne girl's disappearance?"

Dean Bauer clears his throat but otherwise doesn't react. "We don't accuse at Avernia without due cause. However, I'm sure you can look at it from our point of view: Lucy's performance has been consistently declining, she doesn't seem to get along with the other students, and she certainly wasn't happy about the semester's dorm assignment."

I bristle, on edge now with the audience. "Because it was *punishment*—"

The dean waves a hand, cutting me off. "Nevertheless, this simply is not the first time your daughter has been at the center of an...*incident* during her tenure, so it simply seemed most plausible that perhaps she was involved this time or knew something. I don't mean to say she made her roommate disappear, just that there were signs of distress and other ways she could have been responsible."

I glare at him, wishing my stare could burn straight through his skull. Shifting in his chair, the dean runs a hand over his head, his eyes volleying between the three of us.

My father slips his hands into the pockets of his black dress pants. He's larger than life, one of the tallest men I've ever known, and has a presence that exudes charisma and confidence. Dean Bauer can't look away when he speaks.

"Are there not security cameras in the dorms?" my father asks, his blue eyes piercing through the dean. "On campus?"

"Of course. They were the first things pulled by the police. They'd been tampered with and set on a loop around ten Friday night, playing the same footage over and over until about five Saturday morning."

My parents' gazes slide slowly to me.

I grip my knee as it bounces, unease weaving its way around my spine.

"That still doesn't prove anything," my father says after a moment.

"I have an alibi," I add, lifting my chin. "I, um, left the party before it was over. Went back to my room and stayed there the rest of the night."

"And Ms. Hawthorne didn't return at all while you were there?"

"No."

Dean Bauer's cold stare makes my skin flush, but I ignore it as he nods, reaching for a notepad on his desk. "Very well. What about the time in between then and Saturday morning? Can anyone verify your presence in Erebus Hall?"

A warm, familiar voice rasps from the open doorway, "I can."

Chapter 23

Asher

BEATING OFF IN A COMMUNAL SHOWER ISN'T EXACTLY IDEAL, BUT beggars can't be choosers.

After being on the road for the last few years, it's not even the most inconvenient place I've fucked my fist. It's a better alternative to sitting outside the tour bus, waiting for Foxe and whatever groupie or two he met up with to finish.

At least I'm alone. Classes have started for the week, so the dorm's been empty all morning.

Bright blue eyes assault my vision, teary and terrified as they blink up at me.

Pleasure snakes up my spine, slithering along synapses left dormant around *everyone* else I've ever met.

Except her.

My balls grow heavy at the mere thought of her—that coconut scent, the soft planes of her body against mine, her clinging to me in terror. I hadn't realized until then just how much I was missing.

I come hard, thinking about her smooth, pale skin and the smattering of freckles on her face. The way she rasped that fucking nickname from when we were kids, even as she told me to fuck off.

Unfortunately, I've never been very good at following the rules.

When I wrench off the water, wrapping a towel around my waist as I step out into the larger portion of the bathroom, I'm only mildly surprised to find my oldest sister standing by the sinks, hands behind her back as she leans against the wall.

Her dark brown eyes, bracketed by bangs that sweep the ends of her brows and a pair of black feline-framed glasses, remain expressionless as I approach, stuffing a razor into my caddy.

"How long have you been in here?"

"Don't worry. I gave you plenty of time to yourself. Not interested in catching Asher's self-pleasure show again. Once as a teenager was enough."

Snorting, I shoot her a look. "I've never known you to venture into a public bathroom."

She cocks an eyebrow, turning her head to watch me. "What do you think I did when I went here?"

"I assumed you probably bathed in Lake Lerna under the luminescence of a full moon, like all she-wolves. Probably why it's blocked off these days for swimming, right? To keep the packs out?"

Quincy almost cracks a smile. "I think you're getting your *were* lore confused with Fury Hill superstitions."

Dropping my head, I grip the sink with both hands and sigh. "Yeah. I've only been here a few days, and it feels like the town air is warping my brain already."

"Well, don't drink the water. Or bathe in it, for that matter."

I glance over at her without lifting my neck. "You just come from the dean's office?"

"Yep. Lucy's alibi is secured." She looks away, down at the pointed toes of her red heels. "Thanks for making me an accomplice, by the way. I really enjoyed lying to *my boss* and Lucy's parents."

"Still in love with her mom?"

Quincy's pink cheeks blush a deep ruby color. "I was never in love with her. Just had a little crush."

"Oh, that's right, you always had a thing for that Eden girl—"

Her arm whips out, smacking me across the shoulder. "Shut *up*. I'd like to focus on the fact that you asked me to lie about what Lucy was doing Friday night and how you haven't told me anything else."

"You didn't ask."

"Because you said it was urgent. I didn't know there was a…possible murder involved." She crosses her arms, watching as I push a drop of toothpaste onto my toothbrush and then wet the bristles. "What happened?"

"Nothing you need to worry about, Q."

The door to the bathroom swings open, and a blond student in a dark blue bathrobe pauses as he starts to walk in. There's a poppy embroidered on the breast pocket, capturing my attention.

My veins constrict, and I think back to Friday night before I met up with Lucy.

I'd been out there to stash my box and wound up running into someone with a score to settle. Someone who wanted to harm me.

Their shirt displayed the same symbol, and their blood got everywhere.

On *me*.

I'd been drenched by the time I found Lucy.

The student's eyes widen, and he holds up his hands. When he speaks, it grates on my nerves immediately, bringing back all those memories. "Uh, am I interrupt—"

"Get the fuck out," I snap, stalking over. I shove him out the door and slam it in his face, flipping the lock before he can try to come back inside.

Quincy groans, spinning to look at herself in the mirror. She reaches up, adjusting the bun her black hair is tied into. "As pleasant and charming as always. I can see why Dean Bauer made you an RA."

"Like he'd ever deny an *Anderson* anything. He has a fucking perpetual hard-on for our family. Isn't that why he hired you?"

"Don't let your guard down just because Bauer is easily swayed.

Avernia still sees us as antagonists." She drops her chin, staring at the sink. "And they aren't fans of the Wolfes, either."

Blowing out a breath, I lean against the porcelain bowl next to her, nodding. "What's that about, by the way? Everyone I've spoken to on campus so far is pretty much acting like Lucy doesn't even exist. Or they hate her."

"How should I know? This is my first semester teaching, and they definitely didn't tell me shit when I was a student. I spent most of my time trying not to cause trouble and getting Dad to donate lots of money so I'd be invaluable."

"Well, did the dean seem off at all when you told him Lucy'd been with you?"

"I told him she was working as a Daughters of Persephone initiate and that I had her doing grunt work all night after she left the party. He doesn't usually ask questions when I mention the group because organized women scare him."

My expression flattens. *The student organizations on this campus are so goddamn weird.* This whole *place* is weird. "Your ego's really inflated since you got this professor gig."

"Mom always said I was destined for great things." She tosses me a grin, pushing up on her tiptoes to ruffle my hair.

"She says that about all of us," I say, spitting out the toothpaste. "Speaking of—have you heard from Noelle?"

Quincy shakes her head. "Not a peep."

"That's concerning."

"You know how she likes to make her grand entrances. Enrolling in school would be no different."

My mind wanders back to the last time I saw her, during a quick pit stop between Foxe's West Coast shows, and how strangely subdued she'd seemed. Still her upbeat self, but like there was something dark hidden beneath the surface of her skin quietly trying to claw its way out.

The memory of her after our trip to Avernia nearly a decade ago floats to the forefront of my brain, and I think about how cryptic she's been. In the seven years she's been trying to make it in Hollywood, no one's been allowed to even visit her.

Something's off, but she's not the kind of person you can ask. If she isn't willing to tell you outright, she'll clam up and never speak to you again.

I'm sure our parents have it handled either way, and that when she finally joins us here, she'll spill the details.

But I don't like the silence.

"And don't try to change the subject, asshole. I want to know what went down Friday night. Avernia's faculty is in a fucking frenzy, and I want to believe your timely reappearance is a mere coincidence, but...I know better. Did you have anything to do with the girl who's missing? I know we've talked about the disappearances from before you got here, but..."

"Don't read into it, Q."

She lifts her chin. "Kinda sounds like a threat."

"Maybe it is." I snatch my stuff, cradling the shower caddy under my arm. "As long as you're helping me keep Lucy safe, you have nothing else to worry about."

I can tell she wants to keep pressing. As the oldest sister, she's always taken on the role of protector and investigator for me and Noelle, and it's likely killing her that I won't let her in enough to do either of those things.

Especially since she's here, and she *knows* what kind of shit happens at this school. She's seen it firsthand.

But the less she knows about *this*—Celeste's demise and the latest attack on my life in the forest before that—the less trouble it'll cause for her too.

At least that's my hope.

"You know, you promised me an adventure."

I toss Foxe a dirty look over my sketchbook. "No, I did not. I didn't even tell you to fucking come to New Hampshire with me. You just insisted because you're a goddamn parasite."

"Yeesh," he grumbles, squeezing Keats's face between his hands. "Can I assume by your heinous attitude that you've yet to fuck Lulu?"

"I'm not trying to fuck her, you troglodyte."

Which is true, on the surface. Fucking her isn't my main goal, but I wouldn't say no to a little tension relief in the form of her pretty, spiteful tongue either.

But after screwing up more than once over the last few years, I doubt I'll get that chance.

Maybe I should've just leaned into things when she kissed me in the sunflower field. If I were anyone else, I never would've let that opportunity pass me up.

I'd have had her flipped onto her back, my face between her trembling thighs, before she could've comprehended the words I'd *stupidly* uttered out loud.

Then maybe we wouldn't be here at all.

Foxe frowns. "I miss when your insults were less than two syllables."

"Okay, dick."

"See? Isn't that better? It's crisp. Rolls off the tongue nicely."

"Why are you even here?" I snap, slamming the book shut. "Don't you have groupies you could be harassing or parents you should be checking in with?"

"I already video chatted with my mom this morning, thank you." Keats jumps off his chest, landing on the floor before scurrying under the bed. Foxe props his arms behind his head, staring at the ceiling. "As for groupies, I think Lulu was right about the students at this school. No one seems to notice they have a god in their midst."

Snorting humorlessly, I turn back to my desk. "Or maybe they have more than two brain cells to rub together."

"I'll forgive you because I know you're projecting."

Putting the sketchbook down, I swipe my phone from the desk, pulling up my school-sanctioned email. Already, the inbox is overflowing with welcome bullshit from the student government and different orga-nizations trying to lure me in with promises of parties, networking opportunities, and course credits.

As if I need any of that. My degree is practically finished, having spent my time on tour with Foxe taking online classes, and if I never go to another party again, it'll be too soon.

And I definitely don't need to network, especially *here*.

Opening the oldest email thread in the inbox, I scroll up to the forwarded message, clicking on the attachment.

Scans of Fury Hill city plans, several centuries old, and the original Avernia College blueprints. Sections were broken off to allow housing for each founding family member, six structures evenly dispersed at the edge of the bulldozed property, just inside the forest.

There was no lake at that time, just eroding mountains and dense foliage. Two of the houses were demolished in favor of adding Lake Lerna, cutting off some of the access to the cave systems that supposedly run beneath campus.

Of the remaining four houses, one was condemned due to poor engineering and spatial issues, and two were converted into administra-tion buildings.

The last remaining residence was engulfed in flames. An attempt by the others to rid themselves of the man they saw as a problem due to his ambitious nature and strange homeopathic practices.

Cronus Anderson.

The reason we're a target now.

During my first visit here, I'd gathered as much through the ency-clopedia in the Obeliskos, but it hadn't gone into as much depth, nor had I fully believed it.

Even now I'm skeptical, but after being assaulted in the woods again, I'm understanding a little more.

If the curse isn't real, these people certainly think it is. This email, explaining Cronus's role and how even those who associate with his bloodline could be cause for concern, felt too pointed to ignore.

After throwing her to the wolves in the name of safety, I couldn't very well leave Lucy to fend for herself this time.

A high-pitched siren sounds down the hall, causing both Foxe and me to nearly jump out of our skin. He clamps his hands over his ears, sitting up on the bed.

"What the hell is that?" he shouts. "Fire alarm?"

The one in the corner of my room isn't flashing or blaring, so that doesn't seem possible. Unless maintenance cuts corners on those sorts of things, which wouldn't be surprising.

Several loud thuds and crashing noises echo outside. I glance at Foxe; he hops up, throwing on a T-shirt as he bolts across the room.

I get to my feet slowly once he's at the door, grabbing a baseball bat from the corner. Slipping on my boots, I nod for him to open, and we both lean out into the dark hall, squinting at the window at the far end.

We don't see anything at first, though it takes a moment for my eyes to adjust. Once they do, I note that the hallway is bathed in shadows, and there's a solitary figure standing just a few doors down, staring at the wall.

No, not the wall—someone's closed dorm room.

I step outside, gripping the bat tight.

It takes approximately three seconds for me to realize who it is.

Lucy's completely still, the ends of her hair tucked into her cardigan, as if she'd put it on in a hurry.

Foxe walks ahead of me, his stride lazy and confident as he approaches her. "Goddamn, Lulu, if you wanted some attention, all you had to do was—"

He cuts off abruptly when he reaches her side, his face twisting in horror.

My eyebrows draw inward, and I close the distance between us, wondering what the hell their problem is.

I don't get the chance to ask though, because just inside the room are two faceless corpses, hanging by their feet behind the doorframe.

And even though they're mostly unidentifiable, their eyes mere holes in their skulls and their skin mutilated, I recognize the three-headed beast carved into their stomachs and note the waterlogged bloating. Probably from being tossed in Lake Lerna.

One is Lucy's roommate.

The other is the Curator I killed.

Chapter 24

Lucy

THERE'S ONLY ONE PROFESSOR EMPLOYED BY AVERNIA COLLEGE who truly has no qualms when his students show up late, so long as they're doing well in his class.

When I slip inside the back of a dusty auditorium in the Lyceum, and meet the intense jade green eyes of Professor Dupont, I know I've fucked up.

Still, I quietly slide into a seat in the last row, setting my bag in the chair next to me.

I'm not *that* late—by my usual standards at least. No matter how hard I try, I just can't manage my time well. Add in the fact that I spent the better half of the night giving a bland statement to the police after the *nightmare* in my dorm, and being on time hardly seemed like it was an option.

Avernia should be fucking grateful I'm here at all, considering.

It's doubtful Professor Dupont will let me explain that though. Especially since I didn't finish the *Antigone* assignment or any of the ones from the previous six classes.

The man is forgiving to a fault unless he thinks you're falling behind.

A small tear in the knee of my tights draws my attention, and I groan under my breath, pinching the fabric.

Professor Dupont draws a theater on his mobile chalkboard onstage, cross-referencing the places where actors would have stood in ancient Greece.

As I try to focus on what he's saying, my gaze snags on someone several rows ahead of me: a mop of jet-black hair obscures his face, but I'd recognize him anywhere.

I roll my eyes. *Of course he's in here.* Never mind that it's a course requiring an audition for admission and that he's a late addition to the Avernia roster. Everything always seems to work out for him anyway.

Laughter surrounds him like a séance circle, and he sticks out like a tower in the middle. Girls flank his sides, the two seats before him and two behind. One with dark brown skin and tight curls tied back at the nape of her neck—Muna something. Other than Beckett, she's one of the only Curators to speak to me since freshman year.

Considering it's the first I've seen her in this Staging the Greeks course so far, I assume she was the guide assigned to the shiny new toy.

Back home, he abhorred attention; whether people studied him because of who his parents were or because they thought he was cute, scrutiny always got under his skin, drawing violence to the surface like baking soda sucking out a splinter.

Sometimes, I think that's why he stuck so close to my side. Being left alone is so much easier when your existence makes others uncomfortable, though he did seem to get into more fights when I was around.

Not that he ever complained.

A redhead sits next to Muna, his pale, freckled skin almost moon white in the overhead lighting. He's got on a dark sports jacket and oval-framed glasses. He's the only one of the group not paying Asher any mind.

At the edge of the groupie circle, Beckett has one leg crossed over the other, his frame practically spilling onto the other seats as he gawks at Asher. He toys with a strand of hair in front of his face, clearly trying to appear bored, even as his slimy gaze remains on the new student.

Asher and I lock eyes when he turns his head slightly in my direction.

My lungs constrict as if trying to seal themselves off from air, while the events of the night he first showed up play on a loop in my mind.

Ever since then, my brain's been a broken record, rotating between Celeste's screams and Asher's warm brown irises.

My thoughts shift back: Celeste's pleas for those guys to stop and how they seemed to get off on it.

Then Asher's body pressing against mine in the forest as we hid from whoever killed Celeste. How he'd been *covered* in wet crimson, painted in blood like a stuck pig. Soaked in sweat but breathing normally.

He never did explain what that was about.

And then he'd sent me out of the dorm when we discovered the two corpses in my room, insisting I contact the police. I didn't see or hear from him again, and I spent my night in the Obeliskos bathroom while he was God knows where.

Not with me, that's for sure.

Resentment seizes my heart, squeezing it inside my chest. *Would it have been so horrible to stay and comfort me, even if I turned him away? Would trying to make me feel less terrified have been that difficult?*

When my gaze refocuses, I notice Asher's still looking at me.

I don't think he ever looked away.

Unable to deal with that realization, I break contact, facing the stage once more.

Professor Dupont turns back to the class as he launches into his lecture, dusting his hands off on his slacks. The sleeves of his black button-down are rolled up haphazardly, and I can't rip my gaze from the differing lengths.

It feels off, since the man typically seems so polished and put together, and it's all I can look at.

For about ten seconds.

"Now, I know this may seem like a superfluous course to a lot of you. Especially those taking me as an easy credit."

A few students cough out laughs. No one could ever accuse Professor Dupont of being *easy*.

You take his classes because you want to learn from the renowned actor himself, not because you're planning on coasting through.

"But the point of life isn't to just *get by*. There has to be structure. Order. Otherwise, we descend into chaos. We spent the first part of the semester discussing the schools of thought, and how they influenced art in ancient societies, and now we shift into application."

His green eyes find mine as he finishes the sentence, and my hands curl into fists in my lap.

"We'll start with the basic formulation of the birth of a play in ancient Greece. Beginning with its conception and moving on to the archon eponymos proposal. Does anyone know why they were called an eponymos?"

I'm jostled in my seat as someone flops down into the one directly beside me. My peripheral vision shows black hair and a frame of lean muscle, clad in a burgundy knit sweater. A backpack sits half-deflated in his lap, and he pulls out a notebook, flipping to a page with a dozen unfinished sketches on it.

He doesn't look my way, even when I turn my chin fully in his direction. I scan him from head to toe, cataloging every inch to see if anything feels new or jarring. If people regenerate their skin every seven years, he should be about twenty-three percent an entirely different person.

Yet... The scar slashing across his lip remains. The one he got when a food fight with Foxe at school turned brutal. I took an elbow to the face by the tight end of the football team, and Asher shattered the guy's jaw.

There'd been blood everywhere after that. His parents donated a new cafeteria to keep him from being sent off for his aggression.

I don't know what happened to the football player, but it was the first time I looked at Asher and realized he always seemed to have blood on him. It was a staple.

And even though I'd spent my life building my morals around pacifism and activism through peaceful efforts, I realized I didn't much mind how it looked on him.

Back *then*. Before he ruined everything.

Now when he shows up soaked in it, I'm not sure what to think.

Shrinking in my seat, I pull my feet in from the aisle and look at Professor Dupont. After three seconds of trying to focus, my gaze floats over to the group of students Asher left behind, and my heart ricochets in my chest.

They're all staring. Glaring, really.

Especially Beckett.

"Your entourage misses you," I huff under my breath.

Asher doesn't comment.

I shift in my seat, then pull one leg up, folding it beneath me. "Sitting here was a mistake. Campus will probably be talking about you for a week."

Still, he's silent. He picks up his pencil and starts writing in the margins of his notebook, between sketches of faceless characters and monstrous creatures. Anxiety compresses my lungs as I trace the outlines of the drawings, so I quickly look away.

"They're practically *leering*, you know."

"I don't fucking care." He taps his pencil on the desk. "I'm trying to learn."

Putting both feet back on the floor, I squint at the front of the auditorium, attempting to get roped into the lecture once more. But there's a restlessness skittering through my bones, something scratching at the edges of my focus, and I can't stop my gaze from bouncing around the room.

I feel confined, like I'm stuck in a box rather than a folding chair, and there's no way out.

My hand swipes against the desk, brushing off debris from erasers. I repeat the motion idly as I search for something else in the room to pay attention to.

Sweeping turns to tapping, and I don't even realize I'm doing it until a larger hand comes over mine, warm and gentle as it halts me.

His knuckles are bruised and a little scabbed over. I peer at the mangled skin, wondering what the fuck he spends his free time doing.

If he was involved in what happened to Celeste that night—if I should be worried about his sudden reappearance into my life.

When I glance back up, class has been dismissed. Time has passed again without me realizing.

Students exit the room, some slinging backpacks over their shoulders, others cradling textbooks to their chests. Onstage below, Professor Dupont stands with three people in Curator blazers, listening intently as the one in the middle speaks with animated hand gestures.

Asher pulls away, and my fingers are immediately enveloped by the chilly auditorium air. He stuffs his notebook into his backpack, zipping slowly, and doesn't look at me once.

The sharp angles of his face make him look angry. Angrier than he usually is.

"What are you even doing in a theater class?" he asks suddenly, his voice gruff and annoyed. Like he has any right to be.

"It's an elective."

"You're an ecology major. I imagine there were probably a dozen more appropriate courses you could have taken."

My molars grind together. "Who asked for your opinion?"

"Not an opinion. Merely an observation. What benefit do you get from staring at that guy for an hour and a half twice a week?"

I start to retort again but pause instead, considering his words. My gaze shifts to the front where Professor Dupont bids the student goodbye and crouches down, sifting through his messenger bag. A couple of girls off to the side keep stealing looks at him and giggling, admiring from afar.

It's true that the professor is an attractive man and not much older than most of us students. He was hired on right out of grad school and looks like he just stepped off the set of a movie.

Slowly, my eyes swivel back to the man I've known my entire life. *Asher is jealous.*

A snort tumbles out of me. "Noelle spent a lot of time helping me perfect an audition for this class last semester. I *wanted* to step out of my comfort zone. That was the whole reason I chose to come here in the first place, but I guess I wouldn't expect you to remember any of that. Or to care."

He grabs my forearm as I get to my feet and try to push past him, but he's still not looking at me. "I *remember*."

My blood hums, but I shake the feeling off, refusing to let his words affect me. Scoffing, I ignore his claim. "So should I expect you in my Environmental Justice class in a few hours?"

"Would be a safe bet."

Irritation boils under my skin. "At a certain point, this is just harassment."

"At what point?" he snaps, those brown eyes finally meeting mine. They glow with an animalistic intensity, fierce and unyielding as he glowers.

I swallow a tiny gulp. "What?"

He leans in, the scent of his soap surrounding me. It's soft, clean, and so familiar, and I stop breathing because of it. "At what point do *you* consider it harassment, pup? You got all the morals between us growing up, so do tell me where I fall on your scale of impropriety. I'm *dying* to know where your opinion of me stands."

"It's low." I lift my chin, defiance pulsing through my veins. "I told you I don't want anything to do with you."

"Well, that's too damn bad. I didn't ask what you wanted. I asked how you *felt*."

I blink. "How is that different?"

"Your wants are external. Always have been. They contrast with what you feel on the inside."

"Are you trying to gaslight me into thinking I don't actually hate you?" I ask. "Sorry, *pretty boy*, but in this case, my wants and my secret feelings are one and the same."

"You're such a goddamn liar, Lucy."

Rage singes my nerve endings. "How *dare* you call me a liar, you fucking hypocrite?"

"Takes one to know one."

"All I have ever done was tell you the truth, Asher. And all you've ever done is *punish* me for it." My voice breaks, tears springing to my eyes, making me loathe him even more.

His hold on me vanishes, like I've burned him—yet somehow I'm the one in pain.

"Ms. Wolfe," Professor Dupont calls from the stage. He's at the edge, arms crossed over his chest. "Could I see you in my office before you leave?"

My face heats. Asher tenses.

"It'll just be a moment," Professor Dupont adds.

I nod, the muscles in my arms growing taut.

Asher gets up, gripping his backpack in one fist. With the other, he shoves a piece of torn paper into my hand, his brows drawn together and mouth in a firm line.

"You should pay more attention in class."

The crumpled paper hosts his sketches on it but also the notes he took in between. The definition of *eponymos*, the entire basic structure of creating a performance in ancient Greece, as well as a site to visit for test prep.

Notes that I *know* he doesn't need because retaining information has always been effortless for him.

Notes he took for me.

When I look back up to ask about it, Asher's already gone.

Professor Dupont's office is a small room in the Lyceum's annex, down a back hall from the auditorium. With a deep orange love seat, a large mahogany desk, black-and-white film posters plastered on the dark sage walls, and a bust of Shakespeare sitting in the lone window, it somehow manages to feel a lot cozier than the dean's.

There's something disarming about the professor too, despite the knowledge that he's a notoriously tough grader and unforgiving in his performance critiques. But I suppose you'd need to be to keep up a decent reputation around here.

Given the Duponts' family history as major acting industry professionals, it's no surprise he takes his courses so seriously.

"Lucy," he greets as I enter the room, still clutching the notes Asher gave me earlier. "Come in. Have a seat."

He gestures toward a plastic chair across from his desk, and I perch on the edge of it, my stomach churning violently. If this is a progress report, I'm in deep shit.

"Professor Dupont, I can explain—"

"Call me Sutton. Professor makes me sound like I'm a million years old."

I swallow, squeezing my hands in my lap. "Okay…"

But I don't call him that. It feels weird.

I feel weird.

"There's no reason to be nervous," he says, offering a small smile around a giant coffee mug. His dark green eyes are even more intense up close, like the insides of raw gemstones, his jaw just as lethal. No wonder half the campus is in love with him.

"That's what everyone says," I point out, though my tongue is dry.

"And so very few mean it as much as I do."

He sets the mug down, resting his forearms on the desk. His skin has a very slight tan, as if he spent his summer somewhere sunny, and his dark brown hair is slightly tousled from how often he runs his fingers through it while lecturing.

"If you think this is going to be a crucifixion for your repeated tardiness, allow me to put you at ease: in my time teaching this class, I've yet to have a more memorable audition for entry than I did with yours in the spring. That performance, your rendition of *An Ideal Husband*, haunts me still. So no, I don't particularly care whether you show up on time or not."

I don't even remember doing it, my mind screeches. Even though I spent so much time practicing with Noelle and my aunt Ariana, both performers, I have no recollection of getting onstage for him. It's like I blacked out for the monologue and woke up with a pass.

My shoulders relax slightly anyway. "Aren't I technically failing though?"

"Omne initium difficile est. Every beginning is difficult."

"Can this still be considered the beginning, when we're weeks into the semester now?"

"The beginning starts whenever you decide so."

I must have a blank expression on my face, because he leans forward and continues.

"Technically, by Avernia standards, yes. You're failing." He shrugs. "I don't tend to judge by their parameters though. I think doing so can be a bit messy, and there are other ways of testing whether a person is absorbing material. Don't get too hung up on letter grades."

I nod, though I'm not entirely convinced. It's not the first time I've been told something similar and still had the grading scale favor otherwise.

"Simply put, I only called you in here today to see how you were doing."

"With what?"

"Well, it's not every day a fellow student is murdered on campus. Even less common for their bodies to be deposited in a dorm room. That would shake even the strongest soldier, I'd think."

Celeste's face pops up in my vision, taunting me. Eyeless holes stare back as blood pours from the sockets, turning everything in my direct line of sight crimson—

Clearing my throat, I square my shoulders and blink, dispelling the mirage. "I'm okay."

Professor Dupont watches me for several beats, and I can't help wondering what he's looking for. If he finds it.

After a moment, he brings his hands up beneath his chin, balancing it on two extended fingers. "There've been...murmurings, Lucy."

Panic floods my nervous system. "I didn't do it."

He gives a long, slow blink. "I never said you did. I've heard your speeches on civility and ethics, and after you petitioned Fury Hill authorities to stop detaining students simply leaving Lethe's intoxicated, I find it difficult to believe you'd harm your peers. You're an ecological science major. You protested your introductory biology class because they were using fetal pigs, for Christ's sake."

Actions can be deceiving, I almost say. Just because I didn't kill Celeste doesn't mean I'm innocent of everything.

I didn't help her either. That makes me just as bad—maybe even worse—than the ones who took her life.

My heart thumps loudly in my chest. "You know an awful lot about me."

"I make it a point to know a lot about interesting students. Especially ones that cause positive disruptions on campus." He exhales slowly, leaning back. "God, I sound like my father when I say that. Really, Lucy, my only intent in bringing you here was to make sure you were doing okay. I know it's been a rough few weeks."

Yet he's never once come to my defense. "And I said I'm fine."

"It would be understandable if you weren't though. I've skimmed *The Delphic Pages* once or twice this morning." He pauses, smoothing a free hand over his jawline. "I know it was a gruesome sight you stumbled upon."

Meeting his gaze, I pretend the sheen of his irises doesn't remind me of the Primordial Forest. I pretend this entire situation feels normal, him checking on me, and not like some convoluted plot to get me to confess to something I didn't do.

All I've ever wanted was for someone other than my parents to be concerned about my well-being, and now that I've got it, I can't help feeling like it's some sort of trap.

Just how much does he know about the crime scene?

How much does Pythia know, and why?

"I'd probably care more about Pythia's reports if she wasn't always fueling the lies about me," I tell him.

"She? Why do you assume the moderator is a woman?"

Heat fans my face. "Well, it's not that I think the person behind her is, but she's named after the most famous oracle at Delphi, right? And she takes on this personality of prophetess in some capacity, being the first to leak rumors and news schoolwide. So *Pythia*, as a concept, is a woman."

"Interesting." Professor Dupont considers this analysis, rubbing his chin. "I like that idea. I always just figured the dean plucked a random tie-in to ancient Greek culture to impress the alumni."

"I guess that's possible too."

"Indeed. Few care more about appearances than that man."

"Wouldn't surprise me if *he* was Pythia, to be honest."

I'm not really sure why I say it, but Professor Dupont laughs anyway.

"I doubt I'd enjoy it as much if he was. But don't go spreading that around campus," he says after a few seconds, pinning me with a bright smile. "If the department head knew I was a sucker for that gossip site, they'd have my job, I'm sure of it."

I huff out a breath of air that's almost a laugh. As a founding family member of Avernia, Professor Dupont's status at the school is basically written in stone.

If you believe the what they say about the caves, which are etched into the mountains bordering campus, his name is *literally* carved there.

A fate, like so many others in Fury Hill, determined long before he was born.

Beckett's words from the other morning ring in my mind. How he'd been so curious about Celeste and the fact that I *know* it was him I heard out there that night.

Since the professor is his older brother, I can't shake my suspicion that this meeting has more to it than I'm being told.

But if this is how he wants to play, I'm game.

Chapter 25

Asher

I DON'T WAIT OUTSIDE THE AUDITORIUM FOR LUCY.

She wants space, so I'll give her a little. Her finding my presence offensive might be amusing if it wasn't making my life so goddamn difficult.

I'm not willing to leave Lucy at Avernia by herself, even if she doesn't want to see me. That doesn't mean I have to ditch her.

Been there once already. Won't fucking happen again.

Even when I'm not by her side on this godforsaken campus, I'm *aware* of where she is. What she's doing. I have eyes everywhere, and the cardigan I gave back was installed with a small tracking device, courtesy of my dad's cybersecurity friends.

Her safety is my only priority. I won't accept being kept in the dark anymore.

The sky is a muted gray, pelting the stony Avernia pathways with a light drizzle as I take a look at my course schedule. Muna was assigned as some campus escort intended to help integrate me into student life, like I'm at all interested in joining any clubs, trying out for sports, or going to trivia nights at Lethe's.

Frankly, I'm not terribly interested in doing anything that Lucy isn't, which means half the courses on this slip of paper are nonstarters. But since my degree is mostly finished, I needed something to fill in the blanks.

Raucous laughter floats in from behind me, and when a hand clamps down on my shoulder, I fold the schedule against my chest. Annoyance simmers immediately beneath my skin, but I reel it in for a moment while I turn to meet the gaze of the intruder.

The idiotic part of my soul is hopeful I'll see beautiful blue eyes.

Hopeful and naive.

"Asher fucking Anderson in the *flesh*." A guy with black hair steps into my path, his hold on me tightening as he flashes a sharp-toothed grin my way. "I wasn't convinced it was you in class, since you completely ditched us to sit in the back."

He's flanked by a few others, Tiernan and a deeply tan brunette a few inches shorter than me. They're all wearing matching blazers with a theta symbol in the middle of a poppy embroidered on the breast pocket.

I look at them, then back at the one touching me. "Do I know you?"

If they were sitting around me in that auditorium, I wouldn't fucking know. I wasn't paying them any attention.

"*Ouch.* I'd be offended by that if you weren't still brand-new around here." The guy laughs, but I notice the way his fingers dig a little deeper into my arm. "We're friends of Muna's. She said you might be looking for a tour guide? Maybe stuff she can't necessarily show you?"

My chin tilts down, and I glance at where he's *still* gripping me. My stare lingers and finally returns to his, my eyebrows arching.

Waiting.

When he makes no move to retreat, I reach up, grabbing his index finger, and pry it off me. The other four digits follow, and he winces into the movement, grunting when I yank back, making his bone pop.

"I don't need to be shown anything."

"Well, that's what you'd think if your orientation was lacking." He steps away, holding his fingers and nods at the pair behind him. "Sara-Sofia and Tiernan have been on Muna's route before. They know she's kind of boring."

I don't bother glancing at the other two and continue my walk instead. The mouthy guy doesn't move before my shoulder checks his; I barely register the impact, noting his recoil in the corner of my eye.

Still, that's not enough. He jogs to catch up, once again putting himself in front of me. "Look. As an upperclassman, fellow RA, and FFM, it's my duty to really welcome you to Avernia. If you decline, I'll be forced to report the insubordination to Dean Bauer."

"FFM?" A throuple pairing in some of the romance novels my mom reads, but surely that doesn't translate here.

"Founding family member."

Again, I just look at him.

He frowns, the expression on his face growing almost menacing. "Is playing dumb how you got out of trouble the other night?"

That piques my interest. "What's that supposed to mean?"

"In the words of the great George Bernard Shaw," the guy says, practically shouting into the damp air, "'dying is a troublesome business.' Even more so for those left behind with the body."

Tiernan steps up, adjusting the straps of his backpack. I wonder if he's having trouble looking me in the eye because of our last encounter. "We're not exactly strangers to death around here, but you have to admit, a double homicide happening in your dorm, on *your* floor while you're the RA, looks pretty shady."

I press my lips together to keep from laughing outright. "I wasn't aware that I was a suspect."

"You're not," the girl rushes out, her cheeks darkening when my gaze meets hers. "I think what Beckett and Tiernan mean is that Avernia gets spooked easily, and some of us just want to get to know you better. There's a party at our chapter house on Friday—it's the big, ugly Victorian near the edge of campus, right before the fencing cuts off the property line. We'd love it if you came."

The last party I was at burns a hole in my mind, and I consider saying no on principle.

I fucking hate people, parties, and everything about this place.

How I ever survived as a stagehand for a rock star is beyond me.

Still…maybe getting in with these guys wouldn't be such a bad idea. It's technically what I've been wanting anyway, even if these three are incredibly irritating. They'd likely know *something* about what's going on with the murders and their cover-ups.

"All right," I reply. "What's your guest policy?"

"Oh." She looks at the two guys, toying with her ponytail.

"No couples," Tiernan says. "But other than that, you can bring whoever you want."

I stare at them for a long time, weighing my options. Despite them trying to rile me up, it doesn't seem like the school gives much of a shit about what happened in Erebus Hall, considering how everything has gone on as normal. Maybe they've gotten so used to blowing off student deaths that these were no big deal, or perhaps having two Andersons on campus has them frothing at the mouth for a different sort of destruction.

Either way, attending a party *could* be a smart move.

At the least, it'll give Lucy something to do rather than hide out in the library. I'm certain she won't like me attending on my own. She never did when we were kids, tagging along so she could bounce on her heels all night and chase off anyone who wanted to talk to me.

Not that I minded. It was nice to have a guard dog on occasion rather than being one myself.

I wouldn't have wanted to speak to anyone but her anyway.

Pushing past the little group, I continue across the quad. The rain picks up, drizzling harder than moments before and soaking my sweater through.

When I glance back over my shoulder, the group has dispersed, though the dark-haired man remains, staring after me.

Watching.

Waiting, maybe, though I'm not interested in sticking around to find out what for.

Foxe is flipping through one of my sketchbooks on the bed when I get back to my room, with Keats curled up on his bare chest. There's a scar over one pectoral, white and splotchy, from the tattoo he had removed a few months back, and I wonder if he regrets it yet since the rest of his torso is still covered in them.

"Jesus, do you have to be here *all the time*?" I snap, irritated by the day's events so far.

It's not until I close the door and toss my backpack to the floor that I realize he's not alone. Lucy sits by his feet with her knees to her chest, glaring at a tattered book lying open on the mattress.

I stop in my tracks, blinking. Immediately, my gaze swings to my cousin, taking in his disheveled, half-naked appearance.

Lucy's shoes are off, discarded somewhere near the desk. Her sweater is soaked, sticking to her like glue. A part of me wonders how long she's been in here and how she got here before me.

My jaw clenches, mulling over the possibilities. *They're* related too, distantly, but that does nothing to balm the jealousy surging within me.

Foxe smirks, staring up at the ceiling. "Took ya long enough."

I ignore him, looking at Lucy. "Didn't you have a meeting with your professor?"

"Yup." She glances up, eyes narrowing. "Thanks for waiting, by the way."

"You said you wanted nothing to do with me."

"Since when do you actually listen to what I say?" Extending her legs, she leans over the side of the bed, digging into her bag, and yanks out the torn notebook paper I gave her earlier. "And by the way… I don't want you taking notes for me."

"Who should I take them for?"

She gives me a dirty look. "Yourself? Why do I care?"

"But I don't need them."

"Even more reason you shouldn't just take it upon yourself to offer unsolicited help." Her arm falls, and the paper slips from her fingers. "Did you come to Avernia just to make me feel stupid again?"

Again? I take a step forward but stop myself from closing the distance. Agitation swells in her irises, and while I do enjoy pissing her off—always have—I don't want her to run.

This oddly feels like progress. Her being in my room without summoning.

"Maybe I was tired of being around Foxe twenty-four seven," I say. "You try it, and tell me you wouldn't go looking for reprieve."

"No thanks," she spits.

"Hey," Foxe whines. "Don't drag me into your quarrel. I'm just having fun watching you two self-destruct."

Lucy throws her book at him, and he catches it, laughing so loud the window shakes. That almost pulls a smile from her, but she stifles it before the gesture can bloom, as if suddenly remembering I'm here too.

I could throttle him for being the one to almost make her smile, though I guess that's what he's always been good at.

Me, I just make her angry. Like my own emotions are up for grabs, and she takes whatever she can cling to.

"Look," I tell her, spinning around and grabbing the hem of my sweater. I pull it off in one motion, goose bumps prickling where the cool air meets my damp skin. "I don't know what sort of conspiracy theories you're consuming, but I wouldn't put myself through the hell of higher education just to fuck with you. Can we accept the reality that maybe I just wanted to finish my degree in person?"

She huffs, averting her gaze as I turn back around, still shirtless.

I don't miss the light pink stain of her cheeks or how my chest tightens, my lungs clamoring for oxygen at the sight.

The sleeves of her thin black sweater are longer than her arms, and she pulls the ends over her hands, cradling them in her lap. She scrubs the fabric together, fidgeting. Always fidgeting, like her brain just can't shut off. I wonder if she remembered to take her Vyvanse this morning.

"You're…finishing a degree? How? Avernia doesn't transfer credits."

"Not to other places, but they do make exceptions for incoming students."

"What are you majoring in?"

"Visual arts. I've been doing online courses between gigs. If all I could ever do was listen to Foxe write shitty music, I'd have lost my mind. Figured I should try *something*."

"I didn't know," she murmurs.

Shrugging, I wipe a hand down my face. "Yeah, well, you didn't ask."

Her mouth forms a thin line. "It's hard to believe when you were so adamant about not wanting to attend school here ever."

Foxe sits up a little, sliding Keats off him. The cat growls for a split second, then resituates himself on my pillow.

Irritation boils hot in my bones, and I slide my feet in her direction again, letting it pulse through me.

"Why do you keep fixating on that—"

"Because it's the *only* explanation that doesn't mean you ditched me!" Lucy shouts. Her voice, thick and choked, echoes in the small dorm room, ricocheting off my eardrums.

I blink, my body feeling like it's been swallowed by flames. Foxe's eyebrows disappear beneath his hair, but he remains silent.

She clenches her jaw and squeezes her fingers, not looking at me.

Foxe props his arms behind his head, letting out a low whistle. That seems to break the stagnant air around us, and Lucy slips from the bed, grabbing her bag and throwing it over her shoulder.

"Coming here was clearly a mistake." She heads for the door. "Forget I said anything. You just make me—"

My hand lashes out, latching on to her elbow. Keeping her from leaving. "What, Luce? What do I make you?"

She stares at me with wide eyes, a strand of dyed-scarlet hair falling into her face. "I said *forget it*. Let me go. I have to get to class."

But I don't *want* to let her go.

I never did.

Red rims her eyes, which I see are bloodshot now that I'm looking at her more thoroughly.

I'd taken notes for her knowing that she's practically useless when tired. There's no telling when the last time she got any rest was. Her sleep schedule before college wasn't regular, and I imagine the stress of the last three years—and especially since my return—has taken its toll.

I bet she has fucking nightmares. That's probably why she holes up in the library instead of finding alternate accommodations: to stave off sleep entirely.

My heart beats so loud that it drowns out the low patter of rain against the window. Biting down on my tongue, I swallow and let my arm drop, then reach for a T-shirt.

"Stay," I tell her as I tug the fabric on, then shrug into a black corduroy jacket.

Her hand finds the doorknob. "Stop telling me what to do."

She sounds so fucking *defeated*, but more than that, there's a stiffness to her that I recognize. She can't focus on any one thing, her eyes darting around aimlessly, and her hand grips the doorknob so tight, her knuckles bleach.

This has all been too much. Her mind is revolting—shutting down.

"I'll go."

Lucy freezes. Looks over her shoulder at me. Narrows her eyes into little slits. "Don't be stupid, pretty boy. This is your room."

"And you slept where last night?" She doesn't answer, and I nod in affirmation. "That's what I thought. So stay here and do whatever you need to. I know you don't have another class until later this afternoon."

"You're so fucking creepy."

"Hear, hear." Foxe gets up, stretching and cracking his neck. He slings one arm over my shoulder, leaning against me. His breath smells like alcohol, but I don't say so. "Want some company, Lulu?"

"That depends," she says, releasing the knob. "Do you want to be murdered today?"

He touches a hand to his bare chest. "You're so *mean*, Lulu. What happened to you?"

Shoving him off me, I move toward the door, pulling it open and tossing a hoodie in his direction. "Get dressed and let's go."

"Where to?"

I glare at him silently, and he snorts, putting on the jacket. Lucy stares at her feet, unmoving when the door bumps into her.

Even when Foxe strides out and Keats slinks over, rubbing his slightly overweight self against her legs, she doesn't move.

Maybe I should be more concerned about how traumatized she seems and how locked within her body all her emotions are when she used to wear them on her sleeve.

But right now, all I care about is that she's here, in my room, *staying*.

Chapter 26

Lucy

GETTING OVERSTIMULATED IS EMBARRASSING. EVEN WHEN IT happens in front of someone who's seen it a million times and never made you feel weird about it.

The sensation comes on suddenly—one second, you're existing normally, coasting along in a secluded comfortability. The next, your sweater is a little too long or too tight, or the tag is brushing against your neck because you forgot to rip it out. It's too hot and too loud—just *too much*.

There's no other way to describe it except as an onslaught of *everything*. You absorb the minutiae, and it never gets expelled. It builds and builds and builds until you explode.

And the explosion is always accompanied by fiery shame, the flames of which only seem to fan the blaze. Which is why I'm glad Asher doesn't bother trying to stick around and keep talking to me or trying to reason.

Especially now with that half confession tossed between us.

He didn't even apologize, though I'm not sure why I was expecting him to.

Asher Anderson's never been sorry in his life.

Definitely not for hurting me.

Still, he used to be the angry one. *Didn't he?*

Or was I just not paying enough attention?

As soon as the dorm room door closes, I kick off my boots, drop my backpack, and jump into the bed. It's warm from Foxe and smells like a mixture of him and Asher—fresh cotton and spicy cologne.

My bed growing up smelled like this all the time, since they spent most of their evenings in it, either playing with one of our dogs, doing homework, or annoying me and Aurora. My younger siblings were in my bedroom less than those three.

Stretching out beneath the plaid duvet cover, I realize how stiff my bones are from falling asleep while sitting up in the Obeliskos nightly since the *incident*. A shiver racks my body as I bask in the warmth of the lumpy bed; sprinting here in the rain after my meeting with Professor Dupont drenched my sweater, but I'd been too stubborn to change.

Now I'm soaking Asher's mattress, but I don't care. My eyelids are too heavy to afford that luxury for the first time I can remember.

Keats hops up beside me, curling against my legs.

After lying there for a couple of minutes, the clothes clinging to me becomes unbearable. Sliding away from Keats, I slip from the bed, glancing around to find something to change into. The overnight bag Aurora gave me is tucked away in the library, so I can't exactly trudge over there for it. Not without getting rained on again.

A discarded, plain black T-shirt sits on the back of Asher's desk chair.

Balling my hands into fists, I pinch my eyes shut and silently curse whatever ghosts are reveling in my misery in the afterlife.

Quickly, I peel off my wet clothes and yank the dry shirt over my head. The hem falls to the tops of my thighs, but it's better than nothing, I *guess*.

Nothing would send the wrong message entirely.

I hang my skirt, sweater, and tights over the open door of the wardrobe and climb back into bed, shuffling down under the covers. My panties are still damp, but I refuse to remove them.

Heat envelops me, and I sink into the feeling, pretending I don't notice how Asher's scent is *everywhere*. On my skin, invading my senses, blocking out Foxe entirely.

Instead of going to my next class, I fall asleep and don't wake back up until the clock tower chimes its midnight bell, echoing through all of Fury Hill like some sort of bad omen.

Keats rubs his head beneath my chin as my eyes open, and I stroke his soft, silky fur. He purrs, shifting slightly in his slumber, and the desk lamp across the room flickers on.

Startled, I hug the cat closer to my body, my gaze darting to the figure in the room, taking a second to adjust.

At first, I swear it's one of the men from *that* night, somehow having discovered I witnessed their crime, and my heart drops. Fear slices through me like a serrated knife, taking root in the pit of my stomach.

I blink, and suddenly the unfamiliarity is gone, leaving Asher's tall, lean frame instead. He braces a palm against the wooden desk, his hair hanging in wet strands over his forehead and dripping onto the floor.

There's a tear in his T-shirt, obscured until he discards his jacket, and the material is covered in red and brown stains. He reaches up, messing with the hoop piercing in his nose, and then drops his other hand to the desk, huffing out a leaden breath.

I swallow when he moves to take off the shirt, my eyes glued to the cut muscles rippling across his back and shoulder blades. Even his biceps are corded and tight, and my belly flips as I take in his state of undress for the third time since he's been back in my life.

He walks over to the wardrobe, pulling a long-sleeved shirt from inside. Blackish-purple splotches cover his abdomen, decorating his ribs, and my mouth parts at the brutalization of his pale skin.

"It's impolite to stare."

Immediately, my attention drops to Keats's head. I gently trace his pink and black nose, warmth spreading through me when he pushes into the movement. "What happened to you?"

"Foxe happened. Or I happened to him, I don't know. Doesn't matter. It's settled."

"Ominous." I purse my lips, wondering how bad his cousin looks if he's this beaten up. "Is he still alive?"

He doesn't respond for a very long time. Long enough that I look back over at him, studying the rigid length of his spine and the tension threading through his forearms.

Finally, he glances at me. "Is that something you really think I'm capable of?"

I swallow. "I don't know, Asher. I don't know *you*."

Not anymore.

He stares, eventually turning around with a small shake of his head. I guess I don't need to reiterate that I'm still not convinced he had nothing to do with Celeste, even though there's no real reason for me to think that.

Other than his sudden resurgence into my life the same night it happened.

My fingers spread on Keats's fur. "You guys are kind of old to be fighting like you used to, don't you think?"

"We do it less often than when we were younger," he says, shrugging. "Some things just…bring it out of us."

"Of you, you mean. Foxe is a lover through and through."

Asher's jaw works from side to side, and he lets the shirt fall to the ground. "Yeah. I'm usually the problem."

He doesn't say it like he wants me to refute it, which is just as well, because I won't. Asher's an instigator and always has been, though no one aside from his parents has ever seemed able to predict what might set him off.

I lift my chin, tentatively seeking his gaze.

His attention feels too intense, like staring straight into the heart of the sun. It burns me in places I've long since forgotten, and I rip myself away, rolling onto my back. Keats, disturbed by the shift, leaps off the bed and crawls under it.

The ceiling, like all others in Erebus Hall, is covered in water stains. They leak when it rains too much—already, there's a deep, dark patch directly over the bed, threatening in its presence.

Or maybe that's the man across the room. Sometimes, it's hard to tell.

The bed dips, drawing me to the side with it as Asher starts to climb in.

"Hey!" I put my arms up, avoiding contact with his bare skin. "What the hell are you doing?"

"I'm *tired.* I'd like to sleep."

He rolls over, facing the wall without bothering to get beneath the covers. I feel immensely crowded and pull at the blankets, trying to keep a modicum of modesty now that I'm hyperaware of the fact that I'm in nothing but panties and a T-shirt.

His T-shirt.

It's innocent enough, but there's something about being half-naked and squished here with him that makes me feel...*weird.*

My skin buzzes with anticipation. Of what, I don't fucking know, because I'm certainly not planning on jumping his bones.

Even if something deep, deep within me really wants to. A longing tugs low in my abdomen, begging me to turn and have my way with him.

But I don't. Nerves or anger win out, and I just stare at the open sketchbook on his desk.

Unable to rest now, I move to get up.

Asher's voice halts me. "Where are you going?"

"You don't need me taking up space—"

"I do," he says softly, his hand sliding over my forearm, squeezing tight. He's still facing the wall. "Please, Lucy. Stay."

Swallowing so hard I see stars, I sink back into the mattress. For a few moments, I wiggle around, trying to get my bearings.

"This bed really isn't big enough for us both," I mutter, gripping the covers so tight my fingers feel like they might fall off.

"Do you want to get on top of me?"

Heat sears across my chest, eating up my neck and face. "Absolutely not."

"Don't say I didn't try to help."

"Inappropriate suggestions aren't helpful."

"Inappropriate? We shared when we were younger, and you had no problem with it then."

"That was different."

"Oh yeah?" He rolls toward me, propping his cheek on the heel of his hand. "How so?"

In the dim lamp lighting, I can make out the warm brown of his irises, emphasized by the bruising around the right eye. There's a cut on his lip, split next to the scar, and his nose looks a little swollen.

I drop my gaze to the length of my body, ignoring the blush consuming me. "Well, for starters, I didn't hate you back then."

"You don't hate me now."

Huffing, I shift onto my side away from him. Unwilling to let him know that he might be right.

He snorts, and I feel him move again, probably lying on his back. The warmth from his body sets mine completely on edge, my temperature skyrocketing.

I study the worn spines of the books on his desk across the room, volumes of manga and classics he's had for years now. It makes me feel like we're kids all over again, and a part of me preens at that thought.

When we were kids, I didn't question anything. Asher was my best friend, and that was a truth I knew.

It was all that mattered.

Keats's glowing yellow eyes appear at the bedside, and I move my arm, allowing him a place to jump onto. He fits himself into the small space, curling against me as he begins to purr, and I thread my fingers into his lush fur.

"So…what have you been doing all this time?" I ask quietly, hoping to change the subject. "I mean with Foxe and stuff. Besides going to school, apparently. You haven't really been around back home. At least not when I'd visit."

"Didn't think you *wanted* me around." He blows out a long, labored breath. "To be honest, I haven't been doing much outside of classes. Learning animation and traditional art takes up most of my time. Otherwise, I just go for anything that doesn't demand too much from me, since I apparently became Foxe's main roadie at some point."

A smile tugs at my mouth. "I'll bet he loves that."

"The way he complains, you'd think he'd rather have someone else doing it."

"That isn't true," I say around a yawn. "I doubt he trusts anyone more than you."

Asher grunts but doesn't comment. For a while, neither of us speak, and rain begins pattering against the windowpane, lulling me closer to the edge of consciousness.

Until this moment, I hadn't realized how tired I was. The nap I had before he came in helped a little, but I doubt I'll ever be able to fully catch up.

Exhaustion covers me like a weighted blanket, and I let my eyes fall closed, telling myself I'm only staying because there's quite literally nowhere else for me to go.

My room is blocked off, and the library isn't comfortable. If I go to Aurora, she'll just worry and make me feel worse.

Me sleeping here has nothing to do with how good it all feels.

Nothing at all.

"Just like old times, isn't it?"

I peel an eyelid open at his musing, expecting him to say something more. Something that shatters the illusion.

"Don't bother reading into it," I reply softly. "I'll be gone in the morning."

Again, he doesn't respond, and I assume he's fallen asleep. I clutch Keats close, trying to convince myself that it's his fur heating me in places I've never felt before rather than the steady, rhythmic breathing coming from behind me.

But it's the breathing I fall asleep to anyway.

Chapter 27

Asher

MY PHONE BUZZING SOMEWHERE ON THE BED WAKES ME UP, BUT IT'S the arm slung low across my waist that keeps me in place on the tiny mattress.

I'm on my back, the same way I fell asleep, but Lucy's turned completely around. She's facing me now, her hair in total disarray, and her arm is heavy where it lies on my bare skin.

I swallow, glad that the duvet cover is at least pulled up enough to hide my dick, which is raging from the early hour.

And *only* the early hour.

It has nothing to do with the fact that Lucy's T-shirt has risen up, exposing the slight curve of her hip, or the way her body heat is seeping into mine like warm, delicious honey.

Or the fact that she's in nothing but *panties* from the waist down.

Another quick sweep over her sleeping form alerts me to the fact that she's not wearing just any T-shirt, and she wasn't wearing one when I left her in the room yesterday.

That's my shirt. She's wearing *my* clothes.

The hem's lifted, revealing the entirety of her smooth thigh to my hungry gaze. The center is pulled and twisted a bit, sticking to the contour of her tits—perky handfuls I'd love to put in my mouth.

Whoa, Jesus Christ. Where did that come from?

I'm no stranger to wanting Lucy Wolfe. Most of my life has been spent pining silently after her. Our emotional connection has always taken precedence, but the underlying desire was present too after a certain age. It wasn't until after we stopped talking that I realized I *needed* the connection to feel anything.

She's the only person I want to be close to. The only one I've ever dreamed about riding me, sucking me, letting me live between her legs.

Still, this probably isn't the place.

Even if my dick is throbbing, begging me to say otherwise.

Keats is nowhere to be immediately found, which is just as well. He'd get in the way cuddling with her, and she'd welcome it.

Animals flock to Lucy and she to them.

Her family even has a grove of laurel trees on the edge of their property where some of their dead pets have been planted because they love animals *that* much.

I steer clear of the grove though, like with most haunted places. Except if Lucy drags me to their depths, the way she has with Avernia.

Granted, it's not *solely* her fault that I've wound up here. But she's not innocent either. She has to know I'd have followed her anywhere.

Eventually. *Right?* Despite everything…she has to know that us being apart wouldn't have been forever.

Lifting my hand, I gently brush some black and red hair from her face. A knot forms in my throat as I revel in the softness of her skin.

I'd go to the ends of the earth if she asked me to.

When I withdraw, she shifts in her sleep, her fingers flexing over the waistband of my pants. I suck in a gust of air through my teeth, tensing beneath her inadvertent touch.

She squeezes the elastic fabric, her thumb slipping a fraction of an inch beneath.

My body lights up in flames.

If she moves any more, I might combust on the spot.

Heart racing, I lean to the right, easing myself away from her body.

The action has the opposite effect though, and once space opens up between us, gravity pulls her into it.

Into me.

I hold my breath, counting backward from one hundred to calm the hormones raging through me. The tendons in my neck pull to their limit when her fingers graze my skin, and even though I know I should wake her or roll away, I can't seem to fucking move.

My focus is glued to her sleepy exploration. A tiny sound comes from the back of her throat, and she dives deeper, stretching, ghosting over the tip of my dick.

I grit my teeth until they ache. Every fiber of my being vibrates with ridiculous anticipation, sweat beading along my hairline and dripping down my forehead.

After a few seconds, her eyelashes flutter as she starts to wake, and I exhale long and hard.

Blinking, she swivels those blue eyes toward me. For a brief moment, too brief for me to really grasp it, there isn't an ounce of hatred hidden in the glittering sapphire.

But in the same instance, it's back, and I feel completely hollow inside.

"What the *fuck*, Asher?" she snaps, pushing up on her free elbow.

I lift my palms. "Don't look at me. You're the one with her hand in my pants."

Horror etches into the smooth lines of her face. "Oh my God! Why were you just letting me do that, you fucking *perv*."

"*I'm* the perv?" I bark as she snatches her hand away, cradling it against her chest. "You got in my bed half-naked and then started groping me. My hands have been perfectly well-behaved."

"I was asleep, you big dummy!"

"Well, clearly your subconscious has other ideas about what you should be doing."

Breathing hard, she stares down at me, her ass half hanging off the edge of the bed. Her eyes sparkle in the early morning light, ocean waves I want to dive deep into and drown in.

Something in her expression morphs in the quiet that ensues. She's thinking, the cogs in her brain turning, and finally she lets out a shallow breath.

"Did you know Foxe and Aurora hooked up?"

Shifting, I pull more of the comforter into my lap. "What, like recently? Not in my bed, I fucking hope."

"No, not... I mean back when we were younger. She didn't tell me when exactly, but at *some* point before we all graduated."

"Oh yeah, I knew that. Pretty sure all our parents knew." I glance at her, cataloging the strange, mildly perturbed look on her face. She seems like she's just barely straddling the line between reality and the past. "You didn't?"

"How come no one told me?"

"Jesus, I don't know, Luce. Are you the sex police or something? Did we all have to notify you before we engaged in lewd activities?"

She pushes onto her knees, folding her hands in her lap. The T-shirt sits teasingly on the very tops of her thighs, exposing the rest of her pale flesh to my starved gaze, but I do my best not to stare.

Not too much anyway.

"Have you..." She trails off, her teeth snagging on her bottom lip.

One of my eyebrows arches, interest swimming through my veins. "Have I what?"

"Been with anyone," she continues, her cheeks blooming a bright pink. "Like that. Sexually or whatever."

My heart hammers a slow, steady rhythm in my chest. Against my ribs, like it's trying to get out. I sit up a little, propping my head on my hand with my elbow resting on the mattress.

"Are you asking because you don't want to be the only virgin left of our friend group?" I utter, barely able to push the words out. "Or because you want to know if I went to someone else after rejecting you?"

Her eyes lift, anger etching into the corners. She clenches her jaw, her nostrils flaring. "I don't remember propositioning you."

"No? Your hand on my dick in the sunflower field—that wasn't an invitation?"

She's silent for a moment. "I was drunk."

"Not *that* drunk."

"That was years ago."

"I still think about it."

A tense beat of silence pulses between us. She swallows audibly, and I watch her throat work over the gesture. "What, when you're out fucking girls? Is it supposed to make me feel good that you at least envision me instead?"

When she starts to get off the bed, my hand lashes out, locking around her wrist. I tug, wanting—no, *needing*—her closer. She resists, because of fucking course she does, so I move to her.

I lean in, curling a strand of her hair around one of my fingers. "Who said anything about *other girls*, pup?"

"Please." She smacks my hand away, but I just grab her again, keeping her from slinking back. Frustration laces her brow. "I'm not stupid, you know. If Foxe is out there...sowing his oats or whatever, it stands to reason you'd be doing it too. Monkey see, monkey do."

"And if I told you I've never touched another girl the way I wanted to touch you that night, among those ridiculous fucking flowers? Beneath the stars?" My grip on her tightens, and I inch forward so our breaths mingle. "That I've never even *thought* of being with anyone else that way?"

Glassy blue eyes meet mine. "Then I'd say you're a liar."

"Not right now I'm not." Exhaling a shaky breath, I try once more to pull her in my direction.

This time, she comes after only a little hesitance, spilling onto my lap like an overlooked drink. She gets caught on the bedspread, landing with her palms on either side of my hips.

Her face is so close. I could bridge the distance between us right this second, but I don't. My nerves are shot, and even doing this much is taking all the energy I have.

How many times have I dreamed about this moment over the last few years?

"Asher…" Her voice is a warning, low and raspy still from sleep. She glances up at me through long lashes, carefully taking me in. Uncertainty lines her irises, and I fucking *hate* that she's questioning my sincerity.

Hate that I made her feel like she needed to.

"Aren't you curious?" I ask, trying to inject some playfulness into the situation before I bust in my damn pajama pants. I've got to get a grip, and she needs to be eased into the idea of something more with me.

I suspect she's still not fully awake and letting her body do the thinking. When her hands fall to my shoulders, she uses them to adjust herself on my lap, planting her knees on the outsides of my thighs.

She blinks down at where her fingers meet my bare skin. I feel each flex against me, as if she's battling the urge to pull away and end this.

I'm trembling beneath her, but she doesn't move. Almost like she's frozen in place, paralyzed by the sudden shift.

"Touch me," I urge, though I keep my own hands on the bed. "We both know you want to."

"I…" She blows out a shaky breath, licking her lips. "I don't know how. Where do I…"

"Anywhere, pup. Explore to your heart's content."

Biting her bottom lip, she slowly slides down, gliding over my pecs. My nipples tighten as she approaches, goose bumps scattering along my body like tiny time bombs, threatening to detonate the longer her hands are on me.

The T-shirt she wears sits high on her waist, baring the entirety of her thighs to me. I trace them with my eyes, memorizing every inch and wishing I could see *more*. But if I ask for that, it'll spook her, and I'm not ready to end this little bubble we're in.

Hooking her pinkie around my nipple, she gives a gentle squeeze, and I force a heavy swallow. She shifts again, bringing her fabric-covered pussy right on top of my dick; I grit my teeth, and her eyes flicker to mine, a silent question pulsing in their depths.

"Is that..."

My jaw works from side to side, and I glance past her, white-hot embarrassment coating my insides. I don't fucking know why, considering this is the girl who's seen me in far more humiliating situations, except that there's an extra layer to this one. A complication if things don't pan out correctly.

Lucy runs her tongue over her teeth, and her hands come up, her fingers stroking my jaw. Slowly. She cups under my chin, pushing my head so I'm forced to meet her gaze.

"Just from me touching you like this?" she asks, and I note the furious blush staining her cheeks, her nose, crawling across her neck. Like she feels every bit of what I do.

I nod. Just once. Just a small confession.

She moves, lifting her hips a fraction of an inch, before bearing down harder on my lap. The pressure against my swollen cock makes me see stars, and I'm *aching* to grab her and create even more friction.

I taste my heartbeat in my throat when she repeats the motion, grinding on my erection like a wanton wet dream.

"Luce..." I warn. She doesn't know what she's doing—right?

Lifting a shaky hand, she pushes it beneath her T-shirt, cupping her own breast as she continues sashaying her hips, riding me like she's been doing it for years.

With each thrust of her warm pussy against my cock, I can't help wondering why this is the first time we've ever done this. Why I let her get away back then.

"Does that feel good, pup?" My words are a whisper as she clutches my neck, leveraging herself.

Fuck, she *looks* good. Incredible, actually, with a sheen of sweat coating her face, flushed with exertion and excitement.

When she covers my mouth with her palm, abandoning my neck to silence me, I almost come on the spot.

She shoves my head back, pinning me to the mattress, and shifts so she's straddling just one of my thighs. My cock leaks drops of precum, throbbing with impending release, and I know that it won't take much more.

I've never seen anything more fucking beautiful than Lucy Wolfe on top of me, using me for her own pleasure.

I could die happy right here, right now, even if this was all I ever got.

"Ash…I'm…I think I need more…"

My eyebrows shoot up, and I unstick my hands from the mattress, holding one up in question as she keeps my mouth covered.

She looks at my fingers, long and flexible, and gives the tiniest nod. I watch, rapt, as she arches her back, sitting up straighter to grant me access.

Turning my hand over, I slip two fingers beneath her; my eyes roll back in my head when I feel damp panties, rough against my skin, and then I brace my thumb against her clit, letting her find a rhythm she likes.

Her hand moves beneath the T-shirt, and I make a noise low in my throat. Panting, she looks at me and reaches for the hem, slowly—*fuck, so fucking slowly*—lifting, baring one breast to me.

My parched stare drinks in the rosy, diamond-hard nipple dotting her sweet, slightly swollen flesh. The way she drags her thumb over the peak, strumming in a way that makes the pulse between her legs flutter.

She's close, if her sudden hike in breathing is any indication, and I'm holding on by a bare fucking thread. As soon as she cups herself, kneading her breast and letting out a low sound of desperation, I'm gone, my cock jerking in my pants and spraying everything it touches.

The guttural groan that emits from my throat echoes in the room, and as I shift my hand, pressing two fingers against her clit, she seems to follow suit, releasing her breast to grasp my hip and squeeze tight.

Her eyes snap shut, and she continues grinding against me, her hips undulating in a frenzy of need. The sound of her coming is soft and distinct, like a song created just for me, and already my dick is hard again from hearing it.

Breathing heavily, she finally opens her eyes again, scooting away from my waist. I keep my hand between her legs until she forcibly removes it, tucking her hair behind her ears as she sits back on the mattress.

I stare up at the ceiling, euphoria dancing with something dark and unidentifiable in my chest. "That was—"

"Stupid."

My limbs are like jelly, so I just move my head, tracking her as she scrambles from the bed and begins dressing frantically.

"That was a lot of things," I say, narrowing my gaze at her naked back as she tugs on her sweater. "But stupid is not one of them."

She slides her skirt over her hips, spinning around to face me. "Did you think fooling around would make me forgive you?"

My eyes widen. "What the fuck? No, and it wasn't what I—"

"Just forget it, Asher." She holds a hand up, stepping into her boots, and then darts for the door. "This changes nothing."

Chapter 28

Lucy

FLIPPING THE BATHROOM DOOR LOCK, I SLAM MY BACK INTO THE solid surface, slap my hand over my mouth, and let out a silent scream.

What the fuck did I just do?

My legs are still tingling, partly from my sprint to the Obeliskos but mostly from the aftershocks of the best orgasm I've ever given myself.

Well, *sort of* myself.

Asher *barely* even had to touch me. I was on the edge from waking up with my hand in his pants, and the rasp in his deep voice paired with having his half-naked body so close and so warm proved to be a dangerous cocktail.

Needless to say, that won't be happening again.

Slinking away from the door, I move to the sinks across from me, splashing cold water on my face. My heartbeat hasn't slowed down at all since I fled Asher's dorm, and I'm a little afraid it never will.

He came just from watching me. I didn't know it could happen so easily; you hear about men lacking stamina in bed, but they always talk about it in such a negative light.

No one tells you what to do if you find his lack of control *more* arousing.

If I'd spent just a few more minutes in there, I'm positive we'd have gone further into the abyss of regret.

That's why I couldn't stay. My judgment was clouded, and I'm nowhere near ready to forgive him for *ditching* me. Especially when he doesn't seem the least bit sorry.

Not to mention the weird things that have occurred since his appearance on campus. I still don't want to believe he had anything to do with the grisly murders, but it's hard to ignore the timing.

Knots sprout in my stomach at the thought of letting a killer touch me like that. Asher's violent, but cold-blooded homicide? If he cares about me as much as he claims, I can't imagine him doing it.

Which means the real killers are someone else, and I have no leads.

When I finally leave the restroom, I take my backpack and set up at a corner table on the thirteenth floor, prying open my laptop. My dorm room is inaccessible, but the campus police at least threw together a few bags with my shit, which I've been storing in an unused custodial closet.

Aurora thinks Dean Bauer put me up in another dorm, especially since that's what I told my parents to keep them from visiting a second time. Not because I don't appreciate their intervention but because I took the dean's threat very seriously.

I'm on thin ice here. It's best if I just keep my head low and try to graduate with my life intact and as much dignity as possible.

So what if the thought of death—the *image* of it, right before my eyes—keeps me up at night? It's not really that different from the stress of school or my sadness keeping me awake instead.

At least every time I think about Celeste or that unidentified corpse, I feel like the reason is legitimate.

I start to work on my midterm project for Politics of Conservation, even though it's not due for a while, but my mind wanders, and so does my cursor.

Professor Julie Ouellette is one of the founding family members, though currently the only surviving one of her house, and the instructor of this class.

The Delphic Pages posted a thread a few years back about how Julie's dad, a renowned poet laureate, snapped when she was a kid, killing his wife and both his parents, and stuffing the bodies beneath the floorboards of the campus observatory's main deck.

"Because where else would the heir to a literary empire hide a body?" Pythia had quipped.

I wind up on her faculty page on Avernia's website, noting the decrease in course load versus previous semesters. As a Curator sponsor, Professor Ouellette typically has a full schedule, yet the conservation class is the only thing listed outside of mock trial and Fury Hill Historical Society meetings.

In contrast, Professor Dupont—Sutton? I'm not going to call him that—has a packed calendar between theater, humanities, Visio Aternae projects, and unspecified commitments. He's in high demand, it seems, although one could argue his schedule feels a little *pointedly* full.

Almost as if he's trying to make sure his whereabouts are never in question.

Not that I have much reason to suspect him of anything, other than his being a founding family member. Those people are too entrenched in the tainted fabric of this school for me to believe they're all innocent though.

Finally, I end up on Quincy Anderson's faculty page; as the new head of the classics department, she only has a couple of intro-level courses listed, plus the admissions page for the Daughters of Persephone student organization.

There are pictures of her with the initiates, posing behind the Lyceum and Obeliskos where they're renovating the campus gardens. She's smiling in all of them, her calm aura visible even through a lens.

When we were young, I looked up to her most. She was a lot like her dad: the silent but confident type, driven and motivated to carve out the life she wanted for herself.

At one time, I attributed that assurance and determination to academics. That was part of the reason I thought coming here would be life-changing—because she had initially made it seem that way.

Turns out some people are just *born* with these abilities. The skills can be taught, but application is a whole other ball game.

One I've never been very good at playing.

It's no secret that Quincy wound up despising her time as an undergrad; anytime she came home to Aplana, she looked like she'd seen a ghost, her pale skin somehow moon white, her brown eyes sunken and guarded.

She'd never talk about it with anyone outside her family though. Not even me, who spent half my life harboring a crush on the entire Anderson family, though I'd never admitted it to anyone out loud, because Asher wouldn't have liked sharing the attention. Or me finding his family attractive, I'm sure, since he didn't take it well when I kissed him back then either.

I glance at the office hours listed on Quincy's page, wondering why she's back, working under the same dean she claimed to abhor. What could have possibly changed?

Did she come here knowing her brother would be enrolling? To protect him, since the entirety of campus has some strange love-hate relationship with their family?

A photo in the bottom right of the faculty gallery makes me do a double take; I lean in, squinting at the computer screen, trying to ignore the massive knot that materializes in my throat.

Quincy, standing in the quad before the statue of Demeter. It's an older photo and sort of grainy, probably from when she was a student. She's next to a pretty brunette I don't recognize, her dark gaze glued to the other girl's face, her hands wrapped around a small gold talisman.

So small, I almost don't notice its shape until I see the points. The tail curling around her pinkie.

A three-headed beast.

"So how much do you need before the shelter accepts a donation?"

I glance at the glass mason jar on my tabletop, then at Tag Holland, the only student to pass through my line the entire hour I've been set up. A part of me wants to lie and create some sob story, but I'm raising money for the Fury Hill Animal Shelter, which is at capacity and close to picking a euthanasia date to cut down costs and free up space.

If that doesn't appeal to someone without me needing to throw in a whole fucking show, I don't know what else I could even do.

Personally, the thought of an open-intake shelter makes me sick to my stomach. I understand why they exist, but having grown up with my mom's shelters in Aplana, which have a strict no-kill policy, it's hard for me to fathom. Though I suppose the latter is easier to pull off when you have the disposable funds to hire adequate staff and maintain resources.

It's not as if the government gives a single shit about these animals.

Or its people either. To them, and even Avernia alike, if you can't directly contribute to society in a way that benefits those in power, you don't deserve rights or equity.

Which is utter bullshit, but I digress. The government and higher education being disasters is nothing new.

Still, this is why I try to sponsor this high-kill shelter each fall during Avernia's big Philanthropy Week, which we do in lieu of homecoming.

Frankly, despite everything else, Avernia College's decentering of sports is still one of its main appeals for me. That and the fact that credits are nontransferable are the reasons I haven't left.

Plus, I'd rather shoot myself in the face than let Dean Bauer think he'd gotten to me.

Even if I can feel my spirit draining with each passing day the campus murders go overlooked, as if Celeste and Frances Sweetgrass—the Curator found in my room—never existed in the first place.

It's fucking creepy, but it is what it is, I suppose. If they won't make a fuss about it, neither will I.

What's the point when no one would believe me anyway?

"Technically, I can make a donation of any size. The shelter won't say *no*," I tell Tag, watching him run a hand beneath his black wolf cut, pulling strands of hair out of the collar of his shirt. He keeps his dark eyes on mine, listening intently. "But I don't feel good about throwing a hundred or so bucks their way and calling it a day, you know? That'll buy one or two bags of dog food and not much else. Definitely not the robust support they need at this point."

Tag's face falls. "All I've got is a fifty…" He reaches into his back pocket, sliding the bill from his wallet, and stuffs it into the jar. "There. Maybe once people see the first donation, they'll flock over to you and do more."

Doubtful. "Thanks, Tag. I appreciate it."

"Don't thank me with words," he says, placing his palms on the table and leaning down with a small smile. "Why don't you let me take you out? Professor Dupont's putting on his winter play, and auditions are open to the public. We can go and poke fun at the Curators who truly have no business trying to act."

I stare at him.

His grin widens. "I know you want to say no, and you probably think I'll take my donation back if you do. I'm not like that. I would have asked you out either way."

"You don't want to go out with me," I say finally, something unsettling in my stomach, like a boat being thrashed on angry seas.

"Au contraire, mademoiselle. I've wanted to go out with you since freshman orientation. You just never let me talk for more than two minutes at a time, so I've not had the chance."

My face heats as a couple of students walk past, glancing over their shoulders, eavesdropping. They walk away whispering and snickering to each other, and I grind my teeth together to keep from calling them out.

"I don't think a date with me would be good for your social standing," I try again, folding my arms on the table. "It would be rude of me to do that to you."

"See, but that's what I like about you, Lucy. You *care* about that shit."

The seat beside me is suddenly yanked back, and a tall figure plops down into it. His knee, in his black chinos, bumps me, and I ignore the way mine tingles beneath my tights from the contact.

I *definitely* don't let my gaze track upward, lingering slightly over the thigh I had between my legs not long ago. Strong muscle strains against the fabric of his pants, and a bit of sweat percolates between my breasts, dripping from my bra as I recall how sturdy and masculine it felt, how primal and desperate I was—

My hands ball into fists. *Focus, Lucy, for fuck's sake.*

"Oh!" Tag's eyebrows jump as he takes in the intruder. "Lucy, you didn't tell me you had someone helping out this year."

"I was kind enough to volunteer my services," Asher says, and after a few seconds, Foxe meanders over from a booth selling knockoff Girl Scout cookies, with three boxes of chocolate-coconut crisps in his arms.

"Hey, Lulu, how come you're the only one without a line?" he asks, dropping two of the boxes onto the table and tearing into the third. He stuffs a cookie in his mouth, offering the sleeve to Asher, who shakes his head. "Need me to beef things up for you? Draw in a crowd? Some of the *freshmen* know who I am at least, so things aren't a total wash here."

I straighten my back, not bothering to turn and spare either of them a look. "Sorry, Tag, maybe you should come back some other time."

Tag frowns, glancing between the three of us. "Is there a problem, Lucy? Do I need to get security?"

Someone—Foxe—snorts, and Asher scoots forward, balancing his elbows next to mine. "No problems. Right, *Lucy*?"

The way he says my name, even though it's spat through closed teeth, causes something to stir in my stomach. I swallow, forcing a nod.

Asher holds his hands out. "See what I mean? So please, continue your conversation."

"Well..." Tag tugs at his collar, shifting on his feet.

Across the quad, several other booths are now watching us, captivated by Asher's sudden presence at my table, I'm sure. They've never bothered glancing over here before.

I can already feel Pythia's gossip trending the longer we sit here.

Founding Family Member Spares Avernia Pariah Precious Moments of His Time.

The headlines write themselves.

"I'd still really like to go with you, Lucy," Tag says, crossing his arms over his chest. "It would be fun and probably good for you, considering how the semester's gone so far."

"Oh?" Foxe leans in, cookie crumbs flying. "Go where?"

"School play auditions. They're happening soon, and I was thinking we could—"

"She's busy."

My head whips to the side, and I glare at Asher. "No, I'm not."

His eyebrows lift. "That isn't what you said in my bed the other day—"

Reaching beneath the table, I grab his thigh, pinching the inside before he has a chance to stop me. I put all my strength into it, gritting my teeth; he jolts, his hand immediately coming to cover mine as he drags my chair closer.

He grunts, wrenching my fingers from his leg, and then tangles ours together, drawing them into his lap.

Squaring his shoulders, Asher sits back, turning to Tag again. "Sorry about that. You know how Lucy gets when she hasn't eaten."

Anger blots out my vision, blurring the side of Asher's head for a few seconds.

At the same time, my fingers are numb from the elation of holding his hand. Because that's what this is basically; we're intertwined at our palms, and he's got his free hand curled over the two, lazily stroking his thumb along my knuckles.

The number of times I imagined this *very* gesture when we were teenagers is embarrassing and not something I'll ever admit out loud, but for a few seconds, I let younger me indulge.

"I..." Tag clears his throat, stepping back from the table. "Yeah, sorry. I had no idea... I didn't think you dated, Lucy, honestly. I'd never try to slide in on another person's partner."

Sitting forward, my chest aches. "No, Tag, it isn't like that."

"It's okay, really! Don't worry—"

"I'd love to go out with you!"

I blurt the words before I've even finished processing them, suddenly desperate not to have Tag think poorly of me. Like I've been stringing him along or didn't think he was good enough to tell about my boyfriend.

My *nonexistent boyfriend*. I rip my hand from Asher's hold and get up, reaching into the jar to fish out Tag's cash.

Asher's tense beside me, his rage palpable even from a foot away.

Walking around the table, I tuck the money into Tag's palm, giving him what I hope is a kind smile.

When allies here are too few and far between, I can't just let them slip through my fingers.

Tag grins. "Are you sure?"

"As *friends* though," I add, too softly for Asher or Foxe to overhear.

Understanding dawns in Tag's eyes, and he nods emphatically, then looks down at the fifty. "You should keep this—"

I shake my head. "No way. Keep it so you can take me to get some good refectory food before the auditions. Remember, I don't eat anything made from animals or their by-products."

"Then I shall find us the finest vegan food in all of Fury Hill, m'lady!" He gives a fake salute and takes off down the quad, heading for the Lyceum and ducking inside.

Asher's got his arms crossed, glaring at the now-empty jar when I come back to sit at the table. I scoot my chair out of reach, declining the cookies that Foxe tries to offer me.

"Do you enjoy doing things that piss me off?" Asher asks in a low voice.

"Yes," Foxe and I say in unison. I lift my fist, and he bumps his knuckles against mine.

Scoffing, Asher juts his chin at the glass. "You gave away your only donation."

"It was his money."

"Well, great. Now you have none. How are you going to save the fucking animals with nothing?"

That does it. I feel something—a tether, threadbare and struggling—snap deep inside me, releasing a pit of every negative emotion I've been bottling up since his arrival. Everything unspoken in the air over the last three years and the rejections in between—it all comes to a boiling point.

I whirl in my seat, jabbing my finger into the center of his chest. "Why don't you let *me* worry about that and mind your own fucking business? I didn't ask for your help or your opinion or for you to be here at all, so for the love of fucking God, just leave me *alone*."

The urge to toss *pretty boy* in there is strong, but when I turn back toward the quad, my face breaks out in hives with the influx of stares we're getting.

Yep, he is definitely a problem. For multiple reasons.

A thought occurs to me, and I bend, reaching under the table for my backpack. The wooden box Willa and Eli found is at the bottom, and I take it out, shoving it into Asher's arms.

"While we're at it," I say, pushing again for emphasis. I meet his gaze, doing my damnedest to keep my voice from shaking. "Stop leaving your shit in the forest."

Asher pales a little. "Where the hell did you get this?"

"Someone else found it and brought it to me," I say, shrugging. "So whatever's inside, you should really consider if you'd want some random college kid stumbling on it and then don't leave it out for just anyone to grab. That's littering by definition."

"Gonna issue me a citation, warden?"

Anger roils between my ears like the open mouth of a rushing river, yet I don't miss the way his voice dips a little when he says that or how his eyes hood, dropping to my lips.

"I'll report you to your sister," I counter, giving him a saccharine smile. "Maybe when she gets you kicked out, you'll give a shit about the environment. Or me."

Considering the goal of Quincy's student organization is supposedly campus beautification, I know she'd be on my side too. Even though the Andersons are close-knit, there's obviously something tying them here that they don't want to be removed from.

And if they won't explain it to me, if Asher just wants to pick things up where we left off after he ruined my life, he's got another think coming.

I'm not the same codependent girl he shattered back then.

I won't let him close enough to do it again.

Chapter 29

Asher

I WATCH LUCY'S ASS SWING FROM SIDE TO SIDE AS SHE STOMPS AWAY from the quad.

Fuck, she's hot when she's mad at me. Or when she's bossing me around. I can't help but admire the way her short little black skirt hugs her hips, and her tall boots make her legs look miles long.

Getting them wrapped around my waist is all I've been able to think about since she rode my thigh the other morning.

Foxe drops into her now-empty chair, kicking his legs up on the table. He lets out a low whistle, popping another cookie into his mouth. "Boy, does she hate you."

I shoot him a dirty look. "She does not hate me."

"Sure seems like she does." He cocks his head to the side, studying her retreat. "She looks good walking away from you too, huh?"

My arm lashes out, my fist connecting with his injured shoulder. He winces, losing balance for a split second. One of his cookies falls, and he groans.

"Look what you made me do!"

"Quit perving on your fucking *relative*, you cretin."

"What? Is it my fault that our family won some sort of genetic lottery? Am I not allowed to say we're beautiful?" He huffs, scooping up his cookie. "Besides, our moms are cousins. It's not like we're *that* closely related. I bet it wouldn't even be illegal in some places if we fu—"

Turning in my seat, I hike my foot and kick the back leg of his chair. It splinters and explodes, sending him sprawling onto the ground.

I know he's fucking with me. His heart belongs elsewhere.

But the anger doesn't rest.

"One of these days, you're going to seriously maim me," he groans, stretching out on the cobblestone. He lays his head back and stares at the overcast sky, grabbing cookie crumbs and pushing them between his lips.

"That is the hope."

"Psychopath." He looks at me, putting his chin to his chest. "Why'd you bring that box here with you anyway?"

I glance at my lap where the ornate wooden container sits, having already forgotten its presence because everything happened so quickly. Lucy going off on me was distracting in itself, though I wish she wasn't such an issue.

My issue. Not hers. The fact that all I want to do is let her pin me to my mattress again is a *problem*, especially since there are actual things I'm supposed to be doing while I'm at Avernia.

Things I've been neglecting while trying to reinsert myself in Lucy's life.

Clearly, it isn't working.

And this box isn't mine.

"Hello?" Foxe stands up, waving a hand in front of my face. "Can you focus on *me* for five seconds?"

"You asked a fucking question."

"And then you immediately floated off on some Lulu-induced cloud, I'm sure." He huffs, perching on the edge of the table.

"You're being extra needy today."

"I'm but a simple goldfish," he croons, flipping his hair out of his face. "If you don't pay enough attention to me, I'll die."

I narrow my eyes at him, absorbing how disheveled and tired he looks. I'm no stranger to an exhausted Foxe James—when on tour, the man works himself ragged, his dedication to music and performing unmatched—but there's something *off* about him now.

The lack of direct eye contact, the overconsumption of sweets. I know I smelled alcohol on his breath not long after we came to town, but I hadn't thought anything of it. Not enough to mention it, because that's been our deal for years.

We don't really talk about shit. Our fists have always been the driver of conversation between us.

Violence has always been my solution to everything. It's why I wound up in the Primordial Forest the night Lucy's roommate was murdered, trying to stop a wheel from turning—but I'd run out of time to execute my half-assed plan and went to find Lucy instead.

Now, I'm spending all my energy trying to win her over, and the wheel turns anyway, like it would have whether I showed up or not.

Sometimes the wheel turns because it's the natural progression of things. The consequences of a person's actions. Evolution manifesting.

A curse set in motion long before any of us here now were even born.

"Did something happen?" I ask Foxe.

He lifts a shoulder. "What do you mean?"

"I don't know, you just seem—"

"I'm fine," he cuts in, kicking at me with the toe of an expensive loafer. "Don't worry about it. This place is just kind of boring, and I think it's getting to me. No biggie."

Sliding off the table, he stretches his arms over his head. A few girls from a different line giggle among themselves when his shirt rides up, and he shoots them an easy, million-dollar smile.

He's the picture of ease, but as he grabs his boxes of cookies, I can't help the sense of dread that weighs like a lead balloon in my stomach.

When he leaves without another word, I shove all the cash from my pocket into the glass jar—a thousand or so dollars. Not as much as the shelter needs but better than nothing.

On my way out of the quad, I'm stopped by the smug, dark-haired fucker I ran into after my first class with Lucy. He grabs my shoulder again, halting me in my tracks.

"Anderson," he greets with a curt nod, glancing down at my occupied hands. "Ah, reaching out to the far less fortunate, I see."

I shrug out from his grip. "I like animals."

"Oh no, I meant Lucy Wolfe. That shelter's one she sponsors, right?" He chuckles, shaking his head, and points to a fancy booth at the other end of the quad. I see the redhead and the brunette from that same day and realize I don't remember any of their fucking names. "We're down there if you ever feel like supporting a cause that isn't doomed because of the person heading it."

My gaze narrows, suspicion clouding my vision. "You sure like talking about Lucy."

His cheeks pinken slightly. "I don't *like* talking about her. It's just hard to be on campus and not have something to say. She's fucking weird, man. You shouldn't even bother trying to befriend her. No one's ever succeeded."

I inch forward a step. "How exactly is it that *you* tried?"

"Hey, man, don't look at me like that. If you want to do her, she's all yours. I tried a few years back, and she wasn't into it. In fact, she tried to burn down the place we were in just to get away from me."

"Pretty strong message from a pacifist."

He snorts. "Please, is that what she's telling people now? She's a skilled liar, I'll give her that."

There's a flash in my mind—the smell of smoke and the flickering of bright orange flames as they outgrow the little dive bar I've just set on fire.

I remember Lucy in that back room and how she wasn't alone. A man was sitting on the sofa next to her, his hand touching her thigh.

Glancing at his arm, hanging limp at his side, I study one hand. The other is stuffed in his pants pocket, but I recognize the visible knuckles. That face.

The theta emblem on his jacket makes me even more suspicious.

When I meet his eyes again, I take a few seconds, cataloging him for any changes in pupil dilation or breathing. Anything that might suggest he remembers me.

He continues to stare blankly, his eyes bored.

But the boredom feels…almost practiced.

It's too precise.

Tucking the glass jar under my arm, I extend my free hand, doing my best to plaster on a pleasant expression. Not my strongest suit, but my parents did spend a few years trying to coach me in case I decided to try for colleges that wanted to meet in person.

"What'd you say your name was again?"

The guy's face screws up, but he takes my hand anyway. "Beckett," he answers. "Beckett Dupont. President of the Curators, Aquarius, and fellow founding family member."

"Ah. So that's why you're so invested in me."

He squeezes my fingers twice before releasing. "It's a networking thing. Rarely do we ever have so many founding family members on campus as students and faculty, and since this is the first the Duponts have crossed over with Blackwaters and Andersons since your sister was a student, there's a certain responsibility to make contact. Suss you out, so to speak."

"Because you think I'm here to, what? Carry on my namesake's supposed curse?"

"I don't believe in the curse," he tells me, casting a sideways look at his table. "But there are a lot of Fury Hill residents who do. Something to do with botched sacrifices and hubris, I don't know. All I give a shit about is my Curators. We work too hard to keep a good, clean name for a bunch of age-old bullshit to fuck that up."

It's a nice spiel, I suppose, albeit not compelling in the slightest. The Curators and Avernia are doing him no favors as far as story-telling goes.

Still, *this* is what I was looking for. How lucky that he seems to have simply fallen in my lap.

Lucky and far too coincidental.

"So what exactly do you want from me?"

Beckett rolls his shoulders, adjusting the book bag strapped across his chest. "How'd you like to join my ranks?"

Chapter 30

Lucy

"Do you think it's weird if a guy comes really quickly?"

Yuri looks over her anthropology textbook. Since they found Celeste, she's been absorbed in her studies, rarely coming out of Blessed Hall to do anything. Even now, she's only here because Aurora lured her in with the promise of homemade cupcakes, sent up by her mom, my aunt Lenny.

"What, like to see you before class or something?" Yuri asks.

Snorting, Aurora smooths her gloved fingers over the section of hair framing my face, rubbing red dye into the strands. "*Coming* as in what they do when you make them feel really, really good."

Her eyes find mine in the mirror, and she squints at me.

"I do think it's weird you're asking us this before a date though. Got big plans there, cousin?"

"Tag's cute," Yuri adds. "But I didn't think you liked him like that."

I'm not sure why I said anything, except that I can't seem to stop thinking about the day in Asher's dorm. How intoxicating it felt having him come completely undone, just from a few over-the-clothes thrusts of my hips.

I didn't realize sex was so consuming. That being intimate with someone would feel like ripping open your chest to bare your soul and letting them put their hands all over it.

Not that I've never been curious. I kissed and dated girls and boys, tempted to go further but never really finding an opportunity.

It was all a ruse anyway. Not my bisexuality or the attraction I felt but because I was trying to distract myself from the belief that Asher didn't want me back. The one person on the planet who I could see myself going all the way with wasn't interested, and it sucked.

In college, there aren't very many people I'd even consider getting that close to. Especially not after the whole thing at Lethe's.

Still, I'd thought for sure my desire for Asher would have burned out by now. Imagine my surprise when I realize it's the complete opposite, and I'm losing sleep over both the thought of my dead roommate and the outline of my former best friend's cock under my pussy.

I swallow, rubbing my fingernails together and averting my gaze. "This isn't a real date."

"Then why are we all huddled in my room like it is?"

"You made me come here so you could do my hair."

Yuri slams her book shut. "Can we circle back around to the original question and, more importantly, why it's being asked?"

"No, let's just forget I said anything."

"Okay, then can we talk about the elephant in the room?" Aurora spins away, flopping down on the pink comforter tucked into her bed.

The dorms here in Rad Hall are so much nicer than the ones in Erebus and even have singles, which is what Aurora managed to snag.

Unlike Erebus, though, Rad Hall is a constant stream of parties, mostly thrown by non-organization members and lowerclassmen who don't get invited to Curator gatherings.

Bass coming from a lower level makes the floor vibrate, and I lean toward the mirror, checking Aurora's handiwork.

"What elephant?" Yuri asks, pulling her legs up in the bucket chair with her.

"The *celestial* shaped one?" Aurora gives her a look. "We haven't talked at all about the fact that Lucy's roommate was found murdered. Our *friend*. Isn't that weird?"

Unease sinks to the pit of my stomach. I swallow, my leg bouncing as memories pump through my brain, filtering into my vision.

I guess forgetting is too much to ask for.

"Should we be talking about it?" Yuri frowns. "I mean, it's an ongoing investigation…"

"Yeah, but remember what you said about your texts being read on Celeste's end, even days after the police say they suspect she was actually killed?" Aurora fishes a bottle of hot pink nail polish from her nightstand and gives it a shake. "Her phone was dead the night she went missing, which means someone would've had to charge it at some point."

"Maybe whoever…did that," Yuri postulates, rubbing her chin, "kept her phone on?"

"Okay, but then why hasn't anyone found it yet? The police should be able to locate it from GPS or whatever, right?"

"Well, you'd think the person would dump it once they realized… or maybe it died again. My texts have gone unanswered and unread for a while now. Since…"

I feel them look at me, their stares guarded and heavy.

My head swims, my suspicions mounting along with my fear of being found out.

Something is amiss at Avernia College, and it's not *just* the corpses. The fact that the investigation barely even seems to be happening is shady on its own, but add in that, aside from my room, absolutely nothing on campus has changed or been blocked off? Not even the Primordial Forest?

Inhaling, I press on my kneecap, trying to get my leg to stop moving. Panic whispers at my throat, its fingertips ghosting over my skin with the smattering of things I'm keeping hidden.

If I have secrets, it wouldn't be surprising that this school does too.

I should confess, tell them what I saw, even if it means getting into trouble.

Aurora sighs. "All I'm saying is this stuff doesn't add up—"

Shoving my chair back, I get to my feet, yanking the black graphic

T-shirt I brought over my long-sleeved one and tucking both into my skirt.

"Uh, Lucy? What are you doing? We've still got to rinse your hair," Aurora calls out as I bolt for the door.

I don't answer though, because I'm panicking and not really sure how to make it stop.

Pressure mounts in my chest, bearing down like a thousand-pound anvil, and by the time I get to the downstairs lobby, I'm hyperventilating. Struggling to draw in my breaths, even as I rationalize that I've *technically* not done anything wrong and no one knows I was there that night.

No one except Asher and Foxe, that is.

But they won't tell. The only one who has to live with the guilt is me, and if I could just figure out what happened with Celeste and who killed her and why, maybe my silence wouldn't feel so suffocating.

Rain drenches me as I run across campus with nothing but the clothes on my back. The exercise helps calm my nerves a bit, but chaos still reigns in my veins.

Red dye drips down my chest with each step I take; I stop outside the revolving glass door at the entrance to the Obeliskos, wringing out the ends of my hair before making my way to the thirteenth floor.

Kicking open the girls' bathroom door, I veer toward the back stall where all my stuff is stashed, crossing my fingers that nothing's been disturbed.

Bending down, I unwrap a hand towel from my backpack, patting my face lightly, and then scream into the fabric.

The sound is muffled, but I'm sure if there really are ghosts in this building, they hear.

Failure and shame circulate through my nervous system, coagulating near my heart. God, I'm such a fuckup. Maybe I *should* drop—

"Why are you keeping your shit where anyone can take off with it?"

I jump at the sudden voice, whirling around to face the intruder.

Asher leans against the sinks, a hood pulled up over his head. His clothes are wet, his hair hanging limp against his forehead—just like it did in the forest that night.

His brown eyes, usually so warm and evocative, lack any emotion. He just stares at me blankly, his jaw squared, shoulders stiff.

"Are you stalking me or something?" I quip, hugging my bag to my chest.

"Yes. But I was here first."

My mouth drops with his brazen admission, but when he turns, I see a tear in his black jacket, slicing all the way through to mangled flesh beneath. Blood drips from the wound, coating his clothes and hands.

Running a balled-up brown paper towel under the sink, he carefully rubs it against the site, letting out a shaky breath.

"What the hell happened to you?"

"Got caught on the fence leaving campus," he deadpans, not bothering to look at me when he speaks. "Wrought iron's a bitch."

I drop my bag and walk over, peering closer at the cut. It's a nasty gash, jagged and several layers of skin deep.

"The fence did this?"

"That's what I said."

Liar.

God, I can't stand this man.

He chuckles when I tell him as much. "Are you afraid of a little blood, pup?"

"No, but I'm concerned you're going to bleed out because you're not treating this wound correctly." Irritated, I snatch the towel and bat his hands away, pressing both of mine onto the laceration. "Your dad's a doctor, for God's sake."

"It's cute that you care—"Asher's breath hitches, and he cuts off abruptly.

My eyebrows draw inward, knitting above my nose as I concentrate. "That hurt?"

232 SAV R. MILLER

"Obviously."

"Good."

Blood quickly soaks through the paper, so Asher yanks some more from the dispenser, holding the new pieces out to me. I take them, not bothering to smooth anything before holding them to his side.

"Feels like we're sixteen again," he murmurs. "Do you remember the first time you cleaned blood off me?"

"We weren't sixteen. We were *six*."

"Ah, that's right. You were trying to catch that feral dog, and when you couldn't, you came to ask me for help." His mouth twitches. "I had to get twelve stitches in my hand after it attacked me."

"Well, I tried to tell you to approach it slowly, but you lack patience."

"You're one to talk."

Swallowing, I ignore the comment and continue with my task.

He turns his head, and I feel him looking down at me. "You don't miss it? Being young and carefree?"

I miss you. "What was carefree about being ostracized and neglected at school or during extracurricular activities?"

"You weren't ostracized," he says. "You had me."

He doesn't mention Aurora, or Foxe, or my siblings. Just himself.

My eyes burn. "And that was supposed to be enough?"

"It was for me."

"Don't, Asher. You can't rewrite history when I was there. I *wasn't* enough for you." Emotion clogs my throat, and I withdraw to wet more towels. "That's why I came and forged a path at college all on my own. Not because I wanted to, but because there was no other choice."

"Does Aurora know how invisible she is to you?"

"Aurora never promised to stay by my—" Gritting my teeth until a sharp pain shoots through each root, I stop myself. "You know what? I'm not doing this with you. Nothing in our past even matters now. I came to Avernia to forget about you and all the other bullshit."

"Doesn't seem like you're doing much better in the present though."

This part, he says quietly, and I wonder if it's to soften the blow. But the jab lands anyway, right in the center of my aching chest.

"Yeah, well," I reply, pushing against his wound with more force, "some things just don't change, do they?"

We fall silent, and I pull the towel away, exhaling when I see the bleeding has slowed down.

Tossing the soiled paper into the trash, I put my hands on my wet hips, watching as he inspects the cut in the mirror. "You might need stitches again."

"Nah, I'm good." He points at a first aid kit on a sink, then pulls the top open, grabbing a handful of gauze.

My stomach tenses, flipping as he rips open the first packet with his teeth. Twisting, he tries to get a good angle, but the laceration is far enough back on his side that he can't seem to reach it well.

Rolling my eyes, I suck on the inside of my cheek and push his hands out of the way once more, lifting the hem of his jacket and sweater.

I keep going, exposing his toned abdomen and the lean muscle lacing his back, and he lets out a strange noise.

"Are you undressing me, pup?"

"Shut up and take your shirt off."

He quickly obeys, shrugging out of the clothes and letting them fall to the floor.

My heart thumps a staccato rhythm, beating hard against my ribs, as I take the gauze from him. Holding up the roll of medical tape, I stretch out the length for what I need and raise it to his mouth.

Leaning forward, Asher pulls back his lips, baring his teeth, and bites through the tape.

Slowly, the piece tears in two.

A pulse awakens between my legs, and I do my best to suppress the tremor that wrecks my fingers.

I bring my hands to his side again, patching him up the way I've done hundreds of times before. The only difference is that now we know what the other looks like when we come.

"You gonna tell me what really happened?" I ask, pressing the last piece of tape to the edge of the bandage.

His shoulders deflate with a sigh. "Ever start a fight and realize too late that you're the only one without a weapon?"

Scoffing, I bring my eyes to his. "Who do you think you're talking to? I've never been in a fight in my life."

"Except with me."

"Well, that's different. I was always safe with you."

The words come out before I can stop them or fully weigh their meaning. Heat scalds my face, inching down my neck and blooming bright in the center of my stomach like a field of daisies.

One of the sink faucets drips slowly. Asher doesn't reply, and I step back, taking a second to check my handiwork. I smooth my fingers over the gauze before I realize what I'm doing.

Asher's breath hitches, and mine seems to get caught in my throat.

Clearing it, I let my hand fall. "I find it hard to believe Foxe would stab you."

"Not Foxe." He moves closer to the sink, turning his ear to inspect the piercings there and then his nose ring. "Some Curator trash."

Hearing him talk about the Curators like that makes my heart skip a beat. Somewhere, deep down, I hope it was Beckett. "Why are you fighting with Curators?"

He shrugs. "Seems like some of them need a little humility."

"But they stabbed you."

"Barely even a graze."

I push my index finger into the gauze, watching blood swarm to soak the spot. Asher hisses through clenched teeth, whipping around and grabbing my wrist, yanking me into him.

"It won't stop hurting if you keep poking it."

My chin lifts. "Maybe I don't want it to stop hurting."

His chest heaves, his grip on me ironclad. I wouldn't be able to get away right now even if I wanted to, and it takes several seconds of silent self-reflection for me to admit that I *don't* want to.

Despite my anger and loneliness.

Right here, in Asher's orbit, it's warm.

Safe.

I'd stay forever if it didn't mean forgiving him for things he hasn't apologized for.

Still, he doesn't release me, and I don't try to get away.

"You're gonna be late for your date," he sneers, his gaze growing angry.

"How do you even know about that?"

"When it comes to you, I do my research."

"Is that why you're here? To keep me from going?"

Sighing, he drags me in front of him, turning on the sink until steam rises from the flowing water. He fiddles with the cold handle, as if looking for a balance, and then pushes my hips into the sink.

I grunt, catching myself on the edge of the bowl. "Excuse you."

Seconds later, I feel his hand on the back of my head. Fear lashes down my back like a whip, immobilizing me for the briefest moment.

My eyes are level with the faucet when he lowers my face into the bowl, turning me to the side. He lets go again, taking one of the red sections of my hair in both hands.

Gently, he brings the dyed pieces beneath the spray, coaxing the color out with long, nimble fingers.

Crimson water fills the sink, and my vision starts to spin as thoughts of Celeste begin making their way in, trudging up from my throat and threatening to sew it shut—

"Close your eyes."

Sucking in a deep breath, I do as he says, cutting off that sense from the increasing discomfort.

The only problem now is that I'm hyperaware of *him*, especially as he moves so his legs bracket mine, his groin grinding against my hip. I don't feel what I did that day in his dorm, but I *remember* how it felt— how thick and long he seemed—and arousal burns behind the wall of my chest, flowing into my belly and making it hard to remain standing.

We don't speak as he starts to put more of my hair beneath the spray, massaging my scalp with the blunt ends of his fingertips. My breathing gets heavier, and I grip the sink tighter, trying to ignore the storm of volatile emotions swirling in my stomach.

Eventually, he shuts off the water and then spends a few extra minutes wringing out my wet hair. His fingers wrap around the strands, pulling at the roots like a squeegee, and I bite my tongue as I pretend the gesture doesn't feel amazing.

There's no way he'd let me live down a moan right now.

One of his hands finds my back, and he presses softly on my spine at the same time as he's squeezing water from my hair.

My eyes pop open, and I swallow. A shiver skates across my skin.

Asher clears his throat, stepping away. I stand upright, letting out a wobbly breath, and meet his dark gaze in the mirror.

His stare this time is heated. Fiery. I feel it all the way in my toes.

Slowly, I turn around to face him, realizing a second too late that he didn't move far. My shoulder grazes his chest, and I tilt my chin, letting my eyes soak in the strain of muscles in his neck, the splash of dried blood on his jaw, and the scar through his lip.

He gulps audibly, lifting a hand to my face. His thumb swipes over my cheek, then my ear, and he pulls away to show me the red droplets there on his skin.

I can't focus on anything except how close he is, how good he smells.

"Luce," he says in the lowest voice. It's almost a whisper. "Can I . . ."

My mouth is dry as a desert. "I should be getting to my date."

Something shifts in his expression, turning sinister. "Don't."

"Why?" I quirk a brow, the most movement I can manage. "Are you jealous or some—"

"Yes."

He steps in, our chests brushing. Bending down, he plants his hands on either side of the sink, trapping me.

"Yes, I'm *jealous*. I want to be the only one who ever sees you this close."

His hand finds my jaw, angling my head as he leans in.

My chest tightens.

"The only one who touches you like this."

Unsticking my tongue from the roof of my mouth becomes a priority. My gaze darts between his lips and his intense stare, unsure of which to land on.

I should stop him. When he leans in, his eyelashes flutter like he's as nervous as me, and I'm completely stuck, unable to do anything except breathe and watch, my desperation rooting me in place.

"Let me kiss you," he exhales, his fingers sliding over my skin. "Please. If you still want to go on your date after, I'll step aside, but… Fuck, Luce, I need to kiss you right now."

Conscious thought becomes increasingly difficult, but there are dozens of little alarm bells screeching in my mind, warning me away from him. Since he's been back, he's done nothing but cause trouble, and while I'm used to it from him, there's also been a severe lack of explanation.

No apologies. No evidence of remorse for ditching me and getting me framed for a crime.

It's like one day, Asher decided he was going to be my best friend again, and nothing else mattered. None of the in-between was important enough for him to consider.

Swallowing over the knot in my throat, I lift my hands to his chest, flattening my palms. "Does it feel like you might die if you don't kiss me?"

Say yes. Let me know I'm not alone at least.

He nods. Inches closer.

I shove him backward, using every ounce of strength and the advantage of surprise to twist away from him.

"Then die."

Spinning on my heels, I aim for the door, launching myself through it. I get back out to the library, weaving between two aisles, but Asher's faster than me. He grabs my wrist, pushing me against a bookcase.

Forcing me around to face him, his hands immediately cup my cheeks, and he lets out a deviant laugh that ricochets inside my chest.

"Only if you kill me for this," he says before sealing his mouth to mine.

Chapter 31

Lucy

KISSING ASHER ANDERSON, UNFORTUNATELY, FEELS LIKE THE FIRST drink of water after a forty-day drought.

I hate how easy it is to sink into, how my body stretches to fit against his, each plane and ridge conforming so it's like we're becoming a single being.

Long ago, I believed our souls were connected. That he was my missing half, the other part of the equation that made me whole.

When our lips touch, even with all the distance and animosity still between us, the hole he left fills instantly. Like it was never empty in the first place.

His hands slide from my cheeks into my wet hair, threading through the strands as he opens my mouth with his tongue. I claw at his bare skin, avoiding the bandage, trying to bring him closer.

I'm pressed against the shelves with him covering the length of my body, and it still doesn't feel like enough.

A couple of books fall with a loud thud to the floor, disturbed by our sudden frenzy.

My legs part when he shoves his thigh between them, nudging me up so I have to stand on my tiptoes to keep from losing my balance.

"Wait, wait, wait," I rush out as I break away, attempting to control my breathing.

My clothes are still soaked through, sticking to me, and he's half-naked. If someone walked in right now, we'd be in loads of trouble.

"Should we be doing this here?" I ask, because I don't really know what else to say. I'm not convinced we should be doing anything at all, yet I can't peel myself away from him.

"What exactly are we doing?" Asher replies, moving to ghost kisses along the side of my neck, then up the column of my throat.

"You're kissing me."

He pulls back with a big, goofy grin on his face. "Fuck yeah, I am."

Catching my breath becomes impossible.

His lips stretch with my silence. "I've got no intention of stopping either, regardless of what nosy little shit makes their way up here."

My eyes widen at the complete reckless abandon. I don't think I've ever seen him *giddy*, yet his body seems to hum with excitement, bleeding over onto me.

Or maybe it's me vibrating. Aligned like we are, it's difficult to tell the difference.

When he brings his mouth back to mine, it feels like the air evaporates from my lungs. I move an arm, grabbing a shelf to steady myself as his tongue slashes between my lips, tasting and teasing.

The flickering sensation makes my toes curl.

A strangled noise comes from low in my throat as his hands slide out from my hair, then down my back. He lifts me, hooking his arms beneath my ass, and I wrap my legs around him to keep from falling.

This angle… I swallow over my nerves, my pulse intensifying. I can feel it *everywhere*, the same as I feel Asher's touch as if he's stroking more than just my physical form.

My soul is disturbed. Moved by his existence.

It's always been that way. Pretending otherwise is futile.

I kiss him back harder.

He presses my spine firmly into the bookcase, and more heavy volumes tumble to the floor.

Nimble fingers begin working my skirt up my thighs, granting better access for his pelvis to thrust against my pussy. My vision blurs on the edges, my head lolling as he grinds against my clit.

If he really is a virgin, it's a little cruel that he seems to know what he's doing. Meanwhile, my hands shake because I'm not sure where to put them.

Before, he said I could touch him anywhere, but this feels different somehow, more intense, and all I can do is thread my fingers through his hair and hope I don't do something wrong.

"Ash," I mutter into his mouth, nerves crawling up my sides like little spiders.

When he pulls away, he's panting, and it takes me a second to realize I am too. His damp hair is completely disheveled from my touch, and I resist the urge to fix it.

"What?" he whispers, skimming my thighs with his hands. One inches inward, and he shifts, giving himself space to slip between us. "Are you not enjoying this?"

A gasp puffs out of me when his thumb grazes my clit. I squirm as he rubs a gentle rhythm over me, the friction from my tights and panties causing my back to arch, pushing me tighter against him.

"I–I'm supposed to be angry with you," I rasp as tiny wisps of pleasure erupt where he massages me. My hands fall to his biceps, squeezing hard.

"So be angry. I can handle it."

His finger prods bluntly, and then I feel him twisting and tugging. Seconds later, a small ripping sound drags a squeal from me, and he maneuvers my underwear aside, stroking me with his skin on mine.

"But what I can't do," he says softly, testing and pinching, "is stop. Not now that I know how soft you are or how good it feels to have you in my arms."

Digging my nails into his skin, I climb higher, resituating myself on his hips at the same time as I'm trying to escape his touch. Or maybe I'm aiming for more. It's hard to tell.

I writhe in place, a craving opening somewhere deep inside me. An endless cavern of need.

There's a brief pause where he removes himself to offer his index finger to me, touching my bottom lip in question.

Exhaling roughly, I open my mouth, taking it slowly.

He hisses through clenched teeth, watching as I wet his finger—I don't know what the hell I'm doing, but he seems to enjoy the way I flick my tongue around him nonetheless.

After a moment, he withdraws and lets that hand slide between us once more.

Meeting my gaze, he pauses at my entrance.

When I don't give any signs of resistance, he pushes in.

My entire body seizes at the intrusion. The stretch is a little uncomfortable, but nothing particularly painful, which is good.

He gives me a moment to adjust before sliding out and then plunging back in. A muscle jumps in his jaw as he fixes his hold on me, moving so I'm mostly being held up by the bookcase before coasting his free hand along my side and finding my breast through my sweater.

Heat blooms a trail across my face as I realize just how thin my bra is; he cups the full swell, thrumming his thumb over the nipple until I feel it tighten, straining against the lacy fabric.

"I want to see you," he says, gliding beneath the hem of my top and pushing it up, exposing me to the cool, haunted thirteenth-floor air. "Please. I need you."

Desperation bleeds from his words, sending tendrils of arousal spinning through my abdomen. Following his lead, I grip the sweater and hold it in place, allowing him to drink me in. He plays with my breast, yanking on the flimsy material of my bra, and covers the whole thing with his warm palm.

"*Perfection*," he says, his voice laced with something I've never heard from him before.

Awe.

"Do you hear that, pup?" he continues, kneading my chest at the same time as his finger drags in and out of me, pumping lazily, like he's getting a feel for how I react to each stroke. Squelching noises fill the library between huffed, stuttered breaths, and I might be embarrassed about how telling it is if I had any sort of foot in reality at the moment.

But I don't. Long gone are thoughts of Celeste, Tag, and the fact that this is all happening in the Obeliskos—out in the open too, where anyone on campus could waltz in and get us in trouble for public indecency.

I don't fucking care. Asher Anderson *needs* me, and I'm realizing years too late that it's the only thing I've ever really wanted.

My thighs tense, quaking with the dueling sensations of being filled and toyed with. Pressure, white-hot and magnificent, invades my stomach, zipping along my spine and collecting between my legs.

Asher grunts when I shove a hand through his hair, getting better leverage as he works me over. "This little virgin hole is dripping wet, and I'm the first man to ever put anything inside it. What a fucking honor."

"Jesus, Ash." I whine, struggling to string together coherent thoughts. "Are you sure *you've* never—"

I trail off, my mind suddenly assaulted with images of him doing this same thing to others. Foxe supposedly gets around on tour, so what would've stopped Asher from participating in similar activities?

He said I was the only one he ever wanted to touch, but how do I know if that was true?

My heart becomes an uncomfortable entity inside my chest, aching in a way I've never felt before. My limbs grow heavy, sadness starting to work its way into my bloodstream, even as he curls his finger, reaching a spot within me that makes my eyesight darken.

You're a liar, he said in that sunflower field after I kissed him. After I threw myself at him, using what little liquid courage I had at the time to put my feelings into motion.

I'd spent months building up to it, convincing myself that his lack of reciprocation was only in my head, and he crushed me.

Then he ditched me and never apologized for it.

Reaching down, I grab his wrist, halting his movements.

His eyebrows arch. "You want me to stop?"

My mind screams *Yes! Stop while I still have some dignity left!*

But I shake my head, despite my conflicted thoughts. God, I'm a mess, but ending this in the middle of things feels more wrong than the entire situation.

Maybe it's arousal motivating me, or maybe I'm afraid that if he stops now, he won't want to start again.

Instead of making him let me go, I adjust my hips, pulling him in deeper. Where it feels best.

Dropping his chin, he watches me fuck myself for several beats; sweat drips between my breasts, and he swipes over it, spreading the moisture on my nipple.

I have no idea what I'm doing, just chasing whatever makes my heart vibrate, but he's enraptured by the motions anyway. Like I'm some marvelous miracle he's getting to witness up close.

Swallowing audibly, he adds a second finger. The fit is even tighter than before, and my entire body shudders with unabashed bliss.

He angles against my inner muscles, picking up the pace. My arms stretch behind me, my hands grasping at the shelves as my thighs quiver, liquid heat pulsing through my veins.

"Fucking Christ, pup. You like that, don't you?"

My nod is curt, and he pinches my nipple before bringing his hand to the back of my neck as if to keep me steady.

"You're gonna come on my fingers, aren't you?" he asks, a teasing lilt to his voice despite its roughness. "Gonna soak my hand and then walk out of here and go on your little date. You'll be sitting in that auditorium or at dinner or wherever else you go tonight a sticky, needy mess all because of me, and he'll be none the wiser."

His lips find my ear, grazing the shell, before he takes it between his teeth, nibbling lightly. One of my hands flies off the shelf, clutching at his bicep, his shoulder, anything I can to get him closer as elation starts to rain down my spine.

My orgasm collects at the base, spreading like honey through my thighs and culminating at my pussy. I taste my pulse in my throat and cling to him like I might die if I stop.

"O-oh," I choke out, my forehead dropping to his chin. "Asher…"

Along with the rush of a climax, panic winds beside it, trying to lace its fangs into the euphoria. Air escapes me, and I struggle for a moment to separate the two and step out of my head, to allow my release at the hands of a man who has broken me before.

Paranoia and anxiety tell me it'll happen again, but he's making my body feel so good that I want to ignore it.

Tears well up in my eyes. I'm so pathetic.

"Let go, pup. I've got you. I'm not fucking going anywhere."

His voice is a gentle caress, so at odds with the brazen, unbothered person who's been at this school trying to force his way back into my life.

And it's apparently all I need to push myself over the cliff, into a spiral of oblivion that has me writhing against his hand, grinding my clit so the sensations match. I wrap my arms around his neck, my mouth opening on a silent scream as my pussy clamps down on his fingers, and drive my teeth into his shoulder.

"There we go," he murmurs into my hair, a strain in his voice that mirrors my own desire. "Take whatever you need from me."

I want to drink his blood. For our two beings to become one.

Instead, I bite down harder, willing his skin to break.

When I crest fully over that hill, my body deflates, the release taking tension and worry away with it.

This is the second time I've let him help me get off. Boundaries and lines be damned; evidently crossing them, even after almost two decades of friendship, isn't such a big deal.

Asher's lips skim my temple as he withdraws from me. I wince at the loss, ignoring the unease settling in the pit of my stomach.

He puts me down, albeit reluctantly, and pulls my shirt over my breasts after one last lingering look. Heat flares in his brown irises, enough to make my body tingle, as he lifts his arm and places his fingers on his tongue, sucking off the remnants of me.

My pussy throbs, my throat constricting when he gives a salacious grin.

Letting my eyes fall below his waist, I note the distinct outline of his erection, and I'm struck with the memory of rubbing myself on it and how he came from just that alone.

A tremor ripples in my voice when I speak. "Do you…I mean, I can—"

He glances down at his crotch and then gives me a small smirk. "Don't worry about it. I'll take care of myself while you're off having fun with another man. It'll help knowing you won't be able to stop thinking about me, even when he's buying you dinner or making you laugh."

Heat simmers in my stomach. Shit. How am I supposed to concentrate with that image in my mind?

I continue staring at his lap. He steps forward, using his middle finger to tug my chin up.

"Seriously, Luce. I didn't do that just so you could reciprocate."

Releasing me, he moves back, and I snap myself out of the fog of arousal. With my feet now on the floor, I yank my skirt back into place, the hole he tore in my stockings making me feel a little exposed, even though my panties are still intact.

Once I've managed to taper my thoughts a bit, apprehension settles on my shoulders, weighing them down. Asher drags a hand through his hair, letting out a long breath, and I cross my arms over my chest to get a little distance from everything.

My toe taps of its own accord. "What changed?"

Confusion twists his features. "You mean—"

"Between now and in that sunflower field. I… We could've done this then, but you rejected me. Why now?"

For a couple of seconds, he just looks at me, and I wonder if it was a stupid question. Maybe I should learn not to overthink and just live in the moment, but the only time I've ever been able to shut my brain off long enough to do that is when I'm with him.

That realization is preventing me from it now.

When we were kids, I could do it because there was no need to pretend. He didn't give a shit about anything or anyone, so putting on a mask to hide my insecurities and overactive mind wasn't necessary.

It didn't *stop* the endless thoughts or the buzzing beneath my skin that made me want to constantly be in motion, but I could focus on other stuff too when I wasn't occupied with being someone else.

I'd have thought our friendship breakup would've put an end to that sense of safety, but it's almost like we've fallen right back into our old patterns.

With some lewd activities thrown in.

Those are new.

Taking a step toward me, Asher swoops in, gathering me into his arms once more. I go, because I am kind of stupid, and he kisses me again. This time, it's slow, steady, and languid like we have all the time in the world, and I moan into the action, unable to help myself.

"I was an idiot," he tells me, his tongue flicking across my upper lip as he draws back. "That's not an excuse or really a very good explanation, but it's the truth."

"Well, I'm not sure what to do with that."

Seeming sorry and vocalizing remorse are different things. Even if my heart wants to say fuck it and move on, a few kisses aren't enough for absolution.

He sighs. "I know. I...I know it might not seem like it, but I do intend to earn your forgiveness. No matter what I have to do. I won't stop until—"

The lights above us flicker, and he cuts off, tilting his face toward the ceiling.

"It's fine," I say. "These lights are always going out."

As soon as the last word leaves my lips, the entire floor becomes cloaked in thick darkness. We stay still for a few minutes, waiting for them to come back on.

"Avernia is way too expensive of a school for basic shit like this to not be maintained," Asher grumbles, dipping his face into the curve of my neck.

Letting out a shaky breath, my body settles into a dull panic now that I don't have the distraction of seeing his reactions. Instead, memories of the Primordial Forest weeks ago rush back in, and I can hear my roommate's last moments.

I see her faceless corpse hanging in my dorm, along with another's, and the school's dismissal of everything.

"How long do they usually stay off?" Asher asks.

I purse my lips, yanking myself out of the impending spiral. "Depends on how mad the ghosts are, I guess."

"*Ghosts?* Are you saying they're behind this?"

My eyebrow quirks, and I grab his head, pulling him away from my neck. "You don't believe in ghosts, do you?"

"I'm not arrogant enough to think we're totally alone on this planet. Besides, isn't that what makes people human? The soul? Where do you think it goes when you die?"

"Wow. I didn't think I'd live to see the day Asher Anderson cowered away from the supernatural. You didn't believe in them when we were kids."

"Which was naive of me—"

A deafening crash near the entrance to the stairwell interrupts him. I jolt, pressing closer to his chest, my heart pounding as the noise echoes between my ears.

At first, we don't do anything.

Then another crash ricochets through the air, splintering the quiet into a million little pieces. This one sounds more like an explosion, and the floorboards under our feet seem to groan with the force of it.

Asher untangles himself from me. I twist around, peering beneath the shelves; at this point in my college career, I've spent so much time up here that I've acclimated pretty well to viewing this level in the dark.

There's no movement out by the glass cases housing the town archives or past that where the study tables sit in neat, untouched sections.

"We should go," I whisper, tugging on the waistband of his pants.

His shadow turns, and I see his teeth in the very faint light spilling in from the stained glass windows. "Scared, pup, or just trying to get me to a secondary location so you can fuck my brains out?"

Embarrassment fans like flames over my cheeks, though I appreciate the effort to lighten the mood. Normally, that'd be a Foxe thing to do. "I have a date to get to, you know."

"Ah, yes. With that kid from the quad. Will you be telling him about your time with me, or should I walk you to the Lyceum and take care of that for you?"

"I'm taking this one to the grave," I whisper.

"Oh good. In life and in death then."

I can feel his grin in my chest, but something catches my eye through several bookcases, by a couple of old leather armchairs. Three figures materialize in the shadows, but when I blink, they're gone.

Nausea bubbles in my gut, discomfort ringing in my bones. "We need to get out of here."

Asher doesn't question it; he just grabs my hand and drags me into the bathroom, putting his shirt and jacket back on quickly. The lights don't come on in there either, so I'm convinced it's a circuit breaker problem, although I don't really know what that is. Old buildings like this one, though, are bound to have electrical issues.

Surely the outage was just poor wiring.

Ghosts aren't real, and there's no one out to get us.

Right?

The crash, however, I don't have a way to explain. Same with the random figures.

It isn't lost on me that there were three of them, just like that night in the forest. Since foot traffic on this floor is practically nonexistent, especially this time of day, I can't rationalize it any other way.

I hover close to Asher as he slowly leads us toward the stairwell, keeping a hand on the wall while he navigates with the light from his phone. My skin feels pinched, fraught with nerves and the aftermath of an orgasm.

He pushes the metal door open, holding it so I can pass. A motion-detecting emergency light kicks on, illuminating the area, but my legs don't move.

Asher's chin tilts, and he peers down at me. "You all right?"

I stare straight ahead at the landing beneath us.

Where a pool of dark red liquid covers the entire floor.

Chapter 32

Asher

THERE'S A REASON I HAD QUINCY INTERVENE WHEN THE DEAN MET with Lucy earlier in the semester. My virtual interview, hosted over the summer with the middle-aged fuck had been more than enough contact for me.

As I watch him purposely loom over Lucy's defiant form, I'm reminded of just how slimy and irritating he is.

The used utility knife in my pants pocket is heavy against my thigh as I make my way back over to the pair, my fingers itching to drive the blade between his veneers.

If we weren't in public, I'd do it, no questions asked, just for the way he looks at her. Like she's subhuman filth he can't stand the sight of.

"Don't *you* find it a little odd that you are consistently at the literal scene of these crimes, Ms. Wolfe?" Dean Bauer asks, hands on his hips. "One death we might be able to explain away by coincidence, but now the school is being vandalized with what we can only assume, until the lab reports back, is blood? I can't think of a single reason you'd be so close every time, except if you had something to do with it."

Lucy tucks a piece of hair behind her ear, cocking her head to the side. "If you're going to accuse me of stuff, I wish you'd just come out and do it. This game is getting a little old, don't you think?"

"I hardly find illegal activity on campus to be a game, little girl."

Shoving my hands in my pockets, I stroll casually up to them, turning once I've gotten to her side. She stiffens visibly but doesn't try to run away, and I have a flash of two hours ago when my fingers were stuffed inside her sweet, wet pussy and have to actively suppress the shot of arousal that zips down my spine.

The dean's eyes narrow at me, but his shoulders square and he straightens slightly. "Mr. Anderson. It's nice to see you again. How's Erebus Hall treating you? I trust you're settling in well, RA duties and all."

"It's been fine, although I must say there are a number of uneasy residents roaming about as of late. Any updates on the incident in Lucy's dorm room?"

He stares at me silently for a beat, then chuckles. "Unfortunately, I'm not at liberty to share those details with the public. Although if you'd like to come by my office sometime, perhaps we could discuss that and your enrollment in the Curator program. I'd be happy to invite your sister along as well, since we used to have our own little meetings back when she was a student."

There isn't time to question that comment, because I feel Lucy's eyes swing to me, accusation lacing her irises before she even says anything.

"Your *what*?" she demands.

"It's not exactly what it sounds like," I say, scratching the back of my head, even more inclined to just stab this motherfucker, although I don't think Lucy would forgive me for such extreme measures.

Then again, with murder throbbing in her gaze, maybe she wouldn't mind right now.

Dean Bauer claps me on the shoulder, squeezing tight. "I'm just happy to see yet another founding family member join the ranks of Avernia's best and brightest. We certainly don't have the issue of recurrent crime among *those* students."

I smother a laugh of disbelief. It's hard to tell whether he's being serious, though something tells me he knows far more than he lets on. There's no way he's unaware that it was likely Curators who killed Celeste—that has to be why they're suppressing the story.

The way he keeps trying to pin things on Lucy, though, makes me uneasy. It's part of the reason I want to get closer to Curators like Beckett Dupont, who seems to live and breathe gossip, if not also violent crime.

Hence the obviously orchestrated attack earlier, in which some student slashed me with a knife as I made my way back from the forest.

All I'd wanted was to check on the box I left out there. It'd been right in the spot I hid it, proving the one Lucy gave me was a poorly constructed replica. And I'm trying to understand how and why it showed up at all.

It feels like we're being watched, and I don't like that.

My assailant got a few slices in before I was able to regain my footing and smash their hand with my boot. But they ran before I could yank their ski mask off and reveal their identity.

Though all I really needed was to see the flowery theta symbol on his jacket to know who'd sent him.

I'm not sure what Beckett's angle is, especially since he's trying to recruit me, but it makes me think violence is much more engrained into the livelihood of this school than any of us realize.

How else would they be able to get away with so many missing students and unexplained deaths?

The people who pay to go here want to trust the administration. If the powers that be are good enough at covering their tracks, there would never be any reason to question anything.

So they promote their superstitions, distort history, and pick out vulnerable students to blame for their shortcomings. That way, if something seems off, it's not *their* fault, but the fault of the entities they've painted as enemies.

Even an entire bloodline.

Though I'm still not *fully* convinced of a supernatural tie-in, I can't deny the email I received months ago freaked me out. I opted out of attending school here in the first place to keep Lucy safe, but the anonymous sender indicated that as tensions mounted among the higher-ups, even those distantly linked to the Andersons could be in trouble.

Especially if they stood out too much.

If dissension was going to become a capital offense, Lucy would not survive.

That's why I came. I could not have lived with myself if something happened to her.

Lucy's boots scuff against the pavement, and she clears her throat. Her smooth, delicious throat that I'd love to sink my teeth into again, which is why I need the dean—

"Mr. Bauer," she says, interrupting my thoughts. "If you're done with me, I'd like to be on my way now."

"That's *Dean* Bauer," he snaps, lifting his arm to check the bulky Rolex on it. "Though I suppose it is rather late. I'd hate for you to be able to blame your poor attendance in class tomorrow on me."

She doesn't respond, even as he rakes his gaze over her form, noting her disheveled state. Luckily, none of the blood from me seems to have gotten on her despite our little rendezvous, so she doesn't really look suspicious.

I, on the other hand, have a bandaged wound peeking out of a hole in my shirt, but neither the dean nor the police who showed up seem to notice.

"Try to make it through one week without causing trouble," the dean tells her. "There are people in positions much higher than mine who don't exactly take well to constant disruption. Especially from someone who has already proved to be an issue."

Lucy snorts, spinning on her heels so she's facing the dorms. "I'll be sure to keep that in mind, *Mr.* Bauer."

As she stomps off, I take a step toward her, but the dean holds an arm out, halting me. "So, Asher. Now that you've had time to settle in here, what is your real opinion of my school? Your sister picked a good one, eh?"

I keep my gaze on Lucy's retreating form. "If you say so."

"Frankly, it was a bit of a shock when she applied for the teaching position at all. Most of the faculty thought we'd seen the last of her when she graduated."

Turning my head, I refocus on him. "Did she say something that would make you believe that?"

As far as I know, the one time Quincy came home in complete shambles was her only public admission that things were amiss here. Otherwise, she kept on like her college career had been a good experience and never said anything else about it.

Since I wound up not going and she'd gotten out alive, I didn't think it mattered all that much.

Except…

I didn't tell Lucy anything. Just dropped her in with the sharks and hoped they'd smell blood somewhere else.

Meanwhile, the blood stains my hands. Invisible as it is—the feeling of it never ceases.

Dean Bauer exhales, staring up at the Obeliskos. "Quincy was an excellent student, but much like Ms. Wolfe, she had issues…fitting in, I suppose. A college campus operates with dozens of fast-moving parts, and it thrives best when those parts understand each other and work in unison. Your sister wasn't interested in embracing the Anderson name or the responsibilities that come with it, and that's why she started that glorified beautification program, which has been a pain in my ass for nearly a decade. The higher-ups didn't appreciate that. Given how they feel about your family… Well, they're an easily alarmed bunch."

"Seems to be a pretty common denominator in Fury Hill."

"Not to mention the belief in a cursed lineage." He brings his chin down, looking at me. "Do you believe in the curse, boy?"

His attitude keeps shifting, flipping back and forth between cordial administrator and weird little rat.

I don't trust the fucker one bit, so I'm definitely not going to be honest with him.

"I'm afraid I find a curse to be too simplistic for my tastes," I say, rolling back on my heels. "It's too easy for the original families to write off every bad experience at Avernia as a result of some sinister magic."

Hands still in my pockets, I walk forward until the toes of our shoes are touching. He's a few inches shorter than me and perspiring profusely. I wonder if it's not just Quincy that he has issues with, but Anderson blood entirely—does *he* believe in the curse?

That won't do. I don't want him to think it's some centuries-old beef bringing destruction to his cushy little campus.

When this place burns down, I want him to *know* it was me.

"Don't you think that sometimes, bad things that happen are simply the consequences of one's actions? The culmination of corruption coming to a head?" I cock an eyebrow, tracking the bead of sweat that slides down the bridge of his nose. "Misdeeds coming to light?"

"Perhaps, though institutionally, we still frown on vigilante-style justice. If that's the sort of thrill you chase, I fear you'll be joining the ranks of our shunned." The dean clears his throat, reaching up to adjust his tie. "If you're aware of any misdeeds, Mr. Anderson, I implore you to report them to the school board for immediate investigation. There are several active criminal cases open, you know. Each of them has, interestingly, occurred since your arrival."

"Coincidences, I'm sure."

He presses his lips into a thin line and shuffles back a step. "Of course. I wasn't suggesting otherwise."

Giving the library one last lingering glance, he starts off toward the administration buildings across from the quad, pausing just once. He tosses me a look over his shoulder, something unreadable passing through his gaze.

"However…" A pause, and he faces forward again. "I would keep an eye on your friend, Mr. Anderson. If she's not involved in what's going on, it's very clear someone wants us to think she is."

Chapter 33

Lucy

FOXE TOSSES ANOTHER SPITBALL ON THE DESKTOP COMPUTER across from my study table. That's twelve and counting, and if I wasn't trying to do my ecology homework, I'd snap at him to pick them up.

"Are you nine?" I ask when he wads another piece of paper and places it on the tip of his tongue.

"What? It's not *technically* littering if it's indoors," he whines, earning an irritated look from Aurora, who sits at the opposite end of the table with Yuri, holding her textbook close to her face.

When I begged her to join me in the Obeliskos, she agreed, but only if I promised to tell her what was going on with Asher and me.

Unfortunately for her, my promise was made facetiously, since I've been avoiding him since the upstairs incident.

There's nothing going on anyway. Other than a few heavy kisses— kisses I can't stop thinking about, even when I'm sharing Aurora's bed late at night, tossing and turning while she shakes the windows with her snoring—I can't really say anything else has changed.

He hasn't apologized, and frankly, things around him are weird in general. I'm not sure I *want* anything to be happening between us.

One day I'll stop lying to myself.

"So is this really what you do all day?" Foxe continues, folding his arms on the table and resting his head on them. "I always thought college was about parties and getting alcohol poisoning, but you guys *actually* study."

"Your dad is a professor," I note. "Why are you so surprised?"

"That's how he described it growing up."

"Is it possible he lied to entice you?" Yuri asks, popping a big pink bubble against her lips. "Maybe he thought you'd be more inclined to attend if it sounded fun?"

Foxe glances around at the endless rows of wooden tables and chairs, the walls framed by heavy wooden bookshelves and accented by large, overstuffed furniture. At this time of day, foot traffic is pretty steady, but the quiet remains throughout.

The librarian across the large room escorts people out for being too loud, which is probably why she's been glowering at Foxe for half an hour now.

"That *does* sound like something my dad would do," he concedes with a laugh. "Backfired though, didn't it?"

We're shushed *again*, and a thumping noise sounds beneath the table, jolting all of us as Foxe lets out a grunt.

He bares his teeth at Aurora. "*Ow.*"

"Sorry, leg spasm," she replies, lifting her brows as she goes back to her book. "They're triggered by morons who can't shut up."

"You never seemed to mind in high school," he snaps, tension threading through the planes of his face. It's unlike him and totally unnerving. "In fact, I think you rather liked how unceasing my tongue was—"

"Shut *up*," she spits. "You have no right to talk about any of that."

"*No right?* I didn't break *your* heart there, cupcake."

Her cheeks turn the same shade of pink as her lip gloss. "What the hell are you even doing here, *Foxeglove*? Shouldn't you be off with your handler somewhere, being a nuisance to someone who wants you around?"

Foxe's jaw drops at the use of his full name—no one uses it, ever.

The tips of his ears turn red beneath his shaggy brown hair, and a flash of something I've only seen on rare occasions flickers in his eyes for a moment.

But then he scoots his chair away, turning his attention to me.

I give Aurora a look, but she just clenches her teeth, busying herself with something in her backpack.

"You got a test coming up, Lulu?" Foxe asks, leaning in to see what I'm working on.

"Yep. Finals will be here before I know it, and I've spent most of my semester...well, not keeping up with assignments, that's for sure. If I flunk anything this term, I'll have to push graduation because they don't offer most ecosystem restoration courses in the spring. For some reason."

"I thought you were majoring in poli-sci."

Snorting, I shake my head. "I'm *minoring* in it, and only because my dad convinced me I could do some real good with a little political experience in my bag."

"Imagine if we all majored in the stuff our parents made careers out of," Aurora says to me, pointedly ignoring Foxe. "My time would be spent making craft beer and painting."

"Ugh, I'd be teaching Japanese literature. *In* Japan," Yuri adds. "My parents had the whole thing planned out for me until I told them I'd applied for a student visa and was coming here to study."

"I'd be working for the Mafia," a new voice interrupts.

My throat swells up at the deep tone, my toes curling inside my boots when I think back to the last time I heard it—when the owner had his fingers inside me.

Now, those same fingers flatten out on the table as Asher bends, getting in my face. His other hand grips the back of my chair, and suddenly I'm being tilted, my world upending as he suspends me backward, lifting my feet off the ground.

He steadies me at an angle, grinning. "Hey, pup."

"Hi," I say, because it's the polite thing to do.

Not because I care or suddenly forgive him. Especially not after the dean revealed he'd been buddying up to Curators—and here I'd thought his fighting with them meant he understood how much I despise them.

Before I can react, he kisses me in front of *everyone*, slipping his tongue between my lips. A spark flickers in the space between us, and for a split second it's just us two.

His soul and mine, floating somewhere in the ether.

Lifting my hand, I go to pry him off, but my fingers curl into his hair instead, keeping him in place.

Fuck, am I in trouble.

Sense slams into me when he tips my head, deepening the kiss and making my insides turn to jelly. I shove at his chest, breaking contact after a moment, though he doesn't make it easy.

"What the fuck," Aurora whispers.

Yuri blushes. "Your question from the other day makes total sense now."

Clearing my throat as Asher plants my chair back on the floor, I wipe my lips with the tips of shaky fingers, ignoring his expectant gaze. Shit, I can barely think straight now, the buzz from his presence zapping all my focus.

"Are you trying to make me jealous, Ash-tree?" Foxe complains, dropping his forehead to the table. "Because it's working."

"For fuck's sake. It was just a kiss, people. In some countries, that's the standard greeting," Asher says as he plops into a chair on the other side of me.

"Sure," Yuri agrees. "But most of those kisses aren't French."

Hooking his ankle around one of my chair legs, Asher yanks me closer, spreading his knees and fitting me between them. I reach out to keep from falling, my palm landing high on his thigh.

I gulp.

He smirks.

"What're we studying for?"

Shaking my head, I try to peel my fingers off him, but he reaches down and covers my hand with his, keeping them there.

"Asher," I warn in a low voice.

"*Lucy*," he replies, leaning in until our noses are almost touching. "Don't you think we already obliterated some lines? Is a little PDA going to kill you?"

"It might."

"Come on. Just let me be near you."

I can feel everyone else's eyes glued to us as they strain to listen in on our conversation. Heat envelops my face, making me dizzy, and I glance down at our hands. His thumb strokes mine, but he doesn't make a move to push me higher or invade more of my space.

I'm not really sure what I was expecting after I let him finger fuck me upstairs. Maybe that he'd be done, having somehow gotten what he wanted from me, even though we didn't go all the way.

But I guess maybe there's a part of me that will always assume the worst. Once you've been ditched with no explanation, your heart shattered and left flattened on the floor, believing someone wants to stay becomes an insurmountable feat.

I haven't decided if I forgive him yet, or if I even want to. I'm not even positive pursuing *anything* with him is a good idea, especially if he's getting involved with Curator shit, but…

My hand stays on his leg as I return my gaze to my textbook.

"There you go," he murmurs, grinning. "That wasn't so hard, was it?"

"Only because I have more important things to do than argue with you."

He hums, resting his forehead on my shoulder. "Need me to get the test answers?"

"What good would cheating do?"

"It'd make your life a little easier."

"Sure, in the moment. But I'd be missing out on potentially vital information, which could be detrimental down the road. I know you don't care about learning, but *I* like it. Learning is the only way you grow."

Even if it takes me longer to learn some lessons than others.

Asher considers this as the rest of the table devolves into an argument about where to take a snack break.

"You're right," Asher says, nodding. "Read to me then."

I frown. "What? Why?"

"If I remember correctly, reading stuff out loud used to help you concentrate." He lifts his head, raising an eyebrow. "With everything going on, I'll bet you're struggling."

My frown deepens.

"So, use me as your audience. Read the material, and I can quiz you on it after. No pressure. But... Maybe I'll learn something too." His cheeks darken with a blush. "And if not, at least I get to enjoy the sound of your voice."

"You want to listen to me drone on about the management of different soil types?"

"After three years without a word, I want to hear anything you have to say."

My chest throbs, and I grip the textbook tighter. Damn him. "I'm supposed to be mad at you," I note softly.

"That doesn't mean you need to suffer for it," he replies, just as quietly.

Once again, it's just the two of us here in this little bubble. I look into his eyes, tempted to ask about his involvement with the Curators but unwilling to ruin what feels like a *moment*.

I don't have to forgive him just for being helpful.

"All right," I relent, swallowing over the knot in my throat. "But we have to whisper. I don't want to get in trouble with the librarians—they're the real heroes around here."

I'm not paying attention to where I'm going when I leave the Obeliskos later, too wrapped up in my confusing thoughts about Asher and the feelings he evokes within me.

On the one hand, it was nice to sit with him like old times. I've not had such a productive study session in years as I did with him there, listening intently as I went over the final material.

But I can't get the facts and secrets out of my head.

He stayed behind to talk to Foxe, but I have no doubt he'll be after me as soon as he's done. Maybe then I'll have the courage to ask what he's *really* doing here, and why he's getting involved with Curator business.

The sinister possibilities swirl like a hurricane in my mind, heightening my anxiety and quickening my pace. I take a corner, running directly into Professor Dupont as he's coming from the opposite direction.

My chest collides with his, and all the papers he'd been stuffing into his briefcase go flying, scattering across the damp ground. Cringing, apologies spill from my lips, even as I drop to my knees and try to rescue the pages for him.

Professor Dupont laughs, putting a hand on my shoulder. "Lucy, don't worry about it. The fewer papers I salvage, the less of my evening I have to spend grading. Truly, you're doing me a favor."

Relief rushes out of me, taking some of the tension from my body with it. Even if I don't fully trust him, I don't need him as an enemy when his brother is already one.

They're not close, according to Pythia, which makes sense considering the professor practically donates his services as a teacher, and seemingly does little else. When he's not teaching, he's working on screenplays or Visio Aternae's philanthropic ventures as the faculty advisor.

Beckett, meanwhile, thinks he's above altruism and distances himself from those who participate.

Still, of the founding families, the Duponts have the most influence in town while also being the most mysterious. No one knows if their patriarch is even alive, as he hasn't been seen anywhere in months.

The professor acts as a proxy for any founder or council business, which means he'd be directly involved if the family knew about nefarious plots on campus. They have members on the school board, which makes them complicit to whatever is going on in my book.

I just don't know what's going on. A cursed belief bleeding into reality, or something worse?

"Be that as it may," I tell Professor Dupont, my nails scraping against the pavement, "I can't in good conscience leave litter lying around."

My hands pause over the edge of one paper, my gaze getting caught on the insignia stamped at the top.

Not the Visio Aternae emblem—two torches and a key—but the three-headed beast of death.

Dread snakes its way into my veins, making me freeze in place.

Surely that's something he confiscated or a school letter attempting to address the notorious student organization.

"Ah, yes. *Conscience.* That pesky internal monologue of morality is bound to get you into trouble someday." He crouches, draping his arms over his knees, and takes the paper from my fingers.

I glance up, unable to ignore the way his brown dress pants strain against powerful thighs or the corded muscles threading beneath the sleeves of his sweater vest.

Traveling farther still, I trace the contours of his handsome, angular face, meeting those dark green eyes. They seemed lighter and less guarded that day in his office, but now maintaining eye contact feels like staring at some phenomenon that might steal my vision forever if I do it for too long.

Pulling myself together, I blink and quickly shuffle some more papers, holding them out for him.

He takes them, his thumb grazing my knuckles. It's ice-cold, and I shrink away from the touch.

"Sorry," he tells me with a small smile. "Raynaud's. I tend to forget about the dysregulation until someone recoils from me."

I nod, folding my hands in my lap, remaining on my knees. He finishes resituating his papers and then locks his briefcase, exhaling heavily.

"What are you doing out right now?" he asks, pushing some of his dark brown hair back from where it droops into an eyebrow. "Is there someplace I can walk you? Hopefully not to one of Beckett's parties though. They've been getting out of hand lately."

"Yet Avernia allows them to continue."

He lifts a shoulder. "The administration overlooks a lot of shit when you've got the right money and connections. You'd be surprised what you could get away with, Lucy, if you just leaned into your family's name a bit more."

Lifting my chin, I narrow my eyes. "Are you encouraging nepotism and a system that rewards homogeneity over individual identities? Doesn't that seem sort of counterintuitive to what you teach?"

"In the post-Socratic world, the ancient Greeks believed in four principal schools of thought," he says, pushing upright.

I get to my feet, unwilling to let him tower over me.

"The belief that reality just *is*, the drive for pleasure seeking, and the suspension of judgment."

"That's only three."

"Cynicism is one I often leave out, because it feels a bit too rudimentary for me. It's easy to assume that rejecting worldly pleasure might lead to enlightenment or whatever else, because nearly every religious doctrine adopts this idea in some form." He brushes his hands on his pants. "Each post-Socratic philosophy is rooted very heavily in individualism, which is something I value as an educator. I do think there is merit in singular identities and the freedom in which to explore those."

I cross my arms over my chest. *Why does this feel like a lecture I would have skipped?*

"But if you go back further and dive into Platonism, you get slightly different, more community-driven philosophies. That is the period that Avernia tends to draw from. It's why they try to drill connection so hard into their students, because of the belief that virtue, ethics, and justice all stem from the collective. It's difficult to maintain order in modern society if the backbone is purely individualistic."

My mind drifts back to the emblem on the one sheet of paper he's carrying around. The symbol of the anonymous organization that moves in silence and leaves its mark everywhere. On trees, bathroom stalls, and murder victims.

"And which do you subscribe to, Professor?"

He looks over my shoulder, something seeming to capture his

attention; his pupils dilate, and for several seconds, there's this unreadable expression on his face. Something…forlorn, maybe, as if whatever he sees is eternally just slightly out of reach.

But then he gives a tiny shake of his head, and the look is gone, replaced by a mask of professionalism.

I swallow, taken aback by how easily it slides into place.

"Growing up in a family that discouraged any sort of free thinking, I'm of the belief that too much community can turn negative. Especially when it's a community fueled by power, greed, and pedigree." He shrugs, suddenly seeming much older than his late twenties. "When there is no incentive and no benefit for the general public… The people will break off and begin making their own adjustments."

Tag doesn't seem to mind at all that I missed our date. He shows up at my desk in Politics of Conservation, propping his elbows on the edge and grinning while I explain what happened.

Well. I leave out the part about Asher fingering me in the library. Frankly, I've been trying to forget about it myself, and I don't want to make Tag feel like I ditched him solely to fuck around with someone else.

Even though I made it clear the date was platonic, it still feels shitty.

Not to mention the whole blood fiasco. The school didn't officially confirm or deny anything, but I know what blood looks and smells like. And the only way to get that much is for something—or someone—to have been systematically drained of it.

Not to mention the Death's Teeth emblem painted on the wall above it.

"You look like you haven't slept in weeks," Tag says, tapping the desk with a rolled stack of papers. "So I'll be honest. I feel like that's a good punishment for you standing me up."

I rub my eyes, too tired to even care that it's smudging my makeup.

Aurora, whose room I've been crashing in to avoid an invite from Asher, snores like a fucking freight train.

But I wasn't sleeping well before anyway, so it's not like it matters exactly where I spend my nights staring at the ceiling, wondering if I'm in actual danger or if I'm just some beacon for terrible luck.

Maybe Dean Bauer is right, and the incidents are my fault—not by active involvement, of course, but maybe my aura is attracting unfortunate events.

Or maybe someone wants me to leave campus so bad, they're willing to literally slaughter other students to achieve that goal.

No part of me would be surprised if that asshole was Beckett. He clearly sees me as a threat to whatever community he's trying to build here in our last semesters.

"I think I'm losing my mind," I admit, dropping my face into my hands.

"I'm flattered," Tag replies. "But not worth all that. Besides, I wound up having a good time anyway. You're now looking at a volunteer set designer for the play."

My brows lift. "I didn't know you had a set design interest."

"Eh, I don't. But that girl you're friends with, Yuri what's-her-name? She's the coordinator or something, and I'm *very* interested in getting closer to her."

"Moved on from me already?"

He holds up his hands. "Hey, a guy can't wait around forever, though I *will* take payment for your sins in the form of you going to a Curator party with me."

Groaning, I fold my arms on my desk and bury my face in my elbows. I will never understand this campus's obsession with that stupid group or its parties, but since I already ditched him once, I tell him I'll see him later tonight.

Beckett's eyes find me from the front of the classroom where he's been chatting up Professor Ouellette for the past ten minutes, much to her dismay. She's seated behind her desk, pumping hand sanitizer into her palm and listening to him with a mildly irritated look on her face.

The gold ring she wears on her left hand is bright against her brown skin and new. I wonder when that happened and if her partner is aware of the history that comes with the founding families. Even the ones who removed themselves from Fury Hill but have somehow found their way back.

Eventually, Beckett breaks away from the professor, and she turns around to write on the whiteboard. Instead of taking a seat, Beckett meanders over to me, joined by Eli and Tiernan something.

"We missed you at Avernia's midterm budget meeting." Beckett's smarmy smile sends a shiver across my skin as he places a hand on my desk.

I scoff but don't reply, opening up my notes from last week.

"It felt a little weird having discussions about where to allocate school funds without some chick sitting in the back row questioning every single bullet point," Tiernan adds. "You've been a little subdued lately though."

"Guess we have Anderson to thank for that." Beckett cocks a brow, taunting me. "Though I can't figure out for the life of me why a promising student like him would want to slum it with trash."

"Aw, are you jealous?" I lean forward, returning his overly-sweet grin. "You wish it was you he was obsessed with, don't you? I'd heard rumors that you were into powerful men, but I didn't realize that extended to students too."

He narrows his eyes. "Not *all* students. Just that one."

"Why? You do realize he doesn't give a shit about you, right?"

Tiernan crosses his arms. "What, like he cares about you or something? The dude seems seriously unbothered."

Eli doesn't say a word, tracing his index finger over a big AC carved into one of the desks.

My gaze darts between the three of them, anxiety collecting in my chest. Not because of the teasing—that, I'm used to—but because of the tone. The prodding. It feels more like they're out for information than simply trying to fuck with me, and I'm not sure I like the subject.

If Asher is already involved with the Curators, I know he'd have mentioned our history. He tells everyone about us. And if he hasn't, there must be some reason.

When I look at Eli, his green eyes quickly bounce away. *What's a Visio Aternae member doing hanging out with a Curator anyway?* Other than being founding family royalty, I can't imagine the two have much in common.

Unless Eli's considering defecting.

Or being forced to.

"All right, class, settle into your seats, please." Professor Ouellette claps her hands, making a sweeping gesture toward us. She gives Beckett a pointed stare, and he lifts his hands in surrender, backing away from my desk.

"Guess I'll see you at my party later," he says, ignoring Tag's presence entirely. "Think you can stay out of trouble for one night?"

His parting words leave a pit of dread in my stomach, but it's mostly forgotten when the lecture begins, and I try my best to focus, considering my midterm project was unfinished when I submitted it. Professor Ouellette is much less forgiving than Professor Dupont, so I need some sort of effort to keep me from being dropped from the class before the semester ends.

Later, when he comes by Erebus Hall to walk me to the Curator clubhouse, Tag shoves a crumpled paper into my hand, then takes my arm, half dragging me in the direction of the old Victorian.

"You don't have to hold me," I say, tugging away.

"Open it," he replies.

Rolling my eyes, I smooth out the sheet, using my thigh for leverage. Printed in bold black letters at the top are the words FURY HILL ANIMAL SHELTER: DONATION RECEIPT.

I scan quickly, my eyes widening when I get to the bottom, and dig my heels into the ground to stop walking. Tag spins to face me, releasing my arm.

"What the hell is this?" I demand, pointing at the dollar amount listed. "You donated *ten grand* to the shelter?"

Tag purses his lips. "Yes. Yes, I did."

Suspicion claws at my throat. His pout turns into a grin, and then he kicks at a rock aimlessly, shrugging his shoulders.

My eyes narrow. "*You* donated this much? Doesn't your mom own a grocery store in Portland?"

He laughs. "Does that mean I can't fundraise? Ten thousand dollars isn't really that much in the grand scheme of things, you know."

In the adult world, he's not really wrong, but it also doesn't sound like something that someone who grew up living paycheck to paycheck would ever say. It sounds like something that was planted there for him to regurgitate to me.

"You only had fifty at my booth. Now all of a sudden, you've managed to cough up ten grand?"

"I'm a very hard worker. Also, has anyone ever told you that you have trust issues?"

"One person, yes. My *former* best friend." I push a finger into his chest. "Who really gave this money?"

Tag's dark eyes fill with glee. "Seems like maybe you already know."

Letting my arm fall to my side, I look past Tag toward the decrepit Victorian mansion where half the Curators live. It's lit up inside and out, and bass carries across the quad, making the damp air pulsate.

Then I turn back around, staring up at Erebus Hall looming like a haunted palace with the full moon hanging bright behind it. Inhaling deeply, I ball the paper in my fist and spare Tag a brief glance. "Go on without me, all right?"

He hesitates. "You've got a weird look in your eyes—"

"Just go, Holland. Yuri's at the party already, guaranteed. She likes weed and peach candies, like the ones they sell in the refectory. Bring her some, and she's yours forever."

Clicking his tongue, he gives me a half bow before darting off in the opposite direction. I snort when he trips, catching himself before he can fall, and disappears behind the corner of the Lyceum.

Then I go back into the dorm.

Chapter 34

Asher

"I MEAN, YOU CAN'T REALLY DISCOUNT ALL THE PLACES GHOSTS could be hiding here."

Foxe tosses a piece of popcorn into his mouth, chewing so loud that Keats growls at him from his perch on my dresser.

"The caves in those mountains are probably ancient. Older than the dinosaurs or something, and who fucking knows how many people have died in them over the years? Probably why the administration has them blocked off."

Rubbing my eye with my knuckle, I grip my charcoal pencil between two fingers, smudging the lines on the monster sketch in my lap. "What the hell are you even doing out by the *caves*? Shouldn't you be in the studio or something?"

He snorts. "You think Fury Hill, with its population of, like, five people, has a recording studio? My best bet would be driving one state over and seeing if Aiden's home so we could do a little jam sesh, but then I'd be leaving you all by yourself to deal with the weird stuff going on."

"I'm more than capable of handling myself, dipshit."

"Sure, sure, but I'd be lonely."

In truth, I'm starting to regret bringing him along in the first place.

The more people I keep in my company, the more at risk they are of being pulled in to this strange world. The more dangerous things become.

"How do you think Lulu will react to finding out you're cursed?" he ponders, holding a piece of popcorn in offering to Keats, who sneezes at it.

"I'm not cursed."

"Oh right. Your *bloodline* is." Foxe shakes his head, catching the snack between his teeth. "Sheesh, good thing we're related on Grandpa's side. A curse probably wouldn't be too good for my music career."

"Can you call it a career when you haven't done anything with it in months?"

He makes a face, throwing a handful of popcorn at me. "I'm starting to think you don't want me here, cowboy."

I glance up from my sketchbook.

"Pfft. Your life would be shit without me, and you know it." Setting the bowl on the floor, he slinks down farther on the bed, rolling onto his side. "What's your next move anyway? Gonna actually burn down the place like you wanted, or are you content to just silently pine after Lulu and continue to let her run around while killers are loose?"

"I'm not *letting* her do anything." She wouldn't believe me at this point, even if I tried to explain.

Or maybe she would, and I'm just an idiot.

Maybe not fucking telling her is what got us into this mess in the first place.

"The crimes are obviously messages, Ash-tree. Do you not think she'll notice a pattern?"

"Well, it's not like *I'm* the one sending the fucking things."

"No, but you're the reason she's being targeted." He cocks an eyebrow at me, waiting. "Right? That's why you didn't want to come here?"

I don't reply, going back to the sketch. A headless horse with a limbless rider, next to a sea monster and a minotaur. Nonsense, but it takes the anxiety out of everything going on in the real world, if only for a little while.

The closed door starts to rattle as someone pounds on it from the outside, making Foxe jump. I turn my head, watching the doorknob shake as the knocking continues, echoing in the room.

Keats hisses, diving under the bed.

"Methinks you fucked up big-time," Foxe says, climbing out of the bed and walking to the door. He rolls his shoulders as if prepping for a fight, and there's a sliver of hesitancy in both of us before he grabs the knob.

My side aches from where I was stabbed, and I consider the fact that there is very real danger lurking in the shadows on this campus. A group of people, if not the entirety of Avernia College, who are so terrified by what my ancestor did that they're willing to go to great lengths to ensure it doesn't happen again.

Would Lucy have been fine if I hadn't come? I suppose fine is relative, and since she wasn't exactly having the greatest time, there's a possibility that all this would've happened anyway.

She witnessed her roommate's death before anyone but the dean and my sister knew I was enrolled. It's not like I'm the sole cause of what's going on here.

Right?

Though I suppose I'm also not helping matters. One might be able to argue that I've made them worse, but I'd never admit it out loud.

Foxe throws open the door with more gusto than I care for, all things considered.

Somehow, what's waiting at the threshold feels more damning than a killer.

Lucy's eyes, hardened and glowing with anger, find mine immediately. She's in one of her tight little sweaters, this one a deep green that brings out the bright blue in her irises, and a short black skirt like the one she had on in the library. Tights cover her long, toned legs, and even though she's clearly pissed, I can't help the way my dick stiffens at the sight of her.

It's always been like that, if I'm honest. Seeing her just takes my breath away; the reaction between my thighs is simply a bonus.

For me at least. I imagine the woman seething across the room would not find it enticing at the moment.

Or maybe she would. Her anger gets me going, so perhaps there's something in her that would also see the benefit of a rage-induced make-out session.

Fucking Christ, you stupid bastard. Get a goddamn hold of yourself.

"Lucy," I greet in a monotone voice, aware that she's been avoiding me since the library.

"Oh, fuck that." She points an index finger at me, her eyebrows knitting together. "Don't you dare call me *Lucy* like I'm in trouble or some bullshit. You've had your hand so far inside me that I could practically taste it. You are *not* making me feel like a piece of shit by using my full name."

Foxe's jaw *unhinges*, and he swings his gaze to me. "*Oh?*"

"Get the fuck out," I snap at him, flipping my sketchbook shut.

"No, he can stay. This won't take long," Lucy says, stomping inside. She shoves a piece of white paper to my chest, the force making me cough. "Did you do this?"

I take the sheet and toss it into the wastebasket by my desk. "That kid wasn't supposed to fucking tell you."

"He didn't." She crosses her arms. "Why would you do that, Asher? The whole point of me doing the fundraiser was to *raise the funds*. If I wanted to use my parents' money, I would have."

"Why didn't you? They'd save the shelter in an instant."

"Of course they would, you big dummy. That's not the point. I don't ask them for help because I want to be able to do shit by myself. If I have my parents step in every single time I need something, that isn't *my* accomplishment."

"Seems kind of pointless," Foxe chimes in. "You have the means to do actual good in the world but deny the help because of…vanity?"

She whirls on him, glaring. "I'm allowed to want to earn things independently. My parents don't define me, nor does their money. I do things because *I* want to, but if all my efforts are only possible because I had a built-in safety bank, then the risk is canceled out. My dreams and goals belong to my parents. Not me."

"But nepotism rocks," Foxe replies, scratching at his chest. "It gets you opportunities and brand deals and—"

"It isn't *mine!*" she screeches, tears springing to her eyes. Her hands claw at the air, her voice raw. "You don't get it, because you never needed to. You have an identity outside your parents, your friends, your connections. No one cares that your cousin is a famous musician or that your dad is a renowned music professor because they like *you*."

Something burns in my chest.

"I don't have that, Foxe. I can't make friends easily or connect with people on a whim. All I do is make everyone fucking angry or uncomfortable, because I don't know how to do anything else. I am barely a human, and skipping steps to do actual good makes me feel like I'm not even that."

Her voice cracks, and nausea rolls in my stomach.

The room goes silent when she stops speaking. They stare at each other while I study a chip in the wood of my desk.

I've always known there was a disconnect between Lucy and her peers, ever since we were young, and probably partially because of her ADHD. Even after her parents addressed it and got her medicated, the way her brain worked made her see and do things differently.

It was a similar disconnect I felt between myself and others, but where I didn't give a shit what people thought or how they reacted to me, it was quietly eating away at her inside.

A person forced to care so deeply about a world she could never fully break into.

She cared so much it made her dysfunctional. Unrelatable in a society preoccupied with ego.

And rather than start college with her and attempt to help navigate newfound freedom and identity, I fucking ditched her.

I thought she'd be better off, but clearly all it's done is make her miserable.

Me. It's *my* fault she feels this way.

Clearing my throat, I trace the chipped wood with my thumb, dragging the jagged piece through my fingerprint. "I didn't get the money from my parents. Or yours."

Lucy's head jerks to the side, confusion in her watery eyes. Christ, I hate making her cry.

"What do you mean?" she asks, wiping her nose on her sleeve.

"I mean, I donated about a thousand bucks. That was all I had on me." Shrugging, I let my hand fall to my lap, suddenly perturbed by her unwavering attention. "The rest came from the students. Curators, mostly. Beckett Dupont was more than willing to run around for me after I agreed to join his little club."

Lucy's nose scrunches up. "You got the Curators to donate?"

"Figured they'd have the most disposable cash and the influence on campus to make up for whatever they didn't have. It was surprisingly easy, to be honest. They definitely have an issue with you, which I would like to talk about at some point, because it's pissing me off—"

"You actually *raised* ten thousand dollars for the shelter," she whispers, turning to face me fully.

"Well." I lift my chin, meeting those glassy gemstone eyes. Dark ocean water, but clear all the way through. "I did it for you."

Her chest rises and falls with each breath she heaves. She takes a step in my direction and then another until she's standing between my spread legs.

I place my hands on the armrests of my chair, anticipation humming through my veins as I wait for her to slap me.

For the frustration that's been building within to come to a point and for her to finally snap.

But it never comes.

The slap, that is.

Instead, she places her palms on my shoulders, plants her knee between my thighs, and leans down to kiss me.

Chapter 35

Asher

THE MOMENT OUR LIPS TOUCH, MY HANDS FIND HER HIPS, AND I draw her into my lap. She braces her knees on either side of me, fingers gently cradling my jaw, and tilts my head so she can deepen the kiss.

"So should I leave, or..."

I pull back far enough to glare at Foxe over Lucy's shoulder. "Yes, you fucking weirdo."

"Hey, some people want to be watched, I don't know."

Gritting my teeth, I pick up a wooden bookend and chuck it at my cousin. It misses, smacking against the wall and falling on the floor. Laughing hysterically, Foxe slides out the door, closing it behind him.

A few tense seconds pass, the weight of us being alone settling in with the silence.

"I think I might throw up," Lucy says.

Alarm ripples through me. "That is probably something you should do in the trash can. Or down the hall in the bathroom."

Shaking her head, she curls her hands around my neck. "No, it's just... I can't believe I'm doing this. Kissing you...without you objecting. I mean, I know we did stuff in the library, but you initiated it that time."

"And if I ever object to you sucking my face off again, you have full permission to call my mom and let her know to make room in the family plot."

"So… Why did you reject me back then?"

I tap her hip with a thumb. "Is this the conversation you want to have right now?"

"It doesn't need to be a whole *thing*," she rushes out, like she's embarrassed. "But I have spent the last three years wondering, so I just thought maybe…"

When I don't immediately reply, she sighs and starts to get off me. I cup my palms under her ass and haul her up, walking to the bed. Dropping her on the mattress, I yank my shirt off and plant my fists on either side of her head, hovering over her.

My throat itches with need, but I ignore it.

"Don't take that as me saying I don't want to tell you." I brush a strand of hair from her face, tucking it behind her ear, grazing the row of piercings lining the shell and spinning the ruby-studded flat. "We can talk about how I was a fucking dumbass and how I'll never be able to make up for what I did. But…I've been *dying* to kiss you again."

She flutters her eyelashes against her cheeks, brushing the heated pink skin. "Me too."

"Good." I grin, and when she returns the gesture, it strikes me deep in my gut that this is actually happening. That Lucy Aberdeen Wolfe wants to kiss *me*, despite everything. "I'd like to do some other stuff to you while we kiss if that's okay."

Nodding, she digs her teeth into her bottom lip, reaching up to stroke my face. My body trembles, a mix of apprehension and excitement twisting my insides into knots.

"What are you waiting for then?" she whispers. "I want your hands on me."

Lifting a shaky palm, I slide it behind her head, threading through her soft, luxurious hair. I clutch her skull and pull her up, reveling in the gasp that escapes as her back arches to meet me.

My dick jumps behind my zipper as our mouths meet once again, hers widening enough to push her tongue into mine. She flicks in and out over my teeth, and I slip my other arm beneath her waist, fitting her pelvis against me.

She wraps her hands around the back of my neck and then hooks a leg behind my thigh, angling so her pussy rubs me through the layers she has on. Her skirt rises, catching on her hips, and I'm already panting at the thought of tearing it off her.

I squeeze, tugging at her sweater, and slowly glide my way over the curve of her leg, urging her closer. Our kisses ignite a hunger deep in the center of my being, begging me for *more*.

Circling her ankle, I push her calf into her thigh, moving it toward the mattress. Rolling my hips, I use the added space to grind forcefully against her clit, swallowing the strangled sound she makes with the contact.

My hands practically dwarf every inch of her I touch. Releasing her leg, I reach for the hem of her sweater, abandoning her mouth temporarily. With each inch of skin exposed as I push the fabric up, my lips trace the path, leaving a trail of kisses along her stomach.

She sits up, lifting her arms so I can take the sweater off entirely, and then she's just in her skirt, tights, and a flimsy little bralette. Black lace covers her pale, sexy tits, obscuring her pretty pink nipples *just so*. I run my hand down the zipper of my pants, my cock already throbbing, making it difficult to see straight.

I'm aware that being a virgin may put me at a slight disadvantage, not to mention the fact that I've been dreaming about seeing this girl naked for the past seven or so years. Ever since I got my first hard-on watching her swim laps in the pool behind her house and realized my sexual attraction wasn't nonexistent, it just needed a deep connection to kick in.

Still, I didn't come into this unprepared. I've watched porn, I've practiced, I've fucked my hand raw some nights to build up stamina. I even swallowed my pride and asked my dad and uncles for advice, of which their main thing was to focus on *her*.

I can't imagine doing anything else.

My thumb grazes one hardened peak, and her mouth parts on a shaky breath.

"You're so beautiful," I utter.

Her face reddens. "Don't say stuff you don't mean."

Dipping my head, I pull the lace cup toward me, baring her tit, and run the flat of my tongue over it. Saliva paints her skin, and I pull the nipple between my lips, sucking gently.

"I've never been more honest in my entire life," I say around her. "You are the most magnificent creature I've ever laid eyes on."

Her fingers crawl up my neck, tangling in my hair.

Keeping my eyes on her, studying for every slight change in breathing, every flush of her cheeks, each swallowed moan, I score my teeth over her flesh. Just a bit at first, and when a fire seems to blaze in her blue irises, I apply more pressure, biting firmly.

She hisses, her back arching, and pushes more of her tit into my mouth. I lave over the bite, reveling in the red, inflamed imprint, and repeat it on the inside, closer to the center of her chest. Then again on the opposite side and again at the top until there's a desperate trail of teeth marks leading to her collarbone.

"Vampire," she rasps, watching as I move farther down the length of her body, taking her skirt and tights with me. Lifting her hips, she lets me disrobe her lower half, leaving her in only a pair of black lace panties that match her bralette.

"Can't seem to help myself," I say, skimming my lips along her calf, propping it on my shoulder. "When you leave here later, I want everyone on this fucking campus to know my mouth was on you."

"Well, they won't know it was *your* mouth."

"Good point." Letting her leg fall back to the bed, I crawl off and jog to my desk, snatching a charcoal pencil. She rolls her head to the side, eyeing me as I come back with the utensil poised between two fingers.

Grabbing her hip, I flip her over so she's lying on her stomach; she pushes up on her elbows, and I flatten my palm on her lower back, keeping her in place.

Hooking my fingers in the elastic waist of her panties, I drag them down, baring her perfect, round ass. She sucks a breath in when I kneel on the mattress, swatting her thighs apart so I can fit between them.

"Asher..." she trails off, uncertain, trying to close herself to me.

I ignore her and make the *A* on her left ass cheek bigger than necessary. Then again, marking her at all probably isn't *necessary*. There's no way anyone else is getting to see her like this.

Not after I'm done with her.

She'll be lucky if I don't beg her to stay in my bed the rest of the semester—hell, the rest of our *lives*. That's how fucking far gone I already am.

Maybe always have been.

Still, there's some strange, primal part of me that wants her visibly marked. The bites are fine, but there's something delightfully erotic about putting my name on her, even if only temporarily and only where I'll see.

The *s* is smaller but no less prominent. Charcoal glides effortlessly against her skin, and I give my signature a silky-smooth finish.

My dick leaks a bead of precum, and I grit my teeth against it, praying to whatever god might be out there that I don't come in my fucking pants. Again.

Rolling her hips, she curls her body so she's hovering slightly off the bed. Granting me more access to the most intimate parts of her. I take the dull edge of the pencil, sliding it forward, teasing her seam. A shudder works through her when I brush her clit, and then I withdraw, moving to replace the pencil with my mouth instead.

"Hey, wait." She glances at me over her shoulder, her hair falling in front of her face. "Don't do that."

My eyebrows raise, but I pull back, sitting on the edge of the bed. Disappointment washes through me, and a wave of insecurity has me tightening my grip on the pencil, loathing myself for not having done this years ago. Maybe she wouldn't have cared about the inexperience then.

Lucy twists around, getting to her knees. Her swallow is audible as she reaches for me, grabbing my shoulders and shoving me so I'm lying supine on the bed.

Her naked form hovers above mine, her tits right in my face. I strain upward, lashing my tongue against one, reveling in how the nipple hardens even more.

She leans down, kissing me hard and fast before sliding backward. Trembling fingers move to undo the zipper of my pants, and I feel each tooth unlatch one by one, punctuated by a jolt of my cock in response.

The sensation reverberates in my chest, in my bones, like a symphony contained only by massive walls and domed ceilings. My breaths struggle to make their way out of me as she starts to work my pants down, pausing once she's at my knees.

Tilting her head to one side, she studies the sole tattoo I have on my body. The wolf with a crown of roses, about the size of my entire hand, on top of my right thigh.

She doesn't say anything for a moment, and my muscles tighten, apprehension lacing them.

It was a stupid, impulsive decision. Foxe got one that same night, after his last show, but when he got his removed via laser, I opted not to.

There was no removing the Wolfe in my life from the thread of my soul, so what was the point of removing this one from my body?

Now, though, it feels kind of stupid—

Leaning in with her eyes hooded, Lucy runs her tongue over the bottom edge of the line work, maintaining eye contact with me as she licks a path to the top of the design.

My head drops back, hitting the wooden frame of the bed, my mouth falling open on a breathless moan.

Grinning, Lucy drags another swipe of her tongue, this time ending the motion with a bite of her own. She nips at the tattoo, sinking her teeth into me until my cock is fucking throbbing, hard as steel and probably as dangerous right now with how close she is to it.

"This is hot," she murmurs against my inked skin, fluttering her lashes.

My chest feels heavy, arousal spinning a delicate web through my ribs, the vertebrae of my spine, my muscles. Everything is primed, raring to go, and when she comes up for my boxers, tugging them with her teeth, I almost black out from holding back.

Gripping the sheets, I pant when my cock bobs free, and Lucy's eye level with it. Gingerly, she wraps her hand around the base, and the entire length jumps beneath her touch.

"Wait," I manage, taking her by the wrist and yanking her up to me. The searing kiss I give her makes my head spin, and I urge her to flip around so she's facing my legs.

"Um…" She hesitates, peering at me over her shoulder again.

I take one thigh and bring it over my hip so she's straddling me backward, her glistening, swollen pussy on complete display.

"Is this not weird?" she asks softly, splaying her fingers on my thighs. "It's so…intimate."

"Not a thing weird about it, pup. Brace yourself, and feel free to correct if you need something different." Grabbing her ass in both hands, I move in and lick, getting the first real taste of her wetness—that gentle, very slight flavor that men abandon their livelihoods for.

Lucy cries out, her head falling as I lap from clit to hole and then back, squeezing her cheeks and bringing her closer to me.

"*Fuck,*" she moans, her breath tickling the insides of my legs.

"We're getting there." I cover her pussy with my mouth, pushing the flat of my tongue against her seam and flicking the tip against her clit.

As soon as I start to press into her, she grabs hold of my cock, taking the crown between her lips. Her hips writhe against my face, chasing friction and driving the motions to exactly where she needs them. She pumps me with her fist and works her mouth over my crown, twisting her hand up the length.

It takes her a few moments to get the hang of it. She switches hands a few times, applying her thumb on the underside and pushing her tongue into the slit as if gauging every reaction I have. My thighs tremble, release drawing near with everything she does.

Maybe it isn't supposed to be this good your first time. I don't have a frame of reference, but considering how long we've both been waiting to do this to each other, I'm inclined to think that no manner of practice would've made a difference.

The connection, the *need*, is there. Everything is going to feel amazing as a result.

When she takes me deeper, I see a flash of blinding white light.

"There you go," I praise once I've regained sight, noting how she *quivers* with the soft encouragement, gushing on my lips. "Suck me good, pup. Let me make a mess in your throat."

Drool spills out as she retches, practically inhaling me.

I groan into her sopping, sensitive flesh. "Shit, Luce, you're gonna make me—"

She doesn't let me finish, bringing the head of my cock to the back of her throat; she gags, her muscles contracting around the organ for a brief moment before she pulls back, letting her saliva slick all the way down, pooling against my pelvis and her fist.

Pleasure snakes its way through my veins, and I redouble my efforts, working my tongue in and out of her tight channel, drowning in the succulent taste.

Pulling back, I nip at her ass cheek, taking her flesh with my teeth and biting until she jolts from the pressure. A red mark sprouts immediately, and she sucks me faster as if to get back at me for it.

My dick throbs, my orgasm scraping against my insides as I do my best to withhold it. Drawing a finger through her arousal, I push *slowly* into her, lapping at her clit as a violent tremble rattles her entire body.

Her head pops off me when my digit curls in and up, and she tosses me a look over her shoulder, rocking into the motion while her hand continues pumping me, luring my own release in.

I cock an eyebrow, drinking in the sight of her flushed face, the strain lacing her brow. "You almost there?"

She nods, returning her mouth to my dick, her tongue sliding left and right as she dips her head.

"What else do you need?" I ask, the fingers on my free hand digging into her hip, leaving imprints there. This *has* to be good for her in case I don't fucking last—ah, who am I kidding? There's no way I'm lasting three seconds when I finally get to push inside her.

When it comes to Lucy Wolfe, my willpower is practically nonexistent.

"Could you…add another?" she asks, her pussy fluttering with the request.

I obey, widening the space between the two fingers. "Need me to stretch you out, huh? Gotta make sure I fit."

She makes some unintelligible sound that I feel *in* my cock, and when I manage to wriggle a third digit inside, sucking her clit into my mouth as I massage her inner walls, she comes, spasming so hard around me that I almost lose circulation.

"Holy shit," she says, her forehead dropping to my lap.

Giving her a few seconds to fall from the high of her climax, I wait until she relaxes slightly before withdrawing and then lift her hips off me, rolling her onto her back and yanking her to the middle of the twin bed.

"Wait!" Pressing her warm hands to my chest, she halts my movements. "You didn't finish."

"I'm probably three seconds away from impregnating your throat," I grit out, crawling on top of her. "I need to have your pussy *now*."

Dazed blue eyes blink up at me as I kneel, fitting myself between her parted thighs. Hunger pools in her irises when I drag the back of my hand over my mouth, licking the tips of my fingers and moaning at her sweet fucking flavor.

A crimson blush stains her cheeks, crawling down her neck and across her chest. My cock bobs, desperate to sink into her as I give it a rough tug.

I swallow, taking a second to admire the beauty in front of me: smooth, pale skin, perfect perky tits littered with my bite marks, the slight curve of her hips, and the sodden paradise between them.

Never in a million fucking years would I have imagined I'd be here.

Lucy lifts her chin, gnawing on her bottom lip. "You're concentrating really hard, and it's making me nervous."

Smirking, I scoot forward, moving her thighs wider apart. Grabbing my cock just beneath the crown, I slowly drag it up her seam, collecting the slick moisture clinging to her flesh.

I hook a hand behind her knee, shifting again and moving closer. She starts to turn away, but I squeeze her leg, shaking my head. "No, pup. I want you to watch when I slide into you for the first time. When I claim you where no one else will ever be able to."

Her mouth parts, but she nods, propping up on her elbows. I can't look anywhere else, can't make sure she's with me, when the crown pushes in. Letting out a choked noise, I roll my neck, my throat constricting as her wet heat begins to envelop me.

Sweat drips from my forehead onto her stomach, and I drive in another inch. Then another. Putting pressure on her knee, I inhale, tearing my gaze from where we're connected to check on her.

Agony shutters her eyes, and I freeze.

Shit. Is this hurting her?

I know it's *supposed* to—or at least it just usually does—but I'd hoped the foreplay would've been sufficient.

Gritting my teeth, I exhale slowly, moving back. "Maybe we should—"

"No!" She latches on to my forearms, halting my retreat. "I'm okay, really. It's just… You're a lot bigger than I imagined. It's a tight fit, but it's not terrible."

"You imagined my dick, pup?"

She rolls her eyes. "Whatever, pretty boy. Just put it in me already."

"So bossy." Adjusting my hips, I sink in a little more, losing myself in how warm and snug and unbelievably fucking soaked she is.

"That a problem for you?" She pushes the hair from my forehead, gasping when I finally bottom out in her, a tear immediately springing to one eye.

I bite back my own at the sensations rippling around me. I'm lightheaded just from the feel of her. "Not even a little. You can order me around whenever you want, and I'll eat your pussy after as a thank-you."

That makes her laugh, but then I shift slightly, cutting her off. She claws at my forearms, breathing hard through her nose.

Gritting my teeth, I stay as still as I possibly can, letting the instant gratification of filling her dissipate slowly.

"Asher…" she whispers, shivering as my hands glide up her sides.

"Is this okay?"

Lucy nods, and I hear her swallow. My fingertips burn where I touch her, my entire body on edge from having her here like this.

Where she belongs. Where she's *always* belonged.

With me.

"Spread wider," I instruct, pressing one thigh back so her knee is against the mattress. I glance down at where I've disappeared in her and strum a thumb over one of her puckered nipples. "God, look at that. Look how you open for me, taking me in like this is exactly what you were made to do."

I don't know what I'm saying; words just pour out of my mouth as I draw my hips back, testing out the motions of my thrusts. The first one hits her *deep*, and she chokes, her spine arching clear off the bed.

"Yeah? That feel good, pup?"

She nods frantically, so I keep going, arcing my hips in a slow, steady pace.

"This is so…" She breaks off on a staggered moan when I bend down, covering her tit with my mouth. I flatten my tongue and then swirl it around, pulling the peak between my lips and tugging gently.

"So what?" I urge.

Her nostrils flare, and her chest heaves. She meets my gaze through those long, thick lashes, and I suck harder, watching her eyes darken with lust.

"*Hot*," she replies, tangling her fingers in my hair.

"Pull it," I encourage, laving around her nipple, admiring how taut it gets before moving to the other one. I can feel her heartbeat in my chest, and I feel like I'm losing my mind in the best way possible.

"Won't that hurt?"

"God, I hope so."

My hips snap to hers again, more forcefully this time, and a stinging sensation ripples across my scalp as she clenches my roots, morphing into pleasure as it rains down my back.

She seems to relax the more I move in and out, and eventually one of her hands leaves my head, snaking between us to toy with her clit. I let go of her thigh, grabbing the curve of her waist with both hands and changing the angle, my jaw locked so tight to keep from coming that I'm starting to see stars.

Or maybe that's from her and how fucking *incredible* this feels. Her tits bounce with each thrust, and the bed creaks with my motions, knocking into the wall.

If I were a good RA, maybe I'd give a shit that we're disturbing the rest of the floor, but I'm *not* a good RA, and I couldn't give a flying fuck about anything other than this very moment.

After this, I can die happy. Or happier at least.

The ever-present rage that exists within me seems…sated almost. Distracted, perhaps.

Whatever it is, I know I'll be chasing the high forever.

"Oh my God, Asher. You're getting so *deep*."

"Goddamn, Luce, don't say shit like that."

"Why?" Her eyes sparkle, a moan falling from her lips. "Does it make you want to come?"

Each word is shoved out as I keep fucking her, relying on the intrinsic range of motion. I keep watch for any signs of her not liking a certain stroke, but she seems to be enjoying the ride, so I just pick up the pace, lengthening each plunge in and dragging my cock up on the withdrawal.

My vision starts to blur at the edges, that telltale sign of impending climax inching its way up my spine.

"I'm close," I warn.

"*Good.*"

"Fuck, I wanted to last longer." My voice is strained, desperate, pleading. "I need to come."

Her chin dips, and she grins. "Do it then."

"I didn't—I don't have a condom, pup."

"Don't need one. I'm on the pill."

She squeezes her eyes shut, continuing to rub herself, and I feel her tighten around me. It's a smaller vibration than before, but it's there nonetheless, and she leans into it, clamping around me so tight that I almost pass out.

I flatten my palm between her breasts, pinning her firmly to the mattress, driving into her with fast, brutal strokes. They steal the air from both our lungs, and she moans, her fingers moving quicker, until the levee barring her second orgasm bursts, and she comes all over me.

Again.

Goddamn, I will never get tired of this.

Clenching my jaw, I yank out of her at the very last second, grabbing my dick as euphoria begins pulsing through my veins like liquid honey. Pumping myself in short, furious jerks, I let out a tortured groan and watch with heavy fascination as cum spurts from my tip, coating her pussy and belly with sticky, white fluid.

"Jesus *Christ*," I pant, my dick softening in my palm. "Fucking hell, Lucy. Your pussy is *divine.*"

Lucy giggles, scrubbing her palms over her sweaty face. "I can't believe we just did that."

I can't stop a smile from spreading, my mouth stretching so wide it's a little painful. "First time for everything."

"You didn't…" She peeks at me through her fingers. "*You know.* Come in me."

Getting up from the bed, I walk over to my desk and grab a pack of wet wipes, taking two before returning to her side. Shuffling her knees apart, I press the cloth against her abused pussy, cleaning the small streak of blood on one leg that's mixed in with everything else.

She winces, letting her head fall back on the comforter.

"I didn't know you were so keen on being a young mom," I tell her, tossing the wipe into the trash.

Her eyes lift. "Huh?"

"Well." I flop down on the mattress, rolling to face her. "I know how shit you are at remembering to take your pills. *On the pill* for you means you probably have a half-used pack in your bag. I come in you, and in a few months, your dad is chasing me through the woods with a bow and arrow, wondering why I fucked up his baby girl's life so early."

Lucy snorts. "He wouldn't chase you with a... No, you're probably right." Sighing, she scoots closer, and I grab her leg, bringing it over my waist, needing her warmth to remind myself that what just happened wasn't my imagination. "I remember you being strictly anti-kid though. Has that, um, changed at all?"

I push some of the dyed-red hair behind her ear, pinning it back with the black strands. "I don't want them anytime soon. Got shit to do, you know?"

Her shit, mostly. I want Lucy to have the most incredible life before anything like that happens.

I'll probably make an awful dad, but Lucy? She'd be the most incredible mom.

One day, if that's what she wants, I'll make her one.

Only me.

Blinking, I push those thoughts away, because we haven't even talked about anything real, and here I am planning our fucking future together. In my mind, the horizon before us is set in stone, but she could be on another planet entirely.

The fact that she came to me and we fucked isn't really enough of an indication. Maybe she just wanted to get off and still hates my guts for what I did.

I wouldn't blame her. I haven't even apologized.

Yawning, Lucy snuggles closer to me, pushing her forehead beneath my chin. I trace the line of her jaw, watching Keats finally come out from under the bed and head for his food bowl in the corner of the room.

"Hey," I tell her when her eyes close, tapping her cheek. "Don't go to sleep. We need to go shower or pee or something. And talk."

She shakes her head. "No thanks. I'm comfy. And sleepy."

God, she's cute. It seems wrong to let it go, but she feels so good beside me that I can't find it in me to object. Not yet anyway.

"Okay," I say, closing my eyes too as exhaustion makes itself known in my body. I wrap an arm around her waist, fitting her more firmly against me. "Just a few minutes though."

And it's the last thing I say to her before slumber takes over.

Chapter 36

Lucy

I've woken up in Asher's bed hundreds of times before. Thousands even, maybe.

But never with his head between my legs, eating my pussy like it's the first breakfast he's been allowed in decades.

My mouth falls open when his tongue spears into me, and I grip the sheets in both hands, twisting them so one corner slips off the mattress.

"Morning," he mutters against my skin, his fingertips pressing into my thighs to keep them open. "You taste fucking incredible."

I stare down at him, maintaining eye contact while he sucks my clit, my stomach twisting into a thousand little knots. I'm still a little groggy and sore from last night, so the dueling sensations morph with my arousal, creating a strange landscape of bursting color and light behind my eyes when I pinch them closed.

He licks me languidly, like he could spend the entire day doing so. It feels really good, but I'm still reeling a bit from yesterday and all the stuff that went down. The things we left unsaid—

Asher pauses, pulling his head up. "You okay?"

Blinking, I give a curt nod. "Yeah, I'm fine."

He doesn't move for a moment, watching me. I shift, suddenly feeling extremely vulnerable with my bare pussy so close to his scrutiny.

Pursing his lips, he disentangles himself from my legs and taps my knee. "Up."

"Huh?"

"Get up for a second."

Confused, I slip from the bed, standing next to it completely naked. Bracing a forearm over my breasts, I cover my pussy with my free hand, waiting while Asher flips onto his back and scoots to the middle of the mattress. He props his knees up and rolls his head toward me.

"Come. Sit."

I narrow my eyes, not liking the commands, but I go anyway, aiming to perch next to him.

His arm lashes out, stopping me. "No, not there. On my face."

Again, I blink. My chest tightens. "What do you mean?"

"I *mean* put your pretty pussy on my face, pup. Ride me and show me what makes you feel the best."

"But it was fine—"

"Fine isn't good enough for me," he says. "If you're able to check out of the moment, I'm not doing it right. So get up here and flood my tongue yourself."

I don't really know what to do, but I'm more curious than nervous. I think.

Swallowing the lump in my throat, I meekly place my knee on the bed, leaning over his abdomen, and plant a hand by his shoulder. The tattoo on his thigh draws my attention for a moment, and I keep my gaze on it as I swing my leg over his waist, grabbing the headboard.

My heart pounds in my mouth. His hands come to my hips, and he stares at me like I'm the most beautiful thing on the planet. Like there's nowhere else he'd rather look.

Sliding farther back, he urges me up his stomach with pressure on my butt. I crawl the length of him, pausing when I reach his chin.

His palm cracks against my ass cheek, and I jolt forward, hovering over his mouth. "Ow!"

"Shut up and sit, Lucy."

I clench my jaw, ignoring the innate desire to snap back at him, because now we're in a *super* vulnerable position, and I don't want to fuck anything up. The fear that he'll ditch me if I do is very prevalent in my chest, and I'm afraid to acknowledge how deep the relationship trauma goes.

Not yet at least. Come first, ask questions later.

Lowering myself to his mouth, I peer over my shoulder at him and then face the wall when I feel his lips graze my flesh. He licks a feather-light path up my seam to my clit, squeezing me, and then forces me down more.

His tongue laps at me as I slowly begin to move my hips, testing which thrusts feel good and where I like the pressure. Dropping one hand to the mattress, I curl my body over him while leaning into the motions, swiveling my pelvis and guiding Asher's tongue in and out of me.

Having him between my legs earlier was amazing, but *this*? Being on top of him, controlling the literal air he breathes?

This is *intoxicating*. All the sounds he makes, little whimpers and grunts vibrating against my wet skin, his hold on my ass, riding the pace I set. I thread my fingers through his hair, grinding and meeting his heavy-lidded gaze, wondering how I could have ever lived without this.

My body tenses, my nerve endings fraying as moans spill from my lips. Asher groans, snaking an arm around my front, gliding his hand up my stomach to palm my breast. He tugs at my nipple, and I unravel, the friction from his mouth sending shock waves of pleasure radiating down my spine.

Jaw locked, my back arches as my orgasm rolls through me, pulling a sound from my esophagus that's half elated human, half tortured animal.

Slumping, I ease myself off Asher's face. Heat tinges my cheeks with the way his lips and chin glisten with my arousal, and a fire burns low in my belly.

Sliding out from beneath me, he tosses a pillow where his body just was, and flips me onto it. I glance at him over my shoulder as he moves behind me and cry out when he plunges a finger inside my pussy.

He runs his free hand over my ass, flicking me. "My name looks fucking delightful right here. Maybe we should get it tattooed."

I snort. "Hard pass."

"Fine. Get used to me writing it on you every time I've got you naked in my bed then."

With the back of his hand, he wipes his mouth and starts stroking me. My toes curl, and I spread my legs wider to give him better access.

"I'm going to fuck you." The way he says it feels less like a warning and more like a simple fact. Not that I'd be protesting, regardless.

Less than a second later, he's rubbing my clit and pushing the head of his cock against my opening. This time as he slides in, he goes much faster, ramming to the hilt before I can suck in a breath. I'm so turned on, though, that it doesn't seem to matter; the fit, while still snug as hell, only stings for a moment before I'm overwhelmed with the *fullness*.

Dropping my forehead to the mattress, I let out a desperate moan as he begins moving, sawing in and out, his cock massaging my inner muscles until I can't breathe. He places a palm on my lower back, then reaches for my hip, drawing me closer to him so my ass is angled higher.

"Your pussy is so goddamn tight, pup. Makes me wanna blow my whole load seeing it swallow my dick like this." He talks through clenched teeth, and I feel a drop of sweat drip onto my skin.

Him saying he wants to come in me makes my heart pound faster, and my breaths erupt in shorter, furious bursts. I'm panting, and I manage to shove one of my hands between me and the mattress, playing with my clit while he continues his sensual assault, his grunts filling my ears like an erotic tune.

"Tell me this feels amazing," he insists, his lips brushing the back of my neck.

Somehow, he's everywhere at once, invading my senses until my entire world is just *him*.

"*So* amazing. You fuck me so good," I blurt between moans. "Please, *please* don't stop."

"Fucking—*shit*."

Reaching under me, he fans his fingers out on my abdomen, and the dual pressure from the top and bottom, mixed with the brutality of his thrusts, has me coming again in minutes, burying my face in the bedsheets.

At the last second, again, he yanks his cock from me with a pained groan, and his cum splashes against my ass, trickling between my cheeks.

"We are in trouble," he mutters, trailing kisses up my spine. "I'm getting addicted to being inside you."

I roll over, giving him a small grin. "I see no issue with that personally."

He wraps me up in the sheet and takes me to the communal bathroom down the hall, where we fuck two more times, despite my certainty that someone is in there listening to us. Asher just places his palm over my mouth when he slides into me, bucking and grinding until we're both coming against the dirty shower stall.

We clean ourselves after that, although since we didn't stop off anywhere, I have to use the shampoo and body wash he has stashed behind a loose tile. Standing in front of the sinks, I comb through my hair with my fingers, and Asher comes up behind me, resting his chin on top of my head.

Tugging at my towel, he pulls a corner down just enough to expose my breast, kneading it before pinching my nipple. I shove my ass into his dick, and he matches the motion, pinning me against the counter.

"Asher," I breathe, bracing myself.

"Sorry," he says into my neck, inhaling. "You've never smelled like me before. It makes me want to bend you over and do bad things."

"This is awfully forward of someone I've yet to decide if I've forgiven or not," I tell him, cocking an eyebrow.

He sighs. "The ten grand for the shelter wasn't enough?"

"My dad once changed all the furniture in his house and office to match my mom's hair color. *And* he *bought* her a whole shelter." Spinning around, I slide my palms up his chest, wiping away the water droplets painting them. "Your contribution was noted and appreciated but only a start."

Leaning down, he cups my cheeks, pressing an open-mouthed kiss to my lips. His nose ring is cool on my skin as he rubs his face against mine. "How many points does a good old-fashioned apology get me?"

I tilt my head, considering. "Three, depending on how good the apology is."

"If I say I'm sorry while my cock is buried in you?"

"Negative points."

He laughs. "Fair enough. I know how easily swayed you are by that particular appendage now of course. It wouldn't be right."

Rolling my eyes, I push him away as my stomach growls. He runs a hand through his damp hair, adjusting the hoop in his nose.

"For what it's worth," he says, meeting my gaze in the mirror. "There wasn't a second I spent during those three years apart when I didn't regret my decision. I thought I was protecting you... No, that's not true. Not entirely."

I watch as he scratches his throat, seeming to grow uncomfortable while he searches for the words.

"Part of it was me wanting to keep you safe. I thought if you came to Avernia unattached from me, no one would know you even knew who I was, and whatever the students like Beckett Dipshit—"

"Dupont."

"—tried to do or say wouldn't affect you. I was convinced this was a bad place to be an Anderson, and I used that as an excuse to bail." He looks up, shrugging. "But the *truth* was that I was terrified of you resenting me. That night you told me about how I was a crutch and that you needed to figure out how to be your own person... I wanted you to do that. I thought my joining you here would somehow inhibit you from it."

Tears sting my eyes when I remember how personal the rejection felt.

I glance down at the chipped vinyl counter, running a fingernail over it. "So bailing was the preferential option? The *only* option?"

"I didn't know what else to—"

"Bull-fucking-shit, Asher."

Whirling on him, I jab a finger into his chest. A concoction of volatile emotion swirls within me like a violent tornado, and I press into the hollow point beneath his collarbone, anger pulsing through me.

For a second, I latch on to the rage. I let it travel along my limbs like a fireball, consuming me as some sort of catharsis for the girl who spent years wishing he'd show up or at least explain himself.

"I *needed* you." My voice wobbles despite my best efforts, but I don't stop. Not yet. "It was terrifying being out here by myself. I mean, Aurora was here, but she gets along with people. She makes friends easily, and it felt like I was in fucking kindergarten again, standing on the sidelines, waiting for her to invite me to come play."

A tear spills down my cheek, and he silently wipes it away with a thumb.

"With you… I never had to wait for an invitation. You dragged me along no matter what you were doing or who you were doing it with. I felt wanted, and maybe it's stupid, but I *needed* that. Or at least I craved it. Everything else was so much fucking work, and being with you—"

My words get lost in my blubbering, the dam behind my eyes breaking with the onslaught of emotions and sensations, all competing for space in my brain at once. Asher's throat bobs, and he gingerly wraps his arms around my shoulders, pulling me into him.

I sob until the cries turn into coughs and keep my face buried in his chest even after they subside.

Again, I'm reminded of when he found me in the forest, alone and petrified, still reeling from Celeste's death.

"I got so tired," I murmur, sniffling. He doesn't ask *of what*, like he already understands the implication—of trying, failing, being alone. The weight of it was constant, pressing down on my shoulders as if to flatten me.

His hold tightens. "I know, baby."

Baby. Something about that word versus all the other nicknames he's ever given me makes my stomach flip, and I eventually pull away, wiping my nose on my towel.

Squaring my shoulders, I lift my chin. "All right, well. Now that we've taken care of that, we can start with the next part of your apology tour."

"Which is?"

"Breakfast."

"Are there any vegan places on campus, or are we gonna have to ask to borrow Foxe's—"

Something hits the closed bathroom door, a crashing noise making me nearly jump out of my skin. It's locked, so no one can just come in, but when Asher starts to walk over to it, the booming sound happens again, like a large object is being repeatedly thrown up against it.

He reaches for the handle, unlocking it, and I move toward him. His head whips around, and he glares at me. "Stay there."

I frown. "Don't tell me what to do, *pretty boy*. I'm not letting you be clobbered to death while I stand by doing nothing."

"You have no sense of self-preservation," he snaps, a pleading look flickering in his brown eyes. "But *I* would like to preserve you. So stay there a second, for Christ's sake."

Crossing my arms, I lean on the sink, gritting my teeth against the urge to defy him anyway. But if there's something dangerous on the other side of that door, without clothes or a weapon, I'm not going to be much help.

Slowly, he pulls the door open, keeping the front of his foot pressed against the bottom in case it's suddenly shoved wider. He sticks his head out into the hall, glancing left and right silently for several minutes.

My body tenses as I wait, and suddenly I'm back in the forest, fear keeping me paralyzed. It isn't until he lets the door swing shut, coming back and grabbing my face, that I realize I'm trembling.

It's easy to forget about the violent crime when everyone else seems to, doubly so when there's other stuff going on in your personal life. Staying busy means not having to think about the things no one on campus wants to talk about and not having to face the reality that life is more out of your control than you ever noticed before.

"Did you see anything?" I ask.

"Nothing. Probably just a prank."

I let that sink in, wondering if he's being honest. For my sanity, I choose to believe him, but other thoughts still nag me.

"What were you doing in the forest that first day?" I question, even though I'm not sure I really want the answer.

Asher exhales, but he doesn't seem to hesitate, really. More like he's trying to decide how much of his soul to bare.

As if it doesn't already belong to me.

Always has.

"I was looking for you," he says, and when he leans in to kiss me once more, I wonder if it's the whole truth.

And if it really even matters.

Chapter 37

Asher

"WHAT'S YOUR GAME HERE?"

Blinking, I squint into the sunlight spilling between the marble statues lining the quad. An angry blond puts a manicured hand on her hip, glaring at me from behind big, pink designer sunglasses.

"My *game?*" I hold up the sketchbook in my lap, pointing at the wordless comic strip across the page. "I'm not sure this qualifies."

Aurora rolls her eyes. "You know, Foxe is the only person in the world who has ever found you funny."

"Yeah? He tell you that himself?" I balance the book on my legs, brushing some pencil debris off the drawing. "How *is* our favorite rock star, by the way?"

Scoffing, she turns, plopping down on the metal bench beside me. "Rock star is a generous term."

"He does okay."

She doesn't respond, and I wonder if she thinks I don't know about them. As if Foxe would ever be able to keep it a secret.

Across the quad, situated a few feet from the front steps of the Lyceum, Lucy hands out flyers that I mocked up for her, detailing the adoption day she's organizing with the Fury Hill Animal Shelter.

She doesn't smile, and most of her interactions with students involve her simply shoving the flyers into their hands, but I can tell she's excited anyway. When they contacted her about setting it up, she'd immediately called her mom for tips, and for a moment, the darkness at Avernia lifted just a little bit.

I should've known the reprieve would be short-lived.

Stretching my arms over my head, I crack my spine and then lean my hands on the back of the bench, glancing at Aurora. "You don't need to worry about me hurting Lucy, you know."

Aurora's green gaze swivels to mine. "I'm not worried about her. She's stronger than all of us kids put together. Lachlan, Logan, River, you, me, and Foxe? We don't hold a fucking candle to Lucy, and you should be terrified of her."

I am. "Then what's the problem?"

She kicks at the ground with her black Mary Janes. "There's no *problem.* I just…"

"Don't want me to take her from you?"

"Yeah." She bumps her shoulder into mine. "I liked having her to myself for a few years."

"If it's any consolation, you can have Foxe."

Her face screws up. "That is a punishment."

"You could just sell him on the black market. I bet there are some unhinged fans willing to take him off your hands."

"You're such a great best friend. You know that?" She snorts, and it's sort of nice to sit here with her like this.

"Well, isn't this cozy?"

Beckett's entire body blocks the sun and our view of Lucy, along with the frame of some other guy with distant green eyes and dark, messy hair. He's thin and pale even compared to Beckett, his hands shoved in the pockets of his black jeans.

He doesn't look at me, instead focusing on his shoes in front of him.

"God, it is too early in the week to be dealing with your shit, Beckett," Aurora says, pushing her sunglasses into her hair.

"You wish I was here for you, PW," he tells her, bringing his gaze to me. "I hear congratulations are in order for Anderson here."

I cock an eyebrow. "For?"

"Word around *The Delphic Pages* is you and a certain little wolf cub are hooking up. Congrats on being the first person to score." He lifts a hand, palm out, in front of my face. When I don't move, my expression flat, he lets his arm fall to his side. "All right, not a fan of spreading the love. I get it. I'd want to keep her under lock and key too, especially with all the weird shit following her around."

Setting my sketchbook aside, I bend down, pulling the utility knife out of my tube sock. I flip open the blade, drawing a line over my thumb with the sharpened edge; blood beads in the cut immediately, and I drag my tongue over it, sealing the wound, before getting to my feet.

Beckett's eyes widen as I take a step in his direction, grabbing the collar of his corduroy jacket before he can move out of my reach. Fisting the material, I yank him close, bringing the knife perpendicular to his face.

He flushes when the tip grazes at his throat, pinching his eyes shut on a wince as my wrist flicks out, cutting through a loose thread near his neck.

"That was bothering me," I say, returning to the bench beside Aurora.

She snickers, hiding it in a pretend cough.

Beckett's nostrils flare. "*Anyway.* I only came over to make sure you were still planning to pledge for the Curators, considering the recent opening in Visio Aternae that just popped up."

"Visio Aternae?" Aurora frowns. "They don't open spots midyear."

"I know. My brother's a stickler." He rolls his eyes but shrugs. "Still, since that Tag kid's death, I guess they had an uneven number, and it was—"

"Tag Holland?" Sitting up straight, Aurora's eyebrows draw in, confusion marring her face. "What are you talking about?"

Beckett's friend finally chimes in. "Uh...he died after a party the other night. Hazing gone wrong or something." The guy glances between us, then at Beckett. "Do people not know about that?"

"What do I look like to you, Eli? Avernia campus police? Dean Bauer doesn't tell anyone shit, so it wouldn't surprise me at all if he kept this under wraps. It happened on his doorstep, practically. He probably doesn't want to look bad to the school board. Lot of deaths on his watch this semester."

Aurora whips out her phone, her thumbs flying. "Yuri was literally just with him at that party. There's no way she wouldn't have said something."

Eli lifts a shoulder, watching her with an unreadable expression. Or rather watching as she texts. "Maybe she doesn't know."

"Curse of the AC student body." Beckett sighs dramatically, lightly punching my shoulder and grinning. "But hey, plenty of student organizations for you to choose from then, right? Although, you know, Curators do have an added layer of protection."

I stare at his hand until it falls away from me. "You realize I was just attacked by a Curator not long ago. Or have you conveniently forgotten my report of that?"

He only agreed to help with the shelter fundraising after I promised not to go to the higher-ups about the attack.

"An overzealous newbie who has been dealt with." Beckett gives me a solemn nod. "Under my leadership, you'd be safe."

Cocking my head, I study him for a few seconds; there's some faint shading beneath his left eye, possibly a bruise, and a scabbed-over cut on his chin. His knuckles are a little raw, as if he's been getting into physical altercations as of late.

Or perhaps one altercation in particular, though his eyes aren't the right color.

Still, I'm not sure it's a smart idea to write him off entirely. He *knows* things, and whether that's because he's involved in them or because his organization really is the lifeblood of the school, I don't know.

"It sounds like you have the hots for me," I tell Beckett, crossing my legs.

Aurora nods, twisting her mouth up, but doesn't look away from her phone. "It really does, dude."

He almost seems offended for a split second, but then his lips twitch, and he crosses his arms over his chest. "And if I do? I've seen the way you look at me, how badly you wanted me to put you on the inductee roster. It's okay to want this. In fact, Fury Hill would probably be delighted—"

"Not interested."

His face falls. "What, because of *her*?"

Hooking his thumb over his shoulder, he points at Lucy, who's out of flyers and gathering her things now. She spins in a circle, likely looking for her dorm room key, since she's finally allowed back in there, before crouching down and picking something up.

"She's not like you and me, Asher." He sounds jealous, but I'm not sure who of, truth be told. "Jesus, she's not even like fucking Eli, who at least has a real shot at making a name for himself now that he's trying to switch into the Curators."

I glance at Eli, who just blinks back.

"Whatever, man." Beckett turns on his heels when I don't say anything else, shoulder-checking Eli as he starts toward the Lyceum. "Your funeral."

As he walks away with his friend in tow, I can't shake the feeling that he means it.

Chapter 38

Lucy

TAG'S DEAD.

For some reason, I'm having a difficult time wrapping my brain around that tidbit.

There's no memorial service, no formal email from the dean's office, no flags flown at half-mast. Pythia is quiet on that front, detailing the schedule for finals and a wine tasting being held in the basement of the Apollodorus—the second largest library on campus—in a few weeks.

If not for the empty chair in Professor Ouellette's class, I might not even believe the rumor. Yet school feels off, and I feel guilty.

"You didn't kill him," Quincy says, making notations in her desktop calendar. "Actually, you weren't even around for this one, so there's nothing to feel guilty about. Hazing takes dozens of lives across the country every year. Survival of the fittest."

"Yeah, how many kids died when you were a student here?" Asher asks. He's sprawled out on the sofa beside me with a copy of some manga propped open. His mere presence is too large for his sister's cozy little office, his long legs draped over my lap.

"Well, there's never been an official tally." She pauses, toying with the rings on her fingers, her long black nails dark against her pale skin.

"Which is shady for multiple reasons. But there were a lot. Some were…
odd, and others were pretty standard."

Standard deaths. At school.

Yet these two were afraid of being here.

I hook my thumb in one of Asher's shoelaces. "It just feels really…
weird that Avernia doesn't seem at all concerned with the fact that at
least three students have died since the beginning of the semester. Dean
Bauer spends more time harassing me than he does investigating, and I
doubt the Fury Hill police department cares, since no founding family
members have wound up dead."

"Yeah, that hasn't happened since I was a student." Quincy exhales,
blowing her bangs out of her eyes, and pushes her glasses up her nose.

"Who?"

She freezes as if just realizing what she said. "Ah…no one?"

Asher looks at her from over his book. "Sounds like you killed her."

Her?

Does he know who she's talking about?

Quincy shakes her head. "Like you have any room to talk."

My eyebrows shoot into my hairline, my eyes volleying between the
two of them. If Noelle were here, the arguing would never stop, but these
two have never been the kind to express themselves vocally. Asher likes
his fists, and Quincy prefers feigned ignorance.

Their other sister, though, lives for verbal confrontation, and a part
of me wonders what would happen if she *did* enroll here, like she was
apparently threatening to earlier in the semester. Having the three of
them on the same campus would be a recipe for disaster, not to mention
the attention—both negative and not—would be unbearable.

Pushing Asher's legs off my lap, I cross my arms over my chest. "You
guys are keeping secrets from me."

"It's nothing, Lucy, honestly." Quincy's dark brown eyes meet mine,
a silent plea hidden in the depths. Like she wants me to drop it.

My knee starts a slow, steady rhythm. I can't *just drop it*. Not when it's
death keeping me up at night while the school seems unbothered. They're

throwing galas and mixers and prepping for finals while pretending this is a good place to get an education.

"Do you believe Tag died from a hazing incident?" I ask.

Quincy blows her bangs out of her face again. "I believe it's possible."

"And the students before—the unexplained suicides from over the years? The disappearances? You think those are all just casualties of the college experience?"

They exchange a silent look, and it pisses me off.

"Well, if you're not going to tell me, I'll go figure it out on my own." I push from the couch, but Asher grabs my wrist, halting me.

"What do you mean by that exactly?"

I shrug. "I want to know what the fuck is going on here, and I think you two know way more than you let on. I'm already aware of your family curse and the people wanting you dead. It doesn't feel like I'm asking anything *huge*, yet you're leaving things out."

"Maybe I leave things out to keep you fucking safe," he growls.

Quincy shifts in her chair. "Why don't you guys—"

"And *maybe* I don't need you to do that." Yanking my hand out of Asher's grip, I narrow my gaze. "Maybe storing me in the dark, where I'm completely helpless, only risks my safety more. I mean, if you'd told me what happened all those years ago to make your sister hate it here, maybe I wouldn't have come."

Asher rolls his eyes. "Yes, you would have, because you're stubborn, and you wouldn't have just taken our word for it."

"Still would've been better than whatever *you* did."

"Oh, we're really not over that, huh?"

"*Fuck you*, Asher. I don't have to be over it just because you think I should be."

Snapping my mouth shut, I spin on my heel and dart for the door, slipping out quickly. My boots feel heavy as I stalk down the hall of the administration building's second floor, but within seconds, footsteps gain on me, and Asher's body is covering mine, pushing me into a dark alcove as he pins me to the wall.

He kisses me hard and fast, urging his thigh between my legs, applying pressure where I like it most. When he disconnects our mouths, he taps his forehead against mine, pushing stray hairs out of my face.

"Didn't seem like that conversation was finished, pup."

"If you aren't going to tell me anything worthwhile, then why should I even bother?"

"Bellamy Dupont." He says the name quickly and quietly, as if afraid someone might overhear, even though it's the weekend and the building is practically empty. "Ring a bell?"

I shake my head.

"Okay, so then what the hell does her death even matter to you?"

"It matters because I want to know what's going on at this school! I feel like I'm losing my fucking mind with every day that passes and another death goes unsolved. Unnoticed. Don't you care at all, Ash? These are people. They deserve some sort of closure or justice or...*something*."

Celeste's cool gaze and Tag's easygoing smile flash in my mind, and the weight of realization hits slowly, like a dripping faucet.

They aren't coming back.

Ever.

People who took chances on me—they don't get to do that anymore. I don't get to continue relationships with them or spend my time turning down their invites to parties, picking up a menstrual cup from the campus store, or laughing internally when they say something funny or dumb or both.

They're just...gone.

And someone here clearly wants me to believe it's my fault.

Asher sighs. "Bellamy Dupont was that one professor's twin sister. She disappeared under 'mysterious circumstances' and was never found. Officially anyway."

"What does that mean?"

"Lucy..."

I pinch his side. "You owe me."

Gritting his teeth, he groans under his breath, releasing me to lean against the wall. "There is a *rumor* that skeletal remains were found in the caves. The Tenarus entrance, specifically. They say that's the reason the higher-ups insisted the tunnels be sealed off to the public."

"Who spread the rumor?"

"Fuck if I know. Hearsay is a disease on this campus. Everyone thinks my sisters and I are responsible for some centuries-old feud, simply because a bunch of pompous fucks decided they wanted to pin the blame on someone. I guess kids who aren't very attached to their namesake in Fury Hill are an easy target."

My tongue sticks to the roof of my mouth as I consider this. If they were considered a good target for political and ethical blame, I wonder what I would look like to the powers that be.

Someone they could use to get an Anderson onto Avernia soil. The people of Fury Hill are superstitious and vindictive enough to do it, especially when they believe the girl to be a problem anyway.

The fire they all think I started—maybe framing me as the culprit was just the beginning.

"What happened when you visited Quincy when she was a student?" I ask, propping my head on the wall.

"Nothing good." He stares straight ahead, his face impassive, though his eyes hold something distant and sinister.

A chill runs over my skin, and I inch closer, wanting to stoke the fire within rather than watch whatever follows him around silently devouring him from the inside.

He grabs my chin, forcing me to look directly into his eyes. "I want you to know that I will do whatever I need to in order to keep you safe, Luce. *Anything* at all, even if it's something that pisses you off. You are the single most important person in my life. But you're right. Not telling you things doesn't help."

I nod, averting my gaze from the intensity of his. There's still a small inkling of something in the pit of my stomach that makes me feel insecure. Like abandonment is on the horizon. What would it take for him to leave again?

"Okay," I say, because I know it's what he wants.

Squeezing my jaw, he moves his head so we're making eye contact again. "I'm not going anywhere."

This time, I don't reply. I just stare into those warm, deep brown eyes—the eyes I fell for when we were thirteen and he gave me that wooden box to keep my dog's ashes in. The eyes anger fled when he was teaching me to drive and I'd stop for every critter crossing the road or get out to help them along.

Eyes that cut like shattered glass when he said he wasn't coming to Avernia.

Shuffling my feet, I swallow. "I'm terrified that you're lying again."

The admission burns as it exits my mouth, but I need him to hear it. I need to say it. Otherwise, I'm afraid I won't ever actually be able to move on. I can distract myself with a thousand other things and pretend I'm fine, but the *terror* will still exist.

Pain flashes in his gaze. He slides his hand behind my ear, threading his fingers through my hair, and tilts my head back. His kiss is electric, like rain and lightning mixed in one, and he spends a few minutes trying to convince me carnally.

It helps, but…

"I know there's nothing I can say that will change your mind," he whispers when he finally pulls away, rubbing my lip with his thumb. "But I mean it this time, okay? I'm *here*, by your side, forever. I'd sooner kill myself than spend another second of this godforsaken life without you."

My heart thumps slow and hard in my chest, swelling with each word even as my brain tries to ignore them.

I love you, I want to tell him. *I love you, and I know you love me, and that scares me.*

If my time at this school has taught me anything, it's that life is unpredictable and you can't really control most of it. Humans are stupid, make poor decisions, and are painfully mortal.

There's no guarantee.

Love is a gamble, and I've never been very good with odds. My brain likes structure and sure things, and this has the potential to crush me.

But instead of saying any of that, I change the subject. He's right anyway; there is no proving an apology with words. Actions are what matter, so all I can do is try to trust that he means it.

Twisting out of his grip, I take a second to collect myself, leaning against the wall next to him. "Are you still trying to join the Curators?"

His eyes cut to me. "On paper. I think Beckett knows some things, and I'm just trying to figure out what."

"*Well...*" Sliding my hand up his arm, I squeeze his bicep, fluttering my eyelashes. "What if we both infiltrated and tried to get information from Beckett?"

"What sort of information do you want?"

I worry my bottom lip. "I think he was out there that night Celeste was killed. I think...no, I *know* I heard him. Maybe we could try to—"

"No."

"You can't just say no."

"Just did. Stay away from him, pup. I mean it."

"Okay, *Daddy*—"

Spinning, he pushes me against the wall once more, this time hooking his hands under my ass and lifting me into his arms. His kisses make me dizzy, and when he glides along my jaw, tugging on the piercing in my earlobe before swooping to bite just beneath it, I cry out, heat scoring a path up my stomach.

"You start calling me Daddy, I'm going to ensure you make me one."

My stomach flips over, and my legs turn to liquid, warmth spreading through me. "Big talk for someone who is afraid of *my* dad."

"Not afraid," he says, grinding his knee against my clit, making me see stars and planets. The whole galaxy really. "I'm respectful of my elders."

"This conversation isn't over, you know. Making out isn't always going to make me forget things," I say between breaths, still in complete astonishment that we're at this point. It feels so natural to have progressed to this, almost as if we didn't lose any time at all.

I find that frightening.

It will hurt much more when it inevitably crumbles.

"What if I'm just making out with you because I want to?"

Poking his nose ring, I grin. "Then carry on."

Chapter 39

Asher

"Hey, Anderson. Could I talk to you for a second?"

I look up from the list of things an RA is apparently supposed to be doing as Muna traipses over from the other side of the quarry. She tugs on the lapels of her plaid blazer, and I note that the emblem isn't a Curator one but two torches and a key and wonder if that means she's switched organizations.

Aurora said Visio Aternae doesn't take new members mid-semester, but maybe that kid's death really did leave a hole they wanted filled.

The question then is *why*.

"Speak." I lean back on the rock I've designated as mine while I watch over Lucy and her little forest cleanup crew. Their orange vests are completely unflattering, yet as my girl bends down to pocket a shiny rock before turning to bark orders at the other students, I find myself wanting to fuck her in nothing *but* it.

Muna exhales but doesn't try to sit anywhere. She crosses her arms, tossing a glance over her shoulder before shuffling a bit closer. "I need to know you won't go spreading this around. It has to stay between us."

My eyebrows arch. "Do you think *I'm* Pythia or something? My desire to talk to most of the people on this campus is nonexistent."

"Still." She narrows her eyes as if sizing me up. "You're an Anderson. A Fury Hill blue blood."

"Until my sister enrolled here, I didn't even know this town existed."

"Doesn't matter, and you know that. Fury Hill cares, even if you don't."

"They hate us."

"It's not hate exactly. They're afraid of you—that's why you were able to enroll. Some people want to appease your family, while others want to destroy it."

"Are these people aware that we lack superpowers?"

She stares at me, unmoved, and I blink, realizing she's waiting for me to promise secrecy still.

"All right." I cross my ankles. "You have my word that I won't say anything to anyone."

Except Lucy, that is. But the other half of my soul doesn't count, right?

Inhaling slow and deep, Muna pinches her eyes closed for a second and lets her arms fall to her sides. Beyond her, I see Lucy watching us, her chin cocked slightly, as if asking to come over.

I give her a short shake of my head, praying she understands that I'm not dismissing her or keeping her out of the loop. After a prolonged moment, she turns back to her group, heading to get more compostable trash bags.

Muna clears her throat. "Since the beginning of the semester, something's been…off. And not just with the student deaths—programs have been getting secretly rewritten, professors have been dismissed from positions they've held for years, and there's this veil of mystery that the administration is hiding behind. Ever since the fall budget meeting when there were questions about spent funds with no receipts. We're talking *millions* of dollars here, Anderson."

"Is that…supposed to alarm me?" I ask, raising my brows. "I'm an art major, not finance or even political science. My assumption has always been that colleges misappropriate funds, and they *love* slashing more liberal programs to allocate money elsewhere."

"But Avernia is a *liberal* school. It was literally founded on the basis of amplifying the arts, the humanities, and the spirit of mortality. Mortui vivos docent, right? The dead teach the living. That's our motto. Yet it feels like they're doing away with the heart of the school."

"Maybe they're adjusting to fit the times."

Muna shakes her head. "No, it's not a simple reconstruction, it's total annihilation. The programs are being slashed and the money is just disappearing. Employment and policy protocol is being ignored… It's almost like someone wants the school to fall apart and then no longer exist." She rubs her chin, pushing some of her black curls off her shoulder. "The dead can't teach the living if the living have nothing and nowhere to learn."

Looking out past her again, my gaze travels the expanse of the lake, which extends all the way to the mountainside, disappearing beneath. The water is so black, it's impossible to see into.

How anyone retrieved Celeste's body without a legitimate rescue crew ever coming to the scene and drawing attention is beyond me. Especially considering the effort it would have taken to haul her to Erebus, string her up in Lucy's dorm, and never be spotted.

It would *have* to be someone with an inside connection. Someone who could convince the dean or the campus police to look the other way while they carried on with their nefarious acts.

A memory rears its head in my mind.

Foxe is looking for bottled water, so I have to make this quick.

The brunette spits as I remove her gag, glaring at me. Malice drips from her like the blood on her chin, spattering onto her knees below.

Mere minutes on this fucking campus, and already, the reminder of why I didn't want to come here is evident.

Someone has it out for me. Otherwise, what purpose would this bitch have had to attack a random guy in the woods? I wasn't even following her, didn't see her coming, because I was too busy trying to execute my own plan: burn this university down before it can ruin anyone else's life.

The bruising on my side throbs a bit, but nothing too bad. I'm fucking lucky I noticed the knife before she drove it into my shoulder. I don't trust Foxe to know how to properly handle an injury.

Yanking on the girl's ponytail, I make her look up at me, wielding the blade before her. Not my blade, since I don't want this tied to me later. The less DNA left behind during the initial crime, the easier it is to clean up, Dad always says.

"Why did you attack me?" I ask her, keeping my voice low. We're out by the gazebo and abandoned building, the place that's haunted me for years, and I don't want another fucking ambush.

"We've been waiting for you," she hisses, her eyes devoid of anything besides pure hatred.

"Creepy." I pull on her hair again until she whimpers. "Explain what you mean by that."

She shakes her head. "That isn't part of the deal. You don't get to know what's going on before they get you and everyone you love."

"Look, I don't have very much patience. Really, any at all. So if you don't tell me something important in the next three seconds, I'm going to take that as a threat and act accordingly."

A maniacal laugh comes from somewhere deep within her. "Stupid, stupid boy. Just like your sister and your grandmother and your ancestor. People like you think they own the world, when really, it's just waiting to swallow you whole. Cronus Anderson took gleefully from our town, and you and the others will pay for his transgressions."

I make a face, wondering why this student talks like she just stepped out of a novel from the nineteenth century, and shove her away. Exhaling, I bring my hand to my forehead and twist in a circle, trying to decide what the hell I should do.

Coming here was a mistake, but I can't really go back. Especially not with the cryptic email sitting in my inbox, suggesting actual danger to the people I care about. Leaving Lucy and Aurora alone now is not an option.

Not this time.

Still, the people at this college are clearly convinced that this family curse is real or are at least interested in making me think it is. Maybe the idea is that if enough people believe in the curse, fewer will question motives when I wind up dead.

I'm only half paying attention when the little bitch launches herself at my back, slipping her bound hands over my neck as she tries to strangle and tackle me. Unfortunately, I'm half a foot taller and much stronger, so I overpower her easily, shoving her into the ground face-first.

Digging my boot into the back of her skull, I push down until she begins to panic, letting up only enough for her to suck in some frenzied gulps of air. She cries out, and I almost feel bad about doing this for a second as I twirl the knife between my fingers, contemplating.

Pausing, I crouch and wait for her sobs to subside.

"They curate it all, you know…" she manages, glaring at me. "The deaths and deception. They run the papers, the online forums, the local authorities. What you see is not reality. This school, this town… They're cruel. Evil. And they won't rest well knowing you're around. Or knowing I failed."

"Why do they want me dead so badly?" I don't even know who they are, but at this point, the reasoning behind it all feels a bit more important.

"Not dead," she says. "Suffering."

I don't see where the new knife comes from, just see her hand shift from the corner of my eye, and then she's rolling, driving the thing right into her own throat.

The force of it causes blood to splash across my chest and face. She assaults herself multiple times until finally dropping the handle.

Somehow, she's still breathing, despite her head almost being detached from her body. I'm soaked in crimson, staring in disbelief as she clings to life.

Her glassy eyes find mine. Something passes through them. An evil I don't understand.

Chest heaving, I take her knife and finish the job.

And then get to work leaving a message for whoever sent her, noting the distinct screams echoing from somewhere else in the forest. Not Lucy's screams, but she could be next.

When I've finished with the stranger, temporarily hiding her in a carpet I found behind the abandoned house, I take off in search of my former best friend, aware that I have fewer answers, more problems, and no way to explain the blood.

Swallowing down those memories, I look at Muna. "Say I believe you. Who, in theory, do you think is behind the shit going on?"

She scratches at the back of her hand. "Who says I have suspicions?"

"I'm assuming you wouldn't waste my time otherwise."

"At the beginning of the semester, I thought Beckett and some other Curators were acting kind of…weird. They were skipping classes, throwing way more parties than usual, and disappearing for days on end. It's not uncommon for Curators to go off and do their own things, because their parents call them back home a lot for events and stuff, but we're required to submit logs detailing our whereabouts. They weren't requesting leaves to travel. All their absences were off the books.

"We have these weekly meetings that are required for active members to attend, unless there is a well-documented and sponsor-approved excuse, and the dean was suddenly stamping a lot of forms, or students wouldn't show up at all. Curators are *very* serious about their membership; if you're put on probation, there's a good chance you'll be removed, and if you're removed, you can't join again. Most kids don't want to risk their families' wrath."

Ugh. College fucking blows.

"So it seemed odd to me that our president especially was one of those students we couldn't keep track of. But no one's reported his or any other absences to the school board or the Curator chapter heads. No one seems to care about *anything* here, and it's almost like…"

She trails off, and I lean forward, draping my arms over my knees. "Like if they don't care, they figure no one else will either?"

Muna nods. "I know you don't have any reason to believe me, but I also found this."

Checking to make sure we're still alone, she inches forward, shoving a photograph into my hand. It's a full-color picture where rows of students in blazers pose in front of a quad statue where the Curator emblem is spray-painted.

Written on it in bold red marker, covering some familiar faces like Beckett and Tiernan, is a three-headed beast.

Muna points to a back corner of the picture, where a grainy couple stands staring at each other; they're hard to see, but I'd recognize that red and black hair anywhere. Not to mention *me* in front of her.

It's us from not long ago, after we fought and made up in the admin building. The Curators had been in the quad taking their fall membership photo, and I'd had to practically drag Lucy from it to keep her from confronting Beckett.

Every person in the photo is marked out, except for Lucy.

I gnaw on the inside of my cheek, crimson rage spilling into my veins. "Where did you get this?"

"Well, that's the thing," she replies. "I found it in Beckett's dorm. And with him being marked out, it *looks* like he's part of the threatened group, but why would it be in his dorm if that's the case? A threat like this isn't something you take lightly, especially a prominent Dupont kid. They'd be all over the news and school getting to the bottom of things."

Staring hard at the photo, I wait for her to continue, piecing the puzzle slowly together myself.

"I think he's trying to frame Death's Teeth for something, which would make sense given all the markings around school—Death's Teeth's biggest known crime was basic vandalism until this semester, after all the weird shit started happening. Everything else has only ever been rumor, and after you showed up, it turned to blood and murder."

"I thought they were a violent vigilante group? Wouldn't blood be *their* calling card?"

Muna shakes her head. "Nobody knows anything about them really. The school acknowledges them to make things seem legitimate, but no one's ever seen them. All they have is an incomplete chapter application and their emblem."

"The three-headed beast," I say pointlessly, glancing at the photograph again. "So either Beckett is trying to frame Death's Teeth *and* make it look like Lucy is involved, knowing I'll leave if she does, or..."

"He *is* Death's Teeth."

Chapter 40

Lucy

WILLA AND ELI SHARE A SILENT LOOK BEFORE THEY RESUME PICK-
ing up debris from Lake Lerna's bank. I groan when they shift their focus
away from me, crossing my arms over my chest.

"Come *on*, you two. It would be fun."

I'm not used to begging people to go out with me, so their hesitance
is making the anxiety ratchet up in my chest.

Willa laughs, pointing at me with her pickup stick. "Lies. Attending
a Curator house party after what happened at the last one? I like being
alive, thank you."

Eli purses his lips. "Well, they said it was hazing, so…"

"Do you have any personal experience to back that up?" Willa asks.
"You weren't hazed, so how do you know how dangerous it may or may
not have been? What if all those rumors are true about the forest parties
and the rituals they do during them? Death's Teeth isn't the only group
with a reputation, you know."

"Are you…saying Tag was murdered? By *Curators*?" Eli's laugh is
humorless, as much as we've ever gotten from him.

His dismissal makes me even more uneasy.

I know what I heard.

Willa cocks a pierced eyebrow. "Are *you* suggesting we go and find out?"

"It's not like you had other plans," he says, shrugging and giving me a sheepish glance. "As long as you refrain from attempting to be initiated, I think you'll be fine."

"So…" I interject, tilting my head. "We're going?"

"This *sounds* like a trap," Willa replies, squinting at Eli. "How am I supposed to trust someone who defected from Visio Aternae in favor of the Curators? Aren't you, like, on their payroll now or something?"

A small blush crawls up his face. "I didn't defect. My dad suggested I broaden my horizons. You try arguing with the state's top prosecutor."

"Selling your soul is broadening your horizons?" she asks.

He doesn't respond, moving down the embankment.

Willa frowns, turning her back to us as she silently ponders. In truth, I don't *want* to go to the stupid party, but we have a holiday break coming up soon, and in-person classes were canceled for the week due to a last-minute faculty retreat drawing a good portion of the professors away. I don't know when I'll be able to get Beckett alone before we leave.

And I can't travel home with the weight of the unknown on my shoulders. It's too unsettling.

Asher doesn't want me to get involved, but since Beckett and I have a history—albeit, one I fully regret—I figure maybe he'll give me *something*. As long as I don't go anywhere alone with him, I'll be fine.

Hence the invitation to these two.

Willa groans. "Ugh, *fine*. I'll go. Professor Dupont canceled rehearsal for the weekend, so—"

"So slacking off should be okay?"

The three of us jump at the sound of the professor's voice. My head whips to the side as he approaches in a dark green sweater, his brown hair askew, a strange flush to his cheeks. Almost as if he ran here, though he doesn't seem winded in the slightest.

His green eyes find mine, and he nods. "Ms. Wolfe. Glad to see your commitment to wildlife cleanup prevails."

I bow my head back. "Thanks for not telling the dean I enjoy it."

"Oh, I wouldn't dream of spilling secrets." He maintains eye contact for a fraction too long, and I swallow, my mind flickering back to the papers that fell out of his briefcase that day in the quad. The Death's Teeth emblem hidden within. "I prefer it when my students trust me. Makes teaching them much easier."

Willa waves a hand. "If I say I trust you, can I be moved up from understudy in *Hamlet*?"

He glances at her, and she blinks, as if taken aback by having the very attractive man's undivided attention. Before this semester, I wasn't really accustomed to it either. It's unnerving, and that's without whatever he's hiding.

"Did I hear you say you were glad that we didn't have rehearsal this weekend?"

Willa's face pales. Eli shuffles farther down the embankment, distancing himself from the secondhand embarrassment.

"Uh, well…not exactly," she stammers. "I just pointed out that going to a party was possible since we—"

"A party?" Professor Dupont folds his arms over his chest. "Not the Curator one, I hope?"

"Um…" She looks at me for assistance.

I sigh, adjusting my vest. "Yes, that one. Your brother loves his soirees."

Professor Dupont's jaw clenches, highlighting his supreme bone structure. "Indeed he does." He stares off into space for a few seconds, then seems to shake whatever internal struggle he's having and refocuses on us. "Well, ladies, I trust you'll keep out of trouble in the event that you do attend."

"That's always the plan," I mutter, still studying him like a scan under a microscope. "How come you're not at the retreat?"

"Oh, I'm much too busy here. Campus unrest has caused me to stay late in my office many evenings over the last few weeks, allowing students reprieve from the terrible things happening." His gaze simmers as it clashes with mine. "You're always welcome too, Lucy."

I nod, though there's no way i4n hell I'm taking him up on the offer.

There's no doubt that Sutton Dupont is hiding something. Maybe a *lot* of things.

And I bet his brother knows about them.

The first night I get my dorm room key back, I return and see *all* Celeste's stuff is gone. Her parents had come at some point after the crime scene cleaning crew and removed everything, leaving behind a couple of sweaters for Yuri and a pair of gold earrings for me.

Two steps into the room, and my throat closes up. It feels *wrong* being here when she isn't, so I turn around and go down the hall, opening Asher's door.

He's lying in bed with his back against the headboard, clad in a pair of green-and-black plaid pajama pants. His knuckles are dirty, dried ink smudged in the ridges, as he fans his hand across his sketchbook, glancing up when I enter.

"I was wondering when you'd make a booty call," he says, grinning. It wipes off his face in seconds though when he peers closer at me. "Shit. What happened?"

Shaking my head, I open my mouth to explain, but no words come out. Only a fat sob escapes, rendering me a blubbering mess again as I press my fists into my eyes.

No matter what, I see her. Dead and alone because of me.

The mattress creaks as Asher moves. "Lucy."

Sniffling, I suck in a breath of air and let my arms fall. My smile feels watery and forced. "Sorry. I just needed a minute."

When I look back at him, his arms are wide open, legs spread slightly. The sketchbook sits on his nightstand, abandoned in my favor.

My throat burns as I push one foot forward. God, I don't want to need him like this, but I can't help it.

He's always been the safest place in the world for me.

Another smaller sob peals out of me, and I sprint in his direction, launching myself at him. He catches me with a tiny grunt, wrapping me totally in his embrace as I bury my head in his neck.

This is real, *I tell myself. Asher's real. Alive. The heart beating in his throat and chest are proof of that. If nothing else, I have him.*

"I couldn't do it," I mutter into his skin, keeping my eyes closed. "I couldn't be in there by myself."

"That's okay." He strokes a hand over my head. "It hasn't really been that long. These things take time."

"I just…" Staring at the expanse of skin before me, watching it blur, I force down my fear. "I keep thinking about how I just stood *there. They were hurting her, and I didn't do anything. I didn't move, didn't try to get help or intervene."*

Shame swirls around my insides, holding me tight in its ugly grip.

"How can I call myself a good person when at the time someone needed help the most, I was a total fucking coward? I was so concerned with my own well-being that I just let them kill Celeste instead. Maybe if I'd done something, she'd still be here."

Asher tenses under me. "And maybe if you'd tried to help, you'd both *be dead. Avernia would be burned to the ground, and the wildfire would spread, because I'd make it uncontainable."*

Pulling back a little, I meet his furious gaze. Brown irises hardening like raw quartz.

"You'd burn down the school for me?"

"Lucy."

He cups my cheeks, sliding his thumbs over them as more tears fall. My heart aches, pumping so hard against my ribs that it feels like it might break out of me entirely.

"I would raze the earth just for a smile from you. There is nothing I would not do, and especially if you were ever harmed or endangered. I know you hate violence…you would not enjoy the man I'd become in the event of your demise."

Tentatively, I lift my fingers to his lips, brushing the tips over them as he speaks, like I'm trying to imprint his words on my body.

I love you, Asher.

I love you so much.

Please, let what you're saying be true. I want to believe it is.

I would love you no matter what you did.

Sighing, I slump against his chest. "Still. I lasted sixty seconds in my dorm room. It's pathetic."

"You experienced a traumatic event, Luce. You're not pathetic. You're human."

"Same thing." *Wiping my nose, I look up at him.* "You saw it all too, and you're fine."

"She wasn't my friend."

"But you're always fine. Nothing affects you, and it never has." *Straightening, I push my hair from where the tears have glued it to my face and exhale shakily.* "Teach me your ways, O Great One."

The corners of his mouth twitch. "This isn't a dysfunction you need to learn. There's nothing wrong with feeling."

"I know that, I just…wish I didn't sometimes." *I slump forward, my forehead leaning against his chin.* "It's hard."

"Most things that are worth anything in life are hard."

"Ew. You sound like my dad. Or your dad."

That makes him laugh, and he rubs my back in soft, soothing circles. "I'm not always as unaffected as I may appear, you know. You've seen how quick to anger I am. And the years we spent apart? I was a fucking disaster. Plus, were you not listening to what I just said? Every time you so much as cry, it tears me up inside. I care about you, Luce, and I love that you care about people so much."

"You don't think it's stupid?" *I ask in a small voice.*

"Never."

I relax a little, softening against his embrace. The comfort I find in his arms should maybe alarm me, but at the moment, I'm too blissed out from his scent and warmth to really care.

"Can I stay here tonight?"

He shifts, and then the comforter is being pulled up and tucked around my shoulders. His hold on me tightens, and his lips skim my scalp. I get sleepy all of a sudden, my eyelids drooping until they remain closed, so I barely hear his answering whisper against my temple.

"You can stay forever."

A few days later, I'm reading in my dorm room when Foxe kicks my door in. I turn in my desk chair, a bland expression on my face when the handle lodges into the plaster.

Cringing, Foxe drags a hand through his messy, slightly damp hair and yanks the door from the wall. "Fuck, my bad. It was locked."

"So you kicked it?"

"I didn't think you'd let me in if I knocked."

"I wouldn't have."

"You're so *mean*, Lulu. Ash-tree is such a bad influence." Walking over, he flops down onto my bed, and I appreciate how the both of us are expertly ignoring the room divider I've erected by hanging multiple sheets from the tiled ceiling, blocking off Celeste's side from view.

Since I've been granted access to my room again, I've been attempting to spend more time in here, but living with her half being exposed was not an option. Dean Bauer agreed—after a call from my mother threatening to come back to campus—to put a hold on filling my roommate assignment for the time being, so for now it's just me and my thoughts. Flipping my Landscape Ecology textbook shut, I bring my legs into the chair with me and swivel toward Foxe. He's got an arm propped behind his head, the sleeves of his T-shirt rolled up, revealing the plethora of patchwork tattoos on his skin, and a strange expression on his face.

I'm used to a bored, restless Foxe. Happy Foxe, and obnoxious, overly touchy Foxe.

This one looks crestfallen somehow.

Setting my chin on the heel of my hand, I squint at him. "What's wrong with you?"

His gaze shifts to me. "Nothing?"

I cock a brow.

Sighing loudly, he rolls over onto his side, looking at me with big green, puppy-dog eyes. "Asher ditched me to do some errands for his sister, and I'm *dying* here. Turns out school is really goddamn depressing when you're not enrolled."

It's on the tip of my tongue to mention that it's depressing even when you *are*, but I don't. Like me, Foxe barely scraped by in high school, and since he comes from a huge music empire, college was never on his radar anyway.

Problem is Foxe James is also likely part golden retriever, so he goes where his loyalties lie. I suspect that's why he's been hanging around Avernia with Asher rather than continuing to tour by himself.

Considering Aurora's also here and averse to his presence, I'm certain the entire experience has been less than thrilling. It's a wonder he hasn't jumped in Lake Lerna at this point.

"What do you even spend your days doing?" I ask, pulling my sleeves over my knuckles.

"I've got, like, a whole fucking album written. It's the only reason my dad agreed I could come, if I was productive." He makes a face, rolling his eyes. "He and my mom worry all the time about stupid shit I might get into if I'm not occupied. Like I'm a dog that needs constant stimulation."

I wince, realizing I just made that comparison and that it could be applied to me as well. I'd hate it if it was.

"In their defense, you did get into trouble a lot before we graduated," I say. Mostly with illegal betting and underage drinking, but still.

"Sure, but eventually, you'd think they'd learn to trust me again, right? I mean, I keep Asher around to make sure I'm in line, but most of the time, I don't really need him."

There's no conviction to the last few words he utters, as if he doesn't fully believe them.

Foxe and I are codependent. We stuck our flags on ships that could survive tumultuous seas, aware that there'd be times we didn't feel strong enough on our own.

Or maybe too terrified to try.

Sometimes, I think that means he gets me more than Asher or Aurora or my family. There's no substitute for experience.

"Okay," I say, clasping my hands together and pushing to my feet. "Let's go."

"Go where?"

"Party in the quarry. You clearly need human interaction, and I need to not be trapped in here with a wallowing man-child."

He grins, climbing from the bed. "Isn't this the party Asher didn't want you going to?"

Throwing a cardigan over my maroon sweater, I slide my stocking-clad feet into a pair of Doc Martens. "So? He's not the boss of me."

"True. He's always enjoyed being on the receiving end of that."

I pause, giving him an incredulous look. "Something is very wrong with you."

Sighing, he drapes an arm over my shoulders, tugging me close. He's a couple of inches taller than Asher, who's already got eight on me, so I feel miniature next to him.

"There is," he says, his voice solemn in a way that feels alarming. "But let's go get drunk and forget about it. I'll keep ya safe if anyone tries anything weird."

Chapter 41

Lucy

WE DON'T.

Get drunk, that is.

After we arrive at the quarry, I immediately introduce him to Eli and Willa, who recognize him from an EP he released a couple of years ago. He gets excited instantly, snapping back into his regular self like nothing was ever amiss in the first place.

We get beers from one of the people passing them out at the keg, although I make it clear to Foxe that he should *not* be going overboard.

I don't want to baby him, but I also don't want to drag home his goofy, drunk ass later.

Asher would come do it for me, no questions asked, but I don't want to see the look on his face when he learns I went to this party or that I made Foxe join.

Not that he explicitly asked me not to come. When I brought it up, Asher just said he wouldn't be able to go and he'd be more comfortable if I didn't because he doesn't trust Beckett.

Well, neither do I. But I *know* Beckett knows things, and I want the answers. If I wait around for Asher to find them out, I'll be pushing fifty before anything comes to light.

The air does feel extra cool out here tonight though. I can't tell if it's all due to the weather or if the terrain is throwing in a biting chill.

I'm sure it isn't the ghosts, since they don't exist.

A breeze sweeps through the crowd, and I cross my arms against it. *Officially anyway.*

I find Yuri near a row of kegs, nursing a beer. She's got a scarf wrapped around her neck, her black hair tucked into the thick white fabric, and she lights up when she spots me. A girl I recognize from Professor Dupont's class sits next to her, gripping the neck of a vodka bottle.

"Lucy!" Jumping up, Yuri wraps her arms around me, some of her beer sloshing onto my shoulder. "Aurora's not here. Had some last-minute fashion emergency and had to go to the mall in Concord. Although she thought you'd be hanging out with your new *boyfriend*. We didn't think you'd make it." She wiggles her thin, dark brows, poking my side.

"He had other things to do," I reply, my eyes widening. "And he's not my boyfriend."

Truthfully, we haven't really talked about what we *are*, and I don't want to be the needy one who brings it up, even though I desperately crave the label. Having things neatly blocked off makes my brain feel more relaxed, and whatever I have going on with Asher makes my heart happy but is also fucking with me mentally.

I suppose it's that fear too. That he isn't really helping his sister do anything tonight and has just taken off without me.

I'm trying to trust him, but old habits die hard, I guess.

"Ooh, scandalous." Yuri grins, moving to sit back beside her companion. "Friends with bennies then? One-night stand?" She turns to the other girl. "Got any advice for her, Sara-Sofia?"

The girl runs her fingers through thick, luscious brown locks. "Please, like I need Curators reporting back to my very Catholic, Colombian parents that I'm sleeping around instead of focusing on my schoolwork. No thank you."

"You could do both," I suggest.

She gives me a wry smile. "Nah, too much work for me. I figure I'll get my astronomy degree and let them marry me off one day. Easier for all of us."

Cocking my head to the side, I try to place her in my mind but can't. "You really don't care about who they pair you with?"

"They love me, so I know they'd choose a good guy. Honestly, as long as he's not a Curator, I think I'd be set." Sara-Sofia shrugs. "Those guys are *weird*. Always speaking in Latin and talking about performing rituals to honor their ancestors. Like, this is *New Hampshire*. Get a grip."

"*Death to Curators!*" Yuri chants, thrusting her Solo cup in the air. I guess she's already tipsy. Exhaling, she drops her arm and nods, leaning into Sara-Sofia. "They're the *worst*. Can you believe they let that Tag kid drink himself to death? And he was so cute too."

"No need to worry, ladies." Foxe props his elbow on my head. "Plenty of cuteness to go around."

Sara-Sofia snorts, going back to her phone in her lap and the vodka in her hand.

Yuri sizes Foxe up, pursing her lips. Then she looks at me. "I don't see it."

"See what?"

She points a finger between us. "This pair. You guys don't have matching vibes. He's sunshine, and you're *maybe* a new moon."

"I'm so glad you made it out of your funk," I mutter, shoving Foxe away.

"Our moms are cousins," Foxe offers even though no one asked. He slings his hands into his jeans pockets, rocking back on his heels. "So we're just friends."

"And barely that." Grabbing him by the sleeve of his jacket, I drag him away, waving at the two girls over my shoulder. Once we're out of earshot, I push at his chest, sending him stumbling a bit.

He catches himself before tripping over a pile of loose rocks, offense coloring his face. "What the hell was that for?"

"Did you come to this party just to make things awkward with my friends?"

"Well, it would've been more awkward for you if she went on to assume we were dating. Unless…"

He pauses, narrowing his hazel eyes as he leans in, as if inspecting a new vehicle.

"Oh! You *want* them to think that, don't you? I mean, I'm sure my street cred won't weigh as heavily around here as Asher's, but I get it. We can pretend if you want—"

Lifting my leg, I move to knee him in the balls; at the last second, he blocks the blow with his shin, howling with laughter as he ducks away from my reach.

"Holy shit," he says, flipping his dark hair from his forehead. "Wait till I tell Asher that you just tried to assault me. He'll be so fucking excited to know he's really rubbing off on you."

Gritting my teeth, I glance back at Willa and Eli, standing around a small bonfire where we left them. "What happened back there, by the way? My friends weren't good enough for you to keep company?"

"Friends, huh?" He whistles low, looking at them over his shoulder.

I don't know why, but him questioning that makes heat score across my face, shame billowing inside me. *Is it wrong of me to consider them friends?*

"They're all right, I guess. The chick is a little obsessive though, and that Eli dude barely said three words to me the whole time. Besides, I came here to hang out with *you*, Lulu. Aren't you supposed to be scheming or something? Let me help!"

"It's not scheming. I'm just trying to collect some information from some potentially shady characters."

He straightens his spine, cracking his knuckles one by one. "All the more reason for me to come along. You'll need muscle."

"Have you ever won a fight against Asher?"

"Well, that's not really a fair judgment. I'm not supposed to hit him back." Reaching up, he strokes his chin, as if just realizing that the rules they made up when they were kids don't particularly benefit him. "But that's beside the point anyway. I can still hold my own without touching him—"

"*Lucy!*" Willa bounces over to where we're standing, a bottle of beer in her hand. "Some people have suggested taking the party elsewhere. Will you go with us?"

My eyebrows draw in, wondering why they're wanting to move things. One of the multiple bonfires erupts into a sudden fireball, rolling across the rock path, igniting on loose twigs and leaves. It hasn't rained in a few days, so everything is extremely dry, creating a definite hazard.

The ecology major in me wants to stay and monitor the situation, even as a few kids start tossing bottles of alcohol into the raging fire rather than trying to stomp it out.

Idiots. You'd think the incident at Lethe's would have taught them how quickly a fire can spread and become potentially deadly, but no. Lessons from the living aren't good enough for Avernia students.

Maybe this place *is* cursed.

Groaning, I turn and see Beckett scurrying along the edge of the quarry, huddled between two tall figures with their hoods pulled low on their heads. They move in the direction of the mountains, and a trail of others follow.

I relent to Willa, and she hooks her arm in mine, pulling me along so we can catch up with Eli at the back of the follow party. At least Asher can't say I have no sense of self-preservation now.

Foxe hovers close behind me, his hands shoved in his pockets. "New Hampshire is fucking freezing at night."

Eli looks over his shoulder, then reaches into his own coat, pulling out mini bottles of tequila. Willa squeals, launching herself at one, and Eli passes the other two to us, lifting his in a cheers gesture. We all clink, drinking quickly as we quietly continue trailing behind the Curators.

After I've downed my shot, Eli hands me another, and I take it for liquid courage. The back of Beckett's head is plainly visible from where I'm standing, so I tell Foxe and the other two that I'll be right back.

Foxe stumbles a step, but Willa steadies him, beaming up at his tall frame. "Someone can't hold their liquor. What would your fans think, rock star?"

He doesn't say anything, but as I push myself ahead and start weaving through the crowd, I can feel his gaze on me. Watching, taking his role as guard dog very seriously.

My shoulder brushes Beckett's as I reach him, and the small party starts to disperse in a clearing near one of the blocked-off cave openings. Tenarus, I think this one is called. Or Tartarus, maybe. They're so sparsely visited that it's hard to remember, especially when the Primordial Forest is so vast anyway.

Music blares from a large portable speaker set up at one end of the clearing, and things seem to pick back up here, albeit in a much calmer manner than with the main party.

If all Curator functions were as low-key as this, maybe they wouldn't be so bad.

Unless Beckett was in attendance. His presence sours everything, which is proved when he turns to me with a suspicious glint in his eyes, baring his teeth so they're highlighted in the moonlight.

"What the fuck are you doing here?" he demands, grabbing my elbow and yanking me off to the side. "I don't believe you were invited."

"The party was open to everyone," I reply, trying to pull out of his hold. "Pythia posted about it."

He scoffs, releasing me with a shove. "Pythia. That bitch is always spreading shit online. Does she not realize how easily she could get us shut down with her big fucking mouth?"

After my conversation with his brother earlier this semester, I'm not entirely convinced Pythia is a real person rather than some artificial intelligence tool collecting data on the students here and posting on an automated schedule. Her forums are generally filled with gossip that no one ever bothers to check, and *no one* seems to know who the hell is behind the account.

This is what you get when you opt out of paper and into digital.

Chaos.

Shaking his head, Beckett lets his gaze drop down the length of me before he meets my eyes again. "Where's your boyfriend, Wolfe?"

Swallowing, I inch forward a step, casting a quick look over my shoulder to make sure we're not being watched. Foxe, perched on a short rock wall with his hands behind him, stares while Willa and Eli seem to be having some heated discussion right next to him, and even though I know it'll piss him off, I reach and push Beckett deeper into the brush.

I don't want an audience. It probably won't take Foxe but a second to come after me when I don't reappear immediately, so I'll have to work quickly.

My hand falls sluggishly away from Beckett's chest as his back hits a tree trunk. I watch it return to my side, the beer and tequila catching up with my brain already. I can still think and see straight, but I'm definitely tipsy, which gives me enough courage to do this at least.

"Alone with the Curator president?" Beckett gasps, pressing his fingers to the center of his chest. "What would Asher Anderson say?"

I roll my eyes—I think. "You've got me here for the first time in three years, and your thoughts are about him?"

"Can't they be about both?" he asks, lifting his eyebrows. Flames seem to ignite in his irises, and he slinks toward me, brushing some hair from my shoulder. His gaze drops to my lips, and my stomach rolls in protest. "If this is your way of proposing a threesome, I'm more than on board, sweetheart. Tell me where to meet the two of you, and I'll rock both of your worlds."

My mind races, trying to grapple with what he's revealing here, but I can barely register it before other thoughts shoot through my brain, reminding me that I'm here for a reason.

Moving back, I try to keep my expression neutral. "Asher wouldn't be into that."

"Because he isn't into men?"

"No, he is, but he doesn't know you that well, and that'd be a deal-breaker."

Plus, he wouldn't want anyone other than me.

Right?

That's what he's been trying to tell me all along. I've just been too afraid to listen.

Beckett nods. "And you?"

"What about me?"

His foot slides forward, hooking behind mine. Trapping me. Fear clouds my lungs like a thin fog, but I ignore it, aware that we're only feet from the party. All I have to do is scream, and Foxe will come running.

It's weird he hasn't already.

"I'm a little shy," I say, trying to remove myself from his stance, but each time I go to lift my foot, it feels like it's submerged in thick sludge.

"Aw, that's just my type when it comes to girls," Beckett coos, cupping my cheek with one hand. "The shy ones are always secret freaks. Your roommate was one too, so I'm not surprised you all got along."

The hair on my body stands up. "How well did you know Celeste?"

He pauses, thinking. "Not *that* well. We hooked up a few times."

"When was the last time?"

The pause ensues, and the silence between us grows heavier. Or maybe that's me growing heavy, I don't know. My eyelids droop, and I give my head a tiny shake to keep them open.

Beckett lets his hand fall from my face. "What are you asking exactly?"

Maintaining eye contact even as my entire body vibrates with the urge to look elsewhere, I lift my chin and roll my shoulders. "Where were you the night she died?"

For several seconds, he doesn't respond. We just stare at each other, the air turning frigid around us.

Finally, something seems to shift, and he moves back, reaching for the buckle of his pants. "You want to find out, Wolfe, you ask *nicely*."

I continue staring at him, my limbs stuck in place. My mouth feels dry, and opening it to formulate a response takes me a moment. "You want me to suck you off in exchange for an answer?"

He shrugs, not a care in the world. "Suck me off and I'll think about answering. I'm sure that's not your only question."

My nose twitches, but I school my expression, wondering how I might use this to my advantage. It's clear he's super into me and also Asher, so I can't imagine him actually forcing himself on me if he wants to remain in Asher's good graces.

Then again, he was in the forest that day with Celeste, and it seemed like the trio surrounding her turned to brute force when she tried to resist.

So maybe I'm in trouble here.

Or maybe him offering up the most *intimate* and vulnerable part of himself is a mistake on his end.

Submissive wolves, when threatened, will lie on their backs and plead for mercy.

Others bite.

If I get access to him there, I can turn the tables and make him my bitch.

But there's no chance in hell I'm putting my mouth anywhere near his dick. That's for one person now, and one person only.

Maybe I should've listened to him about not coming.

Not that it matters at the moment. I'm in it, and Foxe still hasn't come to my rescue, so I slink forward and drop onto wobbly knees. The position change knocks me off-kilter though, and my vision sways, darkening around the edges.

Beckett's fingers thread through one side of my hair as he brings his pelvis closer, urging me to get him out, but I don't. I can't—my hands won't lift, and my sight isn't correcting itself.

Everything continues to get slower, darker, until I'm no longer seeing anything at all.

Chapter 42

Asher

"DID YOU KNOW THERE ARE MORE THAN SEVEN *HUNDRED* VARIETIES of toxic plants found in the U.S. and Canada alone?" Quincy looks up at me from the old leather-bound book in her lap, toying with its silk bookmark.

I slide my fingers along the pencil marks in my sketchbook, smudging them for texture. "You always did find the weirdest things fascinating."

"Are they weird just because you don't think they're interesting?"

"Yes." Pausing, I glance at her for a second before going back to my drawing. "But also because you're weird. It wouldn't surprise me if you found all the Fury Hill lore about the existence of curses and immortality interesting too."

"Well, it *is* classic lore. I'm pretty much required to find it at least mildly amusing."

"And this is why I don't normally hang out with you."

I can practically feel her eyes roll as she swivels away in her chair to look out the window in her office. Unlike Dean Bauer's, Quincy's overlooks the forest and mountains beyond, nestled in the back of the admin building with the rest of the classics department.

"Hey." She doesn't turn around. "Do you realize how long it's been since we've heard from Noelle?"

My hand freezes. "I assumed she decided she no longer wanted to attend. You know she's fickle."

Quincy taps her book. "Yeah, but when I told her I was coming back to Avernia to teach, she seemed really into the idea of enrolling. Especially when I told her that, if nothing else, the theater department here is prolific. LA hasn't exactly done her any favors."

That much is obvious. Years spent out west, and not a single mainstream production under her belt.

"I used to get phone calls from her at least once a week," Quincy says, spinning back around and closing her book. "But I haven't heard from her in over a month."

"Mom and Dad have talked to her though. Maybe she's just decompressing."

"Maybe. I don't know. It just feels strange, I guess."

"Well, you like worrying about everything, so I'm not surprised you think that."

She chucks an Avernia pen in my direction, and it bounces off my wrist, clattering to the floor. "Whatever, asshole. Where's your other half?"

"If I had to guess, I'd say on her way back from a Curator party." Lifting my chin, I scan the analog clock hanging on the wall above her office door and nod to myself. "I told Foxe to bring her back by ten thirty."

"You let Foxe take her to a party?"

"Well, you needed me to move those goddamn statues around, so I couldn't go." I toss a glare at the heavy marble busts crowding the corner of the room, too large to be stored in here, but Quincy insisted. Something about them being too expensive to leave anywhere else, and since they came from the Daughters of Persephone donation fund, she didn't want to take any chances.

Seems like there are a million other people on campus she could've asked, but I've noticed Quincy doesn't really interact with many faculty members. She especially steers clear of the art department, but I can't be bothered to ask why.

It was her decision to come back here, so I assume she has her reasons.

"I love how helpful you've gotten as an adult." Quincy smiles, pushing her bangs from the frames of her glasses. "Mom will be so proud."

Flipping my sketchbook shut, I stand and grab my jacket, shrugging into it. "I'm leaving."

She gives me a half salute as I exit the office. Darkened, narrow halls lead me to a stairwell, and I come out through an emergency door, facing the Elysian Dorms. At night, their stone walls and gabled roofs look even creepier than usual.

Especially with the moon hanging high in the sky above them, looming like it's waiting on something terrible to happen.

Knowing Avernia, it probably already has.

Erebus Hall is dead when I enter, which isn't necessarily strange for this time of night but still something I note in the back of my mind. As an RA, I guess that's technically part of my duties here, though I've been slacking the entire time I've been enrolled as a student.

In my room, I kick off my shoes and curl up on the bed with my laptop, streaming some horror anime and running my hands over Keats's soft fur. He purrs, butting his head under my chin while we wait for Lucy.

Around eleven, I glance at my phone, noting the lack of calls and texts. It's not unlike her to go a long time without messaging, because she just forgets to reply, but Foxe on the other hand is a bit of a red flag with how often he wants to keep in touch.

I could have just seen him, and he'd be texting again within minutes.

Another half hour creeps by, and I head to Lucy's dorm down the hall. Flattening myself to the floor, I check for lights and shadows beneath the door and am met with neither.

I knock anyway. Just to check. And then I try for the handle; it turns easily, and I push the door open, swallowing over the knot in my throat.

"Luce?" I call out, though it's immediately obvious she isn't here.

Something vicious churns in the pit of my stomach. I glance around at the messy space, knowing she'd kill me if I tried to tidy up, so I keep my hands to myself.

Sitting on her bed, I bury my face in her pillow while I wait, inhaling the scent of coconut.

My heart aches, wanting to be near her already. Next time, Quincy can move her own shit.

Twenty more minutes pass, with me constantly checking my phone in the meantime. A collection of agate lines her desk above ecology textbooks, mostly brown and deep red rocks, just like the ones she collected when we were younger.

A small smile touches my mouth at how very little she's changed since I first fell in love with her.

The smile freezes, and my bones become heavy.

Love?

I stare up at the ceiling, replaying every important moment from our childhood. The first time I can remember seeing her, registering her, and how our connection was instantaneous. Like our souls were aligned by fate, intertwined in the galaxy, and written in the stars.

Even when we were apart, it never felt like that shifted. Even when she hated me, wanted nothing to do with me, the tether was still bound between us, pulling taut until we came back together.

I never should've ditched her in the first place, but I meant what I said to her the other day.

She's it for me. I'll never leave her alone again.

After tonight, that is.

Frustration laces my body, making my muscles grow tight. I drive the heels of my hands into my eyes, annoyed with how neither she nor Foxe have shown up yet. If I'd known he was going to keep her out longer, I wouldn't have been okay with him going at all.

But I knew she wanted to see Beckett, so I figured Foxe was better than nothing. He'd die for her as much as I would.

Tapping my fingers on my chest, I wait five more minutes. Then another five until I realize that maybe I'm still waiting because I don't want to acknowledge a possible alternative.

My thumb hits Lucy's name in my phone contacts, and a buzzing sound comes from across the room. Turning my head, I see a little black rectangle light up, and as the vibrating continues, it slips from the desk onto the floor.

She forgot her phone.

Cursing internally, I push Foxe's name instead; the call immediately goes to voicemail. I try again and again and *again* with the same results each time.

An unsettling sensation begins winding its way up my sternum, and I send Foxe a slew of texts asking where the hell he is.

They don't show as delivered, and paranoia starts to set in, strangling my lungs in its claws.

Getting up from the bed, I sprint down the hall for my shoes and jacket and then run out of the dorm. As I'm leaving, I remember that Beckett gave me his number after class one day, so I scroll through my contacts looking for it and almost mow Aurora over completely.

She ducks on the other side of the door, narrowly avoiding my elbow in her face.

"Jesus, watch where you're—" She cuts off when she realizes it's me, and her face relaxes slightly. Blue eyes look up at me in the moonlight, but they're not as dark or vast as I want them to be. "Oh, hey. I was actually just coming to find you. Have you heard from Foxe today?"

Skidding to a halt, I whirl around. "Have *you*?"

Confusion mars her features. "No, that's why I'm asking. Usually by this time at night, I'm getting dozens of texts from him, so it's kind of weird that he hasn't tried to contact me yet."

"Usually?" I ask, raising an eyebrow. "I didn't know you were speaking at all."

Pink flushes her cheeks. "It's not what it sounds like. Since he came here with you, he messages daily. I don't normally reply, but…"

"You like the attention."

She doesn't respond, pushing her tongue into her cheek.

Rolling my shoulders, I try to ignore the anxiety pooling in them. "Well, I haven't heard from him, so if you know where they may have gone during a Curator party, I'm all ears."

"They?"

"Him and Lucy."

"At a Curator party?" Something strange crosses her face, and her mouth twists up as she pulls her phone out, thumbs flying. After a second, she nods, looking back to me. "Yeah, the party ended, like, an hour ago. They had people cleaning the quarry already according to Yuri and Sara-Sofia."

"Who the fuck is Yuri?"

"A friend who was at the party. With Sara-Sofia."

"Why weren't you there?"

"I had shit to do." She narrows her eyes. "Why weren't *you* there? Aren't you supposed to be Lucy's guard dog or something, not Foxe?"

Grabbing her by the elbow, I drag her along as I start walking toward the Primordial Forest. "Let's just fucking find them, all right?"

Two hours later, and we're still coming up empty.

No one's seen or heard from Lucy or Foxe since the Curator party broke up, and only a few people remember that she was in attendance at all. They don't know where a handful of students took off to, noting that they'd indicated starting another party closer to the mountains, but without daylight or the layout of the forest, finding them feels impossible.

If I'd finished putting tracking devices on all her sweaters and cardigans, this wouldn't be happening. Fuck.

Nausea hardens my stomach, a ball forming in the middle that keeps me on the verge of puking the longer we go without locating them.

Eventually, we come to a stop at the burnt gazebo, and I have a horrid flashback to the awful things that can happen in these woods. Our flashlights illuminate the area, casting shadows along the treeline.

"I think we should call someone," Aurora tells me as she leans against a trunk, rubbing at her throat.

An icy breeze coasts through the air like a ghost passing by, making it colder than before. In the distance, an owl's hoot echoes among the leaves, and my skin feels like it's covered in slime, immobilizing me.

Aurora kicks a rock in my direction. "Hello? Are you listening? Don't you think we should tell someone our cousins are missing?"

I manage to shake my head. "We don't know that they are."

"Oh? What would you call it then?" she snaps.

"It doesn't fucking matter. Avernia campus police won't give a shit. You've seen them handle the other deaths this year."

"So what? You want to just do this on our own?" She makes a face, giving me a once-over. "No offense—or full offense, actually, because I don't give a fuck—but I'm not sure I trust you enough for that."

Whipping out my phone, I pull up the contact we both know we'll need, and hit the call button. She pales, slinking back and slamming her mouth shut.

My heart ricochets in my chest like a stray bullet, apprehension slashing at my insides.

There isn't any other choice. If we go to the dean, he won't be any help considering he *wants* Lucy gone. The police will side with the founding families, and they'd take too long to do anything anyway.

There's only one person in the entire world whose hunting skills would give him the actual means of locating her—who'd travel to hell and back to find her.

Alistair Wolfe answers the video call on the third ring; the camera cuts to his lean face, aged the way my father's is, though when he makes eye contact with me, his takes on a bit of an edge that Dad's lacks.

For as long as I can remember, that edge was there, though it's never felt more deadly than right now.

Still, his blue eyes are exact replicas of his daughter's, and the reminder that I cannot fucking *find her* pounds in my skull.

"This had better be good," he says, his English accent muted and raspy from sleep.

Aurora shoves her face in the camera's frame. "Hi, Uncle Ali!"

"Rory," he coos, his features softening. There's a long, drawn-out pause in which it feels as if we're waiting for something. Or some*one*.

Nobody talks, and Alistair's face quickly becomes solid stone again.

Some rustling comes from his end as he appears to push back sheets and climb from the large four-poster bed he shares with his wife. I hear her softly call out and ask where he's going, though I don't catch his reply as he leaves the room and walks down the hall.

Tapping sounds scatter as he enters his office, and the camera shifts, revealing a chocolate lab with a partially white face trailing behind him. Clearing his throat, Alistair settles in behind his desk, propping his phone up on some sort of stand.

"*Speak*," he demands.

Growing up, everyone always seemed more afraid of his wife, Cora, but to me, she was easier to navigate because she lacked a filter. What you saw was what you got.

Alistair Wolfe spent most of his life in politics. He's a renowned hunter on Aplana Island. He knows how to track his prey, how to lure them in, and how to kill with a single blow.

You'd never see it coming, which makes him far more dangerous.

Add in the fact that I'm positive he's never cared much for me, and I could probably piss myself right now over what I'm about to tell him.

Aurora edges away, her swallow audible.

"Asher." Alistair rubs his eyes and then drags his hand through his black hair. "It's my assumption that you would not bother me in the middle of the night unless something was very wrong, and considering you've been attached to my daughter since she popped out of her mother and she's nowhere to be seen at the moment, I'm inclined to believe it involves her."

"And Foxe." My mouth dries up, trying to keep me from saying the words. "They're missing."

Chapter 43

Lucy

I WAKE UP TO SCREAMING.

Not the distant kind you can tune out or celebratory shouts of excitement and festivities.

The kind that pierces your soul as it rips from a person's throat, guttural and raw and animalistic. A last-ditch attempt at prolonging life.

My body registers it all before my brain has a chance to catch up, and the screams snake their way into my veins, rattling my bones to the marrow. An ache flares behind the right side of my skull, spreading across my temple, and as I slowly manage to work my eyes open, I'm met with darkness.

It takes a few seconds for me to comprehend anything outside the terror. The screaming doesn't cease, as if it's a recording being played on a loop, although it's clearly happening mere feet away.

The volume doesn't quite reach my ears, like I'm in some sort of foggy tunnel or underwater where sound is distorted.

I go to move my arms, but my wrists are stuck together behind my back. Tugging with as much strength as I can muster, I try to slide one from the bind—it feels like rope instead of chains or zip ties—but it's too tight.

The screams finally stop, though they continue echoing around me. *What the hell happened?*

Last thing I remember is Beckett asking me to go down on him. Bile teases the back of my throat as I realize things aren't just fuzzy but completely blacked out, and I swallow over burning trepidation, trying to decide if I feel violated or not.

My mouth is dry, my esophagus stinging as saliva attempts to slide down it, but I don't feel bruised or anything. Not *there* at least.

Slowly, I turn my head. Just enough to peek out when I feel light on the backs of my eyelids.

Dirt is in my direct line of vision, but as I start to adjust to the bright floodlight shining down, I see rock everywhere. Walls of it, curving upward to a low ceiling of more solid rock, smoothed away as if to make this area passable for humans.

In my peripheral is a dark, shadowed figure slumped against the wall, their head practically touching their chin.

After a few seconds, I'm finally able to make out their full silhouette and tall, lanky frame. Foxe's brown hair shields a lot of his face, so I can't immediately discern if he's awake or not.

His hands, though, are also bound behind him.

He's *covered* in blood. More blood than I think I've ever seen, even after his worst fights with Asher. It just pools around him in big crimson puddles, like he's on the set of one of those slasher films my brother loves.

I note tears in the T-shirt he has on and wonder if he's even still alive. It's difficult to see if his chest is rising and falling. He doesn't move at all.

When I slide my gaze from him, I manage to lift my chin enough to take a wider glimpse around the area. We're in some sort of cave, and I have to assume it's one blocked off by Avernia officials, since we were close to one of the openings earlier.

There's not much else in here with us: black trash bags, tools, and large plastic bins. A few standing lights and headlamps, abandoned on the ground across from us. A card table against one wall with a couple of folding chairs pushed beneath it and playing cards spread out on top.

Next to a big kerosene tank, Willa lies flat on her stomach. If I thought Foxe was bloody, Willa is practically unrecognizable, drenched from head to toe in scarlet, her short brown hair no longer brown at all. Everything is red, and it takes me a second to realize the screams were likely coming from her.

She's been stripped naked, her ankles tied to two stalagmites, spreading her wide open. An incision from her vagina to the top of her ass leaks a stream of blood, soaking the ground beneath her.

I retch, unable to stop myself as I take in the state of her. She twitches, straining slightly against her binds, before she gives up in the next second. Almost as if she's trying to save her strength.

Glancing down at myself, I note my clothes, assessing mentally for other injuries. Aside from the splitting headache and the mounting horror, I feel okay, though I find that alarming.

What if they were just waiting for me to wake up?

From the corner of my eye, I see Foxe's leg move, and my head swivels to look at him. He groans softly, rolling his as he lifts his chin.

For a few seconds, we just stare at each other.

"Are you okay?" I whisper finally, each word a struggle.

He shifts, nodding toward his side. "Other than the hole in my side, I guess."

My mouth gapes, my gaze dropping to assess the wound. I can't see it, though, through his shirt. "What the fuck happened?"

Shaking his head, he drops it back against the wall with a grunt. "One second, Willa and Eli were arguing about whether to go to Lethe's after the party, and the next, I was struggling to keep my goddamn eyes open. They tried to prop me up, but then they started feeling funny too, and the next thing I know, we're being dragged down into this creepy-ass cave by some guys in white masks. Assholes stabbed me for no reason. Guess I blacked out at some point."

White masks. Oh God.

My eyes dart around the room, widening at the three of us. "Where is—"

"I don't know." Foxe glares at his feet. "If Willa's any indication though…"

A hard lump lodges in my throat, making breathing difficult. Air filters around it, coming out of me in short, staggered bursts.

Head swimming, I start to push up from where I'm doubled over on my knees and crawl toward Foxe. One of Willa's eyes pop open, and she lets out a strangled noise when she sees me, matching the one I let out when I realize she really *is* alive.

I don't know how she is, but I'm not going to question it.

"We've got to get out of here," I mutter to Foxe, as if he isn't likely thinking the exact same thing. Turning my back to him, I lift my wrists. "You guys have lost a lot of blood, so we need to make it quick. Try breaking this off with your foot. If you put enough pressure in the middle, the bindings might snap or at least give enough slack that I can slip through—"

"I wouldn't do that if I were you."

Like almost every other time I've heard it, Beckett Dupont's voice sends a shiver down my spine. Three hooded figures with white face masks walk through an arched entryway, the one in front coming over to stand in front of me. I can tell it's him, even without looking into his soulless eyes or hearing him speak again.

He kicks Foxe's leg, slamming his heel between my bindings; the force of it pulls me backward, knocking me onto my side. Pain ripples through my rib cage, and I grit my teeth, trying not to let it distract me.

"It's a shame we didn't get to continue our fun before you passed out," Beckett says, crouching and petting my cheek as he pushes his mask into his hair. "I guess your murderer boyfriend won't have to learn you were unfaithful before you die."

The relief that floods through my system with his taunting makes me nauseous, but I latch on to it anyway, knowing that if nothing else, I still have that. A glimmer of hope in this utterly bleak reality.

"Asher isn't a murderer," I reply, snatching my face away from his touch.

Beckett smirks. "Aw, he really doesn't tell you anything, does he? How sad. I can link at *least* two student deaths directly to him. Who knows how many others there are? Celeste, maybe?" He cocks his head, then pinches my skin, giving me a little shake. "Can you really say with a hundred percent certainty that you *know* the man you've been fucking this semester?"

I glare at him but remain silent. It'd be a lie if I said I hadn't wondered often about Asher's life without me or what he was doing the night Celeste died. Him being one of the three who had a direct hand in things wouldn't have been possible, I don't think, given how quickly he showed up after they disappeared, but *some* involvement isn't totally out of the realm of possibility, right?

He's always been violent and angry. Maybe in our three years apart, those qualities exacerbated, and he snapped.

Still, even with that knowledge—would he really *kill* someone without a reason?

Violent and angry doesn't mean there isn't a purpose behind his movements.

But he left you, Lucy. What happened to him in the meantime?

Do you really know him anymore? Is he the boy you fell in love with, or is that just what you're hoping for because you don't want to admit that he could have changed?

Beckett sighs, releasing me with a shove. I roll onto my back, my wrists a strained buffer between my tailbone and the harsh ground, and he scoffs, turning away.

"Doesn't really matter, I guess. Him wanting to be a Curator should be all the proof you need, Wolfe. He's been plotting your downfall like the rest of us."

"That isn't true," Foxe says in a low voice. He meets my gaze. "You *know* he'd never do anything to hurt you."

My heart hammers inside my chest, a metronome of uncertainty.

"And he didn't touch your fucking roommate—"

A blow to Foxe's nose interrupts his sentence; one of the other masked figures drives their knee into his face, and I hear the sickening crunch of bone as Foxe absorbs the force with nothing more than a pained grunt.

My stomach rolls, terror agitating inside like a hurricane.

Beckett gives the masked figure a dirty look. "Can you get a fucking grip? If you start knocking them unconscious again, there won't be any time to do what we brought them here for."

I push up on my elbow, trying to maneuver myself back into a sitting position. My eyes stay on Foxe, watching for signs of concussion—or worse. His head lolls as the other person steps away, pushing him back against the wall. Blood gushes from his nose, which is crooked in a way I don't think it's supposed to be, but he manages a small grin in my direction.

"*I'm fine,*" he mouths, though his eyes are unfocused and glassy.

I force my lips to curl up at the corners, but I think we both know it's a hollow gesture. A poor attempt at adding levity to a situation that will likely not end well.

Beckett snaps his fingers directly in front of my face. "Hey, don't go getting all googly-eyed on me now, Wolfe. We've got shit to do here, and I can't have you getting distracted."

"What *are* we doing?" I ask, yanking my head away from his hand. "I thought you were above all that human sacrifice and demon summoning."

"Don't worry. If I leave you here long enough, Fury Hill legend says *something* will crawl out and devour you. The same way it did my ancestor, who Cronus Anderson dragged here and left to fend for themselves in these caves. Do you think you could find your way out, Lucy?"

"You kidnapped four students to satisfy some weird vendetta from hundreds of years ago?"

Beckett makes a strange face, his eyebrows furrowing, and then he tips his head back and laughs. "Duponts don't forget, you wild beast of a girl. How *could* we when we were nearly wiped out by Anderson interference?"

Foxe groans, his chin dropping. His neck is flushed, dripping still, and Willa doesn't look good either. I don't know how much longer we have before bad shit starts setting in here, but Beckett doesn't seem terribly interested in shutting up.

"Not long after establishing Fury Hill and carving this town into the edge of the White Mountains with their bare hands, five of the six founding family patriarchs came down with these terrible coughing fits. From sunrise to sunset, they spent their hours hacking up pools of blood. They were drowning in it. But *one* patriarch remained completely healthy, leading everyone to the conclusion that Cronus had poisoned the others to gain access to their land and sell it off to outside investors."

"Sounds like they had tuberculosis."

"Sure, if you want to be modern about it. But that still doesn't explain why Cronus, who was in constant contact with the other five, never caught it. It's highly communicable, right? Meanwhile, a triage center was established as more and more of Fury Hill became infected. Guess where that triage center was located?"

Goose bumps scatter along my arms, trickling through my hair like liquid fear. I don't have to answer; I can *feel* it here, like the spirits of whomever died still linger hundreds of years later.

Maybe the Obeliskos *is* haunted.

"Avernia College, this amazing entity the six families had created, became a house of death that no amount of holy relics, priests, or praying seemed able to thwart. Until Cronus suggested an unorthodox method of healing: drinking healthy blood to replenish what had been lost and cancel out the tainted supply. But since nearly everyone in town was affected and no one wanted to volunteer, Cronus offered the livestock on his farm, arguing that meat and other parts were suitable for human consumption, so the blood would be fine as well."

Spinning around, Beckett puts his hands on his hips, his voice echoing through the cave as he continues. One of the other hooded figures inches toward Willa, bending down to slide the sharp edge of a blade along her spine; she cries out, and I feel her anguish in my bones.

"That's what he *said* anyway. But the creatures he brought and professed to be livestock were much larger than any animals the others had seen. Overfed, he told them, so their blood would taste better."

A long, long pause. Beckett watches his companion terrorize my friend, and I clench my jaw against the urge to yell at them to stop. Her raw screams come from between gritted teeth, and she twists to try and escape, but the masked person follows.

"One night," Beckett goes on, facing me again, "after the animals were drained, Jean Dupont felt well enough to venture down the narrow tunnels leading out of the caves, where they were housing the founding patriarchs. He stopped at a small entrance to an adjoining cavern. It was covered with a white sheet, and when he pulled it back, he found Cronus feasting on the corpse of a resident who had passed after drinking the livestock's blood."

"A vampire?" I reply, trying to hold back a laugh. "Really? You think that's what Asher's ancestor was?"

"What other explanation *is* there?" he asks. "In that moment, Cronus seemed half human, half monster. Jean didn't understand what was going on, but he knew he had to get out of there."

"You should really leave the lecturing to your brother," Foxe slurs.

Beckett ignores him. "Petrified, Jean took off running back to where the others were recovering, urging them to leave. He got a Blackwater on his back and a couple of others out of bed, but when they made it to the entrance, there stood Cronus, blood coating his entire body as if he'd bathed in it."

My eyes flicker to Foxe and Willa. *Are they trying to recreate that scene?*

"There was no hesitation when it came to slaughtering the founders. Three of them were brutalized by Cronus's bare hands, and only Jean and William Blackwater remained. Jean succumbed to his illness, which had ramped up as soon as Cronus came into play because, as it turned out, the blood did nothing to cure them."

"Why suggest it in the first place?" I question.

"Some say it was just a theory. Others think it made the corpses taste better, and that was why he'd given them the overfed creatures." Beckett shrugs. "In any case, Jean collapsed before Cronus could finish him off. William was never seen nor heard from again. Like he just disappeared in these caves, his body recovered by the earth.

"Cronus, in turn, would go on to rule Fury Hill under the guise of having been a courageous friend who'd tried helping the other families, because no one knew what had happened inside the caves. All the witnesses died, and Cronus painted the bloodbath as an animal attack."

"Then how do *you* know any of this?" Foxe rasps.

"Cronus wasn't subtle. He went on to marry the Dupont widow and would brag to her about what he'd done. She was too afraid to tell anyone until after he died, but she left journals detailing the events. *My* ancestor, although they never had any children together, thank fuck. I wouldn't want any relation to Asher's freaky nightwalker bloodline."

You should be so lucky. "Is there a point to any of this?"

He cuts me a glare. "The *curse* that snaked its way down the line to your little boyfriend and his siblings is the goddamn point, Wolfe. You think evil energy like that just disappears when a man gets to finish his life peacefully?

"They exhumed Cronus's body after his death and used his organs in a ritual that was supposed to keep his relatives and other evil away from Fury Hill, but one of the people who participated in the ritual sought chaos and sent a curse out instead. One that claimed three Andersons would eventually return to finish off the destruction Cronus had started. Since then, Avernia's been prepared to rectify the curse by whatever means necessary. Their strategy has always been clear: end the three in the place this all began before they can annihilate what has been built."

When Beckett finally finishes, I glance around the cave, raising my eyebrows. "Did you forget to bring Asher or something?"

He scoffs. My nails dig into my palms.

"No, you stupid bitch. But I'm not an idiot. I would never win a fight against that mindless brute. He talks with his fists, and we all know he loves to put out fires by creating bigger ones."

A moment passes, the two of us staring at each other. *He knows.*

He knows Asher set the fire at Lethe's that day three years ago, and he knows it was for me.

How he knows isn't relevant, but it's clear that Beckett is aware Asher's connection to me runs a lot deeper than some random hookups.

Nausea churns in my gut, burning a path up my chest. Shit, shit, *shit.*

Is that why I was blamed? To keep the fire's memory alive and keep school apprehension toward me at the forefront of everyone's minds? If no one liked me, it wouldn't matter when I suddenly went missing.

To anyone other than Asher, who they would attack when he came to find me.

Because he would find me. That much I do know.

I can feel him searching right now in my soul, because that's how deep our bond is. That's how well I know him.

He'd follow me to the ends of the earth, no matter how I'd ventured to them.

Except that's apparently exactly what Beckett and his cohorts want. They think Asher Anderson and his siblings are a blight on the existence of Fury Hill, and they used me to bring him to their level.

This plan has been in motion for *years.*

And I fell right for it.

Swallowing, I push down the mounting panic as it rises in my throat. Freaking out won't do anyone any good, and seduction is no longer an option. I need a practical escape, something I can use to get Foxe out too, and then come back for Willa.

My eyes flicker to her, roving over her form as the second hooded figure joins his buddy, stepping on the bottom of her foot until she pleads with them to stop.

They're the first words she's spoken, punctuated by mouthfuls of blood dribbling down her chin, and my heart aches with the sheer agony rippling through each syllable. After a few moments, the masked pair seems to grow bored; they walk off, disappearing through the one exit in the area. Light spills in, and I wonder how many tunnels and other openings there are here.

A sawing noise echoes through the corridor a few minutes later, drowning out the sound of Willa's sobs. Sadness pierces my chest as I wonder what they're doing to Eli—how they probably started with him and are working their way through us.

"Beckett," I say, lifting my chin. My wrists chafe against the rope, but I work them from side to side behind my back anyway, trying to get enough slack to slip out. "Do you realize how bad this is going to look for you? Maybe the Fury Hill PD can overlook one or two students here and there, but *four* dead people at once? Found in the same area, mutilated and tortured? There's no way that's getting brushed under the rug."

He turns, shrugging. "My family owns this town. I'll be fine. Besides, I'm not technically doing anything. I'm not even really *here*. In a few days, when someone reports one of you missing and Dean Bauer opens an investigation so that he looks good to the school board, they'll find nothing but charred remains."

"You're going to start a fire *underground*? Do you realize that can collapse soil and incinerate the entire Primordial Forest?"

"What the fuck do I care? If I can take out half the acreage around campus, that's even better. Room for developing it instead of letting greedy conservationists keep it for themselves."

"They're greedy, but that isn't?"

His face turns bright red. "I'm *allowed* to be. My entire life has been shaped by how this town acts and how—"

"You're a little boy murdering for his mommy and daddy," I spit, leaning in with a glare. "Your life was shaped by your fucking *privilege*, and it's insulting for you to insinuate otherwise just because you want to look good for your future investors or bosses or whoever else—"

I don't see his hand as it sails through the air toward me, but I certainly feel when it connects with my cheek, sending me flying. Sprawling out on my stomach, my chin bounces off the rocky ground, scraping so hard I see stars.

"Shut the fuck up and just wait for your boyfriend." Beckett slides his mask back into place and pulls his hood over his head. "I don't want to have to do that again."

Silently seething, I watch him head out of our cavern the same way the other two exited and then wait a few more minutes to see if I hear his footsteps returning. When only the sounds of Willa's soft sobs are audible, I spring into action, finally managing to slide one of my wrists through the bindings.

Pain ricochets up the side of my face, but I can't pay attention to that now.

With one arm free, I bring both in front of me; blood drips down my fingers from where I've been rubbed completely raw by the rope, but there's no time to care.

Launching myself across the cave, I land hard on my knees next to Willa, my hands trembling as I lift them, trying to figure out what the hell I'm supposed to do.

I reach up, pushing a finger through a small hole in the shoulder of my sweater, and use every ounce of strength I can muster to tear the sleeve from my arm. Still, as I sit closer to Willa and look her over, I realize her injuries are even worse than I initially thought.

Aside from the gruesome incision connecting her privates, her guts are spilling out of a hole in her side. Her left eye is swollen shut, possibly even missing, and there are several stab wounds decorating her right leg.

Frankly, I don't know how she's alive at all right now.

Carefully, I take the torn sweater piece and slide it beneath her thigh, tying tight above one of the wounds to stop the bleeding. Her injuries must be fresh; otherwise, I can't imagine how she's hanging on.

Her right eye looks up at me when she feels me touching her, and she coughs into the ground. "Lucy, don't—"

The words are *barely* audible.

I shake my head, leaning in to whisper, "I'm going to get you out of here, okay? Don't worry."

My chest tightens as I glance at her bottom, wondering how the fuck I'm supposed to bandage her enough to keep that promise.

A small amount of vomit my mouth as anxiety pushes it up, but I swallow, ignoring the urge to gag.

Turning slightly, I look at Foxe. He's watching us, his own eyes swollen, his nose fully disfigured. "If we can patch her up enough, it might be possible to move her. Do you think you could shoulder some of her weight? I can grab her legs, and you get beneath her arms."

Foxe nods once, his gaze dropping to his lap. He looks fucking exhausted, and I'm trying not to let panic set in, but its claws scratch at the chamber of my heart, begging to be set free.

Foxe is a safety net—always has been. He doesn't take things seriously or frown or experience grim emotions the way others do. I mean, there've been times when I thought something was bothering him, but this is different.

Right now, I hardly recognize him.

Doesn't matter, Lucy. Focus on getting the three of you out, and then you can deal with his issues later.

This is all *my* fault anyway. If I hadn't invited him to the party, begged Willa and Eli to come, or ignored Asher telling me to stay away from Beckett, none of this would have happened.

Whether a savior complex or sheer stupidity, I'm the reason for all of it.

Well, me and Cronus Anderson. The fucker.

Chapter 44

Lucy

I TAKE OFF MY SWEATER, LEAVING MYSELF IN ONLY A THIN BLACK tank top, and attempt to apply pressure to Willa's wounds.

To be honest, I'm not really sure what else to do—Asher's dad is the retired doctor, and I never really had much reason to learn how to treat traumatic injuries like these. Most of Asher's were relegated to bloody noses and the occasional puncture, but this is almost inconceivable.

Her insides are *hanging out*. When I tell her I'm going to try and stop the bleeding between her legs, I push down on the area, unable to avert my gaze from the gaping hole in her side.

How the fuck do you fix that? Do they go back in the way they came out, or will touching them rupture something?

I can't just fucking leave her here though. Even considering it makes me want to vomit.

She'd die here, *alone*.

Just like Celeste did, surrounded by horrible people.

No. I will not do this again. I will not be helpless and useless a second time.

My throat constricts, emotion clogging the airway, and I ball my hands into fists to get a hold of myself. I'm slowly losing my grip on sanity, and right now, none of us can afford that.

"Lucy," Willa chokes out through the side of her mouth, smashed against the ground. "Stop. You need…to go."

I frown. "Don't tell me what I need to do, Willa. *I* tell *you* what to do, remember? I'm your boss."

"Only when…we're cleaning up…garbage."

"Well, close your eyes and pretend then, because I'm not fucking ditching you, and you're not going to ask me to leave you here," I snap, hating the bite of my words but unable—unwilling—to leach it from my tone.

Anger's all I've got at the moment.

"This is probably going to hurt, so just…" My hands hover over her broken, battered body. Fuck. *Fuck.* Tears sting my eyes, but I blink them away, inhaling deeply. I rip off another piece of my sweater, offering it to her. "Can you put this between your teeth? I don't want you to scream and alert those shitheads, wherever they are."

"Where *do* you think they are?" Foxe asks. "What if they come back while you're—"

"I don't *know*, Foxe, okay? I don't know. I'm just…trying here. Keep an eye on the door while I figure out what she can handle."

Willa bites down on the fabric, and as I start to roll her onto her good side, she grunts low in her chest, as if resisting the urge to yell.

Tears mix with the blood on her face—just one side though, and again I wonder about her left eye.

She spits out the sweater, wheezing. "Lucy…I can't—"

"Shut *up*, Willa, for fuck's sake." I release her, and she rolls back. "I'm going to figure something out, all right? Just…just stop fucking talking."

"Fine…but you…owe me a friend date…after," she gasps out.

That makes me laugh despite everything. I wipe some of the blood and grime from her face. "Deal. Where do you want—"

The bullet comes out of fucking *nowhere*.

I don't even see it until it's already lodged in Willa's back, a massive hole that tears through flesh and bone, stealing the air from both our lungs.

Foxe's curse is the only thing I hear as a roaring noise rushes between my ears.

On instinct, I shuffle away and see one of the hooded, masked figures from earlier slip through a thin white sheet hung up to my left, concealing another exit.

The figure gets closer, and as they do, I note the emblem on their hoodie; there's a design that's faded and scratched off, only a couple of lines remaining. It almost looks like a torch, but it's too hard to make out, especially with the other insignia that's been ironed overtop of it.

A three-headed beast.

Death's Teeth in the flesh.

"Lucy," Foxe hisses, but I'm frozen in place, paralyzed and unable to look away as the masked man approaches Willa, points the gun at the back of her head, and pulls the trigger once more.

The popping noise is dulled by the suppressor attachment on the pistol, but I still feel it. Still jump when the bullet leaves the chamber, embedding itself in my friend's skull.

Her one good eye remains wide open. Staring forever right at me.

Silence descends upon the three of us.

I can't move.

I want to but can't.

"Oh, for crying out fucking loud!" Beckett races back into the cavern, his fingers yanking tight on his short hair as he takes in the scene. "What the hell is your problem, Tiernan? We weren't supposed to *kill* her."

The masked figure rolls his eyes. "She was seconds from dying anyway after what—"

"My brother is going to *kill* me, oh my God." Beckett paces back and forth in front of Willa's corpse, biting on his thumbnail, a frenzied look on his face.

A part of me catches the mention of his brother, but right now, I'm truly too far inside my head to register the implication.

Her eye is wide open.

Unblinking.

Forever.

"Oh, quit whining, pussy. We'll just eliminate the witnesses, and he'll never know," Tiernan snaps.

"We need the witnesses, dumbass. And you're not in charge here, I am."

"Fine." Tiernan stalks toward me. "Then, we'll eliminate *one* witness. No one will miss this bitch anyway."

Looking away from Willa isn't possible; I try, but my gaze is fully stuck in position, locked with hers. Life drained from it instantly, like her soul bleeding out the way her body did first.

My sweater is ruined. I loved that one.

I'm going to die down here.

I'm going to *die down here*, and Asher won't even know I loved him.

I mean, maybe he'll know, but I never said it. Fuck, why the hell didn't I tell him? Because I was scared? I've been scared every day of my goddamn life—that shouldn't have mattered.

Coming to Avernia was terrifying, but I did it. Defending myself is nerve-racking, but I do that too, yet three little words were my limit? The line I couldn't cross, all because the fear of abandonment was too strong?

Pathetic really.

I'm fucking pathetic.

A sob rattles my chest, and I try to catch it in my hand, but there's no use. It spills out like old milk, tainting the air and grating against my ears.

I tremble, dropping my palms to the ground. There's nothing else to fucking do—no chance I'm going to be able to dart and get something to fight back with. He'll just shoot me anyway.

My family will miss me.

Asher will. Aurora too. Yuri maybe, and the Fury Hill Animal Shelter.

Foxe—God, will Foxe even recover from this?

What I should've been doing this whole time was getting him freed and then finding a weapon, but I wanted to save Willa.

I thought I *could.*

My arms tremble, my elbows threatening to give out as thick black boots fill my line of vision. There's pressure on my head, and I close my eyes, hoping that wherever Asher is, he can feel my love for him.

If only I hadn't spent so much time ignoring him. I wish he'd told me everything three years ago so none of this would have happened at all.

"*Wait!*" Foxe's voice shatters the silence, and the pressure slips from my skull. I lift my chin, glancing over my shoulder as Foxe staggers to his feet, stumbling toward me. "Wait, don't hurt her. I got her free and then told her we needed to get out of here."

Tiernan and Beckett share a look. "No offense, but we don't really believe you," Tiernan says.

I whip my head in his direction. "Foxe, *shut up*. Don't be an idiot."

His jaw shifts, but he ignores me. "Fine, then realize that there is no one on this planet Asher Anderson cares about more than that girl right there. You kill her, and there's no way you're getting him down here. He'll want proof of life, and your curse will continue on."

"*Foxe—*"

Groaning, Beckett tugs at his hair again, ripping a few strands out. "Shit. *Shit.* He's right, Tiernan, you dumb fuck. Get him out of here."

My eyes widen as the third masked figure reenters, immediately heading for Foxe. They grab beneath Foxe's arm, hauling him away, and tears pour down my cheeks.

"*Stop!* Take me, leave him! He didn't fucking *do* anything!" I shriek, lunging for the exiting pair.

Tiernan fists my hair, and I hiss against the pain as the roots struggle to stay in my scalp, but I still try to go after the others.

"*Foxe!* Please, stop! Leave him out of this!" My screams shred my throat, useless as the masked person ignores me, still dragging Foxe along. "You can't leave me!"

Tiernan lifts his foot, swinging it into my stomach. I double over, clutching the area as a wave of nausea and agony rolls through me. The last I see of Foxe is him shoving the masked figure into a wall, but he's in such bad shape that all the other guy does is push back, and I swear when he wrenches his arm behind him, I watch his shoulder dislocate.

My stomach flips over and over, bile burning my throat.

Everything gets really silent for a long time.

I stare at the ground, dropping my palm and digging my nails into the rocky dirt. "What are they going to do to him?"

Beckett doesn't reply.

Tiernan walks away, toward the back exit he came in from. "Whatever he feels like, I guess. Not his first rodeo, if you catch my drift there, Wolfe."

When the screaming begins, I don't register it at first. My mind is elsewhere, trying to protect me from the noise I guess, even though this is all my fault and I should be forced to listen.

The first notes of Foxe's despair reverberate in my chest.

How will I ever face Asher after this?

A bubble of twisted amusement pops. I won't be seeing him anyway.

Still, the horrific wailing persists, growing in volume. Anguish wafts through the cave tunnels, clouding the one we're in, and I reach up to cover my ears, but it's not enough. His agony is persistent.

I'm stuck. Paralyzed by the echoes of his misery, the choking sounds, and the pleas for it all to stop.

The pleas are the worst.

I've never heard Foxe James beg for anything except for attention. Certainly not mercy.

Tears stream down my face as I continue sitting on my hands and knees, staring at the ground. Images of everything from this semester—Celeste's gang rape and murder in the forest, the corpses in my dorm room, the blood in the Obeliskos. Seeing Willa shot right before me, and now *Foxe* going through unimaginable horrors…

Asher's going to come down here and die too.

My fault.

I put everyone's life in danger, all because I thought this school was worth it.

The tears splatter onto the ground beneath me. A single sob, something inaudible, pulses through my chest, but then my entire body is shaking, my own pain mixing with Foxe's terror and making me *sick*.

"Please," I sputter, my vision blurring. "Please, I can't... I don't want to listen to this."

Tiernan snorts, having reappeared at my side. "Aw, that's too bad. I don't give a shit. We'll call this a little parting gift."

Foxe's wailing continues. He yells for his mom, his dad.

Me.

I bite my lip until it slices open, and the coppery taste mixes with the salt of my tears. Sadness, deep and ceaseless, settles in the very pit of my soul. So deep I don't think I'll ever be able to reach it or clean it out.

Not that it appears that will be an issue after tonight.

"Please," I say once more, whispering it. "Let him go. I'll do—"

Tiernan kicks me again, and this time, I choke on a cocktail of blood and vomit. His foot lifts in my peripheral for a repeat, but I don't have the energy to dodge.

At least the pain distracts me from Foxe, if only for a second.

Before he does anything though, the noises coming from somewhere else in the cave system end.

They drop off entirely, like a record slipping off the track.

Beckett pushes his mask into his hair, his face paling. The three of us wait, listening for more.

It doesn't come.

Laughing, Tiernan lets his foot fall to the ground. "Well, well. Guess the big bad rock star couldn't hold out as long as the others."

The others. Eli and Willa.

Dead.

Everyone is dead.

More vomit spills onto the ground beneath me, and I let out a strangled sound, something caught between a whimper and a howl. An attempt to expel the anguish from my body, though it seems keen on living in my bones.

"*Tiernan,*" Beckett barks, shoving his shoulder. "Go check on them."

Grumbling under his breath, Tiernan grabs his gun from the card table and stalks out.

Beckett paces some more, hands on his hips, muttering to himself about his brother not liking the turn things have taken.

I'm not paying attention though, really.

I just keep staring at the fucking ground, wondering if I glare hard enough, will it open up and swallow me whole?

That would be preferable, I think, to the abyss inside me.

Tiernan doesn't comes back, and eventually Beckett stops. He turns and looks at Willa's corpse. My eyes are swollen from all the crying, and he becomes little more than a blurry blob.

"Okay. *Okay*."

I manage to lift my chin a little bit when Beckett's rambling gets louder, and then he whirls around, coming toward me. Bending, he pulls a pair of scissors from his hoodie and cuts the rope still dangling from one of my wrists, then grabs my jaw and forces me to look at him.

I blink through the tears, gritting my teeth. I don't want to make eye contact with him when he kills me, but I guess I don't get much of a choice.

Not that it matters anymore.

Not that it matters at all.

"You need to go," Beckett says, shaking me roughly. He jabs his thumb over his shoulder to where the white sheet hangs. "Head through there, take the first right and the second left, and eventually you'll come up at Lake Lerna. Stick to the trees and get back to campus, then call the police. *Not* Avernia security or the dean. *Fury Hill*. They'll come much faster."

I try to wrench myself from his grasp, but I'm too weak to do it. "Someone's going to ambush me as soon as I leave."

Beckett's jaw shifts. "No, they're not. I'm risking everything by releasing you, all right? But this… It wasn't supposed to be a fucking bloodbath down here."

"You just wanted to kill Asher."

"Mortui vivos docent. Some things are just bigger than us, Lucy. But if you get out of here, you'll get to live at least."

Snot runs down my chin. "I can't go. Not without Foxe."

"You can't carry deadweight by yourself. Get the fucking cops, and tell them to do it." A long pause, and neither of us moves. "Look, I can't... I don't know how long we have before one of them comes back. And I can't fucking do anything for you when they do. This is already way beyond my control. I only came down here to try and clear my name from your roommate's death and finish the Anderson shit for my old man. Everything else..." He trails off, swallowing. "It wasn't supposed to be like this."

I study him for several beats, noting the glint in his blue irises. He doesn't look away, though I still can't be sure if he's telling the truth.

I heard him that night...didn't I?

But even if this is some big misunderstanding and he was framed somehow for Celeste's death, I can't find it in me to feel an ounce of sympathy.

Chapter 45

Asher

WAITING IS FUCKING TORTURE.

But when I tell Alistair about his missing daughter, he insists on coming to Fury Hill himself. Something about being a hunter and not trusting me to keep her safe anymore.

Which is fair, I guess. I certainly failed in that department. I *keep* failing, it seems, and I'm starting to question my ability in the first place.

Alistair summons everyone—except Ariana and Cash, who never answer the phone at night—for a family meeting while he and Dad get ready. My aunt Violet sits on the dark blue sofa in the Wolfes' living room, sobbing into her hands as Cora and Mom attempt to offer her comfort.

There's none to be had though, really. Her son's missing, and that's my fault too.

Uncle Grayson won't let me forget it either.

"You bring my son back to me in one piece, or I take something of equal value from you."

I don't know how to break it to him that the two most important things in my life are *gone*, but it doesn't matter anyway. All I can focus on is Violet's crying and Cora's attempts to pretend she isn't.

Grayson and Aurora's dad, Jonas, drink whiskey straight from the bottle. Grayson's green eyes stay on me through the whole video call, dark and unyielding.

"This is bloody ridiculous," Jonas says, running a hand through his curly brown hair. "Let the kids go searching on their own, brother. It's going to take a while for you to get up there, even with Kal's jet. We could be losing precious time."

Lenny, Aurora's mom, comes behind her husband, flicking his nose. "Not sure that's as encouraging as you think it is."

"Well, I'm sorry, love. I just hate to think of my niece suffering because her father doesn't trust the boy she loves."

"I don't trust him because of *this fucking shit*," Alistair counters from somewhere off camera.

Shame burns my shoulders, and I run my fingers over Keats's fur, letting the vibrations from his purring soothe me.

"They'll get to them in time," Grayson mutters around his bottle, cocking a dark brown eyebrow at me. "Isn't that right, Asher?"

It sounds like a threat, and when I see Dad come into view to press a kiss to Mom's lips, I wait for him to defend me.

He doesn't.

Anger boils inside my chest even more than usual. My hands curl into fists, and I glance at Aurora, who's sitting on my bed across the room, biting her nails.

Jonas is right. We are losing time here.

But Grayson is *also* right.

I will fucking find those two, and I'll slaughter my way to them if I have to.

Motioning for Aurora to follow, I push Keats from my lap and slip on my shoes, ending the call before someone else tries to guilt-trip me.

I'm not going to sit around like a little kid and wait for my parents to intervene.

They've always been *backup*, not the initial solution.

That hasn't changed just because of the magnitude of my mistake.

So instead of waiting for Alistair and Dad, I head straight for the dean's office. Aurora trails close behind me, her arms crossed over her chest as the moon climbs to different heights in the sky.

The light beneath his office door is on, glowing bright. His secretary doesn't seem to be in this late, so the fact that he is tells me everything I need to know.

Lifting my foot, I aim beside the knob and kick the door open. Dark wood splinters, flying in multiple directions as I step inside.

Dean Bauer leans back in his chair, folding his arms over his stomach and regarding us with a tapered expression.

"Asher," he greets with a nod before moving to Aurora. "Ms. Primrose-Wolfe. What can I help you two with?"

"Where are they?" I spit through clenched teeth.

He blinks slowly, glancing between us. "I'm afraid I don't know what you mean."

Aurora rolls her eyes. "Can you not play dumb right now? Neither of us has the patience to put up with your bullshit."

Dean Bauer rocks back and forth, watching us. A slow, insidious smile spreads across his mouth. "Maybe Death's Teeth got to them. *The Delphic Pages* says they've been itching to spill some more blood. Shame no one knows who they are or where they go though, huh?"

I stalk behind him before he can get to his feet, grabbing the back of his head in my fist. He squeaks, and I revel in the sound for a millisecond before shoving my arm forward and slamming his face into the desk.

His hands come up, trying to pry mine from him, but I add my free one and smash his cheek harder into the wood.

"Tell me where they are," I demand, pulling the utility knife from my pants pocket. I flip open the blade and slide the edge beneath his eye, blood beading instantly in the line I carve. "Or I will slice you open right here and then parade your lifeless body around campus so everyone knows what a spineless, gutless little *shit* you are."

"Asher, please, we can talk about this—"

I twist his head to the other side, repeating the action with the knife on that cheek so he's symmetrical. Tears glide down his skin, mixing with the blood and pooling on his desk.

The anger in my heart burns white-hot—too suffocating for me to revel in his misery.

"What did they do with Lucy?"

"I–I don't *know*! I'm only a sponsor in name. They don't really tell me anything—"

The blade moves to his throat. I dig in more.

"*Fuck*, okay. They're using her to lure you down to the caves. Something about that godforsaken curse, but I swear that's all I know."

"Who's they?" Aurora asks.

"A group of Curators, I think. I'm not… I don't really know. Beckett Dupont, Tiernan O'Beirne, and someone else I can't remember. They requested a permit to conduct Curator business meetings in one of the caves through the Tenarus entrance, and I didn't want to grant it, but the board has final say. I can't go around what they order."

I grind the heel of my hand into his skull. "So the board has no issues with them using the caves to kidnap and probably murder?"

Bauer chuckles darkly. "Who the hell do you think encouraged it?"

Later, campus starts to brighten as Aurora and I trudge across it to meet Alistair and my father. They're both in jeans and coats, arguing quietly when we approach.

Turning, they reveal Muna between them, her hands in her pants pockets.

"Muna Henoke," Alistair says. "Meet—"

"We know each other," I interject, looking at her. "What are you doing here?"

"According to the Avernia website, Muna's the premier expert on the cave system in these mountains," Dad replies. "If Lucy and Foxe are indeed beneath them, like the dean claims, we figure it'd be beneficial to have some idea of what we are going into."

I cock an eyebrow at Muna, and she shrugs. "I like maps, all right? Plus, the Curators kept wanting to do shit in the blocked-off caves, so I was told to read up on them so we didn't get everyone killed immediately upon entry."

"As if there aren't perfectly fine buildings littering this property where they could have their little meetings," Alistair says, his mouth curling in disgust. His blue eyes pierce mine, and he juts his chin in the direction of the forest. "Let's get a bloody fucking move on then."

We trek to where the party was being held last night, looking for footprints. Tracks lead us through more thick foliage and dirt, eventually revealing the first cave entrance, highlighted by broken rocky steps and a hole that doesn't look big enough to fit any of us.

Rushing water from close by fills the air, disturbing the otherwise tranquil scene of Lake Lerna at this point. Its black surface is almost penetrable with the naked eye under the gently rising run.

Aurora swallows. "Maybe someone should stay out here. Keep watch in case you need help or something."

Muna hands the three of us a small map she printed on thin copy paper, pointing to a red circle. "We're here now." She drags her finger along a path inside the mountain, demonstrating where the few interior caverns are that the group may have gone to. "This gets pretty narrow, so you might want to send Asher ahead, since he's the skinniest of you three."

"Also the youngest," Alistair points out. "If the three of us can't make it through, then none of us go in. Simple as that."

Dad rubs the back of his neck, distributing flashlights. "Alistair—"

Holding up a hand, Alistair shakes his head. "No, Kal. I'm not putting *all* our children at risk." He looks at me, his blue eyes making my heart ache. "*We* don't fit, you don't go. Got it?"

I don't reply. Like I'd get this close to Lucy and just leave her in there.

He snatches my shirt at the neck, yanking me close. "Do you *understand?*"

A glance at Dad. He just lifts an eyebrow in agreement.

I nod, then shake out of Alistair's hold.

Dad claps me on the shoulder and turns me toward the cave entrance. He glances at Aurora and then Muna. "If we aren't back in a few hours, call for help."

Aurora hesitates. "Help or *help*?"

The authorities or her father.

Dad gives her a look and then pushes me forward. Alistair leads the charge, ducking down to fit inside the entrance. All of us have to bend slightly, since the cave maybe clears six feet. I bump my head more than once inside the narrow tunnel.

Without our flashlights, it'd be impossible to see anything. Dad keeps his facing backward, illuminating the path as we leave it, while Alistair focuses straight ahead.

The first cavern we come to is totally empty and only accessible if you crawl. None of us are interested, so we move on.

Unease floods my nervous system. It's dark and cramped, and for a long time, the only thing we hear is the dripping of a lone water source somewhere farther down.

At one point, Dad clears his throat, sliding closer to me. I pretend not to feel the claustrophobia prickling against my skin.

"Why in the world didn't you call one of us sooner? I thought your mother and I told you to let us know if things took a turn for the worse at Avernia," he says in a low voice. "Wasn't that your stipulation?"

"No," I reply. "You said not to cause problems for Quincy. I didn't."

"I also asked you to keep Lucy and Foxe safe. I said to keep them close. You were the only one of them fully aware of the danger lurking in the shadows, Asher."

Pausing, I spin around and shove him back a step. My neck cramps, but I ignore it as my anger reaches a peak, boiling over. "Do you think I don't fucking know that, Dad? You think I'm having fun down here looking for the most important people in my life, *hoping* like hell they weren't killed for some stupid thing I never bothered to warn them about?"

Dad's eyes widen.

Still, I keep on, my emotions stirring up word vomit. "I'm not a fucking *idiot*, you know, and I'm not *you*, so save the goddamn lecture for when we get home, all right? I do not need your help right now in feeling like a piece of shit."

With that, I turn and push past Alistair, breaking into a light sprint to gain some distance from the two of them.

The second cavern I find is empty too, but this one we can at least walk through. It splits off into two sections, and I stare at the fork, wondering which to choose.

Footsteps scrape against the ground, approaching me. My shoulders tense, preparing for Dad to lay into me some more, but it doesn't come.

Instead, Alistair stops beside me. "Your father said he'd catch up."

"Okay."

He glances between the two entrances. "Which one?"

I shrug. "Hell if I know."

"Left is *Lucy*," he says, chuckling to himself. He points to one, and we start walking again. "We used to have family trivia nights, and that's what Lachlan and Logan would say whenever Luce answered something wrong. The opposite of right was Lucy to them."

The corners of my mouth twitch. "I remember."

He nods. "I never did like the teasing, but I suppose I was always a bit more sensitive about things when it came to my firstborn. Her mum made me the man I am today, but that little girl... My entire perspective shifted the first time she opened her beautiful eyes and looked at me. It was like seeing myself in a mirror, but I wanted so much more for her than I ever got."

A pebble goes flying as we wind our way through the tunnel.

"Lachlan and Logan, they're attached to their mum, but Lucy needed me more, I think. She was soft and pure, and where her siblings could take the ribbing and the teasing and got along with everyone, Lucy was so terribly human that I was afraid she'd break as soon as she stepped foot outside the house. And the problem was she didn't really seem to get *how* to be human or the fact that it made her so very special to feel and love so deeply. Vulnerability is something that gets people killed in this world, but she never questioned hers."

I feel his eyes on me but remain silent. *That's what I love about her too.*

"It was my job to protect her," he says with a sigh. "But a few weeks after she was born, Elena Anderson brought her infant son to meet the newest addition to the Aplana brat pack."

A reluctant snort huffs out of me. "That the official name?"

"Don't tell your mum or my wife I used it, but that Mafia don uncle of yours actually coined it when he realized there were going to be a lot of spoiled kids on the island."

My mother's younger sister, Stella, and her husband have two kids we see only sporadically throughout the year, since they're much younger than the rest of us and in school across the country.

"Anyway, Elena brings this ruddy-faced babe to meet my daughter and asks Cora if she can put him in the crib. Just for a second. Lucy was wailing, and Cora and I were exhausted, so she agreed." Alistair pauses. "The *second* you touched the mattress, Lucy went silent. We all had to check and make sure she was still breathing—her eyes were open, staring blankly upward, but she looked so peaceful. You were holding onto her onesie, watching her, and I realized that day that I would never stand a chance. You two are connected at the soul, and I've always secretly despised you for that. I used to feel like I was intruding on a bond with my own child, but now, I'm… really goddamn grateful, I suppose, that she's always had you."

My chest tightens, and I feel a little woozy. Digging my nails into my palms, I suck in a deep breath, push the anger down for a moment, and exhale. "I *love* her."

He laughs. "Obviously. You tell her that yet?"

I shake my head.

"Well, don't wait. She deserves to hear it, lad."

And at that exact moment, we hear it—not her, and not a love confession, but the bloodcurdling screams of someone being tortured or maimed.

Male screams.

My heart drops into my stomach, bile pushing into my throat.

"Christ. Is that…"

Foxe.

We move toward the noise, the cramp in my neck spreading to my shoulders and beyond. My stomach flips, the sound obliterating all the negative space around us, shattering it like glass.

It becomes louder for several minutes and then suddenly stops.

Like a flame snuffed out.

Rage pulses behind my eyes, fueling my steps. It's the only thing I cling to as silence fills the cave again, bathing us in its implications.

Alistair tenses beside me, nudging my arm with his elbow. "Up ahead, you see that light?"

I nod, sticking to the wall as much as I can manage, and then peer around the entrance to the cavern, clinging to the dirty stone. A long floodlight casts warm shadows around a room filled with bloodshed: a corpse on the ground, mutilated beyond recognition. Another spot across from it is soaked in red, leading to footprints that I hate are so fucking familiar.

They walk right out of the room.

He isn't in here.

A dark-haired man crouches toward the back in front of a girl with mostly obsidian hair, save for the two crimson streaks framing her face.

I stare for longer than I should, soaking in the sight of her.

Alive.

Battered and bruised, but *alive.*

Pushing off from the wall, I propel myself inside, sprinting before the crouching man can turn or fully register my presence. He's leaned in, speaking to her in soft tones, and I want to rip his spine out with my teeth.

Instead, I tackle him, driving my knee into his back as his face slams onto the ground. Grabbing his hair, I bring his head up and repeat the motion, not stopping when blood sprays where the impact busts his nose wide open. Same as I did before leaving Dean Bauer hours earlier.

The blood gets on my fingers, splashing onto my face and neck, and he's totally unconscious by the time I feel a hand on my shoulder.

I spin around, pushing Alistair off me, and face Lucy.

For several seconds, we just stare at each other on our knees, struck completely silent.

"You came for me?" she whispers.

Her voice makes me lightheaded. "Of fucking course I did, baby."

She brings her free arm up gently—so fucking gently—touching my face with swollen fingers, like she can't believe I'm really here.

Her blue eyes are tinged red and wet. She's been crying—no, *sobbing* more likely.

My chest pinches, and I itch to continue beating Beckett Dupont. I'm trembling with the need to make him hurt, but then she scoots forward and launches herself into my arms.

When she buries her face in my neck, she unleashes a torrent of tears, soaking my skin in a downpour. Her wailing echoes in the cavern, ricocheting off the walls and piercing me in the heart.

She clings to me, her breath hot on my throat. "Foxe—they t-took him. I–I don't know where… I don't know w-what they did, but I don't think…"

A tear slips over my cheek. "I know, baby. I know." I make eye contact with her father, whose eyes are red now too. "I'm so, so fucking sorry."

Chapter 46

Asher

DAD EVENTUALLY MAKES HIS WAY TO WHERE WE ARE, STRETCHING his arms over his head, since the ceiling is much higher here than anywhere else.

He glances around the cavern as he stands beside me, both of us giving Lucy and Alistair a private moment to collect themselves. She's wrapped in her dad's arms, and right now, I can't watch.

Not knowing Grayson and Violet won't get that with Foxe again.

Dad clears his throat. "What I said earlier—"

"It's fine. I know you didn't mean it."

"Oh no, I did mean it."

He turns to me, and I take a second to appreciate the heart-to-hearts happening in here while a corpse casually rots and the corpse-to-be continues to lie unconscious mere feet away. Frankly, I would expect nothing less from us.

"I hold you to a high standard because I know you're capable of attaining it," he says. "For a long time, I was afraid of you, being *my* son. I didn't want you to be like me, and you are in so many ways. But I'm okay with that. I've made my peace with it because you're a better version of me. By a million miles. Sometimes, it just seems like you get stuck on your negative emotions, and they end up ruling when you should be making better decisions. I try not to interfere unless you ask, but when it comes to protecting the people you love, that isn't something to skimp on. Ever. I'm sorry if that feels unfair or if I haven't been the best role model for it, but *that* is the Anderson curse. Taking care of the people who make your life better."

He used to be so quiet, always observing and reserving his thoughts for when he was asked for them. I grew up watching that and internalizing it, learning that sometimes words weren't necessary. Action seemed better, and I loved my fists most.

They got results.

But I've always sort of resented the savior complex he seemed to have. No matter what, day or night, if someone he loved had a problem, he was there for them. Which meant there were a dozen or more people on the planet who took attention away from me.

Stupid, really. Selfish too. He never neglected me, yet I hated that he helped others, like it somehow meant he loved me less.

But he wouldn't be here if he didn't love me. I know that much.

Something tells me he came in the hope of finding his nephew alive and keeping me from Grayson's wrath. Despite his silence on the phone earlier, there's no doubt in my mind he'd never let anyone touch me.

Because he's my dad, and that's what they're supposed to do.

I scrub a hand down the side of my face, nodding. "All right. I get it. Sorry for being a dick."

Dad smirks. "You're my kid. I expect it at this point."

"Hey," Alistair says, finally breaking away from Lucy. "Maybe we should get out of here before the others come back."

My father concurs, and the two of them start the charge out of the cavern. I hang back, taking a few extra seconds to get a better look at Lucy. Her sweater is gone, her tank top and arms covered in blood. There's a purple welt on her wet, red face and trauma hidden behind her wide, guarded blue eyes.

But when I open my arms, she limps to me instantly, and I swear to God I never want to leave her embrace again for as long as I live.

Anger is impossible to hold on to when I'm wrapped up in her.

I keep her close to my side as we walk out behind our dads, but she freezes in place in the tunnel, staring to the left. She doesn't move, even when I gently try to coax her in the opposite direction.

"Lucy," her father urges. "We need to go."

She shakes her head. "I can't."

I glance down, assessing her again. "Is it your leg? I'll just carry you—"

"No," she cuts in. "I don't want to leave those guys down here and risk letting them get away. Not after what…" She trails off, voice wobbling, and she rubs her nose with her hand. "Not after what they did."

My eyebrows arch. Alistair exhales, and Dad purses his lips. "I suppose your father and I could go—"

"*No.* I want to see it. I want them dead, and I want to make sure it sticks."

"Honey…"

Ignoring Alistair, she snatches the gun strapped to Dad's side and shoves past me. The three of us look at one another for a moment, then blink, springing into action after her. I catch up easily, since she's kind of slow right now due to her injuries, and pry the weapon from her hands.

"Don't try to talk me out of it," she deadpans.

"Wouldn't dream of it, pup." I show her how to use the weapon in the glow from Dad's flashlight, aware that she's not unfamiliar with guns because of her dad, but still. I need to do something with my hands.

She watches carefully, placing her fingers where I tell her to. Her breathing is labored, and mine matches it.

The last cavern before a dead end is totally lit up inside; we peer around the wall, noting the table where a tall, lanky man is strapped, lying in a pool of his own blood. He's been stripped naked, and a metal device with a phallic end piece is set up behind him, between his legs.

It's bloody too.

Dad curses under his breath.

Foxe's face is black and blue, turned on its side. His head is restrained with thick Velcro straps, his ankles bolted to the table legs, while a slice in one exposes thick tendon and bone.

Lucy retches quietly, and I bite my tongue until a small piece tears off.

Other than my cousin's lifeless form, there's only one masked figure hanging out. He's sitting in a chair with his back toward us, playing a game on his phone with earbuds in.

He must sense something is off though, because in the next second, he's jumping up and whirling on us. I dive for his ankles, knocking him off his feet, and take out my utility knife, driving it into his stomach repeatedly until he matches what they did to Foxe.

I push the mask and hood off him, revealing that fucking red-headed guy Muna's friends with. His eyes are wide open, unseeing as the life fades.

Lucy spits on him.

Getting back to my feet, I glare at Alistair and my father. "Thanks for the fucking help."

"You had it under control," Alistair says, leaning against the wall.

Dad walks to Foxe, bending for an inspection, and I hear him curse again as I drag Tiernan's body off to the side.

"He's alive," Dad says, his fingers pressed to Foxe's neck. "But we've got to get him out *now*."

Before anyone can move, a gunshot rings through the air, shattering the illusion that maybe we were leaving unscathed. Dad clutches his chest as he's hit, gritting his teeth and staggering against the table.

"*Dad!*" My shout echoes off the walls as another gunshot sends us into darkness. I duck, diving behind Tiernan's corpse, and yank Lucy along with me.

Nobody moves or makes a sound. The atmosphere tightens, thickening around us as my eyes slowly adjust. I don't see a third figure anywhere, so they must be lurking strategically.

Lucy flips onto her hands and knees. She starts to crawl away, and I hook my fingers around her ankle, stopping her.

"What the fuck are you doing?" I hiss, trying to drag her back.

She kicks at me. "I can see really well right now. I spent way too much time in the dark at the Obeliskos this semester, and my eyes are adjusting better from it, I guess. I'm going to go undo Foxe's restraints and check on your dad."

"Lucy, no. Absolutely the fuck not."

Her grin tears my heart into pieces. "I wasn't asking permission, *pretty boy*."

Nostrils flaring, I release her and ball my hands into fists, casting my gaze back around the cavern, searching for the slightest movement. A breeze floats in from behind me, and I turn, keeping crouched low as I make my way toward it.

I feel an electric cord and follow the length, hoping it leads to some sort of light. Alistair has his, but I'm sure he's keeping it off so as not to draw attention to himself.

My hand brushes something smooth and hard, distinctly leather, and I pause. Lifting my chin, I look up, tracing a figure standing just inches from my body.

Shock strikes my chest, and I blink, trying to register what's happening but unable to do so. The clear mouth of a gun presses against my temple, and I swallow, cursing the entire fucking universe for my absolute shit luck.

I close my eyes, but they pop back open when an ear-piercing shriek snaps across the cavern, whipping against me. A flashlight shines on the masked figure as Lucy launches herself at it, bringing a fucking sledgehammer up over her body before swinging it into the guy's head.

He crumples instantly, and I scramble to my feet, blinking with my mouth agape as Lucy drops the tool and stares at him. She blinks too, like she isn't quite sure what she just did. I wrap a hand around her neck and kiss the fuck out of her.

She makes an excited noise in the back of her throat when my tongue parts her lips, but then she smacks me, shoving me toward the masked man as he tries to stand.

Planting my knee in his gut, I take out my knife again and hold it beneath his chin, ripping the mask off in a single flick.

Lucy gasps. "*Eli?*"

He coughs, straining against me, blood pouring from where the sledgehammer tore a chunk from his scalp. His eyes are vibrating. "Fuck, just kill me. Please."

"Oh, I'm going to." I push a little harder, the tip of my blade sinking into his skin.

"Wait!" Lucy says, grabbing my shoulder. She hesitates, and Eli's green eyes find hers, devoid of even a hint of emotion. "What—*why*? I thought you were my friend."

"Look, you don't become a fucking Curator without getting some blood on your hands, all right? It wasn't personal, and it didn't start with you. Your roommate, she was collateral damage. An initiation. Me, Tiernan, and that other kid... What was his name? Tag?"

"*Tag* was there that night?"

"He helped kill her. It was the three of us, although we brought a manipulated recording of Beckett to frame him in case anyone stumbled upon the scene. Imagine my surprise when it was *you*, Lucy. The girl who rarely even left her dorm wound up in the wrong place and time that night, so Tag decided to get close to you to see if you knew anything about it." Eli scoffs. "Problem was Tiernan and I thought he was getting freaked out and wanted to confess to you, so we eliminated that problem as well."

Lucy doesn't say a word.

"My family has never taken me seriously, so I thought, why not sow contention between the founding families? Prey on Beckett's dumb beliefs and have a little fun in the meantime." He sizes Lucy up, cocking an eyebrow. "Too bad I didn't get to finish. I had really big plans for you, if only—"

A flick of my wrist sends the knife through his throat. He gurgles, reaching for me, before falling limp under my hold.

"Oops."

Lucy lets out a long, shaky breath as I stand back up. I push some hair behind her ear, noting the missing piercing in her lobe, which has been slightly torn.

She pouts. "I didn't get to actually kill anyone."

"You don't want that burden, pup."

"How come it's okay for *you* then?"

"Because I don't care about me. My conscience has been dead for a long time." I cup her cheek, tilting her head. "But you? I love that yours is free. I don't want to fucking change a thing about you."

She leans into my touch. "Sounds an awful lot like a love confession, Asher Blake Anderson."

I grin. "Baby, I've loved you my entire life. Seems like you have some catching up to do."

"Okay, quit trying to make us grandparents, and get the hell over here," Alistair snaps.

Dad's propped up against the wall, holding his coat to his shoulder. Relief floods me at the sight of him, and then again when I see Foxe's eyes are open, albeit pretty blank.

"We've got to get these two out of here," Alistair says. "Asher, you and I will shoulder Foxe, and Lucy can walk with your dad. The bleeding is stabilized. We think it's a shallow wound but can't be sure until we have better light. And EMTs, probably."

"Not like I'm a fucking doctor," Dad mutters, getting to his feet.

As Alistair and I maneuver Foxe from the table, I try not to focus much on the fact that he doesn't make a single sound. Not of pain or to crack a joke or anything.

It's unnerving.

What the fuck did they do to him?

I pause once Foxe is situated between Alistair and me, noting the metal table he was just strapped to has three names written in big block letters in blood.

Quincy.

Noelle.

Asher.

And mine is the only one marked out.

Chapter 47

Lucy

ASHER STANDS IN THE DOORWAY OF THE HOTEL SUITE, HANDS IN his pockets.

Dad wanted all of us to head back to Aplana Island, but I refuse to leave before Foxe is in recovery, and Asher agreed. My father booked us all rooms and then disappeared with Aurora and Muna to take care of things back at Avernia.

Whatever those *things* are, I don't know and didn't ask. For once, I'm going to let him take care of it.

I'm wearing a change of clothes that Aurora brought—a fleece pajama short and tank top set—and clutching the hotel blankets like a life raft. I took my regular meds and the painkillers Dad grabbed from my dorm, but still there's a humming in my body that only ever seems to come alive when Asher's around.

This is the first I've seen of him since last night.

He's cleaned up, hair dripping likely from a shower, and I can't stop staring at him—his warm brown eyes, hard as topaz as he casts his gaze around the dull room. The slant of his jaw, the wet strands of hair sticking to his forehead, and the aura that just pulses around him.

Even though I can tell he's still angry, I know I'm safe with him here.

I can breathe. Relax my jaw and unclench my muscles.

Maybe even sleep.

Mom and Aunt Lenny have been calling nonstop since Dad checked me in, asking if they needed to fly to us. I declined, because I don't really want to deal with all that extra attention right now, and I'm afraid that if anyone else asks me if I'm okay, I'm going to explode.

Asher doesn't ask, because he already knows. I see it reflected in his eyes. When he steps inside the room, he gently clicks the door shut, latching the lock.

For a few seconds, we just look at each other. None of this feels real still. I've barely comprehended that Foxe is alive and we got out, much less that Asher's here with me. Angry but so obviously relieved.

I throw back the comforter at the same time as he stalks quickly across the room, snatching me into his arms. He clings so tight that it's difficult to breathe, but I don't say a word, soaking in his fresh, clean scent and letting his warmth ground me.

Burying my face in his neck, I let out a broken whimper. "I'm so sorry."

He pulls back, palming my head. "What the hell are you apologizing for?"

"I didn't listen to you when you told me to stay away from Beckett," I say. "If I'd just stayed put and let you do what you wanted, *none* of this would have happened. I got two people killed, your dad injured, and Foxe..." My eyes sting, and I try to blink the tears away, but they fall regardless. "He stepped in for me. They wanted to take me, and he begged to go in my place."

Dropping my gaze as I admit the last part, a wave of nausea rolls through me, and I try to break from Asher's grip. I can't look at him— not after that.

But he tightens his hold, his face hard as stone. "Don't fucking look away from me, pup. You think that'll do you any good? I *know* you. I can feel the despair taking root in your bones as we speak. I hear your guilt and shame making your brain move a thousand miles a minute. I'm not letting you go so you can curl up in bed and spiral."

I glare at him. "You can't just *force* me to not feel bad about this. Foxe is fighting for his *life* because of me." Another sob, and this time he catches it against his throat, smoothing his hand over my hair. "How can you even stand to touch me right now, knowing that? You should hate me."

"Tried that once. Didn't really work out."

Pulling back, I furrow my eyebrows. "What?"

"When we were thirteen, and I was a stupid little shit who hated seeing you cry. I left your dog's funeral early because I was trying to convince myself that watching you get emotional would be easier if I couldn't stand you."

Offense scratches at my chest. "Wow. So when I made my way to your bedroom seeking comfort, you were thinking about how much you hated me?"

"I *didn't* hate you though. I *couldn't*. Your vulnerability and compassion are what I liked most about you; it wasn't fair to hold them against you just because I was insecure." He pauses, sliding his fingers over my jaw. "Foxe loves all that about you too, you know. He didn't just come to Avernia for me."

Sniffling, I shake my head. "Not helping ease the guilt, pretty boy."

His grin chips away at the frozen pieces of my heart. Just a little, but enough. "What I'm saying is… Foxe made his own decisions down in that cave. Shit decisions I'm going to kick his ass for when he's healed up, but still. You didn't make him do it. And if anything, I'm to fucking blame for bringing him here in the first place. All he wanted to do was spend some quality time with us, and I've been an asshole to him all semester."

My heart shatters with the realization that neither of us was kind to him. Not the way he deserves.

And maybe that's what guilt is—a culmination of events and neglect that causes other people to get hurt. People who would never do it back to you.

Who would sacrifice themselves *for* you.

"What about Beckett?" I ask, finally redirecting the conversation. "Willa and…"

I can't bring myself to say their names, just like I can barely believe what Eli said about Tag.

It hadn't been Beckett at all. Just the other three causing fucking chaos, ruining lives for no reason.

Exhaling, Asher yanks me in the direction of the bed. He perches on the edge of the mattress, pulling me onto his lap. "Fury Hill PD has the entire Primordial Forest on lockdown, though it wouldn't surprise me if everything was cleaned up by Monday. Beckett's being treated at the student health center, and the coroner came to collect the others."

Nodding, I lay my head on his shoulder. "How come I don't feel at all relieved that the police are involved?"

He draws circles on my lower back. "Because you know better."

"Should I withdraw from the school?"

"I don't know, Luce. That's a decision you have to make." Shifting, he moves us so I'm lying flat on the bed and he's hovering over me, his arms bracketing my face. "I'm assuming you had a reason to stick around all this time."

"Avernia credits are nontransferable," I say, rolling my eyes. "I didn't want to waste my parents' money or my time by starting over. But you know, if you'd just *told* me what the fuck was going on all this time, maybe none of this would've happened."

"I know." He shakes his head, clenching his jaw. "I was an idiot, and I fucked up. I'll live with that forever."

Leaning down, he presses a kiss to my clavicle, then drags his lips along the bone until he reaches the other end.

My stomach flutters, and I wince. The painkillers they gave me to help ease the bruising have mostly kicked in, but I don't mind that I can still feel a little. Reminds me that I *am* here.

I made it out of that cave.

Alive.

When Asher rears back up, his handsome face looming above me, I cup both of his cheeks in my hands and pull him in. The first sweep of his mouth over mine is tentative, unsure, but then I push my tongue so it tangles with his, deepening the kiss.

A gentle, nervous caress turns to fervent, needy lust, and soon my fingers thread through his hair and he tugs on my top, revealing a breast for his empty palm. The kneading and teasing of my swollen flesh is the only part of me he touches, and I arch into it, pleasure rippling through my body as if it's not battered at all.

One of my legs hooks around his waist, bringing our pelvises together so I can feel the length of his arousal. I gasp into his mouth as he grinds against my clit for the briefest second, but then Asher's retreating, removing my thigh.

"You're hurt," he says softly, resting his forehead on mine.

"We can be careful," I reply, covering his hand with my own, squeezing my breast.

"I can't keep making your pain worse. Everything that happened tonight is *my* fault. Not yours—"

Shaking my head, I lift my chin, capturing his lips. "We have the rest of our lives to make up for the bullshit of the last three years. But I don't want to think about that right now. I don't want to think about anything at all except how good it feels to have you touch me."

My lashes flutter, and he grips my breast roughly, his eyes blazing with desperation. If I had to guess, I'd say they're a direct mirror of mine.

Finally, he gives in with a heavy exhale, flopping onto his back. I don't have time to question what he's doing before he's shoving his pants down over his hips, kicking out of them, and then dragging his shirt over his head.

I watch, mouth watering, as every inch of his pale skin becomes visible to me. At this point, I've seen him naked dozens of times, yet it feels like the first revelation all over again. Silently, I trace the outline of that wolf on his thigh, my heart pounding against my rib cage as his muscles tense beneath my touch.

With a grunt, he pulls me up to straddle him. His cock lies thick and stiff against his stomach, and I glide my pussy over it, absorbing the way it throbs even through my clothes.

Eyebrows drawing in, Asher slips the straps of my pajama top over my shoulders, letting the fabric pool at my waist. His jaw clenches so hard a dimple forms in his cheek, and I frown, smoothing my thumb over the crease above his nose.

"I can't really get in the mood when you're glaring at me like that," I say.

His nostrils flare, his gaze glued to my stomach. I glance down, cringing inwardly when I realize how badly bruised I am; reddish purple splotches fan over my abdomen, still swollen and tender to the touch, even with the pain meds.

Feeling decidedly not sexy, I reach for my top and start to pull it back up, but Asher places his hands over mine, stopping me.

"No, no. I…" He inhales, closing his eyes for a moment before opening them again on his exhale. "If you're sure you want to do this, I need to see you. You're not the only one who could use a reminder that you're alive, pup."

Nodding, I slowly grind against him, taking his hands and putting them farther back on my hips, where the skin is mostly unblemished.

"But if you wince even a fucking little, we're done here," he tells me, leaning to seal our lips together.

The first touch of his tongue flicking inside my mouth has me moaning, tilting my head to grant him better access. His hold on my hips starts to mobilize, guiding me over his cock the way he did weeks ago in his dorm room.

Electricity jolts through me as my clit rubs against him, the friction of my underwear and shorts causing my pulse to skyrocket. I grow wetter by the second, each thrust timed with his kisses, as if that's what's driving my movement rather than utter need.

Bringing my fingers to his chest, I explore the expanse of smooth skin and taut muscle. His nose ring bumps me at one point, a slight cold bite as he jerks into my touch as if yearning for more.

"Shit," he breathes, pulling away. "I want to put my dick in you so bad."

Pushing up on my knees, I reach between us and tug my clothes to the side. My pussy spreads over his shaft, leaving a trail of glistening arousal, making the motion smoother and smoother.

"Do it," I whisper, leaning so he's forced onto his back, his hands falling to the outsides of my thighs, fingers indenting my flesh. One glide forward and a slight shift up, and when I go an inch backward, his tip slips in. Just for a second, just barely enough for the two of us to simultaneously gasp.

"Are you going to hate me for this tomorrow?"

Narrowing my eyes, I get to my feet above him and shake out of my clothes before resituating myself on top of his cock again. Then I lean over to the nightstand and turn off the bedside lamp, enshrouding us in near darkness, save for a streak of moonlight spilling in from between the curtains.

He's a silhouette now, and there's something about not being able to fully see each other that adds a layer of tension to this. Truly relying on the other senses, when seeing is not the sole cause of belief.

Living is an amalgamation of those senses. His clean, cotton scent, the salty taste of his damp skin as I drag my tongue up his throat. The strangled noise he makes when I fist his cock in my hand, thumbing it inside me without preamble.

Fuck, it burns, and I don't know if it's because I'm still getting used to having his girth in me or because I'm in worse shape than I realized, but I don't let that stop me. Placing my palms on his chest, I lower myself onto him slowly, gritting my teeth.

I need this. It doesn't matter how it feels, only that we're connected and—

Asher reaches between my legs, playing with my clit, and squeezes my thigh. "Slow, baby. Slow."

Something pinches in my chest at his calm command; I obey, even though that defiant piece of me doesn't really want to, working him in as arousal floods through me. His thumb draws lazy circles over my clit, and each inch becomes easier to manage until he's fully seated within, his pelvis soaked from my juices.

I can feel them sticking to us when I begin to move, riding the fullness, the rightness of us being connected like this. My stomach tenses, my nails clawing at his skin, desperate for more.

We settle into a rhythm that has both of us panting, our breaths disappearing into each other's mouths as I lean down to kiss him. He grips my ass in both hands, holding me upright while he drives into me from below, making me dizzy with the sudden brutality.

I bury my face in his neck, pressing my open mouth to his skin and biting down. He hisses, fucking me harder, one of his hands tangling in my hair. I half expect him to pull me away, but instead he seems to hold me in place.

"That's it, baby," he croons in my ear. "Mark me when you come on my dick. Make me feel it all. Make me yours."

Spurred on by his filthy words, I slide my fingers to his throat, increasing the pressure of my bite until he's groaning, massaging my clit faster to push me closer toward the edge. The taste of copper sprinkles on my tongue, and I sit up, reveling in the red imprint of my teeth and the light splash of blood there.

A shot of renewed arousal pulses within me, making my stomach somersault. I remove his hands from my body, pinning them on the mattress by his head, and fuck him back, rotating my hips so each stroke of his cock against my inner muscles makes us cry out.

"Christ, you feel fucking incredible," Asher moans, his forearms flexing under my grip. His eyes hood, growing heavy with lust and impending release, and it fills me with a sense of triumph.

"I really like fucking you," I tell him in a low, sultry voice. At least I hope that's what it sounds like.

"Keep going then, pup," he replies, the tendons in his neck straining. My bitemark blooms red and vicious, and I'm tempted to do it again. Maybe make the other side match.

I've never known what possessiveness really felt like until this very moment. Asher's always sort of made himself available to me, outside the three years we spent apart. So there was never a need to worry.

Now though, fear drives me to unnavigated territory. It's a need unlike anything I've ever known, this instinctive desire to make him mine permanently. Forever.

Like I could crack open his chest and sew myself inside, if that were possible.

Asher's panting grows more labored, and sweat pours down his face as I rock back and forth, the undulation of my hips making him hit that special spot inside me. My vision is blurring, pleasure teasing the corners and crawling its way up my spine, but I don't stop.

"Lucy," he warns, nostrils flaring. "Fuck. Lucy, *shit*. Can…can I *please* come?"

Him asking for permission makes me move faster.

"You need it bad, huh?"

"So bad. I'm so fucking close. *Please*, baby."

I huff, nodding. "Do it, pretty boy. Come for me."

Eyes widening when I don't make a move to climb off him, he lets out a strangled noise. "I'm not wearing anything—"

"*Inside* me. Fill me up, please."

His cock swells, but still he hesitates. His next word is barely more than a whimper, and shocks of arousal spin webs through my veins. "*Lucy.*"

"*Please*," I whine, so close myself that I don't want to stop. I can't stop. "Please, just this once. I'll take a Plan B or something after, but I need this. I need you—need to feel your cum flood my pussy."

"Jesus fucking *Christ*," he groans, his hips bucking as he unravels at the tail end of my plea. Hot, thick spurts of his cum warm my inner muscles, and the soft cry he releases shoves me off the cliff into oblivion.

I ride him through both of our orgasms, my pussy spasming around his cock until it's so drained that he leaks out of me, pooling between us.

Only the sound of our breathing dominates the air for several minutes as we come down from the high of climax. I collapse on top of him, fatigue finally catching up with me, and he lets me lie like that for a while, stroking my back in slow motion.

"Trouble," he says after a while, voice low. "That's what I should've nicknamed you when we were kids. You're a terrible influence."

I peek up at him through my lashes, not wanting to fully open my eyes. "You love it though."

He taps my nose with his index finger. "I love *you*. I'm not sure what I would have done if I'd brought your corpse out of that cave."

"Probably would've burned the school down."

Silence. Then, "Did I ever apologize for the fire at Lethe's?"

I snort. "You've apologized, like, once in your whole life, Asher."

"Right. Well… I'm not sorry for smoking you out of that trashy place, but I *am* sorry for the shit it caused after. If I'd known they were going to blame you, I—"

"Still would've done it, because you're a little bit of a lunatic when you're angry," I finish for him.

He doesn't respond, so I sit up, pressing my palm to his cheek.

"I love you," I say softly, tracing the outline of his mouth with my thumb. "I know you'd never do anything to actually hurt me. Your entire life has pretty much been dedicated to the exact opposite actually."

"Bodyguard since birth," he jokes, although there's still some tension in his words. Between us. All the hurt and anger, the stupidity and the danger—I guess that doesn't just magically disappear when you're in love.

Trust and healing are still things you have to work at, especially when you've been burned before.

But there's no one in the world I'd rather work through the bullshit with than him.

Asher Blake Anderson.

The angry boy who broke my heart when we were younger.

And the one who put it back together again.

Epilogue

Asher

WEEKS LATER, FOXE STILL LOOKS LIKE ABSOLUTE SHIT, BUT AT LEAST he's discharged and able to walk around, albeit with a bit of a limp.

His right arm is in a cast, and bandages cover a decent portion of his abdomen from where stab wounds and burns are still healing. There's also a deep grooved scar between his eyebrows from where they did a skin graft to reconstruct part of his nose.

But…he's here.

Sort of.

As he hobbles around his little apartment on the Aplana Island coast, I stand in the doorway, trying to ascertain what exactly is missing.

The light in his hazel eyes seems to have dulled. He doesn't joke around quite as much, a somber expression having permanently etched itself onto his face. When he smiles, the gesture doesn't quite translate.

"You want anything to drink?" he asks, leaning into his fridge. "My mom left some fresh lemonade when she dropped by this morning."

My eyebrows quirk, and I glance around, noting the growing collection of potted plants covering nearly every flat surface of the living room and kitchen areas. "She come over often?"

"Jesus, twice a day every day. Like she's afraid I'll forget to take my medication unless she's here to watch me do it."

I'd say her bigger fear is him getting hooked on the pain pills, given his history, but I don't mention that. I'm sure he already knows.

"But you love the attention, I bet," I tease, flopping down on the dark green suede couch in his living room. I take the bag from my shoulder and settle it on my lap.

He slumps in a matching armchair, kicking his feet up on the glass coffee table between us. "Feels like I've fully regressed into being a child again, but hey. At least I don't have to make myself supper any time soon."

The smirk he gives is easy. Practiced. Still, I don't comment on it.

"Anyway," he says, shaking himself and leaning back. "Where's your other half today?"

"She went back to Fury Hill to pack up her dorm, since she'll be staying off-campus next semester."

"I didn't think that was allowed."

"Well, it wasn't. Until our moms went up there and threatened Bauer within an inch of his life. He's pretty agreeable now that we all have a bunch of shit on him."

Foxe snorts. "I'll bet he is. It's too bad you still haven't burned the place down yet."

"Working on it."

He nods, blowing out a long breath. "What brings you around then?"

"Can't a guy come check on his best friend without an ulterior motive?"

"Best friend, huh?" He gives me a look. "I know better."

I wring my hands together and then unzip the bag on my lap, pulling out the wooden box that Lucy shoved into my hands all those weeks ago, accusing me of having some nefarious plan with it.

She wasn't wrong, really, although this one had been a duplicate. I'm still not sure how it got there, or who made it, but I'm coming to accept that some things in life just don't get answers.

But the real box was my doing, and the stuff I had tucked inside would have incinerated the forest surrounding the school. That was why I'd brought it.

After receiving that cryptic email, I'd decided to enroll at Avernia—just long enough to burn it to the ground and displace Lucy, forcing her to safety.

Then I got attacked before I could put it into motion. Once I'd taken care of that, I abandoned my goal to find Lucy, afraid that she'd be the next target in the woods. From there, she consumed my life, so I never got around to setting the fire at all.

Now, with the threat to Lucy at least contained for the moment, it hardly seems worth the trouble.

For me anyway.

Holding the box out, I cock an eyebrow at my cousin. "Thought you might want this."

"Your box of paraphernalia? I'm touched, Asher. Truly."

Asher. I think that might be the first time he's called me by my actual name since we were kids.

Guilt blossoms like a fucking botanic garden in my gut, but I ignore it. That emotion does no one any good.

"I'll leave torching Avernia to you if you're interested."

Foxe takes the container, staring down at it silently for several beats. "Do I look like I'm in any condition to be setting things on fire?"

"Doesn't have to be right this second," I tell him. "Or even a year from now. Do it when you're ready, or don't do it at all. Makes no difference to me. I just thought that having the option would help you sleep better at night."

His chin lifts, the red rings around his eyes brightening as the light shifts on his face.

"If I'm having issues sleeping, I know you probably are too." Patting my legs, I push back to my feet.

"You love me," he says, a slow grin breaking out across his face.

It hits me in the center of my chest, that glimmer of the old Foxe. Makes me hopeful that he's still around somewhere inside there.

"Don't read too much into it." Tossing a balled-up pair of socks at him from the coffee table, I head for the apartment's entrance, shrugging on my coat.

"Hey, wait," he says as I open the door, taking in the snow flurries drifting from the gray sky. "What's that on your neck? New tattoo?"

Pausing, I bring my hand to the still-tender spot where neck meets shoulder and smirk to myself.

"Yeah," I reply, recalling how my toes had curled when Lucy's teeth indented my skin with their print. So much so that I got the impressions inked on my skin earlier, eager to be permanently marked by her. "It is."

By the time I make it back to Avernia, Quincy's closing Lucy's dorm room, and the sky is pitch-black. Not even the stars have come out to play tonight.

I meet my sisters in Quincy's office, where Noelle sits on the corner of the desk, swinging her legs back and forth. Her dark brown hair is tucked inside a black hood, her skin glowing with a light sheen of sweat, like she's nervous, though I can't imagine why.

Neither Quincy nor I have been informed as to why she deferred starting school this past semester, but I suppose it doesn't entirely matter now that she's enrolled in the theater program for the spring semester.

For a few months, all three Anderson kids will be in the exact same place, and I try to ignore the unease that crops up in my stomach at that notion, remembering the names in that cave.

Our names. Two unmarked, one crossed out.

It feels as if trouble is only just beginning.

And in a way, I guess it is.

"Do we have everything?" Quincy asks, shutting the office door behind her.

She's wearing a black hoodie, pulled all the way to her chin, and a black knit cap pulled over her forehead. She walks to a filing cabinet against the far wall, tossing Noelle and I each a pair of black gloves.

"Blowtorch, lock-picking shit, kerosene…check." Noelle rummages around in her canvas knapsack, nodding. "But I must remind you two that there is in fact time to back out."

Quincy and I just look at her.

Noelle holds up her hands. "Okay, sorry, I just thought maybe you'd want to send a more…theatrical message, but I forgot I'm dealing with the silent twins."

"Destruction is much more impactful when it happens while you're sleeping," Quincy says, wrenching open the door.

"Not my cup of tea, but I'm happy to be invited." Noelle slings the bag over her shoulder, following our older sister out of the room.

I stare after them both for a few quiet seconds, wondering if this is something I should be dragging them into. Then again, neither of them is innocent.

The blood on an Anderson's hands is there at birth. There's no scrubbing it clean.

Embracing our cursed heritage is the only way to survive.

We wind up outside Dean Bauer's campus home and get to quick work making the first floor of the Victorian building inaccessible, inside and out.

The double-paned windows are already made of bulletproof, reinforced glass according to the blueprints we dug up in the Obeliskos, so breaking one of them won't be possible.

He'll have to climb out of the second story if he wants to survive.

I pour the kerosene in a nice, neat little trail on the wraparound porch, inhaling the pungent odor as I come back to where Quincy and Noelle stand just off the steps. I take a match from the book in my pants pocket, strike one against the strip, and drop it on the porch.

Flames burst from that site and spread instantly, singeing a piece of my hair as I calmly descend the stairs and stand next to my sisters. We look up at the house as a light flips on upstairs, and then several more of the windows illuminate, likely as Bauer discovers the imminent danger he's in.

I'm certain he'll get out, even if it means making a fucking fool of himself. There's no way that bastard is going down without a real fight.

We watch the fire rise, orange and bright yellows mixing with the night sky. Off in the distance, the Obeliskos's clock tower chimes, signaling midnight. One of the windows upstairs opens, and Dean Bauer leans out to scream expletives at the three of us.

"Oof," Noelle says, cringing. "Maybe doing this before I started classes wasn't a good idea."

"He would've hated you either way," Quincy says with finality, spinning on her heels.

Noelle and I follow suit, ignoring the dean's cries the way he ignored everything else going on this semester. I couldn't give less of a fuck if he makes it out or not, frankly.

If Lucy wasn't expecting me at her new apartment soon, I'd walk in and kill the fucker myself. Damn the consequences.

Anger can only be sated so much when it comes to people who've harmed the ones you love.

I fear I'll be angry forever about what happened to Foxe and Lucy, but this helps keep it at bay. For now.

A lone figure stands in the shadows near the Lyceum, a briefcase in hand, watching as flames consume the dean's house. The three of us continue walking as if we don't see a thing.

Professor Dupont's handsome, stoic face is half-lit by some of the streetlights, and as we pass him, Noelle stops in her tracks about a hundred feet away.

She stares, silent.

He looks back.

"Noelle?" Quincy asks, nudging her.

I lean in, noting that Noelle's face has paled, now as moon-white as mine and Quincy's. She blinks rapidly, then gives her head a little shake, and when I glance back over my shoulder, the professor is gone.

"Sorry," Noelle says with a little laugh. "For a second there, I thought I'd seen a ghost."

Her hand trembles when she tucks her hair behind her ears, but then she keeps skipping along, dragging Quincy with her, and I pretend I didn't notice shit.

When I look back at the burning house, I swear I see the professor once again, staring up at it. Hesitating maybe. Or thinking.

But then he walks on, disappearing into the Fury Hill nighttime.

I leave my sisters on campus and head straight for Lucy's apartment, not even bothering to knock when I skip up the steps to the front door. She, Cora, and her sister are all sitting in the living room, arguing over a dog collar.

"Oh good!" Lucy squeals, jumping to her feet with the orange fabric in hand. "Asher can help settle this."

"Please," Logan snorts, rolling her eyes. "He's your boyfriend. Of course he's going to agree with you."

"I'm her boyfriend? I don't remember being asked to date," I say, my eyebrows arching as Lucy comes to a stop inches away from me.

She's in an old T-shirt of mine and a pair of oversize sweatpants, and I want nothing more right now than to peel them off and fuck her on every surface of the apartment.

But I don't, for obvious reasons.

"You guys have been practically married for twenty-two years," Logan continues.

Their mother throws a small white pillow at her youngest child. "As the future mother-in-law then, I think Asher should favor my side. I changed a lot of your diapers as a baby, you know. You pissed on me many, many times."

My nose scrunches up. "Not helping your case, I'm afraid."

"Well, I'm also your mother's best friend, so I can just call her—"

Lucy glares at her mom. "Just because you've enjoyed kissing Elena in the past doesn't mean he owes you anything!"

Cora laughs, twisting the piercing in her nose. "There was no kissing, my sweet child."

Ew. I snatch the collar from Lucy's hands, turning it over. "Whose was this?"

"A foster from right before Luce left for college," Cora says. "Which is why I think it should stay with us. Plus, Lucy loses things."

"Not sentimental things!"

"But I can just put it in your old room for safekeeping," Cora continues. "And maybe if you find your way back there at some point instead of wanting to stay here—"

"*Mom.*"

I'd figured Alistair would have the harder time adjusting to the fact that Lucy wanted to finish her education at Avernia, but in truth, Cora was initially completely against it. Even now, it's clear the collar thing is little more than a ploy to lure Lucy back to Aplana, and I can't say I'm against the idea.

I don't want Lucy here either, but I refuse to make decisions for her anymore, even if they're supposed to be in her best interest. If I want this relationship to work, the trust between us has to go both ways, and I can't intervene every time something comes up.

Except right now.

"If we keep this thing," I say, unhooking it, "I'm just going to want to see it on."

Lucy blinks. "On what?"

My hands whip out, bringing the open collar around the back of Lucy's neck. I drag her to me, grinning wolfishly. "*You*, pup."

"Jesus Christ," Cora says, stomping over. She grabs the collar, then bends and gives her daughter a kiss on the forehead. "Logan and I are going to get out of here before things get any weirder. Love you, baby girl."

"Love you, Mom," Lucy mutters, shoving me back until they're at the door.

Cora turns, pausing in the doorway as Logan slips through it. She mouths something to me, protectiveness flaring in her golden gaze, and I nod.

Keep her safe.

I'd die in order to do so.

When the two are gone, shutting Lucy and me inside the apartment alone, she slings her arms around my neck and kisses me hard.

"You're a pervert," she says against my lips, grinning. "My dad is going to throw a fit when Mom tells him what you said."

"They'll live." I back her over to the faux-leather sofa in the living room, lowering her onto it and climbing between her legs. "Besides, I didn't tell them everything I would've done to you in that collar. Like…I don't know, bending you over the arm of this couch and rutting into you like a wolf in heat. Coming deep inside your sweet, pretty little pussy until you had tears in your eyes and were begging me not to stop."

I nuzzle her neck, nipping at her skin, and she giggles.

"Fair," she whispers, running her fingers through my hair. "You were a very good boy."

"I can be even better," I tell her in a soft voice, slipping my hand beneath her shirt, feeling her nipple pucker under my touch. "Good thing you asked me to move in, huh?"

She pauses, pulling back. Confusion blankets her beautiful glacial eyes. "Wait, what? I didn't…" I just look at her until her jaw falls open, her entire face brightening. "You want to live here with me?"

"Do I need to beg?"

"Well, I wouldn't be opposed…"

I kiss her again and again until we're a dizzy, panting heap of warm, damp flesh. That isn't something I'll ever tire of for as long as I live.

"Does this make you my boyfriend?" she asks as I drag my teeth along her throat.

"I'll be whatever you want me to be, baby."

"Boyfriend it is. We can work up to other stuff maybe." She sighs contentedly, stroking my hair as I make my way to her chest. When she feels the Saniderm on my neck, she freezes, tugging at my shirt. "What is that?"

Sitting up, I pick at the bandage until a corner comes loose, and then

I tear it off the rest of the way, wincing at the slight bite of pain as dry ink and plasma are loosened.

"Is that my *bite mark*?" Lucy asks, eyes wide as she smooths her fingers over the tattoo.

"You left your mark on my heart a long, long time ago," I say, kissing her fingertips. "Just thought I'd make the impact a little more obvious."

And when she seals our mouths once more, I really lean in to the sensation of being in her arms. Of never having to leave them.

Because when I'm here, tangled up in her moonlight, my anger doesn't feel so endless.

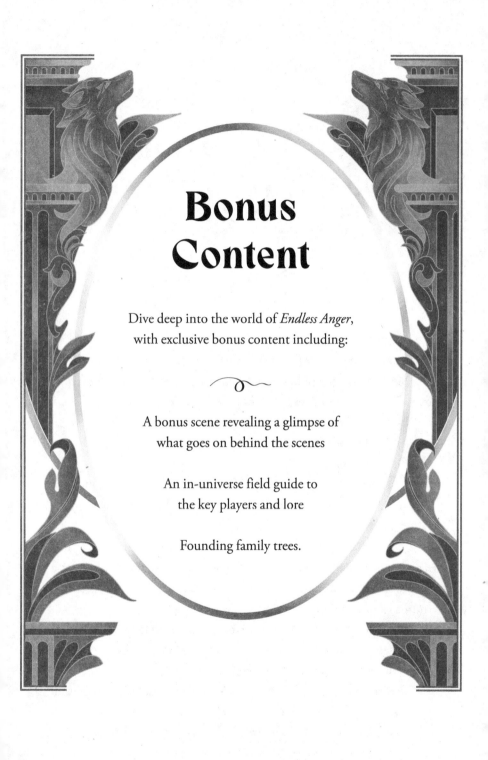

Bonus Content

Dive deep into the world of *Endless Anger*,
with exclusive bonus content including:

A bonus scene revealing a glimpse of
what goes on behind the scenes

An in-universe field guide to
the key players and lore

Founding family trees.

Bonus Scene

Kal

THE LIBRARY IN THE ASPHODEL IS FILLED WITH MY WIFE'S BOOKS.

Since she started publishing, it's the room I go to when I'm feeling overwhelmed and can't exactly go out and murder someone.

Not yet, at least. Technically speaking, I left that life behind when we had Quincy, but the urge rears its head on occasion.

On nights like this one.

I stroll to the big mahogany desk across the room, uncapping an expensive crystal decanter my sister Violet and her husband Grayson gifted us a few Christmases back.

Taking a deep breath, I pour myself four fingers of scotch and immediately down the contents. The throbbing in my head intensifies for a moment as memories from earlier replay in my head: my son, bleeding from a wound in his neck, standing over someone's corpse.

Something I hoped I'd never have to see, especially since I cut as many ties as possible to my own bloody past. But I suppose there are some things that can never be outrun.

Footsteps sound behind me as I pour some more of the alcohol, and my chest tightens as it burns my throat.

"Asher's asleep." Elena's soft voice is like a balm to my battered heart.

I turn toward her, leaning against the desk. She's in a floor-length robe the color of red wine. Its sleeves are sheer, and her dark hair cascades over her breasts, hitting the pomegranate tattoo I know is beneath one.

But it's her eyes I get lost in. Twenty-ish years of marriage, and I never tire of that golden gaze.

Not even when it's irate and blaming me for the mess we're in.

"Good," I reply, slamming the tumbler on the wooden surface. I reach for the decanter again, and she walks over, sliding her hands over mine. Her thumb grazes the pomegranate tattoo on my wrist, and she tugs so I release the glass, turning me toward her.

"Noelle took something to calm her down, so I suspect she'll be out soon. She was pretty shaken up."

"I imagine so."

"Did you call Kieran and Jonas?" she asks, toying with one of the buttons on my shirt. "They took care of everything?"

"Yes. Just got off the phone with Ivers a few minutes ago. No one will know any of our kids were out in that forest today." My eyes flicker to the clock hanging near the door. "Yesterday, I guess. Jesus."

"Quincy's still insisting on staying there."

"Figures. I guess I don't blame her for not wanting to start over elsewhere, since Avernia doesn't fucking transfer credits." I run a hand over my face, exhaling. "I have half a mind to force her back anyway."

"You're not alone, but she knows as much as we do about that school. Maybe more. If she thought she was in trouble, she'd let us know."

Sighing, I look down at her. "How come when I freak out, you relax? What'd you do with my worrywart wife?"

"It's nice to share sometimes. Now, come to bed," she says, hooding her gaze in a way that makes my cock stiffen.

"You want me in it?"

"With all that pent-up energy you're collecting? Absolutely." She smirks, dropping her palm between us as she presses against me. "I know exactly what will make you feel better."

I swallow. "This is my fault, you know. Them getting dragged into this violent, malicious world. Quincy enrolled at Avernia because of me, because of my mom, and now she doesn't want to leave. What if she's next? What if the curse that town talks about is real, and our kids are in danger?"

Elena shakes her head. "Nonsense. Curses aren't real."

"What if we're wrong?" I choke on the word, gritting my teeth against the emotions swarming my throat. "What if we need to be doing more?"

"Asher held his own against a grown assailant with a weapon," she tells me, nuzzling my chest. "Our *fourteen*-year-old son saved himself because you taught him how."

"His thirst for violence comes from you," I mutter, grabbing her hip. "I just showed him how to use it."

"Exactly. Between you and his uncles, danger should be afraid of *him*." She reaches up, our foot of height difference shrinking when she stands on her tip-toes, and cups my chin. "And our girls have the exact same abilities, even if they don't resort to such tactics as readily as their brother. They are smart, capable, and most of all—*ours*. Should anything happen to them, they'll figure a way out. Anderson blood might be tainted according to a few nobodies in New Hampshire, but I happen to know the truth."

I loop my arms around her waist, dragging her into me. "What's that?"

"Anderson blood is *special*." She grins, biting my collarbone and setting my nerves aflame. "Not to mention delicious."

Huffing, I clench my jaw, reaching beneath her ass. She jumps at the same time I lift, and presses a sloppy kiss to my lips as I start out of the library.

I grope the wall with one hand, searching for the light switch, as she tangles her tongue with mine. Fuck, I will never get tired of this.

"You really believe all that?" I ask, continuing the path up to our bedroom.

She nods, pulling away. "I have to. Otherwise, I'd never let our kids leave the house again."

"You trust them."

"I do. And I *love* you." She traces the outline of my mouth with a fingertip. "We might have to let them figure out life on their own a little, but I know that no matter what, their dad can fix anything. No violence or centuries-old curse formed against our family shall prosper."

My answering chuckle vibrates in my chest, and I squeeze her ass tighter. "Quoting the Bible when I've got sin on the mind is a dangerous thing. I could combust."

Her lips curve up. "Let's test that theory."

Deep down, I know she's right, anyway.

There's nothing I wouldn't do to ensure their safety, or to keep them from experiencing even a fraction of what I did when I was young. Maybe I can't protect them from *everything*, but knowledge is a weapon, too. One I hope they use—since something tells me this is far from over.

Pawns

Asher Blake Anderson

KEY DETAILS:
Born March 14th. Pisces. Youngest cursed Anderson child. Art major.
NOTES:
Volatile, violent, protective. ~~Has a cat in dorm.~~ Spends a lot of time alone, or else with his best friend (see: Lucy Wolfe). Not many connections ~~to~~ Fury Hill; could be a ~~simpler~~ target. DO NOT APPROACH UNARMED.

Lucy Aberdeen Wolfe

KEY DETAILS:
Born September 13th. Virgo. Oldest Wolfe child. Ecosystem major, political science minor. ~~Probably not cursed—jury's still out.~~
NOTES:
Kind, naive, prickly. Animals and Asher Anderson are greatest weakness—can be exploited. Few friends, spends a lot of time alone in forest doing cleanups.

Noelle Rose Anderson

KEY DETAILS:
Born August 9th. Leo. Middle cursed Anderson child. Not enrolled at Avernia.

NOTES:
Once spotted near Lake Lerna. Wonder if she knows she wasn't alone out there? ~~No one ever is...~~

Quincy Jane Anderson

KEY DETAILS:
Born April 15th. Aries. Oldest cursed Anderson child. Classics professor—for now.

NOTES:
Founded *Daughters of Persephone*. Said she wouldn't return to Avernia post-grad. Not to be trusted.

Sutton Aleksander Dupont

KEY DETAILS:
Born November 30th. Sagittarius. Oldest Dupont child. Theater professor. Haunted...a lot like our favorite lake.

NOTES:
Dead twin sister—~~definitely gives off guilty vibes~~. Visio Aeternae faculty sponsor. Can often be found hiding in his office or nowhere at all. Keeping an eye on this one.

Beckett Viktor Dupont

KEY DETAILS:
Born February 1st. Aquarius. Second to last Dupont child. Curator president.

NOTES:
~~Weirdly~~ attached to his father. Not well-liked by most who know him. Elitist ~~tool~~. The professor's best, barely-kept secret? Could be useful.

Henry Elijah Blackwater II

KEY DETAILS:
Born February 14th. <u>State prosecutor's son.</u> Quiet, ineffectual (?).
Curator.
NOTES:
Boring to watch, but idle hands...

Tiernan O'Beirne

KEY DETAILS:
Born June 24th. Non-founder bloodline. <u>Associations unclear.</u>
NOTES:
A follower. Can often be found hanging around Beckett, or another
student with leadership qualities. Pawn potential.

Muna Henoke

KEY DETAILS:
Born August 15th. Non-founder bloodline. Irritatingly helpful, Curator
VP.
NOTES:
Has been seen conversing with certain founding family descendants.
~~Possibly compromised.~~

Foxeglove Micah James

KEY DETAILS:
Born April 20th. Taurus. Asher's cousin. Not enrolled at Avernia.
NOTES:
Spends most of his time moping around campus, waiting like a puppy
for someone to give him attention. ~~Seems unstable. Easy target.~~

Aurora Lilith Primrose-Wolfe

KEY DETAILS:
Born May 30th. Gemini. Lucy's cousin. Fashion major.
NOTES:
Seems protective of Lucy and friendly with Asher. Could pose problems, though she is often seen getting distracted by Foxeglove, so perhaps he is a weakness we can use.

Justin Bauer

KEY DETAILS:
Mostly unknown despite Fury Hill upbringing and background. Suspect.
NOTES:
A necessary evil, probably, but I wouldn't mind ~~taking him out...~~

~~REDACTED~~

~~Key Details: REDACTED~~
~~Notes: REDACTED~~

Locations

Avernia College

(uh-VER-nee-uh)

Noun

1. Cursed hunting grounds for vulnerable students, unwelcome to outsiders. An elite, private arts college established ? by the Dupont, Ouellette, Westwood, Blackwater, Anderson, and Abbott families.

2. Named after Avernus, volcanic crater in Italy once believed to be entrance to the Underworld.

Lake Lerna

(lern-uh)

Noun

1. Large body of water between the White Mountains and the Primordial Forest's quarry.

2. Haunted. What goes in does not come back out...usually.

The Obeliskos

(ah-buh-lisk-uhs)

Noun

1. Biggest of three campus libraries.
2. Likely haunted. No ghost sightings reported, but students avoid the thirteenth floor for some reason.

The Lyceum

(lye-SEE-um)

Noun

1. Main academic building for Avernia students.

The Primordial Forest

(pry-MOR-dee-uhl)

Noun

1. Expansive wooded area surrounding Avernia College—stretches across a majority of Fury Hill and over White Mountains.
2. Some archives swear the trees have minds of their own...

Lethe's

(lee-thees)

Noun

1. Bar frequented by Avernia students.
2. Those who go in can expect to forget their time spent.

~~Tenarus Cave~~
~~Tartarus~~
~~The Quarry~~
~~Elysian Dorms~~

Limbs of Fury Hill

Westwood

David
|
Baron —|— Cate
|
Zachary

Blackwater

William
|
Henry Elijah II —|— Christine
| |
Henry Elijah III   Sabrina

Dupont

Jean
|
Claire ———┬——— Jean-Louis
┌──────┬────┴────┬──────┐
Sutton   Bellamy   Beckett   Giselle

Ouellette

Gabriel
|
Julie

Anderson

Cronus
|
Kal ——— Elena
|
Quincy   Noelle   Asher

Abbott

Charles
|
Angelica ——— Zane
|
Lexington   Shelby

Acknowledgments

It's kind of hard to believe this series is multiple years in the making.

Initially, I hadn't planned on writing second-generation stuff at all. I didn't want to age up my characters or mess with their happily-ever-afters, but I'd left crumbs for myself with the Anderson kids. Just in case.

When I finished the Monsters & Muses series, something was nagging me. The world didn't feel complete, but it wasn't until I was casually flipping through a Greek mythology book that I was hit with inspiration: the three Furies (Erinyes), who were daughters of Hades and Persephone in some iterations of the mythos.

Since I'd given *my* Hades and Persephone three children, it felt like the perfect premise, and thus my idea for Erinyes-inspired kids attending a university influenced heavily by the Greek Underworld was born.

More than two years after I began writing *Endless Anger*, and it's finally here. I can't explain just how *good* it feels to be back in this world with fresh faces, but also to have published again at all when I struggled for so long due to burnout and other things going on in my personal life.

But we're back, baby, and there are so many people I could not have done this without.

First and foremost, to my readers: Thank you for everything. Whether this is your first, second, or tenth book of mine, without you

I'm just an introverted hermit making her imaginary friends do things. Thank you for your support, your kindness, and your enthusiasm.

To my best friend, Emily McIntire: Can you believe five whole years have gone by since we met? I literally don't know what I would do without you. Thank you for being my lifeline, my soul sister, and the first eyes on everything I write.

To my PA, Jackie: Thank you for consistently keeping my life in order, for all the paper cuts you've likely gotten from mailing things for me, and for your constant hype and loyalty.

To my agent, Savannah: I'm forever grateful to you for the support and opportunities you've given me. Thank you for always being around to lend an ear or give advice.

To my editor, Mary, and the rest of the team at Sourcebooks Casablanca: This was our first frontlist title together, and *wow*, was I bad at hitting those deadlines. I cannot thank you enough for your kindness, compassion, and understanding, as well as your championship and belief in me. I promise to work on my timeliness (though I will admit, I'm writing this on an all-nighter two days after the deadline again. Oops. Next time!).

To my fairy plotmother, Becca: Thank you for the anxiety-spam texts, letting me spiral and helping me come up with plans, and for being the kindest, sweetest person ever. I owe this entire series to you, truly.

To my therapist: Thank you for trying to keep me sane and being my gossip doctor.

Lastly, to Lord Byron, Poe, and Arrow: Thank you for being my reason to live, even on the really tough days.

About the Author

Sav R. Miller is a *USA Today* bestselling author of adult romance with varying levels of darkness and steam.

In 2018, Sav put her lifelong love of reading and writing to use and graduated with a BA in creative writing and a minor in cultural anthropology. Nowadays, she spends her time giving morally gray characters their happily-ever-afters.

Currently, Sav lives in Kentucky with her dogs Lord Byron, Poe, and Arrow. She loves sitcoms, silence, and sardonic humor.

Website: savmiller.com
Facebook: srmauthor
Instagram: @srmauthor
TikTok: @authorsavrmiller

COMING SOON...

Jealous Rage

~ ᴏ ~

From *USA Today* bestselling author Sav R. Miller comes a dark academia romance inspired by the Greek Furies.

When twenty-five-year-old Elle Anderson enrolls at a strange, secluded private college to be with her siblings and heal from trauma, she accidentally reopens old wounds and forbidden attraction when she comes face to face with the unspeakably hot professor she thought she'd left in the past.

For more info about Sourcebooks's books and authors, visit:
sourcebooks.com

MONSTERS
& MUSES

Welcome to the Monsters & Muses, a series of dark and twisted
modern-day romances inspired by classic Greek myths
by Sav R. Miller, *USA Today* Bestselling Author

PROMISES & POMEGRANATES

Kal Anderson may be cold, but he's burned with obsessive need for Elena since he first saw her…enough to steal her away to his secret island where she can be his and his alone.

VIPERS & VIRTUOSOS

Aiden is a tortured musician who carefully guards his heart…until he meets Riley and loses it, and himself, in her hypnotic blue eyes.

OATHS & OMISSIONS

Lenny Primrose will do anything to be free of her controlling mob boss father…including fake a romance with the assassin who almost killed him.

ARROWS & APOLOGIES

Mayor Alistair Wolfe wasn't supposed to blackmail his one-night stand into working for him…or find himself falling for her more with every forbidden touch.

SOULS & SORROWS

When an ex-ballerina gets herself into a bind at an underground auction, Cash Primrose becomes so enamored that he ends up placing a bid…

LIARS & LIAISONS

Violet Artinos never would've made a move if she'd known the stranger she kissed was her ex's younger brother…or how darkly complicated things could get.